THEY HATE EACH OTHER

Amanda Woody

THEY HATE EACH OTHER

VIKING

VIKING
An imprint of Penguin Random House LLC, New York

First published in the United States of America by Viking,
an imprint of Penguin Random House LLC, 2023
First paperback edition published 2024

Visit us online at PenguinRandomHouse.com.

Library of Congress Cataloging-in-Publication Data is available.

ISBN 9780593403105

Printed in the United States of America

1st Printing

LSCC

Design by Opal Roengchai
Text set in Bodoni Std

To Mom & Dad:

I made it.

Love, PLGP

A NOTE FROM THE AUTHOR

This book is meant to depict queer characters and love in a community that is safe from discrimination based on one's identity. As such, please be aware that the narrative does not allow room for queerphobia of any kind. Thank you!

DYLAN

Jonah Collins is dancing on my kitchen table, and I think . . . yes.

I think I'm about to lose my shit.

I'm impressed I've been holding it together so well. My house has been infested with uninvited partygoers since the last homecoming song, and I've been running around, scrubbing drink stains out of the carpet and picking up after sloppy classmates. Hanna and I only invited a handful of people, so why is half the class here? A thick, bulging vein has been pulsing in my temple for two hours, dangerously close to detonating.

Then, I see him. On my furniture. Dancing to the beat of the music, surrounded by his usual crowd of cheering onlookers.

I stop in my tracks. Inhale. Exhale. Find peace, Dylan.

Jonah is spilling his drink over the rim of his Solo cup. His homecoming tie is wrapped around his forehead, and his pasty white face is flushed, probably from the amount of alcohol he's been looting from the drink table. He pulls Andre up next to him, and they start grinding, and—

No.

I storm through the living room, squirming around people who are hunched with hilarity because, *haha, Jonah Collins is making an ass of himself again, and everything he does makes us laugh, even when it's not really funny!*

I wrestle my way to the inner part of the circle and glare up at them. When Andre sees my expression, he squawks, scrambling down. "I'm sorry!" he cries out. The edges of his dark brown forehead and low drop fade sparkle with sweat, and he's giving me puppy eyes. "Jo-Jo made me do it!"

Andre's sober. That's the power Jonah wields over people—the natural ability to make them sink to his level.

"Go find your girlfriend," I snap at him, before turning my attention back to Jonah. I wonder if she's still ushering people away from the staircase leading upstairs. Regardless, I need her, because Hanna is the only person Jonah listens to.

"Go easy on him," Andre pleads. "He's wasted out of his mind—"

I shoot him another glare that makes him gulp and sends him skittering into the throng behind us.

"Andre?" Jonah whirls around, apparently just now realizing his best friend is no longer grinding up against his back. More liquid sloshes onto the tablecloth, and it takes all my willpower not to wrench it out from under him. "Where'd you . . . ?"

His sharp gray eyes fall to mine. Just like that, his distressed expression flips, and his lip pulls into a grin.

"Oh," he drawls. "It's Prissy Prince himself!"

A hush falls over the crowd. As the focus in the room shifts to me, my muscles tighten like springs. People always get quiet to watch a spectacle between Jonah Collins and Dylan Ramírez. Even if it's usually just Jonah screaming obscene things while I resist flinging him through a window.

"Come to ruin the fun?" Jonah tips his cup into his mouth. Half the drink misses his lips and spills onto his button-down. "As is required in the killjoy job description?"

An "ooh" echoes around the crowd.

"Get down," I mutter through my teeth.

"Two more minutes. Just two more, okay?" Jonah asks, swaying and giggling.

My heart beats against my throat, pumping blood into my head until I'm seeing red. Why? Why does this egotistical jerk cause a scene everywhere he goes? Always running around, leeching attention without a care for anyone but himself. Trying to pick fights with me, as if he'd last five seconds.

"Get off my table," I say, seething, "before I drag you off."

"But you would *never*," he says in mock sternness. "Everyone keeps saying you're this amazing, fan-fucking-tastic guy. Like, a real stand-up gentleman."

Rage is swelling in my chest. The audience is already cheering him on. Because everyone loves Jonah. He says everything with such confidence, you can't help but believe him. Root for him. Unless you're me, and you have to deal with his personality on a daily basis.

I don't know what I'm going to do next—the number of eyes burning into my face makes me want to slink under the table and hide. Suddenly, though, a voice draws our attention.

"Jonah."

Hanna Katsuki is standing at the edge of the table. She looks exactly like she did before the dance, her long black hair curled against the rosy undertones of her shoulders like a princess's, her royal blue dress smooth and unruffled. She's swirling a glass of vodka and Sprite, her weary gaze focused on Jonah, looking like she wishes she was drunker than this. Andre peeks around her shoulder, eyes flicking between us.

Just like that, because he holds no respect for anyone other than imposing women, Jonah concedes. "Yes, ma'am," he says, and my heart drops when he goes to step off the table.

"*Collins!*" I shout, lunging in front of him.

It happens how I expect. Jonah steps forward and realizes the ground isn't under him. He falls with a gasp, but before he can slam his head against the floor, I catch his weight in my chest. His cup smashes between us, pouring sticky pop and alcohol down our shirts.

He looks up at me in bewilderment. People laugh, like he didn't almost just concuss himself. I swallow a scream of loathing frustration as his drink seeps through my clothes.

"Ramírez?" Jonah flutters his eyelashes at me. "You *do* care about me!"

I am going to concuss him myself.

I seize his shirt and drag him behind me, beelining for the door. Jonah doesn't struggle until I swing it open. "Wait, *wait!*" he shouts as I thrust him onto my porch. "What the hell?"

I fish a water bottle out of the cooler next to me and toss it at his feet. "Sober up," I snap, and I slam the door in his face, locking it. When I turn, fuming, I find Andre and Hanna behind me, him nervously adjusting his royal blue tie, her staring at me with one raised brow, clearly about to accuse me of something.

"Do you ever wonder what it might be like?" she asks.

Here we freaking go. "No," I say immediately.

"Joining him? Dancing with friends? Making a ruckus? Having fun?" Hanna takes a sip of her Sprite. "I'm never the loudest person in the room, either, but at least I know how to enjoy myself at a party. Unlike some people who only care about what Jonah Collins is getting himself into."

Ah. I can't go a day without someone insisting Jonah and I should get along. "My version of having fun doesn't involve stomping on people's furniture and twerking for the masses," I grumble.

Hanna looks pointedly at Andre. "Aren't you going to give him company?"

Andre laughs. "Who, the white guy that just got drop-kicked out of the party? Nah."

Hanna stares, unblinking, overwhelming him with her formidable energy until his lanky shoulders buckle, and he shuffles to the door. When Andre swings it open, Jonah's belligerent voice surges into the living room like a tornado gust.

"Hey!" Andre says soothingly, battering him backward. "Jo-Jo, come on, we don't need to go inside right now, shh . . ."

"LET ME PUNCH HIM IN THE SACK—!"

Andre closes the door, cutting him away.

"Menace," I mutter, storming to the staircase. I glance back at Hanna. "I'm changing. Mind making sure nobody burns this place down?"

I hurl myself up the stairs and into my bedroom without waiting for an answer. I slouch onto my bed, prying my dress shirt off. I don't realize how scalding hot I am until the cool air tingles against my skin.

I sit there. For . . . I don't know how long. All I know is I've exhausted my social stamina, and I want this night to be over. I can't say for certain, but I'm 90 percent sure the reason half these people showed up in the first place is because of *him*. Everyone flocks to him and follows him around like he's the most interesting person in the world. I guess most of them only get his personality in short, entertaining spurts. Lucky them.

I must space out pretty good, because when a text brings me back into focus, music is no longer thrumming through my house. Things are eerily quiet, aside from idle chatter out on my driveway and street.

I take no less than one minute to gather my senses before fumbling for my phone. It's from Hanna.

> Managed to get everyone out. Trying to leave
> but Andre and Jonah are arguing in the
> driveway. Lock your doors.

A relieved smile touches my lips. She's technically the one who made me host so I couldn't ditch, but maybe I can forgive her for clearing this place out. The promise of sleep coaxes me to my feet, and I start to the door. But then I hear something. This thudding noise, steadily getting louder. The sound of someone mumbling.

My door swings open so viciously that it slams against the wall stop. It's Jonah Collins.

My jaw snaps shut. His pale face, twisted with rage, is pink under the glow of my bedside lamp. His nose is scrunched with his scowl.

"Leave," I order, because it's way too late to deal with his nasty disposition.

"You threw me out!" Jonah yells. "Into the cold dark night! *What if I died from hypothermia? What if someone kidnapped me because I'm so hot and sexy?*"

As if it isn't a balmy sixty-eight degrees outside. As if any criminals would want his screechy ass. "Why are you still here?" I demand. "What do you want?"

"A fight! *Fight me!*" He drives himself into my bare chest, clearly hoping I'll lose my balance. But I could bench-press two of him, so he doesn't even break my stance.

"Doesn't this get exhausting?" I snarl, prying him off of me. "Being this annoying. Like, don't you ever get tired?"

I figure he's going to hurl another insult, but he staggers back with a groan. For a moment, I'm afraid he's about to puke all over my beige carpet. But he merely moves toward my bed, eyes drooping. "What the hell is with your house? It's so warm." His voice is so slurred I can barely understand it. I watch in bewilderment as he flops onto my mattress and hugs my pillow. "Hey, Prissy Prince. D'you know the valley on Mars . . . it's ten times longer than the Grand Canyon . . . ?"

He passes out.

What?

What the fuck?

I don't know what just happened. Why did he say . . . *any* of that? I realize quickly that I don't care. I'm tired, and anxious, and so angry that it's shortening my breath to frustrated spurts. I storm to the bed, prepared to shake him awake. As I reach out, though, a message from Hanna glows up at me from my phone screen.

> Jonah wants to fight you and Andre can't get him into the car. Sorry. Maybe let him crash on your couch? :)

I'm seeing red again.

Jonah Collins is going to regret waking up tomorrow.

JONAH

I'd sell my soul for the chance to wake up like those cheery assbags in a Disney Channel movie.

Seriously. Is stirring awake to chirping birds so much to ask for? Is it so impossible that I, too, could greet the morning sun, then twirl to my walk-in closet and choose between my cutest outfits? Can't *I* be the one to snag some toast and sprint past my quirky parents because, oh dicks and fiddlesticks, I'm late for school!

Of course not. Because I'm Jonah Collins, and I could never be so lucky.

I can barely pry my face from my soggy, saliva-laden pillow. A throbbing headache expands through my temples and jaw. I squint through my crusty eyes, making out scattered posters on deep burgundy walls. *The Great British Baking Show, Chopped, Hell's Kitchen, Pesadilla en la Cocina, Cake Boss*. The dressers are scattered with tourist trinkets— snow globes, figurines, key chains.

Okay, I'm in someone's bedroom. That's one question answered.

But I'm . . . in my . . .

Underwear?

Oh *shit*.

A curled fist of realization punches me back into last night. Sensations from the after-party nip at my eyes, unraveling and disappearing. Shouting over music. Howling laughter. The sting of alcohol. Sparkles fluttering away from dresses. The glare of my phone screen as I check my texts again.

There's a slight incline in the bed, like there's something weighing down the other side. Half hoping I'm lying beside a gargantuan teddy bear, I flip over, my heart hammering.

Instead, there's a real human lying next to me. Loose black curls tickle his brows, and he's sleeping, one dark brown arm extended under his head, his shirtlessness burning into my retinas. It's . . . It's . . .

Dylan. Fucking. Ramírez.

My jaw unhinges. White, numbing panic burns behind my eyes. I'm fever dreaming, right? No way I'm lying half naked in bed beside my ultimate archenemy without some logical explanation. I have to think . . . *remember* . . .

Okay. I have to go back to square one.

First, my friends and I head to Buffalo Wild Wings for dinner. I order cheese curds, then promptly regret it when I end up in the bathroom, producing curds of my own.

Second, the dance. Music pounds through the cinder block walls of the cafeteria. The DJ pops on a slow song, and my friends break off in pairs, leaving me to dance dramatically by myself, pretending to hold the imaginary waist of a beautiful exchange student. People giggle, fueling my confidence, and then I notice Dylan Ramírez standing away from the crowd, his arms folded grumpily.

The night is suddenly swell.

Third, the after-party. Dylan rarely hosts, so this is the perfect time to cause chaos. Maybe I could "accidentally" bump into one of his thousand-dollar vases or, better yet, steal one. Before I can step through the door, though, he's pulling me aside with his Goliath palm.

"*Hey!*" I yell. "*Unhand me, foul bitch!*"

He smiles coolly. "Break something," he says in a honey-sweet voice, "and you'll regret it. Understand, Collins?"

Oh my God. Is he *threatening my well-being*? I whip my trembling, rage-induced fists out in front of me, prepared to spill blood on his fancy rich-people porch.

His eye roll nearly makes me swing prematurely. "Cute stance," he says, and then he turns to join the party, leaving me flushed and ready to swing at the wall.

Fourth, I'm chugging spiked lemonade, trying to distract myself. From the embarrassment of my wretched singleness. From thoughts of my sisters. From Dylan's presence. He's zigzagging around the party, scowling at everyone within his radius and steering people away from the staircase.

Fifth, I'm checking my phone again, because I can't help it, and—

"Relax, Jo-Jo." Andre's skinny arm slinks around my shoulders, and he gives me a reassuring squeeze that delivers the message. *They're fine.* "Start paying attention to me or I'll cry."

He drags me away from my anxieties, so we're flaunting ourselves in the middle of the party, spreading foolhardiness and laughter.

Sixth . . . ? Oh, yeah. I'm showcasing my sexiest dance moves on a table. At least until I'm on the ground again, courtesy of Dylan, and being shoved into the cold dark night.

Seventh . . .

"Get in the car." Andre's hand steadies me while I teeter, my shirt buttons half-undone. "Mom's pissed that I missed curfew. If you go back, you'll just challenge Ramírez to a death brawl, and he'll kick your ass."

I choke on my horror. Does he really have that little faith in my ability to body a bitch? *My own best friend for all of eternity?* I have to prove him wrong now, so I swivel, wandering up the neatly trimmed lawn to

Dylan's front door and flinging a middle finger up behind me.

"Okay," he calls. "Hanna and I are leaving. Remember to ice your black eyes."

I'm sure I say something witty, but the memory folds away.

Eighth . . . hmm. Eighth was . . . ?

I'm stumbling up a staircase, my steps echoing around his massive, empty house. "Where are you, Ramírez?" I slur, shoving into his bedroom. "I'm gonna challenge . . ."

Ninth. Downturned, deep brown eyes are glaring at me. It's him. The bane of my existence. The rotten core to my apple of life.

Tenth . . . I don't remember. Everything beyond that is a blur, so I blink back into focus, zeroing in on Dylan again. He's still there, a mere foot away. The image hasn't dissolved. Which means . . . we . . . ?

"*No!*" I roar, planting my palm on Dylan's face and thrusting it away. I scramble off of his mattress, struggling to conceal my very irresistible, very unclothed body. *"Absolutely not!"*

"Huh?" Dylan squints through his bleariness, then sits upright, his nose crinkling. "Why did you *strip*?"

I'm too far gone in my horror to fully comprehend his words. Instead, I seize the pillow plagued with my spit and reel it forward like a baseball bat, zipper slapping him with the rage of ten thousand gods of virtue.

"Ay! Collins!"

He lurches out of bed, and I brace for the fight I've been prepared to start with him over the last several years. Dylan has always been bigger and better than me. He's got the higher grades, because he apparently has all the time in the world to study and has zero obligations to anything but himself. He's got the brawnier build, confirmed by Andre, who repeatedly has the gall to tell me I look like a yipping Chihuahua next to him. He has the superior luck—the proof being the house that currently surrounds us.

Basically, all of this is to say that if I can beat him unconscious with this pillow, he can beat me *more* unconscious with it.

I have to knock him out before he counters.

First, I'll aim for his face. As miserable tears of pain blind him, I'll go for the throat. I'll continue this pillow torment until his writhing dissolves into twitching, and then, I'll make my escape.

Good. Good plan. I just have to . . .

I hurl the pillow forward, and he tears it out of my grip.

Bad plan.

I'm about to be maimed. Not only does he have my weapon, but there's nobody around to see him lose the perfect pompous persona he's always wearing like a costume. In a last, desperate attempt to flee, I sprint for the closed door—until his foot hooks around mine, nearly ripping me into the splits. "Ow," I croak. "You little . . ."

Dylan snaps the pillow into my nose, sending me sprawling. "*You* got into *my* bed," he snarls, poised to strike again. "In case you forgot."

There aren't enough words in my brain for me to describe how incredibly impossible that is. Nonetheless, I'm aching too much to tell him how wrong he is, so I maneuver onto my knees, fumbling for my pile of clothes beside the bed. I shove my legs into slacks and hoist my sticky button-down over my shoulders. Hopefully that massive stain down the front will come out in the wash. My "nice" shirts are few and far between.

"Unbelievable." Dylan drags sweatpants to his waist. "I should've thrown you out on the lawn . . ."

I clamber to my feet. My body feels like it weighs triple what it normally does, and my headache is bad enough to blur my vision, but I can't show weakness, so I hold my chin high and say, "I require water."

He stares at me in this "only if I can drown you in it" kind of way. "Okay? And?"

"I'm your esteemed guest!" I snap, marching to the door. "You should take responsibility for—"

Dylan trips me a second time, and I crash against the wood with a thud. I groan, sliding onto my back.

"Of course." He glares down at me with an unpleasant smile. "Anything for my *guest*."

Homecoming. The one night I can go out, have fun, get shamelessly wasted, and forget about my woes.

Like everything in my life, Dylan Ramírez ruined it.

Dylan and I have been archenemies since we were eleven, back when he moved here from Detroit and wrestled into my friend group. Back when Mom was still alive, and I had time to compete with him.

The thing is, he wins. Always. It's been like that since the start, when he slapped me with that +4 in Uno. In our sixth grade band concert, he stole my recorder solo. In eighth grade, everyone went to his Christmas party instead of my birthday bash because he had a chocolate fountain. Freshman year, he nudged me aside to win homecoming prince. Dylan steals *everything*.

And why? He has everything he could ever want. A gigantic, cozy house in a safe neighborhood. The ability to buy overpriced food from the lunch lines without a bead of sweat. Sparkling fresh clothes that make him look pristine and proper and *ugh*. I swear the guy doesn't know how to operate a washing machine, considering how often he's wearing new clothes.

My point? I hate him.

He hates me, too. He says I'm whiny, annoying, too loud, and I over-exaggerate, which I have never done in the history of *ever*. But Hanna is his best friend, and Andre is mine, and their romantic relationship is stable, so we're forced to tolerate each other.

For some sadistic reason (hint: we're bisexual singles within driving distance of each other), our friends have been trying to set us up. Because, *oh, the tension!* Sure, we have that, but it's mostly in a "see how far you can stretch this rubber band before it snaps" kind of way. Regardless, I've wanted to drop-kick him back to Detroit for years.

As I run around Dylan's house, searching for my phone, I pause at the bathroom. I intently examine my neck to make sure he didn't express his innate desire for me in the form of hickeys.

Dylan, who's trudging by with dirty paper plates, scoffs. "Do you really think," he says flatly, "I would ever suck on your crusty skin."

"Um, I am baby-ass smooth, thank you?"

"Please. I've seen your cracked elbows." He crushes the plates into his kitchen trash can, ignoring my squawk of protest, then pulls a glass from an overhead cabinet, filling it with water and holding it out.

"You remember more than me," I mutter.

"Obviously. I wasn't drinking. Though, maybe I should've been." He grimaces. "I wish I could delete last night from my brain."

Reluctantly, I take the glass from him and mutter a thanks. My lack of memory is causing anxiety to tingle under my skin. "So we didn't . . . *do* anything," I say, hesitant. "Right?"

"Of course not," he snaps. "You barged into my room, challenged me to a fight, told me the valley on Mars is longer than the Grand Canyon, and passed out. I didn't feel like sleeping on the couch, so I shoved you over and got in next to you."

My face rises to boiling temperature. I shared a *fun fact* with him? What's wrong with me? I don't disclose my space information to just anyone, let alone Dylan "Who Gave You Permission to Speak to Me" Ramírez. How dare my drunken mouth betray me?

I glug the water, then stride into the living room, still seeking my phone. The pastel furniture and brick fireplace look as fancy as they did when his family first moved here. His TV is the size of my backyard. The windows are expansive and inviting. Everything about this house screams "unnecessarily wealthy."

I head to Dylan's room, hands tingling. It has to be there. Otherwise . . .

The Goddess of Luck blesses me with one spare moment of her time, because as soon as I walk through his door, I hear my "Saturn's Rings" chime beneath his bed. Sighing with relief, I crawl between his nightstand and bed frame, snagging it, then open my conversation with Mik.

> Dad home yet? Mrs. Greene is
> leaving at 9.

> BRAT
> Yep, he's here. Have fun loser!!!

Nothing else, so that's relieving. I do have a text from the betrayer of my heart (I must've changed his contact name last night).

```
ASSHOLE BASTARD WHORE
How was the death brawl? Did it turn
into something . . . sexier? heheh
```

He's included a GIF of two cats licking each other. Grinding my teeth, I swipe to call.

"Good morning, babe." I can almost hear Andre's leering, treasonous smile.

"Don't call me babe." My growl comes more like a squeak. "You were my DD. Why did you leave me with this asshat?"

"You wouldn't get in my car, remember? I thought Mom was going to squeeze through my damn phone and drag me home herself if I didn't get on the road." A beat. Then, "So, how was it? Is his package as big as it looked in the locker room—?"

"Oh no, oh God, no, shut up immediately." I rub my temple. Andre's superpower is riling me up within the first twelve seconds of our conversation. "We didn't do anything weird, okay? It was a mistake."

Andre is quiet. Just when I think the line is dead, "What was a mistake?"

Shit. "What?" I clear my throat. "Nothing. Anyway—"

"So you did *something* with him?"

"No, I—"

"No way." Andre is basically guffawing, now. "I have to tell Hanna, oh my God—"

"Don't say anything!" I reel my head up, slamming it into the corner of Dylan's nightstand and sending a fresh wave of pain rippling through my temples. As I groan and reach for my skull, something drops onto the carpet in front of me. "We didn't do anything, so don't be weird! I have to go."

"No, wait, tell me more, I'm too emotionally invested—!"

I disconnect, cussing and massaging my head. The fallen object before me is a picture frame. As I pick it up, my insides boil with nausea—because of my kiss with the dresser, or because I'm looking at Dylan's child face, I'm not sure. Dylan is probably nine or so and flanked by three people. His mother, a gorgeous Latina woman with soft curls, a tailored suit, and a rusted smile, like it's not often used. His father, a hefty Afro-Latino man with cropped hair and a beaming grin. Dylan, who's peeking shyly at the camera, his hands bunched up in front of him. Then . . .

A teenager slightly older than us now, clutching Dylan's shoulders, wearing a smile similar to Mr. Ramírez's. Warm, wide, and glittering with energy.

I frown. I don't know much about the Ramírez family—only that Dylan's mom is Mexican and grew up in Texas, and that his dad moved to the U.S. from Brazil when he was a child. Beyond that, I don't have any other information. Talking about our families in the friend group is a rare occurrence, and something I actively avoid, unless it's about my sisters.

But it feels like I should've known Dylan has a brother.

I set the picture on the nightstand and return to the kitchen, where Dylan's wiping a stain off a book stuffed with colorful tabs titled *Recetas*.

"So I . . . uh." I clear my throat. "Andre thinks we got nasty last night."

Dylan scowls. "Messed up already? Feels like a record."

Whatever brilliant insult I'm about to generate fizzles when I see the clock above the living room mantle. My chest twinges with unease, and I shuffle around again, looking for my jacket.

"Have a ride home?" he asks, following me.

"My legs."

"But it's raining. Your dad can't pick you up?"

I find my jacket on the coat rack and secure the black buttons, ignoring him.

Dylan watches as sheets of rain douse the street and pummel the windows, then says, "I'll drive you."

My hand is already around the doorknob, but I hesitate. There's nobody around to see his gentlemanly act, so why keep up the image? Why offer something that would force him to spend more time with me?

I decide not to contemplate it. Instead, I salute him and say, "Looks like you've got some cleaning up to do, so no thanks. Deuces!"

I swing it open, but Dylan's hand slams the door before I can squirm through. "How about," he says, voice dangerously calm, "you stop bitching for once, and you thank me?"

My jaw tightens. If I turn around, my face is going to be right in his neck, so I stay still, hating the oppressive heat from his chest mere inches from my back. He doesn't move, either—maybe he's waiting for me to offer my immeasurable gratitude, but I'm not going to give it to him. He probably has some diabolical motivation for wanting to take me home, like to put me in his debt.

Besides, I don't need anyone's help. For *anything*. Especially not his.

"Ridiculous," he mutters. He snags a windbreaker off the coatrack, then pulls me into the rain. He's got a newly leased metallic gray car that makes me grumble with envy.

He stuffs me into the leather passenger seat like a hostage, and then we're off.

Delridge is a small, busy city in the middle of Absolutely Nowhere. In the center, it's any forgettable place, with bars, restaurants, department stores, the occasional neighborhood, and two schools—one for K–8 and one high school. But in the outskirts, it's little more than expansive, twisting country roads, one Amish house, and infinite golden fields.

The ride is quiet. As we encroach on the other side of town, sidewalks begin to fracture. Potholes cut deeper into the asphalt. Weeds reach for the autumn sky, and two-story houses collapse into one-story houses. Jagged wire springs to life in the form of spiraling fences. I don't realize I'm chewing my nail until I taste blood.

"Stop here." We're in the middle of a street, but I pull the door handle anyway.

Dylan sighs. "Just point me in the right direction so I can get back to my life."

Right. His perfect, stress-free life. "Sorry for taking up so much of your precious day," I drawl. "What, do you need to go polish your yacht? Feed your Persian cat? Meet your brother at some thousand-dollar steakhouse—?"

It's like I pulled a trigger. Suddenly, Dylan swerves into a run-down ice cream parlor lot and screeches to a stop.

I stare at him, alarmed. He's unblinking. Deadpan.

"Get out," he whispers.

His seething tone sends a warning tingle up my spine. I fumble for the handle and push the door open, allowing the sound of gushing rain to surge into the car. I'm not sure what conjured this menacing air—it's not like I've never poked at the fact that he's well-off. What's different?

I mentioned his brother.

I've known Dylan a long time (tragically), but I've never interacted with his family. Hanna said his mom is a traveling businesswoman, and his dad is the owner and head chef of a local churrascaria, which I've heard is this ridiculously delicious Brazilian restaurant. Nobody's ever mentioned siblings.

I step onto the asphalt. Rain explodes against my shoes, dampening my slacks. This tension feels worse than before, like I crossed a line and didn't realize it. Maybe I should say something. Like, thank him for the ride after all, or mumble an apology for . . . whatever I did.

Instead, I slam the door and turn away, hugging my sleeves. The tires squeal against the pavement as Dylan swings the car around, kicking it onto the street. My shoulders slump. My pinched eyebrows melt apart.

"My bad," I whisper.

I swivel to the sidewalk and continue the trek home.

DYLAN

I'm not sure how long I sit in my driveway, my breathing startled and shallow. Part of me feels guilty about abandoning Jonah in the rain. Another part feels he's lucky I took him that far.

I lean against the headrest. My brother's name flits around the edges of my thoughts, always there, even when I try to avoid it.

Tomás.

How did Jonah know? My secrets stay where they are, caged and stifled in the back of my head. Especially around arrogant loudmouths who don't know how to function unless everyone is looking at them.

I'm frazzled, which means one thing.

Stress baking.

I head inside. Before yanking out ingredients for pudim de leite condensado, I clean up remaining hints of the party. I scrub at the lemonade stains soaking the counter, empty the coolers, vacuum crumbs and sparkles out of the carpet. I consider picking up Mom's picture above the mantle—the one with her in her quince dress—but it's not like she's ever around to see it, so I leave it tipped over.

I realize how Jonah found out when I go upstairs. The da Costa Ramírez family picture on my bedside table. It's standing up.

I huff in frustration, slapping it facedown.

I return to my kitchen and switch my oven to preheat, then caramelize the sugar, trying to focus on . . . well, anything but *him*. But I can still hear his spiteful yells ricocheting through my house. He's always yelling. God, can't he ever shut up? Andre's squealy, but Jonah's *relentless*. I want to stick a ball gag in his mouth, and not in a sexy way.

School is going to suck. Andre has no doubt unleashed his rumors to our friends at this point, courtesy of Jonah's inability to keep his mouth shut about us sleeping in the same bed. Normally, I'm good at ignoring our friends when they insist we have "couple vibes," but now, we've given them the perfect ammunition for another flurry of smug looks and sly suggestions.

This has been going on since sophomore year. Since I started non-chalantly mentioning that I was bisexual. Jonah has been out (and exceptionally loud) about being the school's "cutest bi-masc guy" since I first moved here in sixth grade.

And . . . sure, maybe his confidence, his willingness to shout it to the skies, was partially what motivated me to do the same. Not to have a whole "coming out" speech in front of my graduation class, but just not to hide it, like I did back in Detroit. It wasn't that people in my old school were outwardly prejudiced, but I was still this quiet, awkward kid who had a maximum of two friends, both of whom stopped texting when I moved away. I didn't want to further ostracize myself by revealing that some of my attraction was reserved for more than just girls.

But, of course, as soon as our friends and acquaintances found out that we shared the same sexuality (and literally nothing else), the pleas for us to try going out began in full force. Even while I was casually dating other people around school.

It's not just because you both like guys, Hanna told me at one point, with a violent eye roll. *It's because you've always had chemistry.*

The only kind of chemistry Jonah and I have is nuclear.

I pour the caramel into my ramekins, and something catches my eye. The drawer next to the sink. It's cracked open. The sealed envelope and faded ink glare up at me.

Lil Dyl

That's the name on the front. It used to be Little Dylan, the Americanized version of my father's old nickname for me (Dylinho), but Tomás decided that was too many syllables and chopped it. "If you become a famous rapper," he said, "you've got a name. You're welcome. I'll take thirty percent of your profits."

He sent this over a year ago. I still haven't opened it.

I bump the drawer closed with my hip, fingers trembling around my whisk as I blend egg yolks. Think about something else. Something . . . anything . . .

Suddenly, I hear keys jangling near the front door, and my heart rate spikes. It has to be Dad. Right? Did he take the rest of the day off for once? He probably got in late last night, since his restaurant closes at midnight and he sometimes hangs with his employees at the bar afterward. He often leaves home early to set up, too, so he definitely saw the party mess on his way in and out.

The door swings in. Sure enough, it's Dad, wearing an apron over his owner's attire, cradling his cell phone between his cheek and shoulder.

"Mantenme informado." He must be talking to a subordinate, because Mom would be scolding him for sounding so authoritative. Most of his Latine staff converse in Spanish, which gives him a good excuse to practice the language to impress Mom's side of the family instead of whining about how nobody in the Midwest speaks Portuguese. Not that he's even fluent anymore—he moved here from Brazil when he was barely seven, and when his mother refused to converse with him in anything other than English to "help him adjust," his fluency deteriorated. All he was allowed to bring with him, really, was his fascination for the food. "Gracias. Volveré en unos diez minutos."

My shoulders slump. He's not sticking around. I shouldn't be surprised, considering this happens every time he walks through the door.

He strides toward me, wearing his famous ear-to-ear grin. "Nice to
see you alive and well. Figured you'd be out cold until two," he booms,
peering into my mixture of ingredients. "A flan kind of day, eh?"

"Yeah . . . it's been rough."

He slings a burly arm around my shoulder and stretches up to kiss my
forehead. I savor this moment, because I'm not sure when it'll happen
again.

"Did you forget something?" I ask sternly.

"Keys to the back office. Had to leave George in charge." He shudders, and now I understand why he's in a hurry. "How was your party?"

"Fine." Even if I wanted to tell him the truth, he doesn't have time
to listen.

His grin turns mischievous. "I peeked into your room this morning."

I can almost feel the color drain from my face. "You didn't."

He fumbles through the drawers for his keys, glancing only once at
the one concealing Tomás's letter. "Who was he?"

"Let's not talk about this," I say shortly. "Nothing happened. He was
drunk, so—"

"*What?*" Dad snatches his keys, then turns on me, nose flaring. "You
got into bed with a *drunk* person?"

"Yes, but we didn't—"

"Dylan Mauricio da Costa Ramírez. You *know* people can't give their
consent when they're intoxicated. Didn't we already have this talk?"

I shudder at the remembrance. Like I could ever forget the humiliating day he decided to sit me down and say, *Let's talk about sex, son.* "I
know! Like I keep trying to say, nothing happened. I just didn't know

where to put him, so I let him share my bed." Irritation creeps into my
chest, and I mutter, "Don't you have to get to work?"

Part of me hopes he'll say no. That he'll be upset enough to sit me
down and scold me. Maybe we'll have the most uncomfortable conversation a father and son can have.

Instead, he says what I expect.

"Yes." He rushes to the front door, tossing one grim look over his
shoulder. "This conversation isn't over, Dylan."

It is. In fact, he's already gone.

I return to baking. I should've picked a more complicated recipe.
This one is easy enough that I don't have to think about what I'm doing.
Baking has always helped take my mind off things—distract me from
intrusive thoughts. It was a mild interest at first, until my therapist told
me pursuing it might help me focus on something other than . . . well.

My phone chimes.

HANNA
Andre said something happened with you and
Jonah. Why am I hearing about it from him??

Immediately, I silence my phone, scowling. There's no way I'll be
able to convince anyone that nothing happened between us. They'll
never stop bugging us, never back down, until . . . I don't know. We give
it a shot, or something. But I'm too emotionally exhausted to contemplate an idea as repulsive as that, so I stow it away.

At least for now.

JONAH

I'm cold and hungover and drenched and this *sucks*.

As I walk, I try not to think about last night. Despite what happened, I had fun. It's not often I can spend so much time with my friends—Andre in particular. He's always swamped in AP homework and student council meetings, being the vice president alongside President Hanna Katsuki. They're Delridge High's power couple, and *busiest* couple, so getting to hang out with them isn't easy.

Not that my own schedule is any help. The only person who seems to have eons of free time on his hands is the Prissy Prince, and he's the last person I'd want to hang out with one-on-one while Andre is driving his brother to lacrosse games, or Hanna is volunteering at the Little League's softball rec center while the varsity team is on break.

The point is, even if my memories from the party are spotty, the moments I do remember are warm and filled with laughter.

It might've been perfect, if I hadn't gone back into Dylan's room.

My house is dainty, and there's tape over one window. The color's faded, the wood's curling, shingles are missing from the roof, the porch is rotting, and the lawn is an expanse of tangled weeds. I could probably do more to make it look less like a fixer-upper, if I had time.

I shake my shoulders out, draw a deep breath, and lift my chin. Adult Mode: Activated.

I head inside, where I'm greeted with the horrifying sight of my sister kicking a soccer ball against the glass door.

"Hey!" I growl.

She squeals and whirls, her brown hair flying around her face. "Jo-

Jo!" She smiles innocently. It used to work a few years ago, but she's twelve—the ripe age of losing squishy cheeks and childlike wonder—so she's not as cute as she thinks.

"Mikayla," I say darkly.

"Hello, my brother." She eyes my sopping wet clothes.

"I can't even afford to fix my window," I snap, kicking my shoes off. "What do I do if you shatter the whole door?"

"I was being gentle! And. Um." Her gray eyes scavenge the ceiling, seeking an excuse. "I need practice, and you won't let me kick in the backyard when you're not home . . ."

"You have *actual* practices, right?" I ask, rubbing my forehead. "Where's Lily?"

"Our room."

"And Dad?" I glance around. He always leaves traces when he comes by—the stinging scent of whiskey, melted ice on the counter, bottle caps. Right now, there's no sign of him.

Mik fidgets, and I can see the truth written all over her face. The sight of it makes my stomach plummet.

"You told me he came home last night," I say sharply.

"I didn't want to ruin your fun!"

"Mrs. Greene left you here *alone*?" I demand. She's the elderly woman who lives across the street and watches Mik and Lily so she can escape her grumpy husband. She usually doesn't walk home until I get there to replace her.

"I . . . might've told her Dad texted me that he was five minutes away and said she could go home." Mik looks everywhere but at my eyes.

Though I'm soaked to the bone, I fold into the couch. My blood rises into my temples, worsening my headache. "You can't stay here alone with Lily," I say, leveling my voice. Normally, I wouldn't be able to, but Adult Mode grants me the power of composure. "What if someone broke in?"

"What if?" she demands. "Not like Dad would do anything about it."

"Mikayla."

My stern voice causes tears to sparkle in her lashes. "Sorry. I just . . . Jonah, I *really* didn't want you to come home."

She's a little twerp. I love her to death. "Hey," I say, bumping her chin up, forcing her to meet my eyes. "Thank you. But you understand why you need to be honest, right? I have to know I can trust your word."

Her lower lip trembles, but she bites it away, nodding.

"I have to get ready for work." Though my whole body is aching, courtesy of the hangover, I rise from the couch. "Ms. Harris is picking you up at one for your game at the dome. Make sure Lily brings a coloring book."

"Don't worry, Jo-Jo." She sticks one thumb in her chest. "I'm the most mature person you know. I got this."

"Says the girl using the glass door as a soccer net." I examine the house again, assessing for damage. The couch footrest is still stuck in its usual half-up, half-down position. The kitchen is cluttered with plates, but nothing unmanageable. "Put towels on the couch, would you? I want that ass imprint gone."

"You're the one dripping rain everywhere!" she hisses, but she trudges to the kitchen anyway. "Making me wipe your butt off the couch . . . so gross . . ."

It's enough punishment for now, so I head down the hall, prying my damp clothes off. I veer into my room and fold a robe over my shoulders, then glance to the taped window. Beside it, angled toward the sky, sits my telescope. As soon as I lay my eyes on it, a pang of nostalgia rocks my stomach. Or maybe it's just the nausea again.

I maneuver toward it through the cramped space, then pick up my feather duster, swiping it along the clean, glossy top. The lens is cracked, so it's useless. But it was a gift from Mom, so it's fine where it is.

I head across the hall, nudging into Mik and Lily's room.

Lily is lying atop her bed, dressed in a pink skirt and one of my old zip-up hoodies, humming over a sketchbook. My sleeves are five inches too long on her nine-year-old arms. You'd think she would stick to wearing her own clothes, considering we've stuffed her wardrobe with new tops, bottoms, and the like since she transitioned last year. Alas, it seems she's only ever truly content when she's drowning in one of my sweatshirts. "Hi, Jo-Jo," she says with a smile that cures my aggravation.

"Hey, Lilypad." I prop myself on her mattress, combing down the curls tangled over her forehead. She's drawing a giraffe, which is the least surprising thing that's happened today. She's got a horrible fascination with those long-necked monstrosities.

"That's the best giraffe you've drawn all week!" I say brightly. "The neck is the perfect height. And I love how fluffy the tail is."

She blushes with satisfaction. "Do you want it?"

I reel back, gaping at her. "You . . . would let me . . . have your amazing, beautiful drawing?" I sniffle, fanning my face. "I'm going to cry."

"I give you pictures all the time," she points out, but she crawls over and throws her arms around me anyway, squeezing. "Don't cry, okay? Also, you're all wet, you know."

Oh, right. I remove her from my lap before dampness can seep into her clothes.

"Um . . . Jo-Jo?" She sits cross-legged, fumbling with her hands. "There's a book fair tomorrow. Ms. Brennan . . . you remember her?"

I nod. Ms. Brennan has been Lily's counselor for almost a year now. She's been a massive resource for Lily at school, where they have private weekly meetings to talk about everything under the sun. Ms. Brennan wrote a letter home not long ago to say that Lily has been doing well, and is feeling more and more like her authentic self as time passes.

It was addressed to me. Not Dad. To which I panicked for over a week, wondering how much Lily has been telling Ms. Brennan about our situation. But there haven't been follow-up questions or repercussions, so maybe Lily is just saying she feels the most comfortable around me, or trusts me to be the one to read updates.

I know it's risky, pairing her with a counselor whose job is to dig deep and ask questions. But ensuring Lily has some kind of support system at school is my biggest priority.

"She found this book she thinks I should get," Lily says lightly. "The main girl is like me. I never read one of those. It looks *reaaaally* good! So maybe . . . I can have a little money?"

The tentative way she asks makes my chest sting. I hate that, no matter how hard I try to hide it, Lily is fully aware of our situation. "Of course." I make sure my smile is bright, warm, and comforting. "I'll put money in your backpack."

I peck her forehead, easing up. Everything's good. Nobody burned the house down. Still, the thought of Mik and Lily spending the night here alone . . .

I don't have time to contemplate what a horrible brother I am, so I dart for the bathroom and suffer through a lukewarm shower (I need to figure out what's going on with the water heater). As I scrub shampoo through my hair, I list out my schedule. Work. If it's slow, maybe I'll get farther in *Pride and Prejudice*. Then, sleep. Then, school. Then, work. Then, piled-up homework. Then, sleep. Repeat. Repeat . . .

I stare at the grout in the tile, eyes drooping, goose bumps raking my arms and legs. I started this school year off pretty well, somehow managing to perfectly balance my personal life with school, homework, and actual work. But I can never seem to maintain it beyond a few weeks, and I fall behind in gradual increments. I've been slipping in certain subjects, especially twelfth grade English. I have no doubt Ms. Davis is going to have some shit to say about it. She's the last person I want to get involved with, but I can't help it. Reading takes more time than, say, solving equations in math, or writing short answers for early childhood education. Naturally, it takes a back seat to subjects I can conquer more quickly.

Once I'm dressed in my server uniform, I call Mrs. Greene. When she says she's about to walk over, I jog to the door.

"Mrs. Greene is watching you until Ms. Harris picks you up for soccer," I tell Mik. "Keep the door locked. Also—"

"I *know*." She rolls her eyes. She looks like Mom when she does that.

I fold open my broken umbrella. The rain is heavier now, so this walk is going to suck.

I stride into the downpour anyway.

I was spotted staggering back into Dylan's house by about five people.

Yet, somehow, everyone knows.

When I get to school on Monday, people are winking, offering congratulations, and slapping my back, like I single-handedly won the homecoming football game. It's like the student body's been pining for us to date since Dylan first thrust his dick into my life.

Nobody believes my story.

"Jonah," Maya says while we walk to precalc, after I've recounted the tale of how I cussed Dylan out and fell asleep immediately afterward. "You and Dylan have more sexual tension than anyone in the school. There's no way you just did some yelling and then crashed."

"It was only a matter of time." Casey, normally my saving grace when it comes to people demanding that Dylan and I taste each other, nods during English. "I try to leave you alone, but now you're spending the night together after parties . . . it's sickeningly adorable."

"I knew you were after Dylan," Rohan says during partner work in sociology. "You're always stripping him with your eyes."

"I am *not*!" I shriek, which makes Ms. Anderson scowl at me.

"Right . . ." Rohan arches one dark brow at me. "Hey, how many inches?"

"*Shut up! Shut up, shut up—*"

"Jonah Collins!" Ms. Anderson snaps.

"I am being harassed," I announce. "May I be removed from this partnership?"

To which she tells me to quit messing around or she'll send me to the office, and I resist the urge to walk there myself.

I don't see Dylan until I'm heading to the cafeteria for lunch with a swarm of students. He stands out in a plaid shirt and beige chinos, with the sleeves rolled up like he's some hot English professor. "Hey," I say, weaseling through the crowd and bumping into him. "Prissy Prince."

I can tell he's refraining from a violent eye roll. "Oh good," he mutters. "It's you."

"What have you been telling everyone?"

"That nothing happened and people are overreacting."

We spill into the cafeteria—the only part of the school I like. The ceiling is paneled high with glass, allowing sunlight to flood in if we're lucky enough to see it. I'm a sucker for glass ceilings, because I imagine, at night, I could watch the stars without worrying about my cheeks freezing. (Not, like, *the* glass ceiling, of course. Shatter those wage gaps, ladies.)

"Oh no," Dylan says, groaning. When I see our lunch table, I grimace.

Our friends are hunched together, talking. Even Casey, who avoids the drama, is tilted in. Maya whips her head back and forth between people so quickly that her microbraids threaten Rohan, who clearly doesn't have the heart to tell her. Andre's the center of attention, and I know. I *know*.

"They're talking about us," Dylan says, mirroring my thoughts.

Hanna is on the outer edge of the group, watching us. She smirks.

"Nope." Suddenly, Dylan has my wrist, and he's pulling me away from the cafeteria.

"Let go!" I hiss, fighting his monstrously strong grip, but he ignores me, nudging me into the bathroom near the main office. It's usually empty, which means it's a great place for emergency dumps. It's also great for private conversations, so long as no one's ripping ass in your ear. "What's your problem?"

"Everything." He kicks the stall doors to make sure they're vacant. He looks flustered, angry, annoyed—like he's at the end of his rope. I wonder if people have been prodding him about Saturday just as much as they've been prodding me. "They're never going to stop harassing us, unless we do something."

"There's nothing we can do." I scowl. "Just keep saying we didn't—"

"That isn't *working*, Collins. It never does!" He gets this look like he's smelling something rank. I have the feeling it's nothing to do with the bathroom. "I . . . have an idea. That could possibly make it go away."

I narrow my eyes. He's looking more uncomfortable by the second.

"They bother us because we won't try going out," he explains. "So, what if we did? We could—*um, no, get back here*."

He catches my shirt collar before I can sprint away.

"*Hell nope!*" I shout, wriggling against his grip.

"Just listen." He releases me, and my momentum nearly carries me into the wall. "What if we pretend something *did* happen after homecoming? We decided to try dating under wraps. But, oh no, they found out anyway!" He shrugs with a fake, playful smile. "Guess we'll go public. We keep it up, and just as they're congratulating themselves for 'setting us up,' boom. We have a blowup. With screaming and crying. Then, we stop talking, and they'll all feel too bad to continue annoying us."

By God, he's serious. "You're telling me," I say slowly, backing away from him, "we should start a Hallmark rom-com."

He blinks at me. "In rom-coms, they fall in love."

I retch violently.

"Exactly," he says. "So, what do you think?"

It's a repulsive idea. There's no way I'd be able to pretend like I'm hopelessly falling for my Ultimate Archenemy of All Time.

Then again, I can't count the number of times people have proposed the idea—Jonah and Dylan becoming *one*.

I tap my worn sole against the tile, deliberating. "We could hold out until graduation." Anything to avoid this horrendous plot.

"Do you think this is going to stop just because we're not in high school anymore?" Dylan asks skeptically. "Our best friends are going out, Collins. This won't end unless they break up, and I don't think either of us wants that."

He's right. Andre and Hanna have been dating for two years, and Andre is the happiest I've ever seen him. And, though she's always been the cool, reserved type, I can tell Hanna's happy as well. She doesn't talk outwardly about it, but from what Andre told me during one of our deep (and rare) best friend conversations in his car, she's always been uncomfortable discussing her asexuality with her partners. Since we were all already friends who knew about it when they started dating, she didn't have to "come out" to him, or fear his response.

He's good at making her feel safe and unrooting her from her stubbornness. She's good at pulling him out of the clouds and grounding him when it matters. I don't want their happiness to end just because I'm sick of Dylan's face. "How long?" I mutter.

"Long enough to convince everyone we gave it a chance. Through winter break, maybe?"

Three months. It's three too long, but if it means putting the harassment and teasing behind us for good . . .

"Okay," I say in resignation, slumping forward. "We pretend to date, and during winter break, we get into a fight and end it."

"Fine."

We regard each other with wary eyes.

"We'll have to . . . act it out," he says grimly. "Do things."

I fold my arms, the thought already churning my stomach. "We don't have to *do* anything."

"Relax, you dip." He gives me a vicious eye roll. "You won't have to ride me in public—"

"Who is riding whom?"

"My point," he cuts in, "is that we have to act lovey-dovey, like a real couple. So when we go out there, you should sit on my lap or something."

My cheeks tingle with warmth. Did that suggestion actually just come out of Dylan Ramírez's mouth? "Why can't *you* sit in *my* lap?" I demand. "Is it because I'm skinny? My thighs are quite sturdy, thank you, and they can totally handle your weight—"

"Dios mío." Dylan clasps his hands and looks skyward. "Uno de estos días lo voy a matar . . ."

Before I can offer an amazing comeback to whatever Spanish insult he hurled at me, the door swings open. When the intruder sees us, he gulps and scurries to a stall.

Dylan and I leave to let him take care of business in peace. Which means it's time to commence our plan, I guess.

Fake it until we crush it. For good.

DYLAN

I didn't think anyone other than Andre and Hanna knew that Jonah spent the night at my house. And yet, I've found myself at the ass-end of ridiculous questions from people that make my blood temperature spike.

Is Jonah as loud in bed as he is everywhere else?

We knew you guys were going to hit it eventually.

I heard you tried the "get it out of our systems" method.

I'm tired of it. I'm tired of *him.* But if we stand any chance of getting people to let this go, we need to work together. So, as Jonah and I reenter the cafeteria, I draw a deep breath. It's only three months. Hopefully the ruse will be worth the mental strain of putting up with him.

"Take my arm," I mumble. Some people are eyeing us, watching us walk together. Reluctantly, Jonah wraps his lean arms around mine, both of which are cold enough to start leeching my body heat. "Come with me to the lunch line. I don't want you going over there and ruining everything with your face."

He huffs, but he must know I'm right, because he doesn't complain. Jonah's face says everything for him. I glance to our lunch table, just in time to see Maya jam her elbow into Rohan's side and point to us. He follows her finger, and his eyes double in size.

No going back now.

When we reach the front of the line, I order my usual protein-heavy sub and apple, then turn my eyes to Jonah. "Not buying anything?" I ask. Now that I'm thinking about it, I can't remember the last time he came to the table with a lunch tray, or even a paper bag from home. I try to avoid thinking about Jonah Collins throughout the day, though, so it's never been something I actively noticed.

He squeezes my arm tighter, like he's trying to crush it. Tragically for him, he's got the strength of a strawberry. "I eat at my job," he says irritably. "It's seventy percent off and more filling than whatever expensive crap they sell here."

"Ah . . . right." He sounds defensive and that's not something I want to deal with, so I guide him to our table without comment. Jonah's clinging to me like I'm a lifeline now, and his face is strained with worry, which makes *me* worry. Will he be able to keep up a consistent act in front of our friends? "Deep breaths," I whisper. "You'll do fine."

Jonah looks up at me, trepidation flickering in his eyes. I want to remind him that we're about to be in his favorite place—the center of attention. So, why is he nervous? Because he needs to lie, maybe?

Jonah examines my level expression, and the tightness relaxes in his jaw. He nods.

I try not to acknowledge that he just used me to center himself.

Finally, we reach the table. Hanna's legs are in Andre's lap, but when he sees Jonah, he lunges to his feet, nearly sending her flying. "Jo-Jo!" he says, grinning widely. "I *knew* you couldn't resist a fine-looking man like Ramírez."

Maya wags her finger at our linked arms. "Nothing happened, my ass," she snaps. "What's that about?"

There's a pause. Rohan's eyes are still bugged. Casey's peeking over their phone at us. Hanna's looking suspiciously between us under her long eyelashes, fumbling with a worn softball hat she was probably asked to remove earlier (like every week), studying us. She's the one I'm most uneasy about. She's always been grounded and observant—a stark contrast to Andre, whose energetic personality nearly rivals Jonah's. I'm more familiar with her Bullshit Detector than anyone.

This won't be easy.

"Um," Jonah says, his voice cracking, and he pushes me into one of the metal-legged chairs. "Don't mind if I do."

He shrugs his backpack off and collapses into my lap.

More silence.

Okay, this probably doesn't look *great*. Because yes, Jonah's smaller than me, but he's not small. He's a five-foot-eight high school senior, sitting pin straight in a six-foot-two guy's lap. There's no goddamn way this looks natural, sweet, or anything I was shooting for. I guess we're going to need to find time to plan how to make our relationship look legitimate.

"No offense," Rohan says, "but what the hell?"

I curl my arm around Jonah's waist to try and make this look less awkward, and feel the shudder of revulsion that rushes up his body. "Since you figured something happened between us during homecoming, we decided not to hide it," I say.

They're still staring. Andre looks like he's vibrating in his seat.

"You see—"

I pinch Jonah's side, squeaking away his sentence. If he keeps his mouth shut, we can get away with this. Calm and steady, I begin to spew bullshit. I tell them Jonah stumbled up to my room, and after a long, deep conversation about our feelings and some other garbage, we decided to try dating. That we were planning on hiding it, until we got to school and realized everybody already knew anyway. They listen, enraptured, clinging to my every word.

Except for Hanna.

Knots twist in my stomach. She's watching Jonah closely, still spinning that hat in her palms. Clearly aware of this, Jonah is looking at everything but her. Only then do I realize how close he is—how many fine details I can see on his face. The rounded tip of his nose. The tired red veins stretching away from his irises. The fine texture of his hair.

"Anyway," I say when I suddenly realize I've stopped talking. "We told each other how we felt and went to bed. That's all."

"Really?" Hanna's voice is steeped in skepticism. "After all the whining and complaining Saturday night, you just . . . came to your senses?"

Shit. We haven't even made it past the first "fake" scene and she's already suspicious? On a whim, I snatch Jonah's hand and begin to massage the length of his thumb. It feels weirdly soft and tender, but I know we'll have to get used to far more, so I don't let it bother me. Hanna looks for smaller clues, so this is a good start. "I didn't expect it either, honestly," I tell her. "But when we were alone, things felt different. Right . . . cariño?"

That word tastes all kinds of wrong on my tongue.

"Right," Jonah wheezes, draping his head in the crook of my neck.

"So basically," Maya says, a slow smile creeping into her cheeks, "we were right."

Which leads to an eruption of laughter, cheers, we-told-you-so's, we-knew-its, and the like. I muster my most convincing smile and squeeze Jonah's palm—I can tell he hates this as much as I do.

Three months. Then, this will be over.

"Let's do a double date!" Andre says, dragging his chair toward us. "My parents are taking Bryce up north for a lacrosse tournament this weekend, so Hanna and I are hanging out at my place on Saturday. We're getting food delivered and drinking my parents out of their booze. You should come!"

"Well. Uh." Jonah fumbles with his hands. "I probably work—"

"Nope! I have your schedule login information, remember?" Andre grins, wagging his phone in Jonah's face. "I take a picture of it every week so I know when to drop in."

Jonah swallows audibly, then turns to me. "What do you think . . . Shnookums?"

Yeah. We're fucked.

"Can't wait," I say weakly.

Just like that, our fates are sealed.

JONAH

Just when I think I've escaped this school day from hell, Dylan catches me on my way out the doors. "Collins," he calls. "Let's talk."

Dylan yanks so hard on my backpack handle that my feet nearly depart the concrete. "Ugh," I growl as he pulls me to the side, so hordes of students can go around us. "Do you drag everyone around like this?"

"Sorry. Sometimes I forget how light you are." He sounds less sorry than he's ever been.

I rub my arms to battle the cool October breeze. The lingering heat of summer is dwindling every day. "What do you want?"

"We should be on the same page about everything if we're going to . . ." Speaking low, Dylan glances at everyone rushing around us to the parking lot. ". . . convince them. Like, how to keep up the act, rules and boundaries. Maybe we can talk at your house—"

"No!" I snap, fleeting panic darting through my body. He draws back, startled. My tone probably sounded more desperate than angry, so I scowl. "Hell no, you can't see where I live."

His jaw does that irritated twitchy thing. Before he can say anything else, I realize my phone is vibrating in my pocket. I pry it out, looking at the caller ID.

Bastard Man.

He sure as hell isn't calling me to ask about my day, so I should probably answer. "Hang on," I say, turning my back to Dylan and ignoring his whiny protest. I lift the phone to my ear. "What?"

"School called." He sounds far away. Not literally. I can hear him fine, but his words are monotonous and more breath than sound, like he can't be bothered to create noise. "Mikayla's in trouble. They're expecting you."

Just like that, he ends the call. Charming.

Thoughts of Mik instantly begin to overwhelm whatever chaos was previously going on in my head, so I start beelining to the main street. If I walk quickly enough, I can get there in twenty—

"Are you seriously walking away?" Dylan's irritable growl reminds me that he's still here. When I glare at him over my shoulder, I realize he's stomping after me like a gigantic toddler. "Where are you going?"

"The K–8 school." I try quickening my pace to lose him, but his annoyingly long track legs don't let me get far.

"We still need to figure a plan out. I'll drive you, and we can talk on the way there."

He's offering me a ride? *Again?* I swivel to examine his expression. There's no hint of pity or sympathy. Nothing to indicate his offer is anything more than a chance to talk.

So I say, "Fine."

I follow him across the asphalt, through the maze of vehicles, hardly noticing as he takes my hand—probably to make us look more convincing in front of the dozens of students clambering into their cars. What's with this guy always being so warm, anyway? And not even in the sweaty, clammy way.

I drop into his passenger seat, gnawing on my nails. I hope Mik's principal will take pity on her for . . . whatever she did. Maybe she talked back to a teacher. Threw a book at someone. Cussed at a lunch lady. Regardless, I hope she doesn't earn another suspension, or I'll have to skip school to watch her. Mrs. Greene comes through as a temporary babysitter, but she's a busy old woman, too.

Dylan is talking. Something about listing out how comfortable we are doing couple things in public, or whatever. I unlock my phone, hoping Mik texted, but she hasn't. Dad got her a phone, but only so I could keep in touch with her so he didn't have to.

"*Well?*" Dylan snaps, hoisting me out of my daze.

"Well what?" I demand.

"I said I'd drive you so we could talk." Dylan frowns. "Normally, you're a pro at running your mouth. Are you ignoring me?"

I decide to do exactly that and lean against my window. They wouldn't *expel* Mik. Right? She's a pest, sure, but she's a good kid. They know that, don't they?

"Seriously, what's wrong?" Dylan demands. I can't tell if he's annoyed or concerned, but the question only agitates me further.

"Nothing." I have it under control. I always do.

"Can I . . . do anything?" he asks, sounding like he's choking on glass.

I should say, "No, but thanks," or "It's fine," or literally anything other than what comes out of my mouth. "You could drive faster, you damn snail."

Ice seeps into the air around him.

I want to apologize, because that was shitty of me, but I can't build the words on my tongue. And I might accidentally say something even worse, so I give up, sealing my lips between my teeth.

Eventually, we come upon the one-story brick school building and its tinted glass windows. With a quick "thanks," I crawl out, sling my backpack over my shoulder, and slam the door. I tromp toward the building, my mood worsened. Dylan gives me ulcers, but . . . I probably didn't need to be like that. Especially since he's the reason I got here so quickly.

After the guard buzzes me in, I beeline to the front office and take a deep breath. Straighten my shoulders. Pop a stern eyebrow.

Adult Mode: Activated.

When I stride into the main office, I'm greeted by the principal's glowering frown. She hates when I come in place of my father. Mik sits before her desk, kicking her tennis shoes, and there's a boy in the seat next to her, nursing a swollen cheekbone on a bag of ice. A scowling woman sits beside him. She looks like the kind of person who thinks a 15 percent tip is generous.

The principal scolds the boy for snapping Mik's training bra. She scolds Mik for punching the boy in the face. There's yelling, mostly on that mom's part. I yell back, because loudness is my specialty. Before I can tell her she's lucky I don't punch that little perv myself, the principal comes between us, looking ready to evolve into a human-size migraine.

"Detention for the next week during lunch, both of you," she says. "No recess privileges, either. Go home."

I exhale quietly. No suspensions. Which means I'm not going to fall further behind in school by staying home with her for multiple days. To be fair, I don't care much about schoolwork and studying. It's not like I'll have the means to go to college without racking up six trillion dollars in debt, so I'm not going to bother. Still, if I don't keep up appearances and have decent enough grades, my teachers are going to take notice.

Especially Ms. Davis. The worst-case scenario.

Mik and the boy offer half-baked apologies to each other. Moments later, we're following the sidewalks home, bracing against the nippy wind rustling our coats.

"Um." This is her first word after minutes of silence.

"Yeah?" I ask darkly.

"I . . . didn't know Dad would send you." She runs her thumbs up and down her backpack straps. "Sorry, Jo-Jo."

"You're lucky they didn't suspend you, or worse," I snap. "Quit taking things into your own hands and go to a teacher next time."

"But *you're* always taking things into *your* own hands."

"I'm an adult," I say stiffly.

"You can't even vote."

"Listen."

She swings her arm around mine, hugging it. I expect she's trying to get on my good side, and yeah, it still works. "Guess Lily's gonna have to ride the bus alone," she mumbles.

I grimace. Lily is the kindest kid in existence, but she's quiet and timid, and prefers to spend her time with a book or sketchpad rather than people. Mik rides the bus home with her every day, and has this dangerous "big sister" energy that keeps some of the older, brattier kids out of their radius.

"I'll walk back later to pick her up," I decide, because I'm not sure I want to sit and wait around for another hour and a half before their school is dismissed.

"I'll come, too."

"Well, I'm not going to leave you alone to break the glass door again."

"Yeesh." She huffs, and a strand of chestnut brown hair flutters to the side of her face. "That was so long ago. Let it go, loser."

I shoot her a dagger-sharp glare. "Really? You have the balls to call me a loser right now?"

"I took yours when you were sleeping."

I can't help it. Adult Mode malfunctions, and I laugh. Mik grins, clearly pleased with herself.

I love this little shit.

DYLAN

I should know by now that if I offer anything to Jonah Collins, he'll just be an ass about it.

I'm still riled up when I get home. Which is new. Mostly, I'm just dreading going inside and getting stuck in a loop of boredom and lack of motivation to do anything about it. Now, though, I'm ready to cure this annoyance and get Jonah's face out of my head.

Except it's not the right face—the one contorted with all the negative things he's known for. It's the one I saw when he was leaning against my car window, eyes glazed with worry. I've never seen him look like that before.

It doesn't excuse his ugly behavior, but it still makes me wonder. What could've happened to make him look so . . . distressed?

I yank on sweats and decide to jog. I've been neglecting that more frequently, with the changing weather and deteriorating sunlight. Running has become a favorite activity, more so than the other sports I've played and dropped in recent years. It's the only one that lets me choose when I want to be social.

I do warmup stretches, stuff my wireless earbuds in, and take off.

As I carve a path through the suburban streets and their tidy lawns and trimmed trees, I can't help but want to plan. I feel like Jonah and I need a detailed itinerary of things to do on Saturday. 6:15—he leans on my shoulder. 6:30—I kiss his cheek. 7:00—he feeds me a fry.

My phone dings. Even now, the feeling makes me wince. I know it's not . . . him. He hasn't texted in over a year. Still, despite the amount of time that's passed, every day hits me equally as painfully as the one before it.

It's from Mom. Probably something about school, grades, or crappy small-talk conversations I should only have with distant relatives.

How was school?

Ding, ding. We have a winner.

I exit our conversation. Then, because I'm feeling particularly bold, I scroll through my messages. I pass Hanna's name, Dad's, Rohan's, George's, a group chat I've muted. Scroll . . . scroll . . . do I still have it . . . ?

Big Tom.

I shouldn't. My thumb trembles, hovering above the name. It's a terrible idea, forcing myself to do this for . . . what reason? I don't even have one.

I open the message screen anyway.

And regret it immediately.

Hey. Comin this time??

You coming with Dad today? Got any plans
tomorrow?? Mom and dad are coming down if
you're interested. Lemme know!

I hear you've been swamped. No worries if you
can't see me.

What've you been up to kid??

Miss you! Call me some time?

Love you, Lil Dyl.

The last text is dated from over a year ago.

I shove the phone into my pocket, heart racing for a reason unrelated to my spontaneous jog. My body begins to go tingly and numb, attempting to submerge me in panic mode. Okay. It's fine. I just have to draw attention to my breath and think about something else. Anything else.

School. I have homework. Precalc. No, is it English? Or both?

Tomás's face unfurls before me, contorted with wrath.

Baking. I should check the pantry. See if we have enough eggs, sugar, semisweet chocolate chips, flour. And . . . flour. Flour. I need flour. For something. For . . .

His voice rings in my ears.

"*¿Cómo te atreves? ¡Te voy a matar, hijo de la chingada! ¡Pudrete en el pinche infierno!*"

Dad. I should think about Dad instead. I wonder if he's out on the floor mingling with guests and enthusiastically teaching them what little Portuguese he remembers, or if he's back in the kitchen. His regret for having been severed from his culture at such a young age comes through most frequently when he's at his churrascaria. Sometimes, it makes me wonder why he wanted us to go by Mom's surname, rather than his. He's secretive about it, but I've always felt that maybe it was a Hail Mary attempt to win over my mom's parents, back when he was still struggling to

gain their approval. I'm not sure why they didn't like him—my parents
don't tell me those kinds of things. But, until they severed contact from
us, he fought to get in their good favor. So much for—

Tomás lifts the baseball bat over his head, chest heaving. Blood
stains the tip.

Mom. Something about her. I just have to think of something to focus
on . . .

He screams, reeling it forward again.

Jonah. Yeah. Him. I have so many thoughts about Jonah Collins that
surely my panic won't find any cracks of still silence to squirm through.
I'll just start listing my infinite number of reasons for why I hate him.
Why does he have to exist so loudly around me? Why does he take plea-
sure in being such a nuisance?

This entire "fake dating" situation is his fault. If he hadn't come back
inside after the party to continue screeching, none of this would've happened, and I wouldn't be worrying about how we're going to pull it off.
Worse, it means that for the duration of our scheme, I can't date anyone.
I had a casual fling with a girl who asked me out this summer, but it
didn't last longer than a couple months. They rarely do. It's not that I
don't like being committed, but . . . when my partners find out how much
baggage I have, they . . . well.

Whatever. I know I'm going to find a person who doesn't mind the
weight I'm carrying.

But I sure as hell won't find them while my ass is glued to Collins.

The buzzing feeling in my body begins to diminish. My breathing no
longer feels like it's on the precipice of leaving my control.

I'm sickened that he's the person who managed to center my thoughts.
Ugh.

I get another text. If it's Mom again, I'm throwing my phone down the nearest drain.

> HANNA
> We're going to Jonah's work for dinner. Want
> to tag along and see your new boo?

Do I want to see Jonah? God, no. And yet . . .

I remember Jonah's face from earlier. Maybe I should've eased up on pushing him to talk, but he needs to be equally as devoted to this as me, even if it means spending time together to figure it out.

Tonight might be a good opportunity to corner him, once Andre and Hanna leave. If what Andre said is true, Jonah only has one free night this week—Saturday. The further we put off plotting, the more likely everything falls apart.

Besides. The thought of being alone tonight sucks.

So I text, Sure.

JONAH

I'm ready to throw up when I see his deplorable face in my booth.

It's bad enough I have to deal with Dylan McDickass Ramírez at school, so why's he at my workplace? With Hanna and Andre, at that. I already have to wear my customer service mask here, and now I'm supposed to throw on another one by pretending to like him?

"Jo-Jo!" Andre leaps up and squeezes my shoulder when I approach the table. He's wearing a Spider-Man sweatshirt with a built-in mask. It's some version I've never seen before, probably from the comics or something, with red sleeves, a blue chest, and a black spider painted across the middle.

"Dork," I say, smirking. I've lost count of his Spidey apparel, and so has he, probably. "Why are you here?"

"Can't I see my husband every once in a while?"

"I divorced you when you wore that naked Batgirl T-shirt." I shove Andre down beside Hanna, who's now looking at him with a newfound repulsion that would have me kneeling in apology. Dylan is across from them in a pale pink flannel button-down, looking exactly like a third wheel. "Any special reason for today's visit?"

"Hanna's parents found some new hole-in-the-wall bar that they wanted to try out tonight, and my parents finally forked over my allowance money from last week, so here we are," Andre says brightly. "Besides, Ramírez was basically begging to see you."

Dylan gives me this emotionless smile that tells me he'd rather choke on something than beg to see me. Hanna glances expectantly between us, her sleek ponytail swinging back and forth behind her softball cap.

Right. We have to be *warm* and *fond* toward each other, so I slip into the booth beside Dylan and offer my cheek. Thankfully, he gets the idea and leans in to peck it. His lips leave a warm imprint above my jaw.

"So, how does it feel?" Andre gives us a leering grin. "Knowing that you lost the battle and finally caved to each other's masculine wiles, all thanks to your two best friends!"

"No need to brag, now," Hanna says, but she's smirking, too.

"How can we not?" Andre demands. "How *long* have we waited for this day, Hanna?"

"Pretty long."

"*Years* long," he clarifies. "Thank us whenever you're ready, boys. Our ears are open to your gratitude!"

Hanna flicks her cap back and gives us a wry smile that tells me she's onto us, and it hasn't even been a day.

Dylan startles me by squeezing my kneecap. Maybe he sensed I was about to say something I'd regret.

I'm afraid Hanna might sneak in a jab or question that might fluster me, so I stand and take their drink orders. Andre gets a glass of Mountain Dew his energetic ass clearly doesn't need. Hanna gets a virgin strawberry daiquiri fit for a queen. Dylan gets the embodiment of his personality—ice water.

I buzz around the restaurant, carrying food, busing tables, displaying my charming smile while actively avoiding my boss, Sherry. She gave me her spare manager card, since I've already worked the legal amount of hours this week and can't use my own. We're busy, so thankfully she's preoccupied behind the bar.

Unfortunately, it means I can't socialize with my friends, but . . . well. Money.

Once they're cashed out, Hanna kisses my cheek, and I soak in the fact that I've peaked as a human. Andre gives me an intense hug and tells me to "hang in there." I tell him the same—I'm sure he and Hanna are about to go home and bury themselves in mounds of AP homework for the next few hours.

I convince myself we'll have some time this Saturday to catch up with each other. Though, I have no idea how likely one-on-one time is, considering we'll be on a . . . ugh. *Double date.*

A minute later, Hanna and Andre are gone. The problem?

They don't take Prissy Prince with them.

"Go home," I order, passing him with an armful of plates. He's propped a laptop and notebook on the table.

"This might be our only chance to talk."

"While I'm *working*?"

"I'm fine waiting until you're off." His eyes flick around the restaurant. "Seems like it's slowing down anyway."

I grumble, moving on. He's right. It's 8:30, when the swarm leaves and random one-tops and two-tops trickle in. Sherry cut me from the floor, too (against my will), so I'm done taking guests.

Once my final table is situated, I bring a giant rack of silverware to Dylan's booth and slap it down.

"Uh?" Dylan says.

"Side work." I sit across from him. "If there's time to talk, it's while I'm rolling silverware."

Dylan watches while I fold napkins and stack utensils. To my dismay, my stomach chooses at that moment to growl obscenely, loud enough that I can hear it over the chipper pop rock playing over the speakers.

"Hungry?" he asks, cocking his eyebrows.

"No."

"Thought you didn't buy lunch because you get discounts here." Dylan looks at me in this accusatory way that makes me feel like I'm being scrutinized. Embarrassment tingles in my stomach.

"I had mozzarella sticks earlier."

"Ah." Dylan nods thoughtfully. "Sounds like a perfectly balanced meal."

"It's dairy and wheat, so yeah, it is," I snap.

He furrows his brows, but thankfully, his focus moves to his laptop. "I outlined discussion topics."

"What's the notebook for?" I ask, smirking.

"In case my laptop freezes," he says defensively.

Incredible. I'm sitting before a living, breathing dork-ass loser. ". . . You're very prepared."

He scoffs at the amusement in my voice. "Better to be overprepared than underprepared."

"Right." I wave my palm. "Continue."

He watches me with wary eyes. Then, "First topic, how to act in front of friends." Dylan pulls out a small hand sanitizer from who knows where, then massages a dollop over his palms. He plucks utensils from the rack, rolling them into a napkin. "I think we can agree lunch didn't go . . . smoothly."

"You told me to sit in your lap!" I cry out.

"But you looked like I was holding you hostage. Lunch will be our biggest test, since that's when everyone's together. Maybe we should make a daily schedule of things to do."

The idea is ridiculous, but I don't want to accidentally flinch if he leans in for a hug I'm not expecting. "Tomorrow, we can meet up outside the cafeteria again," I suggest, flicking his hand away when he goes to roll more silverware. Why is he doing that, anyway? Is he building a résumé of all the things he's helped me with so he can lord it over me? "Hold hands to the table and all that. I'll put my legs in your lap."

"Okay." He nods. "Let's have a side conversation, too. I see couples doing that everywhere. Usually one is, like, playing with the other's fingers. Or looking lovingly into their eyes."

I shudder at the thought. "Finger play is fine."

Dylan stares at me.

"What?" I realize he's biting his lips. "Wait, *what?*"

"Nothing." Clearly fighting a smile as he types, he says, *"Finger play."*

I grumble. "Also, I'll whisper a joke to you, and you'll laugh because of my comedic genius. Couples are always giggling."

He types once more. *"Pretend like Jonah is funny."*

I throw a spoon at him, which he bats onto the table.

Dylan and I draft out the week. We rely on hand holding, head leaning, knee rubbing, and the like. After that, we cover other bases—like, we should meet frequently to discuss how things are going. He can come to the restaurant and wait until I'm off the floor, if needed. Also, we should follow an intimacy timeline. If we're only cheek kissing a month into our relationship, it'll raise red flags. As the days pass, deeper kissing, neck pecking, and . . . ugh. *Looking lovingly into each other's eyes.*

"Okay," Dylan says, and at that point, the silverware is rolled and stacked in the metal basket. "One last thing. We should discuss the breakup and build up to it so nobody thinks it comes out of nowhere."

It's like this guy is plotting a novel. Is there anything he hasn't thought of? "Well," I say, straining my brain. "It could be . . ."

I'm about to come up with the perfect idea, probably, but then, my phone rings. Dylan watches as I fish it from my pocket, tapping his fingers against the table in a ballsy display of impatience. Guess I should make this quick before he sentences me to the gallows, or whatever snotty princes do.

"Mik?" I ask.

"Jonah?" Her voice is hoarse. "Do you . . . know when you'll be home?"

I angle away from Dylan so he can't see my paling face. "Why?"

"Just . . . Dad is home and dropped a glass . . . it wasn't that loud, but Lily had a panic attack . . ."

Ah. Okay. When I next speak, I keep my voice calm. "Be there soon."

I end the call and climb out of the booth.

"You have that look again," Dylan says.

"Have to go." I head toward the bar, where Sherry is cleaning dirty glasses. When she sees my expression, she sighs and says, "Leave your book. I'll get you your tips tomorrow."

I hate doing this. At least I only have one table that needs cleaning, but still. If this happens more frequently, Sherry is going to fire me—a repercussion I can't afford. Especially because she's probably the only manager in Delridge who'd let me work off the clock, beyond the legal hours a minor is allowed to work.

I thank her for understanding, grab my jacket from the employee closet, and return to the restaurant. Dylan is standing in front of the booth, fidgeting. I'm not sure what he's still doing here. "See you tomorrow," I say, and I go to pass him, but he catches my shoulder.

"I know our rides haven't been great," he says. "But do you . . . need one?"

Do I? It would get me home quicker. It would benefit me in multiple ways, probably.

But I can see it. That glint in his eye.

Pity.

My blood is already frothing. "I don't *need* anything," I mutter. I shove past him, then walk to the restaurant door and push into the cool darkness of the evening. Traces of moonlight poke through the spotty clouds, illuminating my pathway.

When I know he can't see me, I start running.

DYLAN

I've been standing at the restaurant, feeling helplessly bewildered, for a couple minutes. Jonah's face is still etched into my brain. And his voice on the phone . . . it was uncharacteristically calm. Jonah speaks with a lot of inflection and force, which is why so many people listen to him. It's like he can funnel his entire theatrical personality into every sentence he speaks.

But this . . . it was so mild. Tempered.

I wander out to my spot in the parking lot and begin to drive.

Maybe it's about his sisters. He's always talking about them with the group. Bragging, like he's a proud parent. One of them made a friend, the other saved a soccer game, one has a new hyper-fixation, the other was voted class clown in mock nominations.

Sometimes, I wonder if Tomás talks about me.

I crawl to a stop under a red traffic light, sighing. Why would he? Mom and Dad probably update him on my life when they visit, but what reason would he have to bring me up to anyone? If not to tell them how I ruined his life and cut communication with him.

Anytime my thoughts near him, my fingers tingle. My throat burns with bile.

I wish I could talk about my brother like Jonah talks about his sisters.

When I get home, the house is empty and dark, as always. Everything is the same, aside from a note Dad left me.

Thumbs up for the pudim de leite condensado! I won't tell George his flan is inferior. Brigadeiro next? Personal request from a Carioca!

I smirk. Even though he doesn't have many memories from his brief time in Rio de Janeiro, and my grandma tried to shun traces of its culture while he grew up in the US (to help him "transition" and "make friends," which is a depressing thought), he's always stubbornly clung to his love for its food. Whenever I make a Brazilian-native treat, he lights up with excitement.

There's an arrow pointing to the back of the note. Frowning, I flip it.

Maybe your boyfriend will enjoy your chocolate too, eh? ;)

I groan, my cheeks burning. I texted him about my "relationship" with Jonah earlier today. He doesn't know it's fake, mostly because he'd never be able to keep a secret that juicy. If he pops in while Hanna and I are home, the last thing I need is for him to blurt, "How's the fake BF?"

The downside to this is that, because he thinks it's real, he's offering me all kinds of unsolicited advice, and asking details about Jonah's life I don't know. But I guess that'll be the point of our future meetups. To figure each other out, so we can convince our friends that things are more than surface level.

Well, if I do it right, brigadeiro cake will take me a few hours. It's a task for tomorrow's Dylan. I lock up and head to my room, shedding my clothes before flopping into bed. I always seem to end the night alone. No parents, no Tomás, no partner. I don't mind it for the most part, but there comes a time when the loneliness really starts to seep in.

I swear I can still feel the imprint of him lying next to me.

I open my messages and find his name. We've never texted individually before today.

You good? I stare at the text, thumb hovering over the send arrow.

I delete it. He's not going to respond anyway.

JONAH

My father is sprawled on the couch, his drooping eyes linked with the local news station, his hand gripping the two most expensive things in this house—a crystal glass filled with amber liquid.

The mere sight of him sucks the energy out of me, leaving me numb.

I don't want to waste any words on him, so I head into the kitchen, where I find Mik stirring mac and cheese, looking like she's aged ten years. "Hey," she mumbles. "She's under her bed. I tried to get her to come out, but . . . you're still the only one she listens to."

I smooth back her knotted hair, then stride down the bedroom hall-way, turning into their room and dropping to my knees. Lily's curled up under the bed frame, face nestled into her stuffed giraffe. "Hey, Lily-pad," I whisper. The sound of my voice causes her face to pop up over the animal's head. Her eyes are watery and red. "I hope you're hungry. Mik's making mac and cheese."

She snuggles up tighter against her animal.

"The ground is cold, huh?" I ask. "Bet you could use a hug."

"No thanks," she murmurs.

I gasp. "You must be *really* sad if you don't want one of my famous hugs."

Her lips wobble into a smile, but she shows no signs of moving. It's not easy to open Lily up once she's curled in on herself. Before she died, Mom was the only one who was able to get her to budge when she hid under her bed. Mik and I were both a little too loud and impatient to gain any real progress with her. But Mom . . . she had that exact level of calmness and lightheartedness that could bring any of us crawling into her arms.

When she passed, someone else had to take up the torch of warmth in our house. Mik was eight and already spiraling into rebellious, wild behavior. Lily didn't have the strength in her arms. Dad was wordlessly sinking deeper into his addiction, unresponsive to my voice.

So, I did it myself. From my memories, I learned how to imitate her—how she handled Mik versus Lily. When they were angry, sad, lonely, hopeful . . . I learned how to adjust to them. How to cool Mik down when she was on fire. How to warm Lily when her light had been reduced to embers. How to make it feel like, even though Mom was gone, they still had someone who could respond to their needs.

I was a thirteen-year-old brat, so I wasn't the most convincing parental replacement. After about a year, though, I settled more easily into the role, and Mik actually began to listen to me. Lily began to seek me out regularly for comfort.

Maybe I became a more convincing role model, or maybe they finally realized that nobody else was going to be a parent for them. I don't know. Over the years, though, and with the addition of "Adult Mode" to my repertoire, I think I've done pretty well at becoming someone they can rely on. I did it without my father. Without any outside familial help. Technically, Mom's sister moved into town after her death, but she never bothered with us before, so I ignored her presence when she came prying.

I didn't need her. Or anybody. I learned how to stop *needing* people years ago. "Have you started reading your new book?" I lie down, just beyond the bed frame, and stretch my hand out, resting it in front of Lily. Just close enough that she can touch me if she wants.

"Mm-hmm," she says quietly. "It's funny."

"Funny like, *this is weird*, or funny like, *I'm going to pee because I'm laughing so hard?*"

She reaches out, setting her palm on mine. "Both."

"Good. Those are the best books."

She crawls closer, so she's a couple feet from me. Her curls are knotted against her forehead. I'm not sure why my sisters always have the messiest hair, no matter how often I comb it out.

I offer my arms to her. "I know that seeing him makes you sad," I whisper. "I know he makes you anxious. I know you don't like how the house feels when he's here. I'm sorry. I promise . . . I'll get us out one day soon, okay? Can you trust me?"

She squirms between my arms, and I pull her into my chest. "I'll always trust you, Jo-Jo," she says gently, and then she begins to cry. For a few minutes, I let her, rubbing her back, whispering that I'm here. Even if I have to drop everything and run across town, I'll always be here.

I scoop her off the floor and settle her on her bed, then pluck a tissue from the bundle on her nightstand and pinch it around her nose. "I'll check on your mac and cheese."

She wiggles underneath the comforter.

When I walk out of the bedroom, I find Mik on the couch, doing math homework. "Where'd he go?" I ask.

"He just left." She sounds exhausted, like every word weighs heavier and heavier on her shoulders.

I move into the kitchen, then dump the mac and cheese into two bowls. I set one beside Mik, then return to Lily and place the other in her eager hands. Once she devours the whole thing, I refill her water glass, tuck her in, kiss the top of her head, and say goodnight, wishing there was something more I could do. Eventually, I force Mik to join her.

Once I have the sink cleaned out, I sit at the kitchen table, pulling books out of my backpack to commence homework torture.

I'm tired.

I stare down at *Pride and Prejudice*, my eyes sagging. I can't get any further behind in school, or my precarious work-school-life balance is going to start slipping away. I've managed to get this far without buckling under the pressure, and I only have until June before I get to put school behind me forever. Then, it'll just be a work-life balance I need to maintain.

Telling myself that doesn't help. My head is becoming heavier, harder to hold up. Every blink burns my eyes.

But I can't pass out. I can't pause. I have to keep moving, keep working, keep treading . . .

Within five minutes, I fall asleep slumped over my books.

I dream about *Pride and Prejudice*. It's about Mr. Darcy (the 2005 movie version) proposing to me in the rain. Someone's pulling down his pants. I think it's Dylan. Keira Knightley is blowing air in my face.

Wait. That's someone else.

I blink my bleary eyes open. For a moment, I'm sure I'm still at my kitchen table, taking a snooze—until I realize that "someone else" is my teacher, and she's smiling at me, her elbows propped on my desk. "Hi," she says.

I yank upright with a choked, "Geh!" I twist around, re-collecting myself as the fluorescent school lighting assaults my pupils. The class is snickering. It's Ms. Davis. Of all the classes to fall asleep during, it had to be hers. Her sharp gray eyes peer into my soul, and she's close enough that I can see her brown roots infiltrating her severe red hair. "Good morning," she says pleasantly. "Shall I fetch you a blanket and a bottle of warm milk?"

More laughter. "Hey," I say, wagging my finger. "I was dreaming about the current read, so count me present."

"Oh?" She straightens up. "Everyone, listen! Jonah is going to tell us about his dream. I'm sure it's far more interesting than the actual book."

I start building my wit, though I'm already at a disadvantage because I'm groggy. But I've never been one to back down from a challenge, especially not from *her*. "So," I say, fully aware that every eye in the room is locked on me. If anything, it fuels my confidence even more. Calling students out during class isn't normally her style, but I've always been a special case. "I'm at the estate, right, when this man visits. He thinks I'm the hottest of my brothers, so he proposes. And I'm sitting there like, my guy. You're my dad's cousin? Gross."

"Such drama." Ms. Davis gestures. "Continue."

I see the competitive flicker in her eyes. She wants to know how much I've read.

"I go to this ball and see this gorgeous guy there. Like, drop-dead rammable. And we share a dance . . ." *Wait, I'm going backward.* "But I find out he was part of this terrible plot to break up my older brother, Josh, and his lover, Brinsley."

Ms. Davis gives me a convinced nod. "The audacity."

"Right?" I scoff loudly. "And then, you wouldn't believe it, the guy *proposes* to me. And he's like, *I guess you're dirt poor, but God, I want to get in those Hanes.* And I'm like, you know what? My mom is about to faint, so I don't have time for you. Bye!"

"And then?" she prompts.

I haven't gotten any further. I sigh in defeat. "That's it."

Her smile turns grim. People are laughing, and it's the only good thing about this moment.

Ms. Davis resumes class. I rub fatigue out of my eyes, refocusing. Why am I so tired? Probably because I fell asleep at the kitchen table, but still. I'm a teenager. Aren't we supposed to have endless youthful energy, or something?

When class ends, I try to squeak out the door with Casey, who's praising my incredible improv.

"Jonah?" Ms. Davis calls. "Stay back, will you?"

Great.

I stop, flicking my middle finger at anyone who giggles or wishes me luck. As soon as they're cleared out, Ms. Davis ambles to the door, pulls it shut, and gestures to the desk next to me, her expression annoyingly neutral.

Groaning, I slump into it. "Sorry for falling asleep, Ms. Davis," I say mechanically. I'm not, but hopefully it'll get me out of here faster.

"I get the formality during class, but you don't have to call me that when we're alone, nephew dearest."

I purse my lips.

"You know, reading your short answers to my prompts is always a highlight of my day." She swings a chair backward in front of my desk, sitting down and folding her arms over the back. I drive my eyes down, avoiding her stare. "Lately, though, they've been getting shorter. Sloppier. Your grade is slipping. And now, you're sleeping during class, when you're usually the loudest voice in the room."

I remain silent. There's nothing I can say here, no excuse I can make, that won't raise her suspicions.

Ms. Davis started working here when I was a freshman, and I managed to avoid her three years in a row. I didn't have a single class with her, and I made sure to surround myself in the hallway with friends so she could never pull me aside to chat with me. But, like always, my luck had to run out. There are only two twelfth grade English teachers in the school, so it was a fifty-fifty chance that I'd get stuck with her.

And here we are.

"Have you been having trouble sleeping?" Her voice is hesitant, and I know why. She knows she doesn't have the right to ask about my life.

"You never worried about me before Mom died, so don't pretend you care now." I want to spit the words at her, but I maintain my calm, cold demeanor. I can't let pent-up emotions lead a conversation with her.

"Forgive me for wanting to check in on my family," she says, with an eye roll that causes a vein to twitch in my forehead. "And quit pretending to know everything about me. Kim and I—"

"Don't." There's ice in my eyes. "Don't say my mom's name."

"Don't act like a child," she says sharply, and that's what gets me to my feet.

I heave my backpack over my shoulder. "I'll read more tonight, so you don't have to single me out again—"

"Sit *down*, Jonah."

My tight jaw quivers with strain. I don't want to hear another word, but I also don't want her to send me to the vice principal for my behavior. So I stand there, frozen in limbo.

"Look at me," she says.

No. She looks exactly like Mom, if Mom were in her early thirties and had dyed hair. She's got the same slender nose, eye shape, widow's peak, chin. I *can't* look at her. Doing that will reopen the grieving wounds I managed to sew up following Mom's death.

I don't have time to sew them again.

Just then, the door opens, and someone else walks into the room—a towering Black man dressed in a tie and dress shirt buttoned to his neck. It's Myron Kelly, the teacher who specializes in family and consumer sciences electives, like child development. Though, he looks more like a gym teacher, with legs thicker than the Bible and arms that could snap necks with one flex. (He wouldn't, though. He's one of those "gentle giants," I think.)

I have Mr. Kelly for early childhood education, half because I wanted a blow-off for senior year and half because I'm all right around kids, so maybe there's a future in it for me. Sure, I'd sell my soul to blast myself into the endless abyss of space, but I'm not a math or science buff, so I've retired that dream.

I stopped thinking about my future a while ago anyway.

"Jonah," Mr. Kelly greets, his cavernous voice shaking the room.

I turn to Ms. Davis, glad for the escape opportunity. "Your husband is here to make out with you, so I'm leaving."

Mr. Kelly chokes. Ms. Davis slaps a palm to her face.

I'm already gone.

DYLAN

When Jonah finally meets me in the mouth of the cafeteria, his face is gnarled in a familiar, grumpy pout, and his narrow shoulders are sagging. He seems exhausted.

"Casey told me you got ripped a new one by Ms. Davis," I say amusedly. I've been leaning against the brick wall, playing with the strings of my Delridge High Varsity Track and Field hoodie, waiting.

"The ripped state of my butt is none of your concern," he says stiffly.

I extend my palm toward one of his clenched fists. "Remember the plan?"

"I'm . . . putting my legs in your lap." He slides his fingers between mine, and we start into the bustling cafeteria. "We need to have a quiet conversation. And . . ."

"Finger play." I smirk. "Don't forget the finger play."

We start toward our lunch table, where everyone is already sitting around, munching food and laughing. His hand tightens subtly around mine, though I'm not sure if he's just nervous, or seeking reassurance. He makes no comment about needing to get food from the lunch line.

"Waiting until work so you can eat again?" I ask as we journey to the table.

"It's not that long of a wait," he says sulkily.

I refrain from sighing. I'm not Jonah's biggest fan, but it still makes me squirm, knowing now how long he goes without eating. Though, maybe he snacks throughout the day, or has a hearty breakfast before coming to school. I don't know all the facts, so I shouldn't be concerned.

We get to the table and sit down among the teasing quips and *aww*s.

I draw my lunch bag out of my backpack, trying to loosen my tight face muscles.

"Holding hands again?" Maya asks, clicking her magnificently long nails together with mischief. "Please make it a habit. It's adorable."

Is it? I'm dubious.

"How'd last night go?" Andre leans over his open AP bio textbook on the table, grinning. "You lovesickos didn't do anything cute after Hanna and I left, right? I'd be pissed if I missed anything."

"We just . . . talked," Jonah says, and since everyone's looking, he swivels in his seat and tosses his legs into my lap. He's too far away, though, so he nearly nails me in the crotch with his heel. I wince, my face clenching with (hopefully subtle) rage, then seize one of his chair legs and wrench the whole thing across the floor until he's beside me.

"Love the enthusiasm," I murmur, so only he can hear, "but be more careful, *cariño*."

I spit the last word at him.

"You just talked?" Hanna sounds highly suspicious. *Again.* Her legs are tucked up on her chair, and she's studying an open notebook in her lap while picking at her bento box. I hope she's just looking over her AP psych notes and not studying all the red flags she's probably been keeping track of since we revealed our "relationship."

I laugh with a hint of strain. "We just stopped hating each other. It'll take time before we start making out in front of you, if that's what you and Andre are looking for."

Hanna nods slowly. "You just . . . stopped."

There's this accusatory tone in her words, and it makes my throat tighten with annoyance. "Yeah." My voice comes fiercer. "We did. Why?

Is that weird? You're the one who kept nagging me about how amazing Jonah and I would be together if we could sort things out."

"I figured the realization would come over time," Hanna says, scowling at me. "Not overnight, on the same day you threw him out of your house. Can you blame me for being confused as hell about all of this?"

My confidence is waning. The entire table is quiet, their eyes moving between us. I point my gaze to my lunch bag, scrambling for a response as I pull out my containers of homemade salsa bruschetta and chicken quinoa salad.

"Emotions . . . were running high," Jonah says, folding his hand over my knee. It anchors me enough to make my muscles untense. "We started off yelling, but that realization *did* come quickly. We were talking, then lying next to each other, and the conversation turned . . . so, now we're here."

I have no idea how he gets that bullshit out without cracking his voice. Maybe because he can sense I'm short-circuiting under the pressure. Hanna studies us in that familiar, painfully thorough way.

"Okay," she says.

Whew.

The table moves on, talking amongst themselves. I sigh, resting my forearms over his shins in my lap. "My bad," I mutter.

"It's fine," he says. "Have to pull my weight if this is going to work."

I almost want to tell him I'm impressed with his ability to save us while I was buckling under the pressure, but I don't want to feed his ego. So, I stay quiet, munching on my food, uncomfortably aware of the fact that Jonah doesn't have any.

I want to distract myself, and maybe this is a good time to have our "private conversation," so I search for a topic to bring up. Unwisely, my brain goes to the next thing I've been wondering about. "So, about last night . . . did you get everything figured out?"

As I expect, I've said the wrong thing. Jonah's atmosphere immediately crystallizes into ice, and he hoists his legs out of my lap. He turns to the table, then tucks his face into his arms like he's going to take a nap.

So much for our plan. "Why do I bother?" I mumble.

He keeps his head down for the rest of lunch.

JONAH

Our double date has arrived.

Dylan and I keep up our acting through the week. We mostly see each other during lunch, so we play up the cutesy-poopsy stuff as much as possible. On Wednesday, he stands when I approach the table, and hugs me hard enough to crack my ribs.

"That hurts, you ass," I snarl in his ear.

"Not my fault you're so delicate," he whispers.

On Thursday, he fiddles with my fingers and kisses my knuckles and it's nasty.

On Friday, I stand with him in the lunch line, where he rests his chin on top of my head and allows me to fold his arms around my waist. We talk to Andre and Rohan in that position, trying not to look tense and awkward, until they have to turn and order.

Tonight's our first real test. We'll be in the spotlight. Hanna's spotlight. She hasn't outright accused us of anything, but there's always uncertainty in her eyes whenever Dylan and I interact.

We'll need to be flawless.

I have everything figured out. Mik and Lily will spend the night at Ms. Harris's house, the soccer mom who I only go to if I'm desperate (she likes to ask questions). Now I just have to get through work.

"Hey," a voice says behind me while my finger hovers above the kitchen screen. It's Jez, my co-worker. "I heard your table order the salmon, not the barbecue burger."

I realize I've submitted the wrong order and cuss. I'm not supposed to use the manager card for corrections without supervision, so I call for

Sherry. No way am I going to jeopardize this job, even if she's the last person I want to see.

"Be on guard," Jez mumbles, striding toward the hot racks. "It's an *extra handsy* day."

Of course.

Sherry exits the office and raises one pencil-thin eyebrow at me. When I ask her to void my order, she peers at the screen over my shoulder, close enough that I can see foundation crunched into the lines around her eyes. She takes her sweet time fulfilling my request, then readjusts my apron knot on my waist, pats my back pocket, and walks away.

My tensed shoulders fall. Ugh. Maybe one day I'll swing at her if I find a better job. But I need to put up with it for now—at least until I'm eighteen.

When my shift ends, I speed home and give myself a thorough scrubbing in the shower before fumbling through my closet for something decent to wear. I know we're just going to Andre's house, but it's still a date, isn't it? So, I probably shouldn't show up in my sweatpants.

One of my shirts has a hole in it. Another is so worn I can barely see the design. One I outgrew a few years ago, because my body insisted on growing vertically.

I settle on a slightly faded black button-down with a leafy design. I pull on jeans that are just dark enough to look appropriate, attempt to smooth out my hair, then head into the living room for the final verdict.

"You're so handsome, Jo-Jo!" Lily says brightly.

"Are you *really* going on a date?" Mik sounds skeptical enough to offend me.

"Yes!" I scoff. "It's a real date with a real human."

"A cute human?" Lily leans forward in excitement.

"He's . . ." More attractive than he deserves? Hot in the most infuriating way possible? Pretty enough you can't help but want to punch him and even the playing field? ". . . cute."

Lily squeals. Mik squints at me in a suspicious Hanna-like way.

I still have ten minutes before I need to walk to Dylan's, so I sit on my bed near my cracked telescope. I brush the feather duster along the body, then flop onto my back. Not being able to peek through it anymore is torturous, even if there's not a whole lot to see in the middle of Delridge.

It's been years since I've gone stargazing, but it hasn't diminished my love of outer space. Big fan of the void, this guy. If someone ever talks dirty to me, they'd better incorporate astronomical terms in there. If they say they're going to heat me up like WR 102 in the constellation Sagittarius until I supernova, I'll pledge my body to them for life.

Originally, it started as a cute, totally reasonable hobby. Mostly because my mom was the obsessed one, and I wanted to be as cool as her, so I took interest.

Until she left this world. Suddenly, the stars were more than a fond observation from afar.

I wonder what Mom might say, if she knew about this plan with Dylan. I try not to think about her often, since it makes my chest feel cold and hollow, but sometimes, I can't help but daydream. How she would respond to things, or solve a crisis, or help me prepare for my first date.

If she knew about the fake dating, she'd probably snort and tell me Dylan's way out of my league. Then she'd warn me not to let teenage hormones spiral out of control. If Dylan came to the house, she'd fill the air with sarcastically loud comments about how handsome he is, and

Can't you date my son for real, Dylan? Nobody else is going to want him.

I'd shake her shoulders and beg her to stop humiliating me. Maybe she'd take me to our special stargazing spot later to apologize, with a tray of her gooey sprinkle brownies. I'd forgive her, like always.

At least, that's how I picture it.

DYLAN

We're going to be late, and it's his fault.

I've been pacing my living room for twenty minutes. I've texted him five times, called him ten. To keep up appearances, we decided we should show up together at Andre's place. Now, though, I'm regretting it.

Doesn't he care about being on time? Probably not. It's all about him, after all. Because he's Jonah Collins. The life of the party, the person everyone looks for. *Where's Collins? Is he coming? When will he be here?*

I collapse on my couch and slam my face into my fluffy cobija. I'm annoyed. And . . . well . . . curious. How can I not be, after the weird things that have been happening? Needing a ride to his sister's school, having to leave work because of some problem at home, skipping lunches. Something . . . doesn't feel right.

I'm not sure why I care. It's none of my business. Though, I have a right to be concerned, since it's interrupting our plot.

I've waited long enough, so I text Andre for Jonah's address, then plug it into my phone and retrieve my container of polvorones de canele from the kitchen. Instinctively, my eyes flick to the drawer. *That* drawer. I can't see through the wood, but I can envision the letter—where it's positioned, how it's angled.

Before anxiety begins to cloud my thoughts, I shake my head. I can't worry about it tonight. I have to focus on how Jonah and I are going to pull this off.

I take off in my car. The sun is descending earlier these days, so even though it's barely dinnertime, the horizon is turning a pale orange that casts a sugary pink glow against the clouds.

I wonder what Jonah will do about transportation during winter. Does he seriously walk everywhere year-round?

When I pull into his driveway, my thoughts taper off. I'm not sure what I was expecting, but I thought it would at least be . . . I don't know. More, maybe. I slide out of my car and, after nearly tripping over a fracture in the driveway, I approach the sagging porch. I give the door a gentle knock, shifting foot to foot as the chilly fall air nips my face.

It creaks open. A young girl squints through the crack. "Who're you?" she demands.

I know I'm at the right house, because she looks exactly like Jonah. The button nose, the tousled brown hair, the pasty skin, the gray eyes. The constipated scowl. "I'm Dylan," I say, smiling uneasily. "Is Jonah here?"

"Dylan?" she asks, nearly rivaling his level of sass. "Like, Dylan Ramírez? Like, Dylan, the biggest jerk in Jo-Jo's life?"

That gets a laugh out of me. Jonah's salt knows no bounds. "That's me."

She tries closing the door, but I wedge my shoe in the crack.

"Wait!" I plead. "I'm here to pick him up for . . . um . . . our date."

She glares at me. "*You're* the one he's going on a date with?"

Unfortunately. "Yep."

"Hmm. This won't last long." She opens the door farther, and I squirm inside before she can change her mind.

It's not much warmer in here. The kitchen is a tiny space infested with chipped wooden cabinets and empty beer bottles. The stained beige wallpaper makes me feel claustrophobic. A narrow hallway stretches to my left, probably for the bedrooms. Another child, younger than the first, sits on the couch, a book pulled close to her rosy cheeks.

"Hi," I say with a small smile. "You're Lily?"

She twists toward me. Floppy brown curls rest low on her forehead, nearly creeping over her curious eyes.

"And you . . ." I turn back to the first girl, who's watching me like I'm about to do something diabolical. "You're Mikayla, right?"

She folds her arms, which I take as confirmation. "This is Dylan," she tells Lily.

"Jonah's friend!" Lily's voice is so bright and sweet I'm almost convinced it's true.

I look back at Mikayla, who's now baring her teeth. "Where's Jonah's bedroom?"

"Back left." She scowls, then tacks on, "But if you pull any funny business, I'll kick you in your throat."

"Um . . . right." She's definitely Jonah's mini-me, though I'm not sure if it's endearing or unfortunate. I maneuver down the hall, massaging my cold palms, and nudge the door open.

Jonah's room is a tight, cramped area, like the rest of the house. But, unsurprisingly, it has far more personality. Several space-themed pictures are pinned to his walls, signed by Lily. Rolled up posters lie tucked in the corner of his room, and a telescope sits at his window. One of the panes is cracked and covered with tape. His floor is a maze of discarded clothes, which I maneuver between until I'm sitting on the edge of his bed. His comforter is a starry sky theme—a chaotic swirl of black and purple dotted with golden twinkles.

Jonah's lying there in a snug coat and his shoes, asleep, his phone inches from his palm.

"Unbelievable," I snap, tapping my knuckle against his cheekbone. He wiggles his nose in response. "*Collins*. Wake up."

To my horror, Jonah rolls closer and nestles his forehead into my upper leg. The corners of his eyes are burned red, like . . . like he was . . . ?

"Did you know," Jonah mumbles, "Neptune gives off more heat . . . than it gets from the sun?"

I blink in surprise, then smirk. What is it with him and telling me random space facts while he's half asleep? I almost wouldn't mind lingering here, conversing with a sleepy Jonah to see what else he might say. But Andre and Hanna are waiting for us, so I tug him upright by his wrist.

"Come on," I say, louder. "Time to leave."

Jonah massages his tired eyes, blinks, and focuses on me. His face twists with horror.

"What the *hell*?" he shrieks.

Ah. There he is.

"What? When did? How did?" Jonah reels away from me. *"Why are you at my house?"*

"You weren't answering your phone, so I had to text Andre for your address." My frustration is already flooding back.

Jonah scrambles off his bed, his breaths coming in short, sputtering bursts. I brace for the string of curse words, preparing to fling a few back at him. In fact, I'm half-ready to sling this jerk over my shoulder and stuff him into my car. We're late as it is, so we don't have room in our schedule for a Collins Temper Tantrum.

Then, suddenly, his phone vibrates. In a flash, he has it to his ear, and a completely different voice is coming out of his mouth. "Hi, Mrs. Greene," he says, pleasant and chipper. "No, sorry, I didn't forget. If you could come over now, that would be fantastic. Thank you again!"

He pockets his phone and closes his eyes. I'm so bewildered by his sudden flip that I can't think of anything to say. He grabs my wrist, then drags me to the living room, where Mikayla and Lily are in quiet conversation. I watch, puzzled, as he pulls his shoulders back and lifts his chin, claiming an authoritative air. "Mrs. Greene is packing her magazines to come over," he says, and it's like he's now aged a decade. "Ms. Harris should be by in an hour to pick you up. I packed your toiletries before work, so don't 'forget' to brush your teeth. I put money in your suitcase so you can pay her back for dinner—"

"Okay, bye." Mikayla waves at him, and he scoffs.

"But—"

"Have fun, Jo-Jo!" Lily says.

"You . . . ugh. Fine." Jonah points at his pocket. "My sound is on, so call if you need—"

"*Bye, Jonah,*" they say simultaneously.

He cusses, then takes my jacket sleeve and hoists me out the front door, his lips set in a thin, unfriendly line.

"Quit dragging me," I order. "You—"

"Just pretend you never saw this." Jonah releases me to gesture at the house, then hooks my eyes with his. "Got it?"

I don't know what his issue is, but I don't feel like arguing. So, I climb into the driver's seat, and Jonah leans against the passenger window, looking away stubbornly.

Whatever.

I back out of his driveway, and we're on our way.

JONAH

I'll never forgive Andre for leaking my address.

I try focusing on the passing environment to steady my unease. The trees are turning to sharper October colors, and the grass is already suffocating under blankets of leaves. The skies are a deep, velvety blue—the kind that happens at dusk, before everything turns black.

I jump when his phone vibrates in the cupholder.

"Mind silencing that?" he asks.

I look at the caller ID. "It's your mom."

He startles me with a scowl. "So?"

". . . Okay." I silence his phone, dropping it back in the cupholder.

It's barely ten minutes to Andre's house, but each of those minutes seems to last twenty. I try not to worry about what Dylan's thinking, though if I had to guess, it's probably about how my house is so shitty and frigid compared to his.

I want to shout that I don't need it. Not his thoughts, not his consideration, not his pity. I want to tell him that I haven't *always* been a broke bitch. Like, sure, we weren't rich when Mom was alive, but with her and Dad's combined incomes, we lived decently enough. Our house was warm. The lawn was manicured. The fridge was stocked. We even had enough to splurge on an occasional fancy meal, or a day trip somewhere fun. I have faint memories of my father tagging along, but they're mostly from when I was in my single digits. Back before Lily was even born. Before he switched his priorities.

Anyway, the point is that Dylan shouldn't be looking down on me just because we're not in the best place financially. He doesn't know anything about my life that led us here. He doesn't know that soon, I'm going to lead us out of it.

I want to yell at him about something. Maybe I will. Just as I'm opening my mouth, though—

"I have a suggestion," he says warily. "Listen to the whole thing before you scream and whine."

I glower at him, preparing to do exactly that.

"We've been doing mild stuff all week," he says. We pull to the curb in front of Andre's house. He shifts the car into park, undoes his buckle, and twists toward me. "Remember when we first talked at your workplace? We agreed our relationship should . . . progress. Which means becoming more intimate as time passes."

I know what he's about to say, but I still nearly dry heave when I hear it.

"I think we should kiss tonight."

Kiss. *Kiss.* How can he say that with such nonchalance? Isn't he equally as repulsed by the idea as I am? "Kiss," I repeat squeakily. "Like, with our lips."

"No, with our dicks." Dylan rolls his eyes. "Yes, with our lips, you fucking dork. Hanna is already seeing red flags. I know she's going to dig deeper. So, let's take this next step. Let's convince them."

I sigh forcefully, hating that he's right, hating that I signed up for this nastiness. "When do we do it?" I grumble.

"I'm not sure. But we should be prepared so it looks natural."

I'm not sure "expecting" it is going to make it look natural, considering I've never kissed anyone (and it's *him*, the blight of my life).

Dylan must come to the same conclusion, because he says, "It probably shouldn't look like our first kiss. So . . ." He fidgets, focusing on my collar, and the realization burns me down to my neck. "Maybe we should . . ."

"Practice," I say, offering my guess.

He thrums his fingers against his knee. The air is so heavy with pressure I swear my head is going to explode. Are we actually going to do this? Right here?

"So . . . lean in, then," he says, gesturing to me.

There's only one way to make this moment go faster, so I shift awkwardly until I'm leaning over the compartment between our seats. My heart is already pulsing uneasiness into my body, and when he closes the space between us, it rolls into my stomach.

"Okay, so . . ." I'm close enough to smell the spice of his bodywash— to see each black curl on his head. How does this guy get *more* attractive the closer I am to him?

"So now . . ." He leans in, closing his eyes. His lips are three inches from mine. Two inches.

"Ha ha!" I wheeze, wrenching backward.

Dylan blinks at me. I blink back.

"You've never been kissed," he says. There's no emotion behind it— no surprise, or disgust, or amusement. He's stating it as fact.

"It doesn't matter," I say irritably, though I'm not sure that's true. I'm burning hot enough to set the car ablaze. I squeeze my eyes shut and lean closer, puckering up. "Come on. Lay one on me, big boy."

I brace for the moment his mouth touches mine, glad I can't see his knowing smirk or his dark brown eyes or his jutting collarbone above his navy blue coat.

"You've riled yourself up," Dylan says calmly. "Relax."

I realize my muscles are wound tight with strain. I try doing as he says, melting the tension in my shoulders and neck. "Okay," I say, then flinch when he smooths his thumbs over my eyebrows.

"These, too," he says, massaging space between my crushed brows until my face is relaxed.

"How's this?" I peek through one eye.

Dylan laughs, and the unexpected sound hits my chest like a Molotov cocktail, cooking me from the inside. He taps his index finger against my lips (I still have them puckered), then says, "Let's leave it for now and worry about it when we're inside."

"But . . . b-but I'm completely relaxed now!" I croak as he nudges open the car door and clambers out. "I'm so calm and collected!"

"Not the words I'd use. Come on, let's get in there before they start to think we got lost."

I know that if we don't practice, our first kiss will probably look awkward, so I kick open the car door and scramble out. "Dylan," I snap, and it takes several large strides for me to catch up to him. I grab his wrist, startling him, then turn him toward me and throw my hands in the air. "How the hell are we supposed to convince them if—?"

My voice breaks away. Dylan's eyes are suddenly glazed—his body is shrinking away from my extended hands. A hint of fear dashes across his face.

I blink, though, and suddenly, it's back to neutral.

"What?" he asks, or rather snarls.

"Nothing," I say quickly. It's certainly not *nothing*, but I can't pry now. Not when we're standing directly outside of Andre's house, about to put on a false display of warm tender sweetness or whatever.

"Let's just get this over with," Dylan mumbles.

He wraps his arm around my shoulders and guides me into the house.

DYLAN

Jonah's drunk.

I'm both annoyed and amused. Jonah's more boisterous when he's intoxicated, and he's insufferable in a crowd, but he can occasionally be entertaining in a small group. And weirdly cuddly. The issue is that he's not being cuddly with *me*.

Jonah is leaning on Andre, hugging him randomly while we pluck bricks from the Jenga Truth or Dare tower on the living room carpet in Andre's empty house. He's gotten "remove an article of clothing" twice, so he's shirtless and left-sock-less. Most of the blocks are innocent enough, though Andre's taken some of the unlabeled ones and Sharpie'd them with lewd suggestions.

"My turn!" Andre pries out a red brick, clearly buzzed out of his mind as well. He winks at Jonah. "Kiss the person to your left."

"Say less." Jonah puckers up. My fingers tighten around my Tito's and lemonade (seriously? Not even a moment of hesitation?), but Andre merely smooches his nose. "That's all?" Jonah whines, which is pretty damn bold considering he couldn't even peck my lips earlier without going into mental overload. "I thought we'd make out!"

"So I can get my ass kicked by Ramírez? Nah." Andre gives a solemn shake of his head. "Besides, what if we kiss, and I have some kind of bi awakening? It's too risky. Every group needs at least one hetero to set everybody . . . heh-heh . . . *straight*." He winks, and Jonah breaks down in ridiculous, hysterical laughter.

I glance at Hanna, who's sipping her strawberry-mango smoothie with a pleasant smile. "Should we cut them off?" I whisper.

"Eh." Her eyes glint with mischief. In moments like these, I think she's more conniving than she lets on.

"Refills!" Jonah and Andre scramble for the kitchen, leaving the two of us in brief silence.

"How are things with your new boyfriend?" She flutters her long lashes at me, and even now, there's something critical in there.

"Um . . . great. He's . . . yeah. There's a lot more to him than I thought."

It's not a lie.

Hanna hugs her knees against her chest. "Honestly, I was starting to think you two would never figure it out," she says, her expression softening. Her gaze becomes far away and pensive. "It disappointed me. Because, even though he's a lot, he's also good. Good at pulling people out of their shells. Making them feel comfortable. He's loyal, fun, and . . . every time I look at him, I think, *he's the kind of person Dylan needs*."

I smile through the pain. In just a few months, I'll never have to listen to this bullshit again.

"You also like being a protector." Hanna looks down the hall to the kitchen. "If anyone could use some protection, it's him."

I follow her eyes. Jonah and Andre are laughing, munching on the cookies I brought. I never noticed before, but without his shirt, Jonah looks . . . smaller. Not malnourished or anything, but his skin is a shade too pale, his arms a hint too slender. Whatever food he spares for himself obviously isn't enough. I wonder what he picked when we passed around Andre's laptop to order delivery from a local Chinese restaurant.

Maybe I should just stop worrying about it. I'm not sure why I even started. Jonah has made it perfectly clear his life is none of my business. And my life is sure as hell none of his.

"Anyway, what about you?" I ask, trying to subtly divert the subject from my love life. "How are you and Andre? Things good?"

She shrugs, and I can tell from the way her lip slants down that she's perfectly aware of what I'm doing. "Things are fine. We've been talking about college a lot. He's trying to gather up the courage to tell his parents he wants to study abroad."

The thought makes me shiver. If I had to study "abroad" anywhere, I'd go to Canada. Windsor is only a few measly hours away—a totally manageable drive. "What about you?" I press. "Are you still undecided?"

"Yeah. But . . . somewhere far from here would be nice." She closes her eyes, like she's envisioning it. "I know Delridge is on the bigger side of 'small town,' but . . . this isn't home for me. I want to be in a city. Somewhere with a lot of energy and activity."

"Somewhere that gives you a full ride for softball, too?" I guess, and she snickers in return.

"That too. The season just ended a couple months ago, but I'm already itching to get back on the field."

"You should give your poor knees a break," I tell her. "Seriously. I don't know how you catchers spend the whole game doing squats. It's like you're doing leg day *every* day."

"My legs are the most powerful part of my body, which I think is pretty hot," she says with a wink. "Maybe if you stopped focusing so much on your upper half, you could try it out and . . . see the benefits."

Thankfully, I don't have to think of a response to whatever she's implying, because Andre and Jonah come skipping back, their red Solo cups restocked and their volume still explosive. Jonah's holding a plate of my cookies. "Did you know these were in there?" he demands. "They're *amazing.*"

"Dylan made them," Hanna chips in.

Jonah's eyes slide to me, shimmering. It's so unexpected that something sparks in my chest. Maybe because this is the first time he's ever looked at me without malice, and my brain doesn't know how to process it. "You made these, Ramz?"

Ramz. He came up with that nickname a few days ago, since the term "babe" makes him want to . . . what did he say? Wrench his intestines out through his mouth, I think. "Yep," I say. "Polvorones de canele. Basically cinnamon cookies."

"They're so *good.*" He flops onto the floor beside me, nearly spilling the tray. "Is this your recipe?"

"It's . . . my brother's, actually. With a couple tweaks. They're his favorite cookie, so—" I realize I'm talking about Tomás casually, way too casually, and cough away my sentence. The air thins in my throat. "Glad you like them."

Maybe Jonah's too drunk to process my words, because he doesn't press it. Instead, he reaches for another cookie, and nibbles it with both hands. "Your turn, Ramz," he says through a mouthful of crumbs.

I tear my eyes away from him, then slip a block out of the bottom of the tower. It's one of Andre's ridiculous concoctions. "Leave a hickey on the person to your left." I arch my brow at Hanna, who instantly decides to play along.

"Guess you have no choice." She grins and tips her head, exposing her neck. There's no way Andre's going to let this slide. I pretend like

I'm about to crawl toward her, and sure enough, he scrambles over with a hiss. Then, he's in my lap.

Wait.

No. Andre's still across from me, chugging his drink.

Jonah's sitting on my thighs. He crosses his legs around my waist, squeezes his arms around my neck, and buries his forehead in my shoulder.

"Collins?" I croak. What the hell is he doing? Is this for show?

"No," he grumbles.

My bewilderment disintegrates. Of course it's for show. He's doing a damn good job of selling it, too, so I should play along, rather than looking like I've been stunned.

Hanna throws a hand over her smile. "Jonah, he needs to do what the block says—"

"No, nope, no thank you," Jonah snarls, shaking his head in my shoulder. "Goodbye!"

Andre's nearly dry heaving with feverish laughter. Hanna's biting her hair to prevent joining him. "Hey," I say softly. "I promise not to make out with Hanna's neck. Look at me, cariño."

Jonah mutters something. I realize, then, that he smells nice. Not like cologne but freshness. Shampoo and soap bubbles. Finally, he lifts his face and glares at me accusingly, his gray eyes drooping slightly. We haven't even had dinner yet and he already looks ready to crash.

"Did you really think I'd do it?" Fully aware that we're still being watched, I smile. "Come on, Collins."

His arms are still latched around my neck, his face hovering inches away, scrutinizing me with suspicion. "Not good enough," he mumbles. "You haven't even said sorry."

"I'm sorry for pretending like I was going to kiss Hanna," I tell him. I think I'm smiling for real now. I can't tell how much of his annoyance is real versus fake, but the thought that *any* of it could be real is pretty amusing.

"Not good enough," he repeats.

He's setting up the opportunity. I can see it in the tenseness of his jaw, like he's bracing. "What else can I do to make you feel better?" I ask, softer. Trying to make myself buy into it as much as Hanna and Andre, on the slightest hope that maybe it won't look as awkward.

"What do you think?" he demands.

I reach up and take his chin between my thumb and index finger, drawing him in. Hoping he won't rip away instinctively, like he did in the car. There's already a pinkish color blooming along his cheekbones, and his eyes are scrunched shut. I guess I can't tease him too much for being nervous, since it's his first one.

I nudge my smile briefly against his lips.

Within the second, I draw away. It was just a peck. And yet, the pink is spreading through his face, and when he opens his eyes, his pupils are dilated.

"Not so bad, right?" I whisper, quietly enough that Andre and Hanna can't hear. Thankfully, Andre's still reeling with laughter, though I have no idea what's so funny at this point. It must be one of those "too drunk to stop" moments.

Rather than responding, Jonah digs his face back into my shoulder, hiding it.

Andre kicks the tower in his laughter, and it tumbles over.

* * *

Andre's place is comfortable. It's got a cozy charm with sunset-orange walls, dark trim, and picture windows. Since his family is up north, we don't have to worry about anyone intruding. Or, I don't have to pretend like I'm good at talking to strangers. Mr. and Mrs. Lewis have always been kind and welcoming, but they're pretty intense about making small talk and learning every detail they possibly can about our lives. Their approach is far different from Mr. and Mrs. Katsuki's, who, like their daughter, figured out quickly that prodding me with too many questions makes me itch.

Our food eventually arrives, and Andre throws on some recent Marvel movie I haven't seen to occupy our attention. It looks like Jonah actually got himself a decent meal with chicken, rice, and veggies, so I don't have to worry about . . . why I'm worrying. I expect the only reason he didn't settle for an appetizer is because Andre chose one of the cheapest places in town to order from.

Maybe that's his attempt to help Jonah in his own subtle, noninvasive way.

After we've polished off my Mexican cinnamon cookies and cleaned Jenga up, Jonah and I maneuver to the bathroom to brush our teeth (Andre's dad is a dentist, so he has several spare brushes). They bid us goodnight, and we move into Andre's brother's bedroom—a small space cluttered with family pictures, lacrosse trophies, and video game posters. A full-size bed, way too small for both of us, honestly, borders the back wall.

"You won't throw up on me in the middle of the night, right?" I ask, beginning to remove my shirt. But I catch another glance of the bed and its tiny dimensions and decide to leave it on.

"If I do, it'll be on purpose." He tugs on a crewneck he borrowed from Andre, then crawls onto the left side of the bed, setting water and his phone on the nightstand. I place mine beside his, then maneuver onto the bed from the right, shoving the comforter toward him. Even watching how he bundles himself up makes me uncomfortably warm. "Think we did okay, Ramz?"

"Hmm?"

"Like, fooling them." Jonah squirms until he's facing me, looking like a tightly wrapped burrito. He's a foot away. I have the urge to slide him farther across the bed, but then he'd probably just end up on the floor. "Did we do okay?"

I sigh. "Considering Hanna keeps bragging about our compatibility, I'd say so."

"Ugh. *Again?*" He groans. He's close enough that I can smell the mint in his words. I'm repulsed by myself for even noticing. "I don't get it. The only time we talk about each other is when we're complaining."

"You are pretty insufferable," I say, nodding.

He wrinkles his nose. "You're worse. I promise."

I don't know why he has to say it like that, with his face all squinted and bothered. He looks like a little kid who doesn't know how to articulate himself, so he relies on his expressions. Before I can stop myself (thanks to the alcohol, probably), I blurt, "What's with you pretending you're cute today, anyway? It's horrible."

"Cute?" he squeaks.

"Well. Like . . ." I scramble to think of something less embarrassing. "Not *cute*, exactly. Just, like. You weren't being completely annoying for once. Like when you were eating my cookies like a chipmunk. And then you hugged me during Jenga."

He processes this, clearly straining through the alcohol as well.

"Well . . . what's with *you*?" he snaps back. "You were going to give Hanna a hickey? Right in front of me?"

I arch my eyebrow. "Were you jealous?"

"I was *pretending* to be jealous," he seethes.

"Are you sure?" I ask, resisting a teasing grin. It's always been easy to rile him up. "I mean, you *are* the one who set up that kiss during Jenga. You weren't feeling possessive?"

Jonah looks like he may, in fact, throw up on me. "I did it just to get it out of the way! I still think you're a rusty dildo."

"Well . . ." I know I'm going to regret saying it, because the idea is horrifying. I shove it out of my mouth anyway, knowing full well that he won't. "If we want to keep things up, we should practice."

"We tried practicing in the car, and you ran away," he says huffily.

"I decided to drop it because you looked anxious," I snap. "Now that your first kiss is out of the way, maybe you won't be as freaked out next time—"

Suddenly, the bedroom door creaks open. My "pretend" mode activates, and I lurch for Jonah, wrapping my arms around him.

Andre's head squirms between the crack. "You two aren't being gross, right?"

"N-no," Jonah chokes out, very convincingly.

"Good. I'm washing those sheets tomorrow, but . . . you know."

"I promise not to do Jonah in your brother's bed," I say, biting through a smile when Jonah curses under his breath.

"Perfect. Night, lovebirds."

He closes the door, consuming us in quiet darkness.

Jonah melts against me in relief. He still smells nice, after everything. It's irritating. Why do I keep getting distracted by these ridiculous, minuscule things? So what if he smells crisp and soapy? It doesn't hide the scent of his rotten character.

"Uh . . . Dylan." Faintly, I feel Jonah tap on my collarbone. "You're crushing me."

I am? I slacken my grip, but rather than moving away, Jonah sprawls his palm against my chest.

"You're shaking," he says. "Are you good?"

Shit. Not that question. Not that awful, terrible question that forces me to acknowledge it. My heart thumps faster, my eyes go fuzzy. Really? Why here? Why now? Just because Andre startled us? That's not a good enough reason for this to happen. The blankets are becoming too heavy, too itchy. They're pinching my airway and crushing my chest. Suddenly, I can't breathe.

"Dylan?"

I can't. I can't breathe.

"Dylan."

I can't breathe, I can't breathe, I can't *fucking breathe*—

"Hey. Do you have an inhaler somewhere? Are you having some kind of asthma attack?" Jonah is scrutinizing me, strangely calm if he thinks that's what's going on.

"No," I manage to force out. "Just can't . . . just c-can't . . . br . . . eathe . . ."

"You're definitely breathing. I can hear it. Are you . . . having a panic attack?"

Jonah's voice pierces the cloud in my head. *A panic attack.* Right. Of course. I've felt it a million times, and yet, it always fools me into thinking it's something else that's killing me.

"Hey." He fans his hand across my cheek, angling my face, forcing us to lock eyes. His are calm. Focused. "What do you need?"

Buzzing, suffocating whiteness zips through my body in agonizing waves. The alcohol sits thickly, nauseatingly, in my stomach. "To get out."

I'm not sure how coherent I am, but Jonah must understand, because he shoves the sheets so they're tangled at our feet. He climbs out of bed, and then he's next to me, taking my palms, tugging. He draws me toward the door, walking backward, his eyes still fixed on me. I can't look away—they're the only thing centering me.

I blink, and we're in the hallway. Silence rattles in my ears. He guides me through the living room, through the front door, to the stone porch facing the street. The rush of cold air douses me in a soothing, brisk wave, and the sounds of nightlife infiltrate my ears—the chirping of insects that haven't yet died, the scraping of half-naked tree branches in the breeze.

"The stars are bright tonight," Jonah says, sitting us on the porch step.

I look up. A handful of stars sprinkle the sky, and the moon is a luminescent crescent, but otherwise, I can't see very many.

"Did you know . . . the moon has earthquakes?" He leans back on his palms, bare feet tapping the stone. "Well, moonquakes. Ours last a couple minutes, but the moon's can last up to an hour."

"Oh," I whisper. Through the pounding.

"Do you need anything?"

". . . Sorry, what?"

"Do you need anything?"

Why is his voice so soothing? The world is sharpening. I can feel air entering my lungs. I'm still gasping, but I'm breathing. "No," I say, and finally, I feel the weight of the word.

Jonah hugs his knees. He's already shivering again.

"How do you know?" I murmur. "How to handle . . . this."

"Lily has panic attacks sometimes." Jonah reaches beyond the porch and tugs grass blades out of the lawn, twirling them between his fingers. "I know the signs."

There's silence for a while. The environment helps clear my muddled thoughts and dispel the tightness in my chest. My heart is still hammering, but otherwise, I'm okay. It was quick. Sometimes, they're much longer.

"Sorry," I say quietly.

"You don't have to say that."

"I . . . they're not frequent," I tell him, defensiveness clinging to my words. "It's always random, when my guard is down. So, yeah. Thanks for . . . anyway. Can I do anything to make it up to you?"

His eyes glint with mischief. "Well," he says, tapping his fingers like an evil mastermind. "You could bake me more cookies."

My eyebrows fly up into my forehead. "Cookies?"

"Yeah. Those cinnamon cookies were impeccable." Jonah fans a palm over his stomach with a longing sigh. "Since when have you been a sweets guy, anyway? I always took you to be the salty, bitter type."

"Didn't you see the baking posters in my room after homecoming?" I ask skeptically.

The ghost of a smile lifts his lips. "I was more concentrated on getting out, to be honest."

I lean back on my hands as well. My pinkie grazes his. I'm not sure if he notices. I'm not sure why I don't move it.

"You mentioned something about the cookies," he says, his voice hesitant. "Like, they're your brother's favorite?"

So, he did hear my slipup earlier. "Yeah," I whisper.

"What's his name? I've never heard you say it."

"It's . . ." His name is on the back of my tongue, but forcing it out of my mouth drains my strength. "Tomás."

Jonah cranes his neck to look up again. "I saw that picture of your family. He looks like your dad. Same smile, sharp features. Like, all angles and ridges."

"Yeah . . ." I can't tell if this situation makes me want to laugh or panic. I can't believe I'm having a casual conversation about Tomás for the first time in . . . how long? The thought is making me squirm, but I shake my head, trying to shoo away the anxiety. It shouldn't matter if I tell Jonah. It's not like telling him about Tomás, mentioning my past, will change his opinion of me. He hates me enough as it is— there can't possibly be room for more hatred, right?

Maybe Jonah can feel my palm beginning to tremble, because he gives my pinkie a subtle nudge. Reminding me of his presence, I guess.

"Does he live nearby?" he prompts.

"Um. Not really. He's in Detroit. It's only a couple hours from here, but . . . not exactly right around the corner."

"Does he ever visit?"

"No."

"Why not?"

"Because of me," I admit, looking down at my knees.

"Really?" He sounds dubious.

"Really." Surface-level conversation might be okay, but nothing deeper. I can't handle it. I'll start thinking about the letter, and how much I've disappointed him, and hurt him, and . . . and if I had just stood up for myself . . . maybe he wouldn't have found out what was happening to me . . . maybe he wouldn't have gotten as angry.

Maybe he wouldn't have picked up the bat.

Jonah's eyes watch me with a certain carefulness that tells me he's aware of my discomfort. He shifts the conversation. "It feels like homecoming again, doesn't it? Us, alone, intoxicated. It's a bad formula."

"I was sober, actually," I tell him.

Jonah rubs his chin thoughtfully. "So that means you willingly crawled into bed with me."

"Like I was going to sacrifice my entire mattress to you?" I scoff. "You're lucky I didn't kick you out."

"Nah. You'd never." Jonah rolls his other hand dismissively through the air. "You're Dylan Fucking Ramírez. The 'polite' and 'gentlemanly' and 'good-at-all-things' prince of Delridge High. The perfect boy with the perfect life."

He says it with enough contempt that it aggravates me. "I'm good at things that don't matter," I snap. "Sports. Baking. Studying. But you . . . you're good at the important things."

"Such as?" He stares at me with suspicion. I can see every eyelash, every vein of icy gray in his irises.

"Being social. Likable." I lower my voice, hoping he can't hear the envy. "Making connections. Making an impression."

"You realize you're one of the most popular guys in school, right?" he asks.

"Because I'm attractive," I say, and he snorts, which sparks anger in my chest. "What?"

"Oh, nothing. Just didn't expect you to come out and say it." He cocks his head at me with a pleasant, incredibly vexing smile. "I thought you were supposed to be the humble type?"

"I'm not saying it in a braggy way," I growl. Of course he has to make a snide comment when I'm feeling all . . . vulnerable, or whatever. "It's a shallow reason that makes people want to be around me. And the fact that I hang out with you and student council. But . . . I don't have . . ."

My fists are starting to curl. I'm not sure what I'm about to say—only that my annoyance is still spiraling upward. Because, other than looks, and other than my choice of friends, there's nothing else about me that draws people in. But him . . . *Jonah* . . .

Everything about him is inviting. He can make connections with one nod and a grin. As soon as he joins a group, the center shifts around him. There's always someone laughing within his giant radius. Not a single person in the school hasn't heard his name, and not a single person, other than me, seems to despise his firecracker personality.

How am I supposed to compete with that? I don't necessarily *want* to, since being around too many people gives me brain rashes, but . . . it wouldn't be the worst thing if people looked at me and thought anything other than *Oh, there's the brooding hot guy.*

I don't even brood. Maybe I sulk, but *brood*?

"Whatever," I eventually snap, because I can't think of a way to condense my thoughts, and I definitely don't want to share them with him. "I'm not perfect, and my life sure as hell isn't either. So stop saying that."

"But . . . it *is* perfect," Jonah protests. "I mean . . . you have all the resources you need. You've got the looks, the giant house, the money, the clothes, the—"

"So what?" I demand. "Why do you think I don't face problems in my life just because my family has money? You don't know a damn thing about me." I scoff and shake my head, because I don't want to have this conversation right now. Nonetheless, I think he needs to hear it, so I gesture to the back of his hand, then to the back of mine, and say, "There are several things I face that you never will."

When my eyes find his again, I realize he's watching me with that same methodical expression from when we were in bed. He opens his mouth, and I brace, my brain scrambling to figure out what I might hear, and if I have the energy to push back or let it go.

He says, "I . . . didn't think about that."

I pull my knee into my chest, unresponsive.

"I guess . . . like, sometimes I get used to the fact that we live in this open, progressive town—"

"I came here from one of the top ten most progressive cities in the country," I cut in. "I faced the same issues in Detroit that I do in Delridge. No matter how far left or right your hometown leans, brown kids like me are going to have walls and obstacles that white kids like you can just walk through like they're invisible. Even if we're more financially stable. Even if we have more clothes, a bigger house, or whatever. When any person looks at me, the first thing they see isn't my wealth. It's my skin. And that's something you'll never understand."

I turn my eyes to the grass, reluctantly retreating from his studious gaze. But I keep going.

"It's why I had to find a new thera . . . uh, school counselor." I pause, clearing my throat. It's not like I'm embarrassed about it, or anything, but it's also not something I feel like sharing with him. "Throw some non-heterosexuality into the equation and things get *more* difficult. It's why some of my past relationships have fallen through. Those are things you don't see, and they're things you'll never have to deal with. My life isn't perfect. It never has been. So quit whining and saying it is."

Jonah looks thoughtful. Slowly, he nods. Maybe I shouldn't be surprised by this, but he's always been the type to get worked up and fiery over just about anything. Then again, I've never seen him during a serious conversation. I didn't even know he could have them.

"I'm sorry," he says, and it sounds genuine. "I didn't realize . . . I've been, like, belittling these problems you face. All because you're not . . . you know. A pasty-ass white boy like me."

And, okay. I can't help it. I toss my head back and laugh.

"What?" he asks nervously.

"You're ridiculous."

"What?" There it is. The tinge of defensiveness. "What did I say? Dylan! *Dylan! How am I supposed to listen and learn if all you're going to do is laugh?*"

So I laugh harder. He's definitely teasing now. "Your word choice is so ungraceful," I tell him, grinning.

"Sorry I'm not Robert Fucking Frost'ing my apology to you," Jonah snaps, his eyes rolling skyward. "Just know that I mean it, okay? I'll stop assuming ignorant things about your life. And . . ."

Jonah scratches his nail against the porch, glancing around awkwardly. He's back to being nervous.

". . . if there's anything else I say or do . . . you can totally call me out. If you're comfortable with that. I mean, not that you need my permission, or that it's your job to tell me when I'm saying something out of line, because it's definitely not. Like, I don't want to put my behavior on you, but it's just that you've never said anything before, even though I'm sure some ugliness has slipped out of my mouth at some point, so if you want to call me out, even though you totally don't have to—"

"Good to know," I say, cutting through the ramble with a small smirk.

I could probably poke him further about it (seeing Jonah Collins squirm is kind of amusing), but I realize then that his arms are prickled with goose bumps, and he's shivering harder. So I stand, offer my palm, and say, "Let's go inside." He reluctantly gives me his hand so I can pull him to his feet. We lock the door and creep into the bedroom, then slide under the covers. I think I'm okay. I don't sense another panic attack coming. Jonah rubs his hands together behind me, trying to warm up.

"Thanks, by the way," I whisper.

"For what?"

"For . . ." I swallow, a sudden knot forming at the base of my throat. "For being there. For not . . . running away. Or being weirded out."

For several seconds, Jonah is quiet. At first, I think he fell asleep, but then I hear him squirming, and when I flip over, I realize he's done the same, so we're facing each other. This bed . . .

It's still too small.

"Sorry you've had to deal with people who run away, rather than try to help you through your attacks," he murmurs.

"Huh? Oh, no, it's okay." I laugh, but it's weak and pathetic and totally unconvincing. "Like, some people just don't get it. Or they don't want to deal with that. I understand. When your boyfriend has random freak-outs, I see how that could be too much."

"Those kinds of people don't deserve your time," he says, matter-of-fact. "A partner is supposed to be there for you and help you when you're struggling. Not turn their back on you."

His tone is so serious, I can't help but fidget. "You seem pretty sure about that, considering you've never dated before," I say lightly.

"Don't need experience to know how I should treat another human being."

I don't know how to respond to that. Jonah Collins has caught me off guard once again.

He closes his eyes and snuggles up with the comforter without another word.

The night passes in silence. I watch his body steadily rise and fall with his breathing. He moves to tuck the blankets deeper under his chin, but otherwise, he's a stationary sleeper. A contrast from his always-moving persona when he's awake.

If there's anyone who could use protection, it's him.

Looking at him is too distracting, so I flip away, staring at the wall, repeating his words in my head until I manage to fall asleep.

The next morning, I drop Jonah off at his house, and he says nothing more than "Thanks."

I return home and bring my empty cookie container to the kitchen sink. My eyes gravitate toward the drawer.

I told Jonah my brother's name. I almost started talking about him. I might've been able to keep going, if I hadn't cut myself off out of fear of spiraling.

My fingers stumble over the handle, shaking, studying its familiar texture.

I don't know what prompts me. Maybe lingering boldness from last night.

I pull. It slides open.

Tomás's letter stares up at me. The familiar handwriting. The familiar name. His voice sweeps through my head.

"Lil Dyl!"

Regret and relief churn together in a nauseating blur in the thick of my chest. I stagger to the living room, trying to come to terms with what I just did. It seems so menial and pathetic. Opening a drawer. And yet . . .

I slump onto my couch, rubbing my temple.

And yet.

JONAH

I'm thoroughly distracted at work. I make tea in the coffeepot. I punt a basket of tempura green beans on my way out of the kitchen. I trip and spill water on Sherry's blouse. I don't feel too bad about that one.

My tips are awful, because my head's full of garbage.

And by garbage, I mean Dylan Ramírez.

Neither of us have mentioned what happened that night on Andre's porch. It's Friday, so it's been nearly a week since our double date. I've been pondering what I learned about him in those few minutes, and why he was suddenly so . . . open with me. I guess getting through a panic attack with someone at your side makes you feel like you can be vulnerable with them. Not that it makes anything different between us.

Still . . . I never realized how privileged I sounded when I waltzed around, complaining about his perfect life. He's right. Maybe I'm not as financially well-off as my friends, but there are still countless problems that Dylan—Andre, Maya, Hanna, Rohan—have to deal with on a constant basis that I won't ever experience.

I feel like a jerk for the fact that he even had to point it out to me. But . . . I appreciate that he did.

Tragically, I'm becoming more used to being his boyfriend in public. It's less difficult for me to throw my legs in his lap, to lean in and peck him on the lips. I'm getting better at shrugging the teasing off. As an added layer to our relationship, he's been bringing me samples of baked goods—cookies, cake slices, and other things.

"I swear it's not pity food. I need a taste tester," he says pleadingly when I narrow my eyes. "I don't eat sweets, really. Baking just . . . keeps me busy."

If it helps him improve in some way, I shouldn't be stubborn. Even if most of my feedback is useless, since I'm so caught up in the deliciousness, I can't think of any criticism.

As my Friday night shift drags on, I keep thinking about how Dylan has a brother who doesn't come around anymore and how he's apparently used to his partners abandoning him when he has panic attacks, and why does he have panic attacks, anyway?

Most of all, why am I wondering about it in the first place, like it's any of my business?

When I come around the corner to greet my new table, I groan.

"Jonah!" Ms. Davis's smile glitters. Her dyed fiery hair is knotted into a sloppy bun, and Mr. Kelly is sitting across from her, dressed (unsurprisingly) in a sweater vest and tie.

"Hello," I say flatly.

"Wow. No enthusiasm for your aunt?"

"Nice to see you, Jonah," Mr. Kelly cuts in.

I turn to him. As much as my aunt annoys me, I do like Mr. Kelly. He's always staying late at school to talk to kids when they need a counselor who isn't . . . well, a counselor. I considered utilizing him for venting, once, but if he's as secretive around his wife as Andre is around Hanna, Ms. Davis will know everything about my life within ten minutes of my conversation with him.

"I didn't know you worked here," Ms. Davis says, thumbing through her menu. "Every time we've tried coming in, the restaurant has been on a wait. But I decided to be proactive for once and called to make a reservation!"

She sounds proud of herself. I don't know what it is with millennials and making phone calls.

"Anyway," she continues, "how are Mikayla and—?"

"Lily," I cut in. "Mik and Lily are fine. Drinks?"

Ms. Davis blinks, processing my words. I tense, but she merely looks down at her clasped fingers on the table and asks, "When?"

"She began her transition about a year ago, if that's what you're asking."

"Ah . . . has it been that long since I've asked about them . . . ?" Ms. Davis sighs, I think at herself, then moves along. "And your father?"

"He's fine. Drinks?"

"Two Diets, please," Mr. Kelly says, saving me from her torment.

I dart into the kitchen to fill their drinks. Once I have their orders in the system, I continue pushing through my shift, attempting to stay focused. Ms. Davis tries to hound me as I tend my tables, but thankfully, Mr. Kelly keeps her distracted. I'm not sure if he's doing it for my sake, or if he conveniently has something to ask her every time I'm passing by, but I appreciate it nonetheless.

When I next exit the kitchen, I forget to yell "door," and slam into Sherry. My plates wobble, but she wraps an arm around me to steady me, and her palm catches me where it shouldn't. "Careful," she says sternly.

I cough in protest, spinning toward my table as she continues into the kitchen.

I immediately crash into Mr. Kelly.

He grabs me before I nearly drop my plates a second time. "Sorry, Jonah," he says, but he's not looking at me. He's glaring over my head at Sherry through the window in the kitchen door, a menacing flicker in his eyes I've never seen—one that nearly makes me shiver.

"Your food . . . will be out soon," I say weakly.

His jaw shifts. In a stern teacher voice, he asks, "Does that happen often?"

I raise my brows, feigning innocence. "What?"

After a lingering moment, in which he dissects my face too thoroughly for comfort, he continues toward the restrooms. I sigh, then proceed to the correct table and give them their food.

On my way back, Ms. Davis snags my apron. "Wait a moment," she pleads. "Don't you have any time for a quick chat?"

I press my lips, pulling free of her grip. "I'm busy, Ms. Davis."

"I told you, you don't have to call me that when we're alone." She pokes at the bun on the back of her head, her voice steeped in wariness. "Out of curiosity, does your father still—?"

"Jo-Jo!" a voice calls out.

My brain goes numb. That sound. That nickname. What . . . ?

I turn, just as Lily lunges at me, squeezing her arms around my waist. I stare at her in puzzlement, trying to process her appearance. She's dressed in a long pink skirt and one of my old zip-up hoodies— her favorite combination. "Lilypad?" I whisper. "What . . . ? Where's Mik?"

"Mrs. Greene says one of her girlfriends broke her foot, so she had to drive her to the hospital." Lily's curls bounce as she rocks back and forth. "She called you but you didn't answer. So she dropped us off to stay with you at work!"

Behind her, Mik is ambling toward us, hands shoved in her pockets. "Hey, dork," she says.

I'm ripping through my brain, seeking the lever for Adult Mode, but I'm frozen. They're not supposed to be here. I don't have time to watch them. We're on a wait list, and every booth in the restaurant is full or soon to be seated.

"Mikayla! Lily!" Ms. Davis says brightly.

The girls peek around me. Lily must not recognize her, because she shifts behind me, gripping my belt loop. The last time they probably saw each other was four years ago, when Ms. Davis came to our old house after the funeral to tell us she was moving into town.

"Aunt Noelle?" Mik's jaw drops.

"It's been so long." Ms. Davis's eyes glitter, and she peeks around my shoulder to better see Lily. "I *love* your skirt. Are those sequins? Every skirt should have sparkles or sequins, in my opinion."

Lily's cheeks turn pink, and she slowly releases my belt loop. I'm still stuck, unable to comprehend what's going on. Three of my worlds are colliding—school, work, and home. I don't like the way my stomach is sinking.

"And this is my husband, Myron," Ms. Davis says.

Mr. Kelly has now joined the steadily growing crowd around us. "Hello," he says, readjusting his glasses. "I have no idea what's happening."

Mik and Lily both gasp, craning their necks to see his face. "Whoa," Mik hisses. "You're like, *huge* huge."

"Six-foot-five," Ms. Davis says, winking up at him. "But he won't step on you, as long as you're nice to him."

Lily giggles.

"Like he could ever step on me," Mik says, scoffing. "I'm way too fast."

"Myron, these are my nieces, Mikayla and Lily." Ms. Davis points to them, leaving a moment for him to nod politely to each of them, before returning her attention to me. "So, what's this about a broken foot? Was that a babysitter?"

"I . . ." I've now identified that sinking feeling as *overwhelmed*. I mentally slap myself out of my stunned state, trying to find my center. "Yes, that was the babysitter."

"She brought them . . . to you?" Ms. Davis scrunches her eyebrows.

I'm not sure which excuse I should conjure up. Would she believe me if I told her Dad is out of town? Could I even get the words out of my mouth without stumbling over the lie?

When I don't have a proper response, she gestures to the table. "If they're comfortable, they can sit with us while you work. Right, Myron?"

"I'm just happy to be here," he says.

I deliberate my next move. It's a horrible idea. If Ms. Davis starts asking questions, and they begin to open up about our home situation . . .

CPS . . .

I shudder. Nope. I don't need those three letters in my head.

But there's nowhere for them to sit, and with the amount of traffic swarming in and out, I can't properly keep an eye on them. This way, they're with two people I know. So, I draw my sisters away from the booth and crouch, looking between them. "Stay with them until I'm off," I whisper. "But if she asks about Dad, tell her he's fine. We're fine."

Lily fiddles with her fingers, clearly not happy with the fact that I'm telling her to lie. The thought makes my chest ache, but we have to do this. I'm not going to let anyone take me away from my girls.

Mik sighs, patting Lily's head. "Jo-Jo knows what he's doing. He always does. Right?"

"Right," Lily says softly.

So, Mik slides into the booth beside Ms. Davis, and Lily snuggles in beside Mr. Kelly. Praying that conversations stay surface level, I continue darting around, swiping credit cards, inputting entrées, delivering desserts. I try staying focused, but each time I pass their table, conversation flutters through my ears. As I feared, Ms. Davis is asking questions.

". . . grade are you in . . . ?"

". . . position do you play in soccer . . . ?"

". . . giraffes your favorite animal . . . ?"

I don't hear anything about our living situation, and Mik seems at ease, which is good. Meanwhile, Lily gravitates closer and closer to Mr. Kelly, until she's sitting on his leg and poking at his thick arm. Whatever he's talking about must be entertaining, because she hasn't stopped smiling since she sat down.

The only real conversation I get is when I'm taking the order of the table across from them. As I write things down, their voices flutter into my ears.

"When did you get married?" Lily asks. Normally, her voice is quiet and hesitant, but now, she's speaking at a normal level. I can't remember the last time I heard her so clearly.

"Yeah, seriously?" Mik's irritated voice demands. "You didn't even invite us to your wedding? That sucks, no offense."

Ms. Davis laughs, but it's fragile. "It was just a tiny, personal wedding this past spring. Myron's parents and a few of his siblings came, but they were the only witnesses. I sent out one invitation, and it was to you guys. But . . ." She audibly clears her throat. "It might've gotten lost in the mail."

I feel another pang of guilt. Faintly, I remember a fancy invitation arriving for us last winter when I was going through the mail. I must've thrown it out without a second thought. Either because we couldn't commit, or because I was still bitter with her for not trying to get to know us before Mom's death. Probably a mixture of both.

"Did you have a pretty dress?" Lily asks eagerly.

"Pretty expensive, yeah."

"Who walked you down the aisle?"

"Well . . ." I can hear Ms. Davis speaking through a small smile. "I always hoped one day your mother might. But, you know. Life happens. So, Myron's brother Jamal was kind enough to do it."

I walk toward the kitchen, staring dazedly at my notebook. My grandparents—her parents—have been dead for years. Both of them were only children, so they didn't have siblings that Ms. Davis and Mom could call "aunt" and "uncle." If they had any extended family, Mom never kept in touch with them, and it sounds like Ms. Davis didn't, either. That means she didn't have a single family member at her wedding.

When I return to their table to collect everyone's dirty plates, Ms. Davis says, "Put their food on our tab."

"They're not your kids," I say calmly, "but thank you for offering."

"It's been years since I've seen them. The least I can do is cover dinner." Ms. Davis fumbles through her purse. "By the way, they aren't your kids, either."

I look at Mr. Kelly expectantly, hoping he can step in. He's in the middle of braiding Lily's hair. "Don't look at me for help," he says, with barely a glance up. "She's got a point."

"Exactly!" Ms. Davis lifts her hand, clearly expecting a high five. "As husband and wife, we're a team. United in marriage and—"

"I'm not high-fiving you for owning a seventeen-year-old."

Ms. Davis huffs and lowers her palm in defeat.

I swallow my indignation and beeline for the kitchen. My stubbornness wants to keep Mik's and Lily's food on a separate check so I can pay for it later, but the longer I fight her on it, the more time she has to dig into our lives.

So, when I bring the check, it has four entrées on it. Once they've paid, I wish them a good night. Now that the restaurant is slowing, tables are clearing up, including the employee booth in the back corner. I'll have my sisters sit there when Ms. Davis and Mr. Kelly leave.

Except, they don't. They continue lingering, talking, laughing. Mik seems more invested now, and Lily looks as comfortable as I've ever seen her.

I start doing side work in the back, popping out occasionally to check on them. I text Andre to see if he's available to pick us up. I don't like inconveniencing him, and I've walked home plenty at night before, but I'd prefer not to with my sisters. He's also the only one who's seen my house, aside from Dylan, who I want to deal with as little as possible.

Thankfully, he's free for once. As soon as I'm cashed out, and I've tipped the weekend busboy, I throw my jacket on and head for the booth. Lily and Mr. Kelly are playing tic-tac-toe on her kid's menu. Ms. Davis and Mik are talking boys.

"Ready?" I ask, and the two climb out of the booth.

"That was fun," Lily says happily. "I like Aunt Noelle and Mr. Myron."

Of course she does. Lily likes everybody. "Thanks for looking after them," I say, looking vaguely between the adults. "And for the tip. See you Monday."

I take my sisters' wrists and pull them to the doors. Andre's car is humming out front.

"Aunt Noelle . . . is cool," Mik mumbles.

"She's really cool!" Lily says, practically glowing. "I like her hair. I wonder if my hair could be red one day. Or pink. Maybe when I'm not little. Mr. Myron is so big, I bet he could kick down a tree. I got to tell him all about my book, too! And guess what? He says he has another book like mine, and he'll give it to you so I can have it. You don't even have to spend money! I can't believe I get to read *two* books with trans girls in a row!"

I'm not sure I've ever heard this many words out of her mouth at once. The thought makes it difficult to swallow. Is this how she would speak . . . and act . . . ? If we weren't . . . ?

"That's great, Lily," I say gently.

I shepherd them into Andre's car, and when I open the back door, an energetic, instrumental rock soundtrack (probably from some recent video game) spills into the air. He whoops when he sees them, and they squeal back. He can energize my sisters quicker than anybody.

"Thanks for picking us up," I say wearily, slumping into the passenger seat.

"All good." He smiles at me, but there are bags under his eyes. "I needed the break."

I lean over the middle compartment and nudge his shoulder with my head. "Care to share?"

"Just usual shit. Homework. Trying to plan out this teachers-versus-students basketball tournament. Tallying up all the prom theme suggestions. Trying to lock in the teachers for the pie-in-the-face fundraiser event." He bumps my head with his.

"The never-ending stress of student council," I say weakly.

"Yep." He peeks over at me. "Rough night for you, too?"

I nod with a heavy sigh. "Rough night for me, too," I whisper. I don't ask him if he has time for a mutual venting session. I know he's already used what precious few moments of free time he has to come and pick me up, and I don't want to hold him up any further. We drive off just as Ms. Davis and Mr. Kelly are leaving the restaurant. I catch her eye through the passenger window.

She's frowning.

DYLAN

It's a nightmare.

It's the most intense one I've had in weeks. Around me is a flurry of fists and feet, and though I can't feel pain, I feel impact. The air being wrenched from my lungs. The numbing pulse left by each blow. Mangled Spanish burns in my ears. I don't know what I did wrong, I don't know what to do, I don't know how to make it stop—

When I wake, I'm a shivering, sweating heap, yelling Tomás's name, my breathing haggard.

My bedroom door flings open, and there stands my father's burly silhouette. He walks briskly to the bed and sits down in his T-shirt and boxers, reaching for my palm. I fumble for his hand, and when his grip curls around mine, my heartbeat slows.

"Haven't heard you shout like that in months," he whispers.

I sit upright and curl my arms around my knees. "Sorry for waking you," I mumble.

"I wasn't asleep. Just got home twenty minutes ago." He rubs my knee, watching me through the darkness. I can smell the grill and wood-fire on him. "Dyl . . ."

"Don't say it." I can hear the lecture coming.

"I'll say it, and you'll listen," he says sternly. "You should schedule an appointment with Jenna. I can do it for you—"

"I'm *fine*," I snap, flopping down and twisting away from him. I'm not, but who wants to talk about therapy after midnight?

"I . . . saw the drawer was open." He sounds like he's verbally tiptoeing through glass. "You did that, didn't you? If thinking about Tomás haunts you this much—"

"I said I'm fine!" I snarl. "Sitting around with my therapist won't magically stop my nightmares. Go away."

I regret it as soon as I say it, but I shove my face in my pillow anyway, cutting away the discussion. Dad must know that any further conversation is a lost cause, so he pats the back of my head and rises to his feet. The sound of him shuffling to the door makes my eyes burn. Why did I say that to him? I'm not usually the kind of person who snaps like that. Why am I acting like such a jerk when he's just trying to help?

"Sorry," I croak.

"I know." He sighs solemnly. After a lengthy pause, he whispers, "You already know this, but Tomás misses the hell out of you."

With that, he closes the door, plunging me in darkness.

Of course I shoved him away in one of the few rare moments he was actually here for me. Queasy, I roll over and seize my phone from my nightstand. There's a voice mail waiting for me from Mom. Without deliberating, I hit play. I need to hear someone else's voice right now.

"Sorry for calling so late." She pauses. *"The weather's nice on the Gulf. I walked along the shore this morning."* Another pause. *"Perhaps a conference will line up with your spring break. You and Henrique could come, if I can convince that stubborn man to leave his restaurant."* A third pause. *"How are your grades? Have you used your allowance money for anything fun?"* A fourth. *"Que descanses bien. Espero que tengas un buen día mañana."*

The messages are usually like that. Awkward. Rambling. Like she doesn't know what to say.

My thumb hovers over the green call button.

. . . Nah. She's probably asleep now. I'm not sure what I'd say anyway.

I move around my room, seeking distraction. I unfold and refold my clothes and talk to myself, listing things I should clean this weekend while Dad's in Detroit. Trying to use the old methods I once learned from my therapist on keeping myself grounded.

Tomás misses the hell out of you.

It's not working. Fingers etch imprints into my throat. I hear leather snapping against skin, knuckles cracking against bone.

I can't. I can't do this. I collapse onto the floor and press my back to the bed frame.

This *sucks*.

Things get unbearably quiet. I'm a trembling, sweating mass, crushed beneath the weight of electrifying numbness, fighting through the cement thickening in my lungs. It's heavy and awful. I'm scared. I'm going to die, and no one's going to care, or remember me, or miss me.

And maybe that's how it should be.

It trickles through me in slow, agonizing waves, reaching into every crevice in my body. I knead my palms into my dry, bloodshot eyes. It's never going to stop.

Then, I hear a voice. Faint. Irritated. Coming from my fingers, which are now in my lap. I realize my phone screen is on, and I'm in the middle of a call.

"Uh, hello?" they're saying. "What do you want, Prissy Prince?"

Prissy . . . ?

Oh. It's him.

I drag my phone to my ear, though it weighs about fifty pounds. It takes a moment to gather any sound, but I manage to croak, "You're awake?"

"Depends. Is this a booty call?"

Startled laughter shoots out of my mouth. The haze is beginning to thin. "Why are you up? It's one in the morning."

"Finishing homework." He sounds groggy. "Why'd you call this late? Your voice sounds weird."

"I . . . was hoping we could talk about tomorrow again," I blurt. It's the only excuse I can pluck from the cloud of panic filling my head. "I'm picking you up at eleven for the soccer game, right?"

At first, Jonah is quiet. Then, slowly, "I'll run through it again. Just focus on my voice."

He can tell. Just by the way I'm speaking.

So he goes through all the steps we've already planned, and all the little moments we'll share. Andre will be at Mikayla's game, so we decided I should join, too. That way, we can take selfies to send to the group chat, and to show Hanna we're hanging out without her watching. As he speaks, I cling to every syllable, every intonation. He's using that calm, reassuring voice from last Saturday, when we were in Andre's brother's bed.

I slump onto the floor, and soon after, my breath stops rattling in my lungs. I feel like I've been squeezed of every last drop of energy.

I fall asleep to Jonah's voice.

JONAH

"Hey. Dork. Prissy Prince."

I click my pen, staring with drooping eyes at my phone.

He doesn't answer. But I can hear the faintest sound of his breath coming through. It's long and quiet—I think he's asleep.

"You call me and pass out?" I scowl, pulling my blanket tighter around my shoulders. "I'm not entertaining enough to hold your attention?"

No response.

"Insulting you isn't fun if you don't yell at me." My pen clacks uselessly onto my book. I'm not sure why I'm still talking when he clearly isn't here to listen anymore. Nor am I sure why I'm the person he called during a panic attack.

Why not Hanna? Or his parents? Surely they're not the people who treat him like his attacks are a burden, right?

Why me?

There's this weird little tingle in my stomach. I chalk it up to the pot stickers I had for dinner.

I don't intend to spend another night slumped over my kitchen table. But his predictable inhales and exhales are soothing in this weird, ASMR-type way. I'll never tell him.

I fall asleep to his breathing.

DYLAN

The house is still cold, but Jonah's family heats it with their frenetic energy.

"Jackets!" Jonah yells while his sisters rush through the house. I stand awkwardly in the doorway, swinging my keys, watching the chaos. "Mik, your soccer ball."

"Got it!" she says, grabbing it in the corner of the living room. She's dressed in a maroon and gold jersey, and her hair has been tightly braided. I wonder if Jonah did it for her.

"Lily, your coloring book."

"Got it!"

"Mik, you're wearing one tennis shoe and one cleat."

"Whoops!" Mikayla rushes to the shoe rack next to the door, popping her sneaker off.

"Dylan, your—" Jonah stops, blinks a few times, and then scoffs at me. "Wait, what are you doing in here? I said we'd come out to the car in a minute."

"I know, but . . ." I shrug, because I know finishing that sentence will probably cause him to explode with rage. *But I didn't know if you might need help with anything.*

Thankfully, he's too distracted to follow up, and soon after, we're all packing into my sedan. I plug the outdoor soccer complex into my phone, and we're off.

Jonah smears his hands over his face. Mikayla's knees dig into the seat behind me, and Lily is already shifting through her colored pencils.

"Thanks for the ride," he mumbles through his fingers. "Even if it's just for show."

"Sure."

So then we get there and . . . wow. Jonah's loud on a daily basis, but I've never heard him reach such ear-numbing heights. I sit between him and Lily on the bleachers, watching while he howls his support, encouraged by Andre's hooting and clapping. Mikayla stands with her goalie gloves outstretched, her braid bouncing against her jersey.

"*Get it out of there!*" Jonah screeches as the other team dribbles down the field. The parents on the other team, and even some on the same team, give him irritated glances. Either he doesn't notice or he doesn't care. I'm entertained by both of these ideas.

Unfortunately, the morning sunshine has been replaced by sagging, bulky clouds, and it's beginning to drizzle. Lily peeks up at me when I pull her fluffy pink hood over her hair. "Don't want your bangs getting frizzy, right?" I ask.

She smiles and nods.

Jonah, on the other hand, is wearing the flimsiest jacket Delridge has ever seen. The rain glues strands of hair to his forehead, darkening its color, and he's shivering again. Maybe that's why he's constantly moving—to generate heat.

Well, it would look good in front of Andre, so I shed my puffy coat and drape it around Jonah's shoulders.

He whips toward me, frowning. "What are you doing?"

"Giving my boyfriend my jacket." I glance pointedly at Andre, who's already giggling at our exchange.

"But . . . you'll get cold!" he protests.

I flip the hood over his forehead, which droops toward his nose. "I don't get cold."

Jonah glances between us, makes a low growling noise he probably thinks is intimidating, and stuffs his arms through the jacket. "Jesus, what temperature do you run at?" he mutters, zipping it up. "It's two hundred degrees in here."

I want to snap at him for complaining—can't he be grateful for *anything*?—but then he wriggles his face into the collar and hugs it around himself. Maybe he's actually complimenting me in his own weird, whiny way.

"Wait, that shit is so cute, let me take a picture." Andre whips out his phone. "Mom is gonna love this."

"I'll kick you in your neck," Jonah says, seething.

"Go ahead. But let me send the picture first. She's been waiting for your ass to date Dylan just as long as I have."

I turn my attention to the field and catch Mikayla giving us a cheery wave from the net. I remember when I used to be in her position. A goalie defending the net, waving up at my family back when I decided to give soccer a try. I was searching for one of those "activities" my therapist suggested to keep my mind off things. Sometimes, Tomás drove all the way up to Delridge just to see me play.

I can still see him in the stands, waving, shuffling foot to foot, because he was too excited to sit. I can still hear him shouting whenever I neared the ball.

His grin wavered the more he came to see me. The more we linked eyes while he stood in the crowd. The worse I performed. The harder it was to focus.

He stopped coming. I excelled.

Then I quit.

"Mik, you were *amazing*!" Jonah cries out.

Mikayla jogs up to us, grinning widely, her face and legs smudged with dirt. "Good thing we won," she says, high-fiving each of us in turn. "Can't believe I got that yellow card, though . . ."

"You grabbed the ball and yelled, *not today, loser*!"

"And?"

I'm still distracted from the invasive soccer thoughts from earlier, but that gets a smile out of me. I always figured being around the Collins family would be a nightmare, but honestly, they're pretty entertaining. Jonah slings his arm around her, pulling her to the parking lot while Andre carries Lily on his shoulders, allowing her to ruffle his hair and giggle.

"Want your jacket back?"

I blink out of my daze. Jonah is looking up at me with a slight frown, pinching the heavy, fuzzy material around his shoulders.

"I don't need it," I tell him. "You're the one who runs at a crisp fifty degrees."

"Sorry I don't operate at a hospital-admitting fever temperature."

Andre snickers at us, and I jump. I'd nearly forgotten he was there. This isn't good—I need to focus more on keeping up appearances and less about how this place reminds me of Tomás.

"Jo-Jo?" Mikayla kicks the asphalt with her cleats as we continue toward the cars, her eyes trained downward. "The girls are going to that ice rink down the street. In case . . . um. You want to go?"

Jonah's jaw flexes. He plucks a wallet from his pocket, fumbling through it. Then, with a painfully weak smile, he says, "Of course we can go."

Andre, Mikayla, and Lily cheer with happiness. Jonah tells them to go off—he and I will meet them there—and the suggestion is met without resistance. Together, the three of them skip off to Andre's car.

"We should plan," Jonah says. "Since this wasn't in the itinerary."

I shake out of my stupor again, realizing we're alone. I keep spacing out, listening and barely processing. We're going . . . where? To an ice rink?

We hop into my car, and I follow Andre onto the main road. He must be pumping music, because Mikayla's and Lily's heads are bobbing in the back seat. I'm sure it's probably some soundtrack from a show or video game—I can't remember ever hearing Andre listen to music with actual words in it. At lunch, sometimes he'll blast whatever soundtrack he's feeling while studying his textbooks or highlighting his notes. Last time he tried to pump himself up for an AP bio quiz, the *Attack on Titan* season one soundtrack was ringing in my ears for a week.

"Whatever we do, it doesn't involve skating," Jonah says sharply. "I'm not getting on the ice."

Cool. Great. So I'm supposed to skate with everyone while he sits alone on the bleachers? "What's your issue with skating?"

"Like I'm really supposed to keep my balance on ice with two butcher knives attached to my feet?" he demands.

I raise my eyebrow. Skeptically, I ask, "You've never been in a rink before, have you?"

Jonah grumbles and twists forward, which I take as confirmation.

When I look over at him, though, half of his face is partially buried in his (my) jacket collar, and he's peeking sideways at me.

"What?" I ask, amused.

"Just . . . trying to think of ways we can appear couple-y." He fidgets. "And . . . maybe wondering why you're acting all anxious."

My brief smirk flips to a frown. How is it that, after a couple panic attacks, this guy can see through my walls so easily? I can sense his impatience, and I have the feeling he's not going to leave it alone, so I roll my eyes and say, "The soccer field reminded me of when I used to play. My brother showed up for games. Sometimes we'd get nieve frita afterward, but . . . whatever. That's all."

"Nieve frita?"

I snort at his pronunciation, which makes his cheeks redden. "Like fried ice cream," I explain. "If Mom ever came, she'd whine about how it wasn't really a traditional Mexican dessert. Tomás would order two portions out of spite, and talk about how amazing it was in this awful, butchered Spanish to annoy her, and . . ." I falter, realizing I'm smiling. What the hell have I been rambling about? To *him*? Quickly, I say, "Never mind."

"Never . . . what?" Jonah shakes his head, clearly bewildered. "Why do you shut down every time you start talking about Tomás?"

"I shouldn't have talked about him at all," I snap, and before I can swallow the nasty words, they tumble out of my mouth. "Especially not with you."

Jonah doesn't speak for a moment. Maybe I should reel it back, because that was a shitty thing to say, but my teeth are locked together, strained. "Sorry for caring," he mutters eventually.

"You didn't have to pretend to in the first place," I say sharply.

Jonah doesn't respond to my outburst. I kind of wish he would, so I have an excuse to feel angry instead of guilty.

The rest of the ride is silent.

JONAH

So, this is how I die. With two big, glittering brown eyes holding skates toward me and whispering, "Please, Jo-Jo?"

Andre knows my weakness is Lily's angelic face and pleading voice. He definitely put her up to this, and I'll hate him forever.

"Okay, Lilypad," I say unwillingly.

Then my body is moving for me, pulling an extra pair of disposable socks up my feet, and Maya is tying my skates, because you should cross the straps *under* the holes not *over* the holes, and this day can suck my entire ass. Andre decided to invite the rest of our friends along on this venture, and because he naturally draws a yes from everybody, everyone gets to witness my failure on the ice.

Five minutes later, my sisters are skating around the public rink like child pros. Mik stays clustered with friends, all of them looking ridiculous with their dirt-smeared clothes. Lily holds Casey's hand, waving whenever she sees me. She seems in even brighter spirits than usual, and though it might be because we're out and about, I'm more sure it's because Casey said they have a whole supply of old, sparkly barrettes Lily can have if she wants. Andre and Hanna are together, and Hanna looks completely out of her element, her face tight with strain, her arms wrapped tight around Andre's while he laughs at her.

As for me . . . I'm not much better off.

"Kill me," I rasp, hands trembling around Rohan's and Maya's while they draw me onto the ice.

"Just keep your ankles upright," Rohan croaks while Maya wheezes with laughter.

"His face," she chokes out. "Oh my God, his *face*."

I whip my head around, taking the rink in. College guys in matching crewnecks are racing each other on hockey skates. Some people look as awkward as me, and cling desperately to the wall. They're mostly under the age of ten.

"Push, don't just lift," Maya instructs, and suddenly, she and Rohan wrench out from under me, skating away. "Like this!"

"*Wait! Stop! You dickweeds!*" I shriek, coasting to a stop in the middle of the rink. Everyone nearby stares as I reach for Maya, still screaming, teetering forward with inch-long baby steps. They're both nearly doubled over in laughter.

So then I trip, obviously, and I know my kneecaps are going to crack against the ice.

Two giant hands catch my arms, stopping me midplummet. Dylan stares down at me, his expression unidentifiable, his dark eyes glinting under the fluorescent lighting. "So," he says, ignoring Maya's and Rohan's wolf whistles as they skate off. "You're on the ice."

"Not because I want to be," I say snippily.

"I know. It's because of Lily." His lip quirks. "Your weakness."

He sounds diabolical, but he's skating backward now, tugging me along, and I'm too distracted with staying upright to growl. "How'd you learn to skate?" I mumble.

"I used to play hockey."

I scoff. "Are there any sports you haven't played?"

He considers it, then says, "Golf."

I turn my eyes to the logo on his chest. I'm still seething from our conversation, which isn't great for our visible chemistry. Anyone looking at us can probably tell there's tension.

Dylan scrapes to a sudden stop. I don't know how to slow my momentum, so I crash uselessly into his chest. Before I can fall, I throw my arms around his back, squeezing.

"What the hell?" I hiss. "Don't do that!"

"How's it going, lovelies?" someone asks, and I peek over to see Andre and Hanna skating by. She's giving *help me* eyes. I wish I could have that honor. Too bad I can't even help myself.

"Just teaching Jonah how to skate," Dylan says mildly.

He taps my chin up so my face is closer to his, and there's this infuriating smile on his face. Wait. Is this jerk actually setting up a kiss right now? What is this? Revenge? When I didn't even do anything wrong?

He lowers his face so I can reach, and with a subtle huff of anger, I stretch up, meeting his smooth, warm lips. His hand fans over the back of my neck, tugging. My heart pinballs around my chest, then catches fire, then explodes, sending shards of white-hot heat into the rest of my body.

This wasn't part of the plan! I want to screech, but then I remember we *have* no plans, because he was too busy being pissed at me to talk it out in the car.

His tongue scrapes briefly between my parted lips, and only when I squeak in surprise (and nearly pass away because *what, what, what, what*—?) does he pull away, still smiling his whore smile.

"Right." Andre winks at him. "Teaching him. Sure. Seems like you're in no rush. I wouldn't be, either, if Jo-Jo was hugging me like that."

I realize my arms are still hooked around his back. "Go away," I snarl to Andre, but then they actually do, so I croak, "Wait, take me with you!"

I'm too late.

I whip my head back to Dylan, glaring up at him with the unforgiving wrath of a desert sun. "You piece of fuck," I say, seething.

"What?" His expression is back to being neutral.

"Who said I wanted to kiss you?" I demand.

He stares at me, unblinking. "We locked eyes and it seemed like you were on board, so I leaned in."

On board? In what world would the unbridled fury in my eyes indicate that I'm *on board*? "You held me against your lips like a prisoner," I say spitefully.

"Sorry." He looks like he means it, but I want to kick his skates out from under him anyway. "If I promise not to let you fall, will you stop trying to crack my spine?"

I can feel irritation seeping off of him, now. I should probably get angrier, but seeing his distant eyes triggers a sensation in me. It's . . . I think it's . . .

Guilt?

Of course he's pissed. It clearly took a lot of strength for him to even mention his brother after our date at Andre's. And there I was, prodding him, trapping him in a car with no escape, peeling at his layers without even asking if he was comfortable.

"Take me to the exit," I whisper.

Dylan tugs me by my wrists to the entryway of the rink. As soon as the railing is within reach, he releases me and turns to continue on.

"Wait!" I reach for him, grabbing his wrist and swiveling him back to me. Before he can yell at me, I blurt, "I'm sorry for making you talk about Tomás."

Dylan stares at me like I've just spoken fluent Spanish.

"I know it's touchy," I say, looking around awkwardly. "I would've gotten mad, too. So. Yeah."

The ice freezing Dylan's face begins to thaw. He sighs, exasperated, then yanks me sideways so we're not in the entryway. He leans me back against the railing, probably so I have something to grab, but it warms my face anyway. With his hands caging me in, I feel . . . cornered. But not necessarily in a bad way.

Oh, Jesus. What the *hell* am I thinking about?

"You didn't push," he says, relenting. His face is close enough that I have to use all of my mental strength to focus on his words, rather than the downturned corners of his eyes, or his annoyingly long lashes. "Sometimes, thinking about Tomás makes me . . . weird. I don't always act like myself. I shouldn't have snapped at you and said you don't care."

"I *do* care," I say grumpily. For some reason, I hope my breath still smells like spearmint toothpaste. Or . . . well. I should probably be hoping that my breath smells like garlic and onions, because he's completely invading my personal space.

"Yeah." Finally, Dylan smiles. "You care about everything, all the time, way too damn much."

I don't know if that's a compliment or an insult. He laughs at my suspicious expression, threading his fingers through mine.

"I'm sorry, too, by the way," he says. "For trying to piss you off by setting up a kiss when neither of us clearly wanted it. My dad went on and on about consent during our . . . ugh . . . *talk*." He shudders. "It was shitty of me to force you into that situation. So, yeah. Sorry."

I stare at our intertwined hands. I have to pay attention to his voice. His words. Process them. I have to respond. Say something. Anything. Words. "Um," I say, the heat of his hand somehow radiating throughout my whole body. "It's fine . . . kiss was good, so . . ."

Oh my God. Not *that*.

"Good?" Dylan's eyebrows fly further into his forehead, and his smile turns into the worst, most disgustingly amused grin I've ever seen.

"No," I say immediately.

"So I should use my tongue more often."

"I will chew it off."

He laughs. "Well, either way, we should still find time to practice. Just because I know how to kiss doesn't mean I can carry both of us through it during the fake dating. If we practice, you'll look less like an amateur."

I have plenty of negative things to say to that, but then he pulls me away from the railing, sliding us further into the rink.

"Come on," he says, still snickering. "Let's play pretend."

I guess the practice kissing is an issue I can deal with another day.

I resign myself to the fact that I'm going to crack at least six bones before we leave the rink. But Dylan's grip is strong enough to prevent me from folding onto the ice like a lawn chair. My ankles begin to ache, but with time, I find I'm moving more easily, and he can loosen his grasp. Eventually, I don't need to lean on him at all. I'm not skating, exactly— it's more like I'm standing straighter while he pulls.

I never accepted his promise from earlier, but he keeps it anyway.

He doesn't let me fall.

DYLAN

"This sucks. I hate everything. My legs hurt."

"Boo-hoo," I respond, helping Jonah wobble to a bench outside of the skating rink. I plop him down and pull his feet into my lap so I can unlace his skates. Nearby, Mik's team is gossiping up a storm, and Lily sits with them, listening with a chipper smile. Hanna is already back in her combat boots, jamming her middle finger in Andre's face anytime he tries to apologize and hug her. Thankfully, Maya, Casey, and Rohan left to go back to studying, so we're not under too many eyes.

"I can't believe you made me stay out there," Jonah whines. "I'm in a terrible, horrible, no good, very bad mood."

"You did fine," I tell him, kneading my thumbs into his ankle. To his credit, it does feel like his skin is puffing up, but he's clearly over-playing it. He watches my hands, his lower lip jutting out in a stubborn pout. "Though you definitely bruised my arms, with how tight you were hanging on."

"Sorry for not being coordinated on ice daggers," he grumbles.

Once we've stepped back into our shoes, Jonah gathers the skates and takes them to the counter. I watch him go with a sigh. Well, we didn't do too bad, considering we didn't have a plan. Other than our kiss, we were too focused on skating to act adorable and romance-y, but hopefully it was all believable.

Something grazes my fingers. Lily is suddenly next to me, kicking her legs.

"Hey," I say, smiling. "Did you have fun?"

"Mm-hmm." Lily looks over at Jonah. There's a hint of solemnness in her eyes. The kind that's too mature for a nine-year-old kid. "Dylan, are you falling in love with Jo-Jo?"

I nearly choke on my own air. "Wh-what? Ah, no—well, I don't . . ."

I wasn't prepared for this question. I don't want to get her hopes up, only for it all to fall apart when Jonah and I have our breakup. But she's also looking at me with such eagerness I can't help but want to make her happy. I get how Jonah falls for it so easily.

"Let's give it more time," I say.

Lily nods in understanding. "Jo-Jo's kind of hard to get used to. Mik, too."

She's so serious about it that I laugh. I look back at Jonah, just in time to see Andre piggybacking him toward us, his face twisted with what I'm sure is completely real and not-at-all overexaggerated agony.

"Ramz, carry me to the parking lot," Jonah moans when Andre drops him onto the bench. "My feet are broken."

The brat knows I won't refuse when Andre is next to us. He's fluttering his eyelashes in this cutesy, innocent way that makes me want to shove him out on the ice and let him find his own way home.

"Sure, cariño." I stand and snag him around the waist, then hoist him up, planting him over my shoulder.

"Hey!" he cries out. *"I meant a piggyback ride! Or princess style!"*

Andre and Hanna are already snickering. "See you on Monday," I say, and I carry Jonah, screaming and kicking, to the exit. Mik and Lily follow, both trying not to dissolve into giggles.

"Dylan Prissy Prince Ramírez!" Jonah yells when we're outside.

"Are your feet broken or not?" I ask calmly.

"Get dicked!"

"That's not a nice thing to say in front of your sisters."

"He's said worse," Mik tells me.

"Jo-Jo has a huge potty mouth," Lily adds.

I can't help but grin. Something about these kids puts me in a good mood, even if they are related to the writhing gremlin on my shoulder. Maybe I've tortured Jonah enough today, though, so I reluctantly deposit him on his feet, allowing him freedom.

"You . . ." His face is the color of strawberries. "I'm going to . . ."

He steps toward me, but his knee buckles. Before he can strike concrete, I snatch his arm.

"Collins?" I ask, slightly alarmed.

He's even brighter red. "I told you my feet are sore!"

You said they were broken, I think, sighing. Nonetheless, I rotate and crouch down, bracing for his weight. "Get on, then."

". . . Really?"

"Really."

Hesitantly, Jonah slinks his arms around my neck. I hoist his thighs up around me and stand without difficulty.

We start to the car. Strands of Jonah's hair and bits of fur on his hood graze my jawline. He latches his chin in my shoulder, and I realize, then, that he's more tired than he's letting on. I can feel the way his legs are quivering.

"I thought you'd be used to exercise, having to run around at the restaurant," I say.

Jonah sighs, his breath tickling my ear. The feeling gives me goose bumps, but they're not the disgusted kind I might've expected a few weeks ago. In fact, now that I've noticed it . . . I can't pry my focus away from it. His breathing. It's quiet, steady.

I wonder what it would sound like quick and shallow.

"That's adrenaline," Jonah says, though I've already forgotten what we were talking about. My face and ears are flaming hot. Hopefully he can't feel it radiating from my neck. "And I'm not on ice when I'm running around the restaurant. Or skates."

I don't have a response. I'm too busy trying to pull far, far away from the weird place my thoughts just diverted to.

Moments later, we make it to my car and begin to head back to Delridge. About ten minutes into our twenty-minute drive, I peek into the rearview mirror. "You okay back there?" I ask, but Mik and Lily shush me. "What—?"

"He's sleeping," Mik hisses.

I glance over. Indeed, Jonah's curled up, his head tucked under the headrest, breathing deeply. My jacket acts like a massive blanket for him. "Does he ever get any sleep?" I whisper.

Mik and Lily stare at each other. I wonder if I've asked a forbidden question. Then Mik says, "Every time I wake up at night, he's in the kitchen. Like, cleaning, doing homework, making lunches." She fidgets. "When we try to help . . ."

"He gets upset," I figure.

She nods.

We pull into his driveway. I wave goodbye to Mik and Lily as they clamber out. When they shut the car doors, Jonah begins to stir, but then falls back under.

I'm . . . not sure what to do, honestly. Should I wake him up? That seems like the best solution, but Mik's words tingle in the back of my head. Should I sit here and let him sleep a while, then? No, that's ridiculous. And creepy.

I guess I'll do what he wanted at the rink. Princess style it is.

I step out of my car and circle around to his side, popping open the door. I lean over him, unbuckling him, watching him breathe deeply. At least he's unfurled himself now, so it's not difficult for me to scoop his knees up in my right arm, then squirm my left behind his back. As painstakingly slow as I can, I lift him up against my chest. His head rolls sideways onto my collarbone.

"What," he mutters, his eyes still shut.

"Shh."

"The fuck."

"I'm bringing you inside," I whisper, nudging the car door closed with my foot. "Be grateful, little shit."

He doesn't answer. His body still rises and falls with the steady rhythm of sleep. Trying not to jostle him, I carry him up into the house. Mik and Lily must have retreated to their bedrooms, because they're nowhere in sight.

There's a man sitting in his living room.

I pause, my heartbeat quickening. His limbs are skinny, and he has a swollen face riddled with red patches. A few flimsy strands of hair cling to the top of his head. When he twists to observe me, I notice his eyes are drooping. They're almost . . . vacant.

I expect he's going to demand who I am, and why I'm carrying his unconscious son.

Instead, his eyes move back to the television.

I don't want to question it. Not right now. So I move down the hall until I'm at Jonah's bedroom. I shoulder him briefly into one arm so I can throw back his comforter and sheets, then lay him down on the mattress. I try not to let my thoughts wander anywhere foreign as I draw the blankets to his shoulders.

He's all bundled in. Breathing serenely. The crack in his window causes a draft, but it's not too cold today, so hopefully it won't be enough to wake him.

So now I should . . . leave?

Well, yeah. Fucking duh. What am I going to do, stand here and watch him sleep? Slide in next to him and cuddle up?

I suppose a nap wouldn't be the worst . . .

I palm my temples, sighing, and turn around. No way in hell am I ever willingly crawling into a bed with Jonah Collins again unless it's for show. It's what got us into this fake dating scheme in the first place. Besides, I don't need him trying to assault me with his pillow, like he did when he woke up after homecoming.

Though . . . would he? It's only been a couple weeks, but the vibe between us is . . . different. Not by much, but just enough that maybe he wouldn't attack me if he woke up and saw me lying next to him.

Ugh. I need to get out of here before my thoughts get any weirder today. As I start to the door, though, his hand lashes out, seizing my wrist. I jump in surprise, whirling back to him.

He's blinking slow, his eyes half-open, looking up at me through his slender lashes. "You carried me to bed," he mumbles.

When he says it out loud, I realize how ridiculous it is. "Sure."

"You . . . really are a prince, huh?" A lazy smile comes to his lips, burning embarrassment into me.

"It just seemed like you needed the sleep," I say defensively.

Jonah releases me and snuggles up on his side, closing his eyes again, that smile still playing at his mouth. "Such a kind and noble gentleman you are," he whispers.

I'm about to snap that he can't ever seem to ease up on his

insults, but then he continues on, his voice soft and raspy.

"Thanks for driving us around. I promise to pay you for gas next week."

You don't have to, I think, but there's no point in saying it.

"We haven't planned for next week," he tacks on, yawning.

"We can worry about that some other time," I say sternly. "Get some sleep."

He curls up tighter under his covers. Seriously, why is he trying to act all small and sweet right now? It's not working. "I work tomorrow night, if you want to stop by . . . maybe eight thirty?"

I give him a thumbs-up. "It's a date."

He wrestles one hand free to give me a thumbs-down. "It's not."

"See you tomorrow." Again, I turn toward the door to leave, and again, he tosses his hand out, grabbing my wrist. Only this time, he yanks, forcing me to stagger back. I clip the edge of the bed and all but fall directly on top of him. "Hey!" I snap, a foot from his tired face, anger thrumming under my skin. "Don't be so—"

Jonah grabs my shirt collar and yanks down. He bites my lower lip painfully hard, and a horrifying rush of tingles races through my body.

"What?" I hiss, wrenching back. Is he half-asleep? Does he think he's dreaming? What kind of logical explanation does he have for—?

"Payback," he says, smirking.

My brain explodes along the inside of my skull. Incapable of thought, I stagger away from him, spin around, and make a break for the door. This time, he doesn't manage to grab me.

I swear I can still hear him snickering as I tumble into my car and zoom away.

JONAH

They're back.

Words can't express my abhorrence when I approach my last table of the night and find a redheaded woman and gigantic man in a bow tie waiting for me.

"Jonah," Ms. Davis says, smiling widely.

"Please leave," I greet.

She huffs. She's wearing a baggy sweatshirt and leggings, and in this casual garb, she looks barely older than a college student. I wonder if this is how Mom looked at thirty-three. She never kept pictures of her life at the house—or, I didn't find any when we searched it after her death. When I was struggling to cling to any scrap of her existence I could find, before settling for my telescope.

"Good evening," Mr. Kelly says, polite as always. Why's he so spiffed up when it looks like Ms. Davis just climbed out of bed?

"You were both just here," I grumble.

"We loved your service so much we decided to come back," Ms. Davis says brightly.

Yeah, right. Clearly they want to snoop around after what happened on Friday, when Mik and Lily got dumped at the restaurant. Thankfully, since they're my last table, I can preoccupy myself with side work rather than talking to her.

If all goes well, they'll be gone by the time Dylan arrives with my sisters. He texted me earlier to ask if I wanted him to pick them up on the way in, and while I normally would've said no, it might be good to give Mrs. Greene a night off. I get the employee discount for family, too, so letting them eat here won't be too pricey. I already have two booths cleared off, where Dylan and I can plot the week while Mik and Lily are distracted with food and games.

"What are we drinking?" I ask.

"I'm getting an adult beverage." She wags her finger at me. "Don't tell your little friends Ms. Davis drinks."

"Everyone knows teachers get wasted on weekends," I say wearily.

"*What?*"

"Bourbon and ginger ale, please," Mr. Kelly says, smiling. "Noelle will have vodka and cranberry."

"With a *lime*." Ms. Davis gives him a cutting glare. She blows a loose strand of hair out of her face, and for a second, she looks so much like Mik that I'm stunned. She meets my eyes, though, and I blink back into focus.

"Okay." I turn and head to the kitchen, plugging their orders in with Sherry's card. I've been extra careful, because she's been extra annoying. As I walked in today, one of my co-workers was walking out, and caught my shoulder.

Guard up. She took every chance to get close to us and her breath smells like moldy gouda.

When I bring them their drinks, Ms. Davis immediately begins to chug. "This is perfect!" she says. "It's my favorite drink. We settle for simple and cheap around these parts."

"Cool." I flip open my book. "What's for din—?"

"How about you?" Ms. Davis leans on her palm. I have the feeling she pregamed before she got here. "Any favorite adult beverages, Jonah?"

"No," I say, though the real answer is *the sweeter the better*.

She looks intently at her menu. "What about your father? Is his favorite the same?"

My body stiffens. I can see right through it. She doesn't want to know what he drinks—she wants to know *if* he drinks. How does she even know about that? She's digging. She's worried. That pathway can only lead in one direction.

Child Protective Services.

I'm so close to turning eighteen. I'm so close to being an adult, to having the ability to work full-time and focus on building a better life for us. I've been meticulously avoiding Ms. Davis ever since she moved here, and now, just because she sees me more often, she feels entitled to start unraveling everything I've weaved around me?

I'm not good at lying. The harder I try, the more obvious it gets. But my sisters are depending on me, so I flatten my face and say, "He doesn't drink, so I don't know."

Ms. Davis taps the edge of the menu against the table, her expression unreadable. Mr. Kelly is studying me as well, which is almost worse. He literally specializes in family issues and red flags, so it's equally as bad if I can't convince him.

I don't bother with customer service quips as they order. I dart into the back and input their food, my quivering fingers stumbling over the screen. Determined to avoid conversation, I busy myself with sweeping the back, cutting lemon wedges, restocking condiments. I don't even ask if they need refills—I can't give them any opportunities to corner me. But then their food comes out, and if I don't deliver it myself, Ms. Davis will suspect I'm avoiding her. So, I take the dishes to the table, my heart hammering.

"Here," I say, setting the food down. "Anything else?"

Ms. Davis pokes at her pasta noodles. "Say, how many hours do you work a week?"

"I'm part-time," I say, a little too quickly. They exchange glances.

"That manager . . ." Ms. Davis spears the noodle and examines it intently. "She's rather friendly with her employees."

I swallow with difficulty. Faintly, I remember Mr. Kelly walking by when Sherry helped steady me in the worst way possible. Is that something he shared with Ms. Davis? Or has Sherry been walking around the restaurant, being "friendly" in full view of the guests? She's certainly done it before. "She's nice," I say. "No complaints."

Mr. Kelly's normally docile expression is gone in place of furrowed brows and grim eyes.

"Where are your sisters? With a babysitter again?" Ms. Davis presses.

Yes. "Dad's home with them." My voice cracks, and I know I need to get out of here before I unravel any further. I step back, promptly running into someone who's coming up behind me.

"Jonah! Do we have a family member here tonight? How lovely."

Every muscle in my body clenches. It's Sherry.

"Hi," Ms. Davis says sweetly, extending her hand. "I'm Noelle, his aunt."

"Well, of course! You two look so alike, I knew you must be family." Sherry brushes back my hair, her nails scratching against my scalp. Ms. Davis's smile dissolves. Mr. Kelly's demeanor darkens. "Your nephew is one of my hardest workers. You can see it in his tips! Or maybe it's his pretty face?"

She's moving to wrap her arm around my waist. Right in front of them. With no hesitation.

"Enough."

Mr. Kelly's voice comes in a venomous growl. His face is strained with hostility. Instantly, Sherry's hand freezes, mere inches away from me.

"Excuse me, sir?" she asks tightly.

"Do you think your employees like being touched?" he asks, and though he speaks low, his voice is the kind of deep tone that carries. We're already beginning to draw stares from other tables. "*Don't* put your hands on Jonah again."

"What . . . ?" Sherry's nostrils flare. "How dare . . . ? Are you insinuating that I . . . ? *Ridiculous!*"

"Don't pretend to play innocent," Mr. Kelly snarls, louder, and Ms. Davis reaches over the table, placing her palm over her husband's.

"Myron," she says, and though her voice is soft, her glare is sharp on Sherry's reddened face.

Sherry backs away, panting. Several tables are quiet around us— phones are rising through the air.

"Jonah," Sherry mutters. "Cash out with Jez and go home."

She storms into the kitchen. The farther she gets, the thinner the air feels in my lungs, until I'm nearly gasping for it. I whirl on them, shivering with rage. "What have you done?" I ask, breathing heavy.

Ms. Davis's eyes soften. "Honey—"

"No, stop, how *dare* you?" I stagger back, the weight of realization crushing me. "What makes you think you can . . . ? What if . . . ? What if you both just got me *fired*?"

"Jonah, take a deep breath," Mr. Kelly says, and though his voice has returned to its calming state, it does nothing to soothe me. My skin is boiling hot and my eyes are glassing with water.

But not here.

"Jonah, please," Ms. Davis says gently, and I see that look in her eyes. Pity. "We just want to talk—"

"*Hell no*," I say, seething, stepping further away. More words begin to tumble out of my mouth without breath, pause, or thought. "We're not family, Ms. Davis. I've never needed you before, and I sure as shit don't need you now. I've been fine doing this on my own, so *just get the hell out of my life!*"

I don't mean to let the anger slip through. But there it is, in full view, damning me further.

Ms. Davis tilts her head to one side, and whispers, "Doing *what* on your own?"

I don't have the emotional strength to answer, so I speed-walk away. I barely have enough sense to throw my apron and book into the kitchen and grab my jacket, before sprinting to the doors. For the first time in my life, I don't care about my tips.

I just have to get away from here.

I slam out into the night, sprinting across the parking lot. It's quiet, and the air is bitterly cold, stiffening my skin, freezing the scream in my throat.

Doing what on your own?

A blaring horn and squealing tires stop me in my tracks. I squint into the light, watching as the driver climbs out, probably to cuss me out.

"Collins?"

The headlights silhouette Dylan in dusty gold, shadowing his expression.

"Are you . . . leaving?" He takes a hesitant step forward. "I know we're a little early . . . we came to see if things were slow . . ."

Of fucking course he's early. Why wouldn't he be? Whether it's joining track just in time to beat me in the two-hundred-meter dash, or showing up in front of me while I'm on the precipice of a mental breakdown, Dylan Ramírez always magically appears right when I least want to see him.

My jaw is trembling. I storm toward him, thinking I'll shriek at him for something, or jam my middle fingers in his face, or shove him. "You," I hiss when I'm two feet away, gasping for air. "I swear . . . I . . . you're . . ."

It's the perfect time for him to laugh at me and ask why I'm on the verge of crying. I prepare to fling my fist at him, but then he whispers, "What's wrong?"

My breath catches. The tears unglue themselves from my eyes and begin to scorch my cheeks. "Fuck you," I choke out, backing away. "I don't have t-time for your bullshit . . . have to go make them dinner . . . so fuck *off* . . ."

I try to twist and run away, but Dylan catches the crook of my elbow. "They're with me, remember?" he asks carefully. "Breathe. Okay? There's a KFC down the road. They have mac and cheese for Lily. Just . . . don't walk home in the dark when you're distracted. I could've hit you."

They have mac and cheese for Lily.

Why? What is it about that quick, simple line that floods my chest with so much anguish and . . . appreciation? I don't want any positive feelings toward Dylan. I especially shouldn't want to lean against him right now.

But he looks so sturdy.

I cough on a sob, and I stagger forward against him, stuffing my face into his jacket and using it to muffle the scream I've kept trapped until now. Hesitantly, his arms rise around my back, and he envelops me against him. My mouth is moving, but my words are incoherent. I'm trying to tell him what happened, but I only hear one sentence, over and over.

"I miss my mom," I cry. "I miss my mom . . ."

"Shh." Dylan's voice rolls through me in gentle vibrations. "Just breathe . . . shh . . ."

I try, but I'm swallowing air. I'm fired. No one else will let me work off the clock. I won't be able to buy the girls new clothes and food. I won't be able to buy Lily new books or sketchpads, I won't be able to afford Mik's soccer fees. Ms. Davis will contact CPS, and they'll take my sisters away, and I can't, I can't do this, I *can't*—

Dylan scoops my face into his hands, warm despite the temperature. "In through your nose," he says softly.

I pinch my lips between my teeth, watching him breathe, trying to mirror him.

"Good. Exhale through your mouth."

I do. It's shuddery and weak.

"Yeah." He gives me an encouraging smile. "In through the nose . . . okay, hold it . . . exhale."

The crushing sensation flees my chest. He slides his thumbs along my cheekbones, stroking my tears, and the rest of my strength, away. He's treating me so kindly, touching me so gingerly, it makes me want to cry again out of frustration. There's no one around to trick. Why is he sparing *any* warmth for me? Is it just to calm me down so we can continue planning the fake dating agenda?

Yes . . . that has to be it.

The back door of his car opens. "Jo-Jo?" Mik's frail voice says.

I can't let either of them see me like this. I'm their rock. The one they depend on. They can't see any side of me that might shatter the illusion, so I shrink into Dylan's chest, trying to hide against his built figure.

Dylan draws my forehead to his coat, shifting so I'm concealed behind him. "Jonah's fine," he says. "Give us a minute?"

Mik is quiet for a moment. Then, the door closes.

"Thanks," I say weakly. "You didn't have to . . . do this."

Dylan sighs, and his breath flutters the top of my hair. "I know what it's like when people turn away from you at your lowest points," he mumbles. "So. Yeah."

He gives me a noticeable squeeze before dropping his arms, allowing me to step away. The chilly wind instantly cuts back into my face and hands.

"Ready to go?" he asks.

No. I feel disgusting. My face is slimy, and my eyes are puffier than the Pillsbury Doughboy. But my sisters are probably hungry, so I nod, walking around the passenger side, collecting myself enough to initiate Adult Mode.

I crawl into his car. The girls don't say anything, but I can hear Lily sniffling. I hope they didn't see my meltdown, and that they're just responding to the negative atmosphere.

As Dylan buckles in, I turn to them, flashing a bright grin. "Anyone want fried chicken and mac and cheese?"

This perks them up instantly, and they cheer.

I know how to make them feel better. I know how to handle things. I know how to stay balanced. No matter what happens, nobody can take that away from me.

We peel out of the restaurant parking lot, leaving it behind.

DYLAN

Jonah pretends like all is well. We pick up KFC and eat in my car, chatting, trying to restore a casual mood. But under the interior lights, I can see traces of his breakdown. His eyes are swollen, his nose is bright red. I want to pry deeper, but I know he won't talk, especially in front of his sisters.

How long has this situation been going on? How long has his exhaustion been there, lightly cloaked under a false, confident exterior?

I watch him reach around the seat, threatening to tickle Lily's shins while she laughs. The way he interacts with her, with both of them, makes me smile. I never realized Jonah was such a protector. That he's so involved with his sisters. It's endearing, and yet, watching them plunges shards of glass into my chest. Because it reminds me of my own childhood.

Tomás was the Jonah in our relationship. I was the Lily. Boisterous and loud against reserved and mild. When I was really young, his volume could scare me to tears. He'd call me a baby, but then he'd scoop me up, swing me around, and make me laugh until I couldn't breathe.

He was always doing that. Picking me up. Throwing me into the air. Giving me piggyback rides. I was ten years younger than him, so I frequently took advantage of his size.

He stopped coming near me, though, after everything. After he realized I couldn't stop seeing it. The bloodied bat. His venomous eyes.

I'm the reason we can't share these bonds anymore. The reason he doesn't visit, or come to family events, or call me. My throat closes, so I refocus on the road. Jonah is stuffing money into my cupholder, thanking me for the KFC. I wish he'd let me pay. I have plenty of allowance money from whenever I clean the house (or don't, since they're not around enough to notice). But the last thing I want to do is upset him again when he's clearly in a fragile state.

I pull into their driveway, and the girls lunge out, jogging to the door. Jonah sits in the passenger seat, looking like he's ready to crumble into dust.

"We didn't get to talk at the restaurant," he mumbles. "So you can come in. If you want."

I feel like that's the last thing on his mind, but maybe he needs the distraction, so I nod. I've been holding something in my car since last night, too, so it's a good time to give it to him. Jonah exits as well, narrowing his eyes as I move to my trunk.

"What's that?" he demands when I hoist a giant cardboard box onto my shoulder.

"You'll see." I flick my hand at him. "Go on."

He squints more earnestly, then spins around and stomps into his house.

"Brat," I mumble with a smirk, following him.

It's still uncomfortable. It's too cold, too dim and lifeless. But it's not my house, so I don't mind. While the girls sprint to the kitchen to eat the sugar cookies I brought over when I picked them up, Jonah and I head to his bedroom. The man I saw yesterday, who I still assume is Jonah's dad, doesn't appear to be here.

"So? What's with the box?" he asks, nudging the door closed behind me.

I plop it on the floor. "Open it."

While he grumbles and falls over it, I wander up to the walls, exam-

ining Lily's space and astronaut pictures (as well as a random one of
a giraffe). I head for the telescope propped next to his fogged, broken
window and peek into it. The lens is cracked.

When I turn to see Jonah's progress, I find him pulling the electric
blanket out of the box.

"It was . . . sitting in my basement." I try not to sound nervous. "It
should keep you warm. Since your room is so ass-numbingly cold."

Jonah doesn't answer. He pulls his starry comforter back, and I help
him spread the blanket out, tucking it in. He plugs it into the wall, and
within seconds, it's heating up under our palms.

"Glad it still works," I say, because I don't know how to break the
silence.

Jonah slumps onto the edge of his bed, tucking his knees to his
chest. I sit next to him, wishing he wasn't so uncharacteristically quiet.
Is he mad? Relieved? Or taking it in? For once, I can't read his expression. He looks sideways at me, and though he's frowning, it's not in his
familiar, spiteful way. "You saw this . . . and thought of me?" he asks
quietly.

"Yeah."

He searches my face, like he's looking for a lie. Suddenly, his hand
reaches out. I know he won't hurt me, but an image comes to mind. A
man's palm colliding with my stinging face—a knee meeting my aching
ribs. I'm curled up, bracing, while gruff, vicious Spanish assaults my
ears, so unlike my mother's. So unlike my brother's.

¡Si abres la pinche boca, te lo juro que te voy a matar!

Jonah's hand awakens me, dragging me out of my stupor. He hoists
me closer by my shirt and plants his lips on my left cheek. "Thanks,
Ramz," he mumbles, his words grazing my ear.

I'm too startled for words. Did he just . . . kiss me? On my face? *Willingly?*

Maybe Jonah stunned himself, too, because he rips away, his eyes widen, and he blushes deeply. "That was weird," he croaks. "Sorry. It's just. Thoughtful of you."

I can't muster an answer. My cheek is burning from the imprint of his lips. My ear tingles from the warmth of his words.

Jonah scrambles to his feet, chewing his nails. "I'll toss the box," he squeaks out, and he scoops it off the floor, swings the door open, and charges into the hallway.

I sit there, numb. Trying to process everything that just happened. Jonah looking solemn but grateful. Jonah searching my face. Jonah kissing my cheek. I can't seem to wrap my head around any of it, so hesitantly, my hands move out, fanning across the electric blanket. I can't say why I felt so strongly about giving this to him—only that maybe, with it, he could rest easier.

Just when I'm considering going to look for him, he reappears at the door. His expression is suddenly deadpan, and this atmosphere . . . something's wrong.

"What?" I ask nervously.

He strides into the room, sits beside me, and jams a crumpled paper into my palm. I unfurl it with nervous fingers.

It's a shipping receipt. Dated yesterday.

Shit.

"Where did . . . ?" I swallow. I searched the whole box for one.

"Tucked in the instruction manual."

". . . Jonah—"

"You lied." His voice is dull. Emotionless.

"You wouldn't have accepted it otherwise," I say, curling my knuckles. Frustration is already bubbling up in my chest, preparing me for a fight.

"Get out." He stands, as do I, and suddenly, he's ripping the blanket off his bed, yanking the plug out of the wall. "And take your pity gift with you."

He tries to stuff it into my arms, but I let it drop in front of me. *Pity gift.* Is he serious? Does he truly think that any attempt to help him is some display of charity? "It's here, so use it," I say fiercely. "I saw it and thought it could help. That's all."

He squares his shoulders and snarls, "Get. Out."

"What is it with you and money?" I demand. "Is it pride? You're obviously having a shitty night, so why can't you take this one thing?" I want to grab his arms and shake him around—to try and make him see that his stance on this is only going to make him drown.

But he won't see sense. Because he's Jonah Collins. So I may as well give up now.

I storm out of his bedroom, nearly barreling Mik and Lily over, who are lurking in the hallway. I mumble an apology, then continue past them to the front door. As I'm pulling my keys out and wrenching the knob, though, a hand falls to the door, slamming it shut.

"Where are you going?" Mik demands.

I'm fuming too much to respond.

"Gonna check on him," Lily murmurs, shuffling down the hall to Jonah's room.

Mik collapses cross-legged on the floor, then pats the space beside her as an invitation. "Sit with me, asshat."

"I have to go," I tell her sternly.

"Why?"

"Because Jonah doesn't want me here. And I don't want to be here, either." I grab the door handle, but Mik doesn't move from her position. I could probably wrench it open and slide her, but I don't want to be a jerk. So, I slump onto the ground next to her with a weary sigh.

"You know . . . Jonah's a good brother." Mik tucks one knee to her chest. "When he's not a complete dong, I mean. He pays for my soccer and gets me clothes I want at the store. He even gets me my favorite brand of brownies when we go grocery shopping, if he's in a good mood."

She pauses to blow a straggly strand of hair out of her face.

"He always knows how to make us feel better. And . . . we try to be there for him, too, but it's not easy when he sees us as kids." Mik sounds like speaking about this is draining her of strength. "We lean on him a lot, but he . . . doesn't have that. A person to lean on. It's just been him. Alone. There's Andre, but he's always so busy. Jo-Jo says he's fine, but he's a crappy liar, so . . . maybe you could be that person?"

I'm not surprised by this information. Jonah's situation has always felt . . . off. The way he refuses to talk about his home life, the way he reacted when I first saw his house. None of it excuses the fact that he's a stubborn ass who can't accept help, but . . .

Maybe I need to give him a break. At least for tonight. Besides, we still have to pretend we're falling for each other, and nothing good will come of us being in a fight.

"So, what, you want me to go make up with him?" I ask, arching my brow.

"Make up with him. Make out with him. I don't need to know the details." Mik shrugs so nonchalantly that it gets laughter out of me.

"Fine. But if he tells me to leave again, I have to leave. Okay?"

Mik massages her chin, contemplating my deal, then nods. "Fine."

No getting out of this now. I rise to my feet and make my way down the hall, peeking in through his cracked-open door. Jonah is lying sideways on his covers, still in his work uniform, facing the window. The electric blanket lies in a heap on the floor. Lily sits on the mattress behind him, humming an incoherent tune and patting his head—until she sees me and immediately scrambles off the bed.

"You're not going to yell at him, right?" she whispers. Her eyes are so desperate and watery, it makes my heart twinge. These girls . . . they'd fight through hell and back for their brother.

"I promise I won't yell at him," I say with a soft smile.

"Oh. Good." She pulls me farther into the room by my hand, then shuffles into the hall and closes the door behind her, leaving us alone.

Jonah doesn't turn or acknowledge my presence.

"I shouldn't have lied," I murmur. I inch closer to the bed, scooping the blanket up along the way. "I saw it online, and thought you'd like it, so I got same-day shipping and—"

"Why do you care?" His voice is barely audible. "We're fake dating."

It's a fair point. And a question I've been asking myself the last several days. *Why do I care?* The conclusion I've come to, lately, is that whether or not our relationship is fake, and whether or not I despise his raucous-ass personality, I can't ignore the fact that there's someone in my social circle who can't sleep comfortably warm at night.

That's the excuse I've been telling myself, anyway.

I decide there's no response that can satisfy him. I plug the blanket into the wall, click it on, and place it in a pile on his bed. I sit down on the mattress behind him. My anger has simmered into exhaustion at this point, and it seems like his has, too.

"We should talk about this week, since you won't leave," Jonah mutters. "Maya's throwing that Halloween party on Saturday, and—"

"Let's not talk about the fake dating right now," I say tentatively.

He rolls over to face me, blinking his drooping eyes. "Then why are you here?"

"I . . ." I don't know. Because Mik told me to make up with him? Because we need to reconcile here and now if we want to keep up the ruse? No . . . neither of those are entirely true. So I sputter out the truth. "It feels like, maybe, you shouldn't be alone right now."

Jonah stares at me, processing this. Then, his lips waver into a sudden, unexpected smirk.

"What?" I ask defensively.

"Nothing. That was just weirdly romantic of you." He wiggles his feet under the electric blanket. Slowly but surely, the aggravated energy in the room begins to dissipate. "So, you don't want to talk about the fake dating. What do we do, then?"

He's watching carefully for my response. "I don't know," I admit. "Have anything in mind?"

"Well . . ." He heaves a massive, irritable sigh, and his eyes move, very noticeably, to my lips. "You're the one who keeps saying we should practice kissing. I guess now's a good time."

Now? Is he delirious with fatigue? "I figured you wouldn't be the one to bring it up," I say skeptically. "Since you consider me your archenemy for all of eternity or whatever."

"You are," he says, nodding. "And yeah, I'd rather pass away than kiss you. But I'm getting good practice from you, too. Like, stuff I can take with me. Once I find another partner, I don't want to be a complete newbie at everything."

"So . . . you want to practice kiss not to fool our friends but to gain experience." My tensed muscles slacken with both relief and irritation. Apparently, I'm just a pawn to him. Though, technically we're using each other as pawns, with the dating scheme.

"We have to kiss in front of everyone anyway. And practicing will make us look more convincing," he points out. "There just happens to be an extra benefit for me."

As he's talking, pale pink blooms in his cheeks. At least he's embarrassed about wanting to use me for his own gain. Or, I assume that's why he's blushing.

"Fine." I prop myself up so I'm sitting against his headboard. I pat my thighs. "Sit here."

The pink color extends into his ears. "Why?" he squeaks.

"You want to practice on me? Then we do it how I want," I say sternly.

Jonah mutters something but sits upright and shifts his weight sideways into my lap, facing me. He catches my eye, says, "This is weird," and immediately begins to scramble away.

"You're the one who wanted to do this," I snap, catching his arm.

"I know!" He looks highly uncomfortable. "Just feels strange, since there's no one to see . . . I mean, it's *you*."

His hesitation should relieve me, but I'm just annoyed at this point. "Close your eyes and picture someone hot, then," I tell him. "Someone from school. Or your celebrity crush."

Jonah clamps his eyes shut tightly. The skin around them is still swollen from when he was crying. There's a slight tremor in his hands. From cold, I assume, so I lean around him to grab the electric blanket, biting back laughter when he puckers his lips. He must've thought I was leaning in for the kiss.

I unfurl the blanket, pull it up my knees, and drape it over the top of his head. He peeks through one eye, frowning as I tug it around his shoulders and arms, cloaking him in it. At least this way I won't be kissing an icicle.

"Where should I put my hands?" he asks, avoiding my eyes.

"Depends. I don't mind the chest, around the neck, in the hair. But you should ask to see where they're comfortable being touched. Don't always assume."

"Okay." Jonah nods. "Good point. So . . ."

Hesitantly, he slings his arms around my neck. His nose is nearly grazing mine. There's nowhere else for him to look other than my face now, so he closes his eyes again.

I stare at him, blinking slow. Taking this in. Jonah Collins, in my lap, tantalizingly close, the blanket draped around him like a veil, his cheeks radiating warmth despite the rest of his body.

"What next?" he asks, the words sprawling against my lips.

It takes me a moment to realize I'm supposed to respond. "Are there any places . . . you don't want to be touched?"

"No." Jonah's voice is barely audible. "Y—they can touch me anywhere they want."

I draw a slow, deep breath through my nose. Focus on the task. No way am I about to get horny for this asshole just because he's close. I squeeze my eyes, sifting through the hot people I know, trying to come up with one who might be close to Jonah in height and weight.

"We can start?" he asks.

"Yes," I say, despite the fact that I haven't found the ideal person to picture, despite the fact that I'm not ready at all.

He closes the remaining few inches, pressing his lips to mine. My hand rises instinctively to cup his cheek, and the soft material of the blanket grazes the back of my palm.

Hmm. It's not good enough. It'll look too boring and surface level this way—not nearly intimate enough. Jonah's mouth is nearly sealed shut, so I use my thumb to tug on his lower lip. "Part them," I whisper.

A noticeable shiver moves through his body. He does as requested, and now, we've graduated from pecking. My other hand moves to the waist of his slacks, and I knot my fingers in one of his belt loops. His uniform . . . it smells like a culmination of things. Sanitizer, leather from booths, polish from tables, smokiness from the grill. It's an overwhelming scent. One to match an overwhelming personality.

It takes strength to break away from him, and even then, I feel him leaning in, trying to close the gap. "Breathe," I tell him.

Maybe he realizes he's panting, because he pauses, his chest rising and falling against mine. I keep my eyes closed. I don't know what might happen to my wandering thoughts if I look at him right now, while he's warm and flushed and catching his breath.

I take the edges of the blanket around him and pull, guiding him back to my lips. Anything to get this over with sooner—to get Jonah Collins out of my lap. He's taking more risks, getting comfortable with using his teeth and tongue as I use them myself. I nibble his lower lip, properly showing him how to bite (since his surprise attack yesterday nearly caused my mouth to puff up, and I don't want to go around looking like I just got punched in the face). I press my tongue against him, widening his kiss, opening his mouth. The blanket slides down the back of his neck, down his spine, but I'm not sure he needs it anymore. His skin is hot to the touch. I know because my fingers are tracing the length of his neck, down to the collar of his shirt.

I try not to think about the fact that someone else is going to do this with him one day. I don't know why it's so distracting. Maybe because I don't like the thought of being used as someone's kissing dummy.

"You should feel what it's like," I say, my mouth moving without thought. "So you can use it on your partner. In the future."

"What what's like?" he asks, his voice raspy. Inviting.

"Hickeys." I don't know why I say that. I shouldn't care. I *don't* care about whoever he's going to be making out with in the future. The only reason I'm doing this at all is so we can uphold our image more easily.

My breathing is quick. My palms are shaking. I should probably do it, then. I should move forward, press my lips to his neck, show him how to do it. But . . . But something . . . isn't . . .

"Dylan?"

Something . . . isn't right.

"Dylan," Jonah says again, and his voice is sharper, clearer. "Open your eyes, okay?"

His thumbs suddenly touch my cheekbones, and I flinch, hitting the back of my head against the headboard. Ouch. Fuck.

"Hey." His voice is soothing, calm, gentle. "Look at me."

"Por favor, déjame." I don't know why I whisper that. I can't make sense of any of my words, none of my thoughts feel right. "Dije que me dejaras . . . por favor, parale . . ."

What's happening? Am I having a heart attack? A stroke? I don't know what I'm saying, I don't know why I'm shaking, I don't know where I am, I don't—

"Here," his voice says, and he has my hand, fanning it against his neck, pressing my fingers into his skin. My eyes fly open, and I meet Jonah's gaze. His forehead is beaded with sweat and his cheeks are lightly flushed, but his expression is calm.

"Jonah," I sigh.

"Yeah. It's me." He pushes my palm deeper into his neck. "You can feel it, right?"

What? What am I feeling?

There's a quick, steady rhythm beating against my fingers.

Oh. Jonah's heartbeat.

I drive all of my attention to it. The weight of his heart in my palm. The heat of his skin against mine. The way his body moves with his breathing.

All at once, I realize I'm going to be okay.

I stare at him uselessly, water brimming in my eyes. I can't believe this. Embarrassment rips a hole through my chest, and my lower lip trembles. I'm so pathetic. Another panic attack? In front of him? Isn't that three now? What's *wrong* with me?

"Sorry," I croak, and I stuff my hands over my face. "I'm not always like this."

Jonah curls his hands around my wrists, lowering them. I don't want to look at his face. He's going to be aggravated that he had to calm me down. He'll be looking at me in disgust, knowing he still has to put up with me until December. Or maybe he'll be scowling because I failed miserably in distracting him from his shitty night.

But then his palm comes up—slowly, this time, so I see it coming—and it frames my cheek. He tugs, tilting my face up, and holds me there until I meet his eyes.

He's still calm. Not annoyed. Not scared. Not scolding me for making him worry. Not averting his eyes. Not squirming with discomfort because he had to witness that. Just . . .

Calm.

Jonah crawls off my lap, then sits beside me, resting his back against the headboard. He grips my palm, then positions my thumb against the base of his wrist. "Push down," he says mildly.

I do. His heartbeat pulses through my fingers. His presence—his living, breathing existence at my side—helps ground me in this moment.

For a while, neither of us speak. Other than the creaking of his sisters moving around the house, and the sound of my irregular breathing, everything is quiet. Jonah's eyes sag further with each minute, and soon, he's slumping. His heart rate is slowing ever so slightly.

I release him and whisper, "You should change if you're going to fall asleep. Or take your work stuff off. It'll be wrinkled for your next shift—"

"I think I was fired," he says flatly.

This information sinks into my chest. He slides down the headboard until he's lying on his back, then picks at something invisible on his pillow. "I'm sorry," I murmur.

"Not your fault. It's just . . . um. It's not a great situation, since I'm . . ." Jonah doesn't seem to want to finish his sentence. I do it for him.

"You're their provider."

I already know this. But seeing him nod and confirm it makes the fact hit all the deeper.

"I buy their food. Their clothes. Art supplies for Lily. Soccer fees for Mik. It's ridiculously expensive, but I want them to . . . have experiences. Be kids." Jonah continues to pick at that nonexistent thread on his pillow. I wonder if it's because he doesn't want to meet my eyes. "My dad makes house and phone payments. He does taxes. Otherwise, he spends his time in bars and hotels."

His pause is heavy. I don't know what to say, so I shift so I'm lying down, then roll to face him, propping myself on one elbow.

"I'm sure you already knew this stuff," Jonah says matter-of-factly, pushing away the blanket to unbutton his shirt. I realize he's already kicked off his slacks, and soon, he'll be in boxers. Quickly, I steer my eyes to the ceiling. "Or you guessed it."

"Some of it," I say.

There's another few minutes of silence. I don't know what to say. How to console him. How can I, with everything he's going through? His hand is lying next to me, and he doesn't complain when I pick it up, kneading my fingers back into his wrist to find his pulse again.

It's quickened. I wonder if he was nervous, telling me that.

There's nothing I can do to make his situation easier. Even if there was, he wouldn't accept it without complaint. But, at the very least, maybe I can reciprocate. Make him feel less . . . alone. Besides, I've never been able to talk about my situation with someone who's also been through it all. I love Hanna, but sometimes sharing with her is difficult. I feel like I'm unloading on her, trying to explain what it's like to carry so much weight.

But Jonah carries a lot of weight, too. He understands what it's like. So, maybe that means I won't have to work as hard to make him understand me.

"I don't have panic attacks that often," I say softly. "Lately, though,

I've been feeling more anxious. Because, seeing how you are with your sisters . . . it makes me think about Tomás. It makes me wish we could be like you. We used to be, before I ruined it."

Jonah frowns. The blanket is back to his shoulders now, but everything above his collarbone is exposed.

"I think I was . . . nine?" I clear my throat. I allow his pulse to anchor me to Earth, to Delridge, to this street, this bed. "Tomás was transferring to a university, so he couldn't babysit me anymore. My mom's brother recently moved to metro Detroit, so when she went to work, she dropped me off with him. They had sort of been estranged before then. But he was close, so it was convenient."

Jonah waits. I squeeze his wrist tighter, hoping he doesn't mind.

"My tío was violent," I mumble. "When he was angry . . . he lashed out. I used to wear baggy clothes so my parents wouldn't see the bruises. He said if I told them . . . he would . . ."

"Don't force yourself," Jonah says quietly.

I exhale slow and nod. Moving along. I don't need to go into all the details. "Um. Long story short, Tomás came home from college one weekend and could tell something was wrong. He found out what Tío Ramón was doing, and he . . ."

I wince. Again, the image pierces my brain. My brother's cheery, grinning face gnarled with fury. Blood soaking in the wood of his baseball bat.

"The lawyer played up the *he was defending a child* thing, but Tomás put my tío in a monthlong coma with a weapon," I continue, my voice wobbly and frail. When I look down, I realize I've instinctively pressed Jonah's hand to my chest. He doesn't pull away, so I guess it's okay.

"After his sentence, Tomás stayed in Detroit when my parents decided we should start over in Delridge. We've gotten more distant, and . . . it's been a year since we talked. He wrote me this letter, but . . ." I try speaking past the lump in my throat. "I can't open it."

Jonah analyzes me with curious eyes. Just as I'm beginning to panic about whether or not I just trauma dumped, he says softly, "Thanks for telling me. I know it was hard."

"Well, you opened up about your situation," I point out. "And you've had to deal with my problems multiple times, now. I figure it's only fair for me to tell you why."

Jonah shakes his head. "It doesn't bother me like you think."

"What?"

"Your panic attacks. They aren't a burden." He squirms closer, bringing the heat of the blanket with him. "You piss me off for plenty of reasons, but that's not one of them. So don't ever worry about having one around me."

My jaw quivers. Several voices from the past begin to scorch in the back of my head.

I just don't have time to deal with that on top of everything else. I'm sorry.

It scares me when you get like that. Like, what if you hit me or something? I hope you understand.

I can't be with someone who's going to randomly lose their shit. What if we're in public?

I refocus on Jonah. I can tell he's struggling to keep his eyes open. "Go to sleep," I tell him, because I don't have any other words that can truly grasp what I'm feeling right now. I'm not even sure *what* I'm feeling.

"Can't . . . have things to do . . ." He graces me with a massive yawn. "We haven't discussed this week, either."

"We'll figure it out." I rest his extended palm against the bed. I wouldn't mind continuing to talk to him, but I can tell the day's events are weighing on him. I should allow him to escape into sleep. "Goodnight, brat."

He scoffs, but I can already tell he's fading. "Ramz . . ."

I brace for whatever might come out of his mouth. Then, "Did you know . . . Pluto is smaller than the United States?"

A space fact.

I toss my head back and laugh. Jonah falls asleep before I can even answer.

JONAH

I'm under the sheets. When did I crawl under the sheets? My shades are closed and my room is dark, aside from the hallway night-light creeping under my door. The electric blanket acts as a second comforter.

"I tucked Lily in," a voice whispers.

What? Who? I try squirming into a sitting position, but two arms close around mine, easing me back into the mattress. I'm too warm and cozy to complain.

"See you at school," the voice murmurs, pressing the blanket firmly under my chin. The back of my neck tingles.

"Okay," I say quietly, snuggling my head back into my pillow. "Thanks . . . Ramz . . ."

I pass out.

DYLAN

I sit propped on one of my island stools, one knee folded into my chest, my bloodshot eyes focused on the drawer. I've been staring at the letter for twenty minutes. Every time I blink, it's like I'm seeing it again for the first time. Panic tingles around the edges of my chest, waiting for a moment to drive its stake through me.

It's been a while since I've told anybody about what happened. Confiding in Jonah makes me feel like I've allowed air to escape from the highly pressurized can of anxiety in my head. It was *easy,* too. When I told Hanna about Tomás and my tío, I had nightmares for a week. With Jonah, though . . . it was little more than a skittering heart.

I groan, shoving my forehead into my knee. He didn't ask for details, or say much about the situation. I probably went overboard and freaked him out.

I should sleep. It's one o'clock in the morning. Dad's in bed, and Mom's off somewhere, having left earlier today. Apparently, she and Dad went to visit Tomás this weekend, so I never ran into her. I imagine their car ride to Detroit was probably him singing poor renditions of Motown enthusiastically while she sat beside him, silent, expressionless.

I've never understood their relationship. They're complete opposites—he's warm, wild, and full of life, while she's cold, regal, and unfazed by anything. And, despite being an affectionate person, Dad approaches her with the caution of a deer. I can't remember the last time I even saw them hug.

"It's about boundaries, kid," Dad said when I nudged him about it once. "Your mother isn't a person who likes to be touched. I respect that."

He said it like that should clear everything up. Like I would suddenly understand why they decided to stay together despite being nearly as incompatible as, say, Jonah and me.

I sigh, standing up. Getting up for school is going to suck, so I should sleep, rather than sit here and stare at this thing I can't open.

My fingers are next to the drawer handle. The writing is glaring.

Lil Dyl

I can't read it. Not now. But . . .

I extend my hand, grazing the envelope. The texture is enough to cause bile to scorch my throat. I stagger back, clutching the countertop, my heart reeling.

"Sorry," I breathe, though I don't feel the sound leave my lips. "I'm sorry . . ."

I rush out of the kitchen. I don't sleep for the rest of the night.

But it's the first time I've touched the letter in months.

JONAH

SHERRY

I have your tips from yesterday. You may
return to work, but ensure your family
doesn't cause further commotions. I trust
you'll discuss their behavior with them.

I wake to the most relieving text message of my life. I daresay it even puts me in a good mood. I'm so thrilled I nearly skip to the bus, and even add a smiley face to my text to Dylan about what special thing we should do during lunch. To which he asks if I'm being held hostage, and I send him the middle finger emoji.

But then I get to English, and my smile twists into a glower.

Right. She's still my teacher.

Ms. Davis eyes me through the period. I keep my mouth shut, my face down, my pen moving. I have an opportunity to tell the class Mr. Darcy is probably a sub and I don't even *take* it.

As soon as the bell rings, I'm speed-walking to the door with Casey.

"Jonah, stay," Ms. Davis calls.

I cuss.

"Again?" Casey whispers as I wave them past me.

"Won't be long," I mutter.

"Oooh-kay. No worries—I'm sure Dylan will save you a spot in his lap."

They shuffle away alongside everyone else. I know the drill by now, so I collapse into a nearby seat and toss my backpack onto the ground. "Yes?" I ask stiffly.

Ms. Davis moves in front of my desk, readjusting her flowery cardigan. Her crimson hair is knotted into a swirly bun. "Jonah," she says, softer than I expect. "I'm sorry we caused a scene yesterday. Myron mentioned he'd seen her behave inappropriately with you before, and we couldn't watch it happen right in front of us."

"Like you said, she's friendly," I mutter. "It's better than her yelling at us."

Her posture tightens. "Nobody should be touching you without your consent *or* yelling at you. Does your father know about what's been happening?"

Startled, angry laughter escapes my mouth. Her frown cuts deeper into her face.

"What's funny about this?" she demands.

"Nothing. Just . . . don't know why you suddenly care so much."

She takes a long, heavy breath, then drags a chair to the front of my desk, sitting opposite me. "Look," she says wearily. "I know I haven't been present. Kim and I had issues, particularly concerning your father. So, I've been keeping my distance. And that . . . is my mistake."

She pauses, and my eyes are drawn to movement in her lap, where she's spinning a gel pen agitatedly between her fingers. Is she . . . nervous?

"I thought maybe he was doing a decent job of raising you, considering you wanted nothing to do with me," she says, shrugging. "I thought, okay, Kim wasn't lying. I guess, against all my doubts, this man is actually a good father. So, I'll leave them alone, and if they ever feel comfortable enough to reach out, I'll be here. If they ever want to build a relationship with me, I'll let them make the first move. Otherwise, the Collins family is none of my business, as Kim always said."

The pen falls motionless in her lap.

"But then you entered senior year, and landed in my classroom." She observes me with careful eyes. "Since the start of the semester, I've watched the circles under your eyes get darker. I've watched your grade slip, like you're having trouble keeping up. Then Friday happened . . . and last night. Something isn't sitting right with me."

Ice accumulates in my blood. "I don't have to answer your questions," I say, but I'm stunned. Mom never told me why she had a falling-out with her sister. To find out it may have had something to do with my father . . . that can't be the only reason, right?

"True," she says, "but as your aunt *and* teacher, I'm within my rights to investigate."

The oxygen suddenly feels like syrup in my lungs. "No," I croak, too quickly to stop the desperation in my voice. "You can't threaten to involve Child Protective Services—"

"What?" Ms. Davis's brows rocket upward. "I would never involve you in that kind of situation. CPS is the last thing on my mind. But . . . why is it the first thing on yours?"

I'm backing myself into a corner. Digging a deeper hole. "It's fine," I say flatly. "We're fine. Don't worry about us. After years of never visiting, or calling, or checking in, you can't suddenly decide everything is okay between us. We don't owe you anything."

She rubs her temples, which I take as my cue to stand. I pull my backpack to my shoulder and trudge to the door.

"I don't want you to see me as a threat, Jonah," she whispers. "I . . . shouldn't have distanced myself from you and your family. I shouldn't have given up on you so quickly." I hear a shaky breath. "But at the first sign of being unwanted, I backed away. In fact, I used it as an excuse to try to move on. To stop looking for that connection to my sister and start over. And I'm . . . sorry, Jonah. I'm sorry."

I swallow past the knot in my throat.

I walk out, leaving her behind.

On Saturday afternoon before Maya's Halloween party, I arrive at Dylan's house with my costume and a bottle of my father's rum.

"You walked?" Dylan asks when he finds me at the front door. His floppy curls are damp and hanging low over his forehead, and he's wearing a tank top and sweatpants. The hint of spice wafting off him tells me he probably just showered.

"I drove," I say, swinging keys around my index finger. My dad's beaten-up car sits parked on the street. "I dropped Mik and Lily off at Ms. Harris's for the night, then came here."

"Your dad's cool with that?" he asks skeptically.

"Not sure. He was passed out on the couch when I left. But he's got plenty at home to occupy him for tonight." I step inside and kick off my shoes. He takes the bottle of rum, and I drop my bag and fold onto his couch, curling up. I don't *want* to be here earlier than Andre and Hanna, but we haven't had much time to plan our public appearance for the party, so we figured we should talk things over. And besides . . . after Sunday night, I've decided he's slightly less intolerable than I thought he was.

"What's your costume, Collins?" Dylan calls from the kitchen. "Alarm clock? Bullhorn?"

He's still pretty fucking intolerable, though.

"Tee-hee," I snap. "I'm going in my costume from last year."

". . . That spy costume?"

"*Sexy* spy costume," I correct.

He approaches me with a tray of sugary brown cashew-shaped cookies. "The one you tried wearing to school," he says, setting it down. I notice the subtle way his eyes brush over me, like he's imagining me wearing it. "The one that got you sent home."

"Their loss." I bite into a cookie, and my eyes flutter. "What is this deliciousness?"

"Cajuzinho."

". . . Uh."

"Cashew candy," he clarifies, smirking at my blank expression. "Dad said they sometimes have these at birthday parties in Brazil. You can make them with chocolate, walnuts, coconut . . ."

I munch another one. "Tastes like peanuts, though. Not cashews."

"You like them?"

I nod in earnest. "Your baking skills are the only good thing about you."

He rolls his eyes and snatches the tray away from me before I can steal any others, bringing it to the kitchen.

"Your parents aren't home?" I ask when he plops down on the opposite side of the couch.

"Dad is in Detroit until tomorrow. Mom is in . . . Boston, I think? Miami? Dayton? Who knows." He glances at the mantle above the fireplace. I catch sight of an upended picture—one with a girl in a gorgeous, fluffy, pink-white dress standing beside a stern couple.

"Those are your grandparents?" I guess.

"On my mom's side, yes."

There's a hint of bitterness to his words. "Do you ever see them?" I ask cautiously.

"Nah." A sour smirk plays at his lips. "They're in Texas. And everything that happened drove a stake between us."

I knit my eyebrows. "Wouldn't something like that . . . I don't know. Bring a family together?"

"Tomás nearly killed my tío," Dylan mumbles, eyes glazing over on the TV. A rerun of *Cake Boss* is playing on mute. "I don't know much about my mom's past, but apparently my grandparents favor him over her, so they're bitter."

My mouth hangs open. "Even after what your tío did to you?"

Dylan shrugs, but I can tell the weight doesn't leave his shoulders. "Mom was never close to her parents, so I wasn't close to them, either. Her cousins come around, but other than that . . . she's not good at being a *family* person."

I take a moment to absorb how awful that is. "Where . . . ?" I hesitate, hoping I'm not crossing any boundaries, then ask, "Where is your tío now?"

"No idea. He moved away from Detroit and we haven't heard from him since. I don't give a shit if he's living his best life or lying in a gutter somewhere." His voice is flat, and I think maybe I did cross a line, because he says, "Anyway. Tonight."

"Tonight," I echo.

"Maybe we should make out in front of people or something. You did fine when we were practicing, so I think we can make it convincing."

The remembrance of Sunday night—of his palm at my waist, his mouth frantic and yearning against mine, his taste of lip balm—nearly causes redness to flood into my face. I still can't believe that was a real, actual thing that we did with our own free will. "When should we do it?" I ask, trying to sound casual.

"Whenever there are eyes on us," he suggests.

"Please, Ramz." I give him finger guns and a playful grin. "There are always eyes on me."

"I know, and it's usually because you're being annoying as shit."

I have plenty of amazing and well-thought-out comebacks, but then I notice tension in his jawline. He's looking determinedly away, and something occurs to me. "You really hate attention, huh?"

His eyes widen a fraction. "What?"

"I always thought you were just being a grump about social situations," I say, leaning toward him. "But it's more like you're anxious in big groups? Is that it?"

He shifts with discomfort. "I don't like when a lot of people are looking at me, if that's what you're insinuating," he grumbles. "But that's most people. You're an outlier."

"So I'm special. Unique." I lift my chin with a haughty smirk. "Not like other girls."

Dylan presses a hand over his face, probably to hide his uncontrollable laughter, then says, "Let's just start making the pregame sandwiches. Andre and Hanna should be here in an hour."

We head to the kitchen, and I watch as he throws cheeses, meats, and condiments onto the counter. "Speaking of the making out thing," he says, pulling a loaf of French bread out of his pantry. "You . . . seemed like you were into it."

"I wasn't," I wheeze out, already humiliated.

"Right. Sure. I was wondering who you were picturing." His voice sounds strange, like he's forcing nonchalance.

The heat, as always, is moving directly into my face. Why is he asking me about this? To judge my taste in humans? "No one in particular. I was just. Um. Focusing. On learning."

"Oh," he says, without a single flinch in his neutral expression.

I want to move this conversation along, so I start pulling out drawers to look for a bread knife. When I grab the one nearest to the sink, though, Dylan lunges over, snatching my hand.

"Don't," he says quickly. "That's where . . . um . . ."

"Tomás's letter?" I assume.

He mutters something I take as confirmation, then pulls out a cutting board.

Once everything is in front of us, I fumble around to throw things together. Dylan chops tomato and onion beside me, clearly comfortable in this space. I wonder how much time he spends here, cooking and baking, mere feet from that drawer. I wonder how much time he spends in echoing silence.

"What?" he demands. I realize I'm staring.

"Nothing." I whip away, avoiding eye contact. "Just thinking . . . Can I ask you something else? Like, about your tío."

His fingers stiffen around his cutting knife. Nonetheless, he nods.

"How did your parents react when they found out?"

Dylan sighs. "My dad did what you'd expect. He held me, cried for me. He slept in my room every night for months. But my mom . . . she didn't look at me for weeks."

I smear mayo along the bread, glancing up. His eyes are glassing over.

"She wouldn't talk to me," he whispers. "Or come near me. I felt like I'd shamed her or something."

I place the sandwich in the panini maker, contemplating this. "I had a moment like that with my mom," I say lightly. "If you want to hear it."

He shifts his jaw around, then gives a curt nod.

"I was ten, I think," I tell him. "Mom was carrying Mik downstairs and slipped. Mik fell out of her arm and hit the ground. Mom held her when she cried, but afterward, she handed Mik to me and left the house for a few hours. When she came back, she wouldn't come near us. Because she felt so guilty."

Dylan is quiet.

"So," I continue, "maybe that's what your mom went through, on a way bigger scale."

His face hardens. "I don't care," he snaps. "I needed her, and she pretended like I didn't exist. And now she's this chief financial officer—whatever her damn title is—and I never see her. She calls me at these impossible hours. And when she *does* show up, it's like she's so drained she doesn't want to see us. So, I don't care anymore. I'd be fine if I never saw h—"

"Don't."

Dylan sputters off.

"Don't finish that," I say quietly.

He slumps forward with guilt. "Sorry."

I pull out more bread, mindlessly loading it with whatever my palms can find. "Guilt . . . is really powerful," I say, proceeding with caution. "And feeling it after something so traumatic might cause someone to . . . I don't know. Pull away? Or push someone else away?"

I glance at the drawer, then at him. He merely grunts in reply. Maybe he'll see the connection one day, but I don't want to force him there.

As we finish up, I try to avoid keeping tabs on the ingredients we're using, or portioning out how much I can eat before I'll start feeling guilty. But it's hard. I'm accustomed to keeping track, counting the resources and dollars. Dylan will say I don't need to pay him, but he doesn't get it. I have to prove I can keep things under control. Not only to people around me, but to myself. And if I accept handouts, that means . . . I have to acknowledge I . . . I need . . .

Anyway.

The sun begins to set, and Dylan and I have run out of details to solidify. The make-out will come randomly, probably after we've had drinks. We'll be seen disappearing into a room for a few minutes so people think we're getting frisky. We'll find a spot on Maya's couch, where I'll sit in his lap, because apparently he thinks his weight will crush me into fine dust if we do it vice versa.

Finally, the doorbell rings. Andre bursts inside, grinning merrily.

"Let's get boozy, bitches!"

DYLAN

It's Hanna's turn to DD, so Jonah, Andre, and I are already a few drinks deep when we go upstairs to change.

I climb into my generic black pirate costume, faced away from Jonah in my room while he audibly struggles into his own costume. I zip my buckled boots to my knees and adjust the puffed sleeves cinched at my wrists. I button my waistcoat and slap a tri-tipped hat over my hair.

When I turn, I swallow. Jonah's decked out in a skintight faux leather bodysuit cut down the front, exposing a V-shaped sliver of his chest. He's wearing a plastic utility belt, knee-high boots, and arm bracers.

"Sexy spy," he says confidently, tousling his hair. "I bought it the week after Halloween two years ago, when everything was, like, seventy percent off. I was afraid I couldn't pull it off as much as a femme person or boob-haver, but then I was like, as long as I'm the most confident person in the room, that's all that matters, right?"

"Uh . . . right." I blink a few times. He's *definitely* pulling it off. "Do you normally go to the women's section of Halloween party stores?"

"Obviously. Where else am I supposed to find something to show off my goods?"

I'm not sure which *goods* he's referring to (I've never seen any). But this feeling inside of me is very new and very uncomfortable, so I chalk it up to the rum and whirl away, my ears burning. "I can't believe you wore that to school last year," I mutter.

"You can't?" he asks skeptically.

I definitely can.

Andre dresses up as Spider-Man, but it's an entirely black suit with a funky-looking white spider stretching across the center. Either it's one of the comic variations or from the original trilogy that I have little to no recollection of. Hanna's wearing a zip-up hoodie over a vampire costume, her eye makeup black as night and her lipstick crisp red. Jonah has been giving her "please bite my throat out" glances.

By the time we get there, Maya's mansion and lawn are flooded with people. The music is nauseatingly loud, every beat trembling in my bones, rushing through my veins. We find our friends near the front porch in a ring of people sipping out of red Solo cups. Rohan is a bottle of mustard. Casey is an "en-bee" with yellow, white, purple, and black stripes to match the nonbinary flag. Maya steals the show as Princess Tiana in the glittering, strapless blue dress from the movie.

"Make yourselves at home!" she calls out, lifting a bottle of bourbon in the air. "Drinks are on the island in the kitchen!"

She brings it straight to her lips. My respect for her continues to grow.

Jonah and I worm past staggering, drunken classmates, then wander until we locate the kitchen. I place two Solo cups in front of us, dish ice into both, and grab the nearest vodka, dumping it into Jonah's.

"Wow, Ramz. You remember my go-to," he says as I top it off with pink lemonade. I avoid looking at him—I have been since he put that costume on. It hugs him so tightly it looks like he's teetering rather than walking.

"It's not difficult to remember," I say, pouring rum and Coke into mine.

"No vodka this time?"

"Nah." I squeeze a lime wedge into my drink and stir. "I like to mix things up. Keep people on their toes and all."

Jonah rolls his eyes, smirking. "Right. Because if Dylan Ramírez is anything other than moody and snobbish, it's *unpredictable*."

Ass.

We find our way back to the group. Andre has already claimed the center of attention, leading the age-old conversation about which Spider-Man movie is superior. Jonah immediately jumps in to claim *The Amazing Spider-Man* gets his vote.

"Only because you had a crush on both Andrew Garfield and Emma Stone at the time, so you were basically having a movie-long orgasm," Andre snaps.

"And?" Jonah's voice is playful. I can tell he knows how passionate Andre is about the subject.

"Your opinion doesn't count. Especially not when Zendaya exists so obviously before your ungrateful eyes." Andre peers up at me. "What about you, Ramírez?"

His words clatter around in my head. I knew this would happen. Since I'm next to Jonah, I can't hide. My eyes wander the sea of people—there are eleven of us cluttered under the front porch columns. Eleven isn't bad.

"Um . . ." I frown, trying to pick the movies apart. "Probably . . ."

"Dylan likes *Spider-Verse*," Jonah says, and just like that, the eyes are off me. He's not wrong— it's the only movie I remember any details from. Have I told Jonah that before?

Andre nods in agreement. "You have fine taste."

He begins to rant about how important it is that Miles Morales has stepped out of Peter Parker's shadow in recent years, releasing me from the conversation. Hanna watches him ramble, a small smile on her lips.

I take a long, deep swig of my drink, hoping it'll propel me through a night of standing with one arm in the spotlight (the one around Jonah's shoulders).

I realize quickly, though, I may not have to worry. As the four of us wander from group to group, sliding into random conversations and dipping to explore the mansion, I'm not having to speak as much as I feared. Jonah dominates every topic, not allowing a single moment of awkward silence that might cause anyone to engage me. The more light he steals, the wider he grins.

I've never understood him. How does he glide so fluidly into every group and conversation? How does he claim every room he's in with a smile and wave? Beyond all that, how does he feel *comfortable* in that position? He's like Tomás. Rowdy and unruly and never having to scramble for attention. It just . . . comes to them.

We breeze past a game of Never Have I Ever, past couples making out against walls, past groups clustered together on spiral staircases. Sometimes, we split off from Hanna and Andre, but we always make sure they're within seeing distance. A beer pong table is set up in the home theater room, which Jonah jumps into for only a second to throw a ball. He makes it, and the room cheers like he single-handedly won the game for everyone.

Eventually, we make it to the backyard—a massive, grassy lawn with a glowing pool stamped in the center. It's off-limits, since the heating function needs repairing, and with everyone drinking, Maya doesn't want people climbing in. Anyone else would probably be disregarded, but the entire school knows better than to test the class treasurer's patience. Especially when she's not sober.

It's a chilly October night. The cool air stings my face, but the rest of me is tucked warm and snug under my costume. The alcohol helps, though it isn't doing much for Jonah, who instantly begins to shiver when we step outside. We head to one of the tables surrounding the pool, where Casey, Andre, Hanna, and Rohan are chatting. We draw two chairs around them and sit.

I'm beginning to feel . . . at ease. For several minutes, we sit and talk, watching the varsity football team play catch near the pool, taunting their chances of staying dry.

"This place is unreal." Jonah swirls his drink. "Who needs three bathrooms on the ground floor? Do you piss in one and take a dump in another, just because you can?"

Everyone laughs, but I hear traces of genuine distress in his voice. The size and scope of this place bothers him.

"Refills?" I ask when he checks his phone for the fourth time in two minutes. I can tell he's starting to worry about his sisters.

"Yeah." He sighs, standing and placing his phone on the chair. "I'm reserving this seat. Same for Ramz." He snatches my phone and plants it on my chair, then grabs my pinkie, drawing me toward the house. As soon as they're out of listening range, he hisses, "I think it's going well. But we should find time for the . . . you know . . ."

He makes a smooch noise, and I snort.

"We have time," I say, taking the last gulp of my drink. I'm tingly and warm and in good spirits. "Letting it happen naturally is the best way to do things."

"But it *won't* happen naturally," he says as we circle the perimeter of the pool. "We're not really dating, so—"

"*Josh, behind you!*" a voice shouts.

Suddenly, something heavy slams into me, yanking me out of Jonah's grip and sending me staggering. I try steadying myself, until I realize the ground is no longer under my foot. It's water.

Shit.

I plummet sideways into the icy pool. Water races up around me, submerging me and my costume, dampening my hearing. Quickly, I kick upward until I break the surface, gasping. My hair is matted to my forehead—my pirate hat is floating away.

The entire backyard is laughing.

I'm so numb I can barely process how to keep myself afloat. I'm shaking violently. One of the football players—Josh Hammoud—is holding the ball, looking down at me with distress, his lips forming the same words over and over. *I'm sorry, I'm sorry, Ramírez.*

This is humiliating. There are at least fifty people out here, all staring directly at me, and . . .

Wait. No. Not at me.

Slowly, I look sideways.

Jonah is in the pool with me. He's screaming, flailing around, hurling curse words into the air, splashing water over the edge of the pool. *"You taint!"* he roars at Josh. *"You pushed us in! Biphobia! This is biphobia!"*

"I didn't even touch you, Collins!" Josh snaps, before refocusing on me. "Sorry, Dylan. I wasn't looking . . ."

I'm not listening. I'm staring at Jonah, who's shivering harder than me, soaking up everyone's interest, putting on a show.

"Two lovebirds in the pool!" Andre's voice rings out, and everyone *ooh*s and *aww*s.

I blink, and suddenly, Jonah's floating right next to me, water dripping down his face and glittering in his eyelashes. His grin is full of mischief. He's at ease, despite the frigid temperature of the water clawing at his skin.

I'm still stunned. I know everyone is watching, but I don't care. The world is sliding away—the excess sounds of whooping and laughing, the sting of the icy pool. He meets my eyes, and there's a shift in his expression. His playfulness dissolves into something more . . . focused.

I wonder if that's how I look right now. I wonder if he feels the same way. If, right now, I'm the only person he can see.

"Thank you," I whisper.

His gaze falls to my lips. "It was nothing," he says quietly.

I smile. "It was something."

We move forward in sync. I frame his face in my hands and pull. He wraps his arms around my neck, squeezing.

I kiss Jonah Collins harder than I've ever kissed anyone.

JONAH

I'm still shivering by the time Hanna drops Dylan and me off at his house. My bones feel slick with ice, my body aches, and my lips are pale purple. Thankfully, Maya was able to spare us some of her brother's clothes (all while scolding and cussing us out for breaking her one rule at the party), but the guy is a linebacker for the JV football team, so the apparel did nothing but slide around my shoulders and sag at my waist.

Dylan must've noticed I was having a hard time getting comfortable after our pool stunt, because he suggested we leave. Normally, I'm one of the last people to ditch a party, but I didn't mind this time. Even though we accomplished only one part of our plan—making out in front of people—I could feel alcohol exhaustion creeping in.

"Okay," I say through a giant yawn when we enter his living room. "Guess I'll get going—"

"No," he says. I blink up at him in surprise, and he swallows loudly before saying, "You should . . . spend the night. Even if you're not tipsy anymore, you shouldn't drive when you're this tired. Mik and Lily aren't even home, right? There's no reason for you to rush back."

I process this through the fatigued haze in my head. "You want me to stay," I say, for clarity. "Like, longer. Is that right?"

He considers this, then says, "It's more like I don't want you getting in your car and then running into a lamppost when you fall asleep at the wheel."

I heave a massive sigh. I'm not sure why I'm irritated about *that* being his reasoning. "Fine. I'll sleep on your couch—"

"We can share my bed."

He says it so boldly, so confidently, that for a second, I can only stare at him in bewilderment. Part of me wants to make a sly joke about how eager he apparently is to get into bed with yours truly. The other, more stubborn part takes hold, though, and I say, "It's fine. You have that gigantic tiger blanket on your couch—"

"You don't understand," Dylan interrupts, shaking his head. "If my dad comes home and sees you there, he'll ask all kinds of uncomfortable questions."

Oh. Best to avoid that, I guess.

I should probably wash the chlorine off my skin, so I take his offer to use his shower, then scrub the inside of my mouth with toothpaste. When I next creep into his room, hair damp and body wrapped in a towel, he tosses me spare clothes. He's dressed in boxer shorts.

His clothes are longer than Maya's brother's, but not as baggy. When I'm fully dressed, I glance around his room, taking it in properly. It's cozier than I remember—a simple, clean place with a few touristy knickknacks, presumably from his mom's trips. The family picture on his nightstand is facedown.

When we're both washed up and minty fresh, Dylan turns off the light. I stand at his window, massaging goose bumps from my arms, staring through the slanted blinds at the night sky.

"Thanks for letting me spend the night," I say, since the silence is already overwhelming.

"It's fine." He fluffs his pillows. "I owe you for what happened at the pool."

"Don't know what you mean."

He gives me an annoyed, knowing look. I fight a smile, turning my attention skyward again. There's not much to see tonight—the haze of the town lights drowns most of the twinkling.

"Did you know," I say, "that if you put Saturn in a bucket of water, it would float?"

Dylan ambles up behind me, peering out as well. The warmth of his chest presses up against my back. "That'd have to be one big-ass bucket."

I don't realize how close he is until his chin brushes against my hair. "I used to be obsessed with fun facts," I tell him, leaning forward against the windowsill. Wondering if he'll follow. "I'd stare at the stars and moon for *hours* with my telescope."

He moves with me, as I anticipated, and the thought makes my body temperature rise. "The broken one?" he asks, his soft voice precariously close to my ear.

"Yeah. It . . . got busted when we moved houses." I have to force my mouth to conjure the words—to stop fixating on his proximity to me. "But it was from my mom, so . . . you know."

"Right." Suddenly, his hands graze my upper arms, sneaking below my T-shirt sleeves. "Any other facts, Chilly One?"

I rotate toward him, craning my neck. "Really?" I ask excitedly. He's not just making fun of me? I have an entire stash of them, locked and loaded.

My enthusiasm must startle him, because he stares at me wordlessly. Then, "Tell me something about . . . Venus."

"Did you know Venus's day is longer than its year?" I ask immediately. "It takes two hundred and forty-three days to rotate once."

He offers an impressed nod. Then, "Jupiter?"

"Did you know it has seventy-nine moons?"

"That's a lot of moons." He leans down, like he's trying to get a better look at my face. I press my hands back against the wall beside the window, though there's really nowhere for me to go. "Neptune?"

"Did you know that Neptune's moon Triton is constantly moving closer to the planet?" I ask brightly. "Some scientists think Neptune's gravitational pull will eventually shred Triton apart, and it'll become another ring. Which means Neptune could have more rings than *Saturn*."

"Wow." Dylan says the word, but the distracted look in his eyes makes me feel like he didn't even hear me. He rests his arms on the wall beside my head, trapping me between them. "Pluto?"

I hesitate. The moonlight from the window soaks his face in a cool, silvery glow. Pluto. He said Pluto, right? "Um . . . did you know . . . one day on Pluto is over one hundred and fifty hours?"

"I didn't." His face inches closer, and I move my head back instinctively, bumping the wall.

"What are you doing?" I whisper.

"Mars?"

He's ignoring me. Or maybe he's just not hearing me. I should get angry, but all I can sputter is, "It's . . . Mars . . . the sunsets . . . are blue."

The tip of his nose skims mine. "The galaxy?" he murmurs.

My chest is pounding. The room is quiet, aside from my shortened breaths. I look between his eyes, reaching for a fact, any fact, but my mind is a void. "I don't know."

His palms come inward to skim my neck. His thumbs latch under my chin, propping it up. Guiding my face closer. "You can't think of one thing?" he asks.

"I . . ." The words are scrambled in my head. "Did you know . . . ?"

His lips brush my parted ones. I exhale shakily against his mouth. His collarbone is smooth under my fingertips. I don't remember putting my hands there. I can't muster any words—I'm captured under his eyes.

He leans into his kiss, deepening it. My heart bucks against his, separated by the thin layer of cotton that won't stay up on my shoulders. Mint slides against my tongue, mingling with the woodsy scent of his shampoo. His hands drift the length of my arms, leaving goose bumps in their wake, and frame my hips, tugging them against his own.

And he's warm. He's so *warm.* Suddenly, I want to be wrapped in it. To feel this heat against every inch of my body—to shiver, once, for a different reason.

There's a parting moment, in which his forehead is still pressed to mine, and I'm breathing those tight, raspy breaths, and I'm eyeing his lips while gnawing my own. He mouths, *You're safe.*

And I . . . I don't know what to do. My head is a mess of incoherent thoughts and shifting, unrecognizable feelings. He turns, easing me onto his mattress, and I scrape my fingers up through his soft, damp curls, drawing him down. His hands brace the crooks of my knees around his hips. A shudder rolls up my spine, and maybe he feels it, because he smiles.

"Wait," my mouth says.

Dylan draws back, dazed.

"There's . . . no one to see." My voice is weak, raspy. "There's no one to trick here . . ."

Dylan's eyes wander my face like he's never seen it before.

"It's fake," I whisper. "Remember?"

Dylan's muscles tense at my sides. "Of . . . Of course it's fake," he says sharply. "It's just practice. This is practice. Right? For after we break up, and you find someone else to date."

My eyes dart between his. "Practice?"

"What else?" he demands, desperate, like he's hoping I can explain it away.

But I can't explain anything. Not the way seeing him propped over me makes me feel. Not the way every part of me tingles and burns with some emotion I've never felt. Not the way my heart pleads for more, or the way my brain is telling me this person looks good, he looks so damn *good*, and he's so *warm*, and everything is so soft and inviting and—

"For practice," I rasp.

He bends over, kissing me again, his knuckles nudging my chin higher. I drive my palms down the nape of his neck, exploring the soft, shifting ridges of his back.

"For practice," he murmurs against my lips.

Practice. Right. Of course. That means I should be picturing someone, right? A hot celebrity, or some attractive person from our class? I swallow an involuntary noise as his fingers creep beneath my shirt and brush my waist.

Someone else. Anyone else.

He presses his lips to the edge of my mouth, the slant of my jaw, the hollow of my neck.

Someone . . . there has to be *someone* I can think of . . .

Everywhere he touches is searing hot—every time he shifts, I'm disoriented.

Not Dylan. Not the way his hair twists above his eyes, the way his irises freeze me and set me ablaze simultaneously, the way his arms look on either side of me.

Fuck. *Fuck.*

Not *him.*

I slide my hand over his lips. Cutting him away. "Saying it doesn't make it true," I whisper.

Dylan looks away guiltily.

"We hate each other," I persist, though the words feel pathetic and empty. "Remember?"

Irritation flashes in his face. He draws back completely, allowing cool air to swirl between us. "Is that still how you feel about me?" he snaps.

I prop myself up on my elbows. "Isn't the whole point of this to make sure we don't have to talk to each other again?" I ask feebly.

Dylan backs away from the bed, reorienting himself. "Whatever," he mumbles.

He strides out of the room.

I crawl under his sheets, burying myself in the fluff of his mattress. *It's Dylan Ramírez*, I think, despite my flushed face. *It's Dylan Prissy Prince Ramírez.* But it doesn't matter how many times I mentally insult him or remind myself of my animosity.

My heart never stops pounding.

DYLAN

Why?

Why, though? But *why*?

Why, why, why, why—?

I hunch over the bathroom sink, slapping my flustered face with cold water. I'm glad Jonah stopped us; otherwise, things could've gone too far.

But what made us lose our senses in the first place? More specifically, *me*? I was the one who initiated it. Who crept closer, drawn in by the silver reflecting in his eyes, the scent of my body wash on his skin. The pearly smoothness of his collarbone under the window. My T-shirt sleeves sliding off his shoulders, his hair ruffled with shower water. The way his face shone brighter than the moon when I asked for space facts.

I pat myself dry, sighing.

I can't face him right now, so I wander downstairs. It's two in the morning, but that's never stopped me from panic baking before.

Someone's in my kitchen.

My feet scrape to a stop. I recognize the back of her head. In fact, I'm more familiar with it than the front. She pulls something out of her purse—a new molcajete I'll probably have to cure myself, if we ever want to make anything in it. She's always bringing home these useless trinkets and objects from her trips. She places it next to my plate of cajuzinho.

I shift backward, and the floor creaks.

She peeks over her shoulder. "Dylan."

". . . Hi, Mom."

She turns to me. She's wearing a jet-black pantsuit and heels, and

her curls are gathered into a strict bun. Her eyes search my face analyti-
cally, but her expression is neutral, like always. "You've been ignoring
my texts," she says.

"Not ignoring," I lie. "You just . . . text when I can't answer. I forget
to respond."

"Ah." I'm not sure she buys it. "How is your boyfriend?"

I reel back. That's not on her normal checklist of questions to pester
me with. "Heh?"

"Henrique said you have a boyfriend." Her eyes sharpen with sternness. "Is that his car outside?"

Of course he would be eager to spill the details of my love life to
Mom. "Yeah," I say.

She pauses. Then, horrifyingly enough, "You're practicing safe sex,
I assume?"

"Oh my *God*." I shudder, scrubbing my hands over my face. "I'm
leaving."

"Very well." She almost sounds disappointed. Barely. Her voice
doesn't often rise above monotony. "I'm taking a friend out for breakfast,
so I won't see you until the afternoon."

If then. I didn't even know she had friends.

I leap back up the staircase, escaping the uncomfortable energy. I
push into my bedroom and remember there's an entirely different uncomfortable energy waiting for me.

Jonah's hiding under my comforter.

"You awake?" I whisper, knowing full well he's awake. "I . . . I'm not
sure how it got to that point. But it's my fault."

He doesn't answer.

"Probably just . . . hormones and alcohol." I lie down atop the covers, as far away from him as possible. "Not like that excuses it. I made you uncomfortable, didn't I? I'm sor—"

"I have one." Jonah's peeking out at me from beneath the comforter. "A fun fact about the galaxy."

A fun . . . ? Oh. *Oh.* I forgot I'd even asked about that. I roll onto my side, facing him, pointedly ignoring the invasive fluttering going on in my stomach. "Yeah?"

"Did you know . . . the Milky Way smells like raspberries?" His face pokes higher over the blanket. "Astronomers found ethyl formate inside this dust cloud at the center of the galaxy. The stuff that gives raspberries their flavor. So, yeah. Isn't that interesting?"

He waits for my response.

I've never paid the night sky much attention. It's too overwhelming, too panic-inducing. Too lonely. "That's amazing," I whisper.

Jonah turns his back to me. I turn my back to him.

No, I've never liked the stars.

Maybe, though, they're not so bad.

When I wake, there's a note on the kitchen counter.

Thanks for letting me spend the night. Happy Halloween.

I'm not sure how Jonah managed to get out of bed and lock the door behind him without waking me. He must've been trying intently to leave without having to talk to me.

I sigh, leaning against the counter where we made sandwiches. Where he asked about my family. My mom . . .

Guilt . . . is really powerful. And feeling it after something so trau-matic might cause someone to . . . I don't know. Pull away? Or push someone else away?

I grind my teeth, glancing at the drawer with the letter. I wanted to snap that they're completely different scenarios. That I have every right to be annoyed with my mom, regardless of what her excuse is. Regard-less of if I've made the same mistakes.

I slowly pull the drawer outward. It's easier now, like someone greased the slider. My fingers fan over the envelope, then lift. My hand still trembles, and my throat still burns, but I'm touching it.

I don't know what's been changing with me, lately. Why I've become so bold. The only difference between then and now is the fake dating, and yet, because of it, I've been busier. Making plans, going out, attend-ing group hangouts and dates and . . . socializing.

I haven't been alone as often.

Maybe these events have been giving me purpose again. Or things to look forward to, when I previously sulked in self-pity and boredom. I know I shouldn't be looking forward to anything that makes me have to deal with Jonah. And yet . . .

I'm holding the letter. Unfolding the back flap.

Okay, now I'm dropping the letter, and slamming the drawer shut.

Not yet.

But almost.

"Ms. Davis wants to talk to you."

I stare blankly at my history teacher at the end of class as the other students filter out. "Who?"

"Ms. Davis," he says. "Room 232. She asked me to send you to her after class."

I frown, shouldering my backpack. I expect it's some mistake, but I head for her classroom anyway. I've never had her, but I've heard good things from classmates—mostly concerning the fact that, apparently, she's hot.

When I walk into her room during passing time, she's fluttering around, tucking in chairs, dressed in high heels, a pencil skirt, and a blouse. Her dyed red hair is curled, and her gray eyes are framed in black ink and mascara. Something about her features . . . her jumpy movements, too . . . is familiar.

"Ms. Davis?" I ask, knocking on her door.

She looks up with a smile. "Ah, Dylan. Mind closing the door? This is my prep period, but you never know when someone might bust in to whine about their grade."

This is weird. Nonetheless, I do as requested, until the chatter of the hallway is cut away.

Finally, she finishes her cleanup and turns toward me. "I've heard through the grapevine that you're Jonah Collins's boyfriend, and one of his closest friends. Is that true?" she asks.

I stagger back. Of all the things I'd been hypothesizing, this was the last question I expected. "Yes," I say hesitantly, though I can't help but wonder what "grapevine" she's referring to. "Why?"

"I've been wanting to talk to him, but he's been avoiding me," she explains, rubbing her forehead. "I don't want to reach out to people he cares about behind his back. But to get to the bottom of things, I've decided to take these measures."

Measures? "Sorry," I say, "but I have no idea what you're talking about."

Ms. Davis blinks in surprise. Then, she laughs, palming her forehead. "Of course," she says softly. "Why would he tell anyone about me? I've been rambling . . ." She fixes me with another look and says, "I'm Jonah's aunt."

My mouth drops open. No wonder she seemed so familiar. She looks exactly like an adult Mik with dyed hair. "I didn't know he had family in the area," I admit. Since we started this whole thing, I thought Jonah was completely on his own, with no extended family. Now, though . . .

"I have a couple questions," she says. "You don't have to answer them if you're uncomfortable, but . . . it would be really helpful if you could. Is that okay?"

It certainly doesn't feel *okay*, talking to Jonah's aunt while he isn't here. But something about this situation—her stern atmosphere—makes me feel like I don't have a choice, despite her insistence that I do. "I . . . fine," I say.

Ms. Davis grips the back of a desk chair with tight fingers, like she's using it to steady herself. "Does Jonah typically eat during lunch?"

What would lead her to ask that? "I'm . . . not sure I should—"

"Please." Her eyes lower. "It's a matter of health and safety."

My heart thrums quicker. A responsible adult is *concerned* about Jonah. "He doesn't," I say quietly. "Sometimes I bring homemade sweets for him to try, but other than that, no."

She nods, like she was expecting this. "Does he have dietary restrictions? Allergies?"

"I don't think so."

"Okay. Thank you, Dylan." She turns to her desk.

I guess that's that. I head to the door and proceed into the hallway, trying to wrap my head around this. This whole time, Jonah's had someone he could reach out to. A family member who could help him carry his burdens—the responsibility of his sisters. Why isn't he using her?

No. I know why. It's because, over the last few years, he's convinced himself that he's the only one with the ability to handle them.

He's wrong, of course. But he won't ever be able to see that. And on the rare chance that he does, he'll never admit it.

I pause and look over my shoulder. "Ms. Davis?" I say.

She raises her eyebrow.

"Jonah . . . is the kind of person who drives away anyone who wants to help." I tear my eyes from her, swallowing. "Please don't let him."

I leave, closing the door behind me.

JONAH

Ms. Davis physically restrains me from escaping her class by yanking on my backpack handle and dragging me back inside.

"Wait, *wait!*" I plead as my classmates snicker. "Someone save me!"

"Enough," she snaps, twirling me toward her desk. As soon as everyone's gone, she reaches into a cooler stashed below her chair and plops a brown paper bag on the desk. "Myron and I decided we're going out for lunch. Take this."

I stare at it, my heart lurching. Is this . . . her lunch? Obviously, but why would she be giving it to me unless . . . ?

"I have my own lunch," I lie.

"Do you?" Her expression is laced with something I recognize, and detest, so I crunch my hand around the bag.

"I don't need it," I mutter, slamming it into the trash.

"Pick it up." She's using her stern teacher voice now. As if that's going to work on me.

"Who said I don't have something to eat?" I demand.

"*Enough*, Jonah."

I'm nearly shaking with anger. Still, yelling isn't going to serve me here, so I try to reason this out. If I don't take the food, will she be more persistent? If I *do* take it, will she back off for a while? Is that what she wants? To feel helpful so she can pat herself on the back and move forward with her life?

Reluctantly, I reach down, picking it out of the trash.

"Good." She rotates to her desktop computer. "Enjoy."

I want to throw the whole thing at her. But I've already taken the loss on this one, so I stride to the door and grab the handle. "Who told you I don't eat lunch?" I ask darkly.

She doesn't look at me. "I happened to notice as I was walking through the cafeteria once that you didn't have food in front of you."

"So, from that *one* time, you assumed I never eat."

". . . Yes." Her voice is flat. Like mine, when I'm holding back.

My fist curls tighter around the bag. "Shitty lying runs in the family, I guess," I mutter.

She shows no response.

I storm out of the room, hating that my stomach is already aching from the mere prospect of having food. It's not like I'm *starving* myself. It's just that I like portioning out my food at home. If I waste too many ingredients on myself, it means I'll have to go shopping more frequently. It's called budgeting. Why doesn't anyone understand?

I plop down at my empty lunch table—everyone must still be in line—and start pulling items out of Ms. Davis's paper bag. It's a turkey, bacon, and provolone sandwich lathered with mustard and mayo. As I munch on the sandwich and crunch through the apple and chips, I realize there's something else tucked inside the bag. A handwritten checklist.

❑ Salami
❑ Turkey
❑ Ham
❑ Onion
❑ Lettuce
❑ Tomato

❑ Pickle

❑ Condiments/Cheeses/Other?

————————————————————————

The one you're eating was Kim's favorite. Please bring this back to
me by the end of the day.

My jaw snaps shut. What, I'm supposed to check these off so she can
bring me food every day? If I do that, am I not basically admitting I don't
have enough to feed myself? I *do*, but I would rather preserve it for more
important things.

I pretend I haven't seen it and stuff the bag in the trash, then leave
lunch early to go and seethe in the library.

On Tuesday, Ms. Davis passes out her weekly short answer assignment
for the current reading. When she sets mine down, there's an arrow on
the bottom, pointing to the back. I flip it.

She's rewritten the checklist.

I glare at her as she returns to her desk. I have the urge to crumple
it and stuff it into my backpack, but I can't succumb to bursts of im-
maturity. She's onto me, so I have to show her I have a level head—I'm
a responsible adult.

Reluctantly, I check off the ingredients I like, and as everyone drops
their papers into the decorative basket on her desk at the end of class, I
lag behind. I place mine directly in front of her.

"Thank you, Jonah," she says. "And here."

She reaches below her desk and pulls out another paper bag.

I take it and leave without a word. Maybe, somehow, my lack of resistance will ease her suspicions. Otherwise . . . I don't know what else to do.

"You brought that yourself, Jo-Jo?" Andre asks when I sit at the table, scooting closer to me in his chair.

"Why do you sound surprised?" I grumble.

"Because you never bring your lunch."

I scoff, nudging him away. "Whatever."

I turn to the food in front of me and begin to munch.

It's good. Again.

DYLAN

Wednesday morning, I catch Andre as he's coming in from the school parking lot, swinging his keys and whistling what sounds like an epic theme song from some movie. I'm not sure how the guy is always in high spirits, even when he's grounded. When I slide in front of him, his lips stop, still puckered, and he looks up.

"Morning, Ramírez," he says.

"Hey." I fidget, staring at the strings of his hoodie. "Do you . . . have a minute?"

"Ten of them, before first period starts."

"Right." I glance around as more students file through the glass doors, then gesture at him. He squeezes his eyebrows together, but nonetheless, he follows me until we're standing behind one of the pillars studded around the cafeteria.

"What's up?" he asks hesitantly. He's probably wondering why I want to talk to him instead of Hanna.

"It's about Jonah," I admit. "Not about our relationship or anything. Just . . . about him. About his life."

Understanding dawns on his face. He sighs with weariness, leaning back against the pillar and crossing his arms. "Reaching a breaking point?" he asks expectantly. "You feel stuck? Don't know what to do?"

I open my mouth to protest, then close it. He's not wrong. "How do you . . . deal with it?" I ask quietly. "I've just been going along with him because I don't want to fight."

"I learned a long time ago that if I wanted to stay friends with Jonah, I needed to shut up about his homelife." There's this tired grimness

I've never seen before in Andre's expression. He must do a good job of concealing it, if he's known about this for years. "I don't come around to his house unless I'm asked to. I don't ask him if he needs help with anything. He's made a point of snapping at me anytime I get too close to the subject, so I avoid it completely."

"Did you . . . ?" I rub the back of my neck, swallowing. "Did you ever feel like you needed to . . . get an adult involved?"

"What adult?" Andre asks skeptically.

"Like, his aunt. Ms. Davis."

Andre blinks at me several times, registering this, then says, "Ramírez, there's so much shit Jonah doesn't talk about. He's my best friend, and this is the first time I'm hearing that he has any family in the area." He massages the bridge of his nose, and I twinge with guilt.

"He didn't tell me, either," I admit. "I found out from her."

Andre releases another hefty sigh. "I've seen her in the halls. She's got that dark red hair. I always thought she looked familiar."

"Yeah, and she's been prying," I tell him, shuffling around with discomfort. "I've talked to her. About him."

Andre's eyes widen with surprise. "You're playing with fire, Ramírez," he says sternly.

"I know. Don't tell him," I plead.

"Of course I won't."

Whew. One less thing to be anxious about. "So you never thought of going to an adult to see if they could help?" I press, watching as he thumbs his backpack strap. "Someone, like, financially stable? More mature?"

"There were times I wanted to, yeah," he says, frowning. "But honestly . . . I didn't know who to reach out to. I figured if I went to a teacher, or my pastor, or, hell, even my parents, they wouldn't be able to do anything in the long run other than call CPS and investigate the situation. And that's Jonah's biggest fear."

Yeah. That checks out, considering how much he loves his sisters.

"I'm not sure what you're getting involved with, but just be careful," Andre says in a low voice, stepping forward to pat my shoulder. "You've got a good heart. But Jo-Jo won't see it that way if he finds out you're meddling."

He pauses, looking down at his sneakers. A weak smile forms on his face.

"It sounds like you have an opportunity to help him, though," he says quietly. "Guess you have to decide if it's worth the sacrifice of losing him."

With that, he walks away, leaving me with a million thoughts and an aching chest.

I can't recall a single moment of class time. The only words I've been hearing are Andre's, over and over, digging deeper into my brain.

You have to decide if it's worth the sacrifice of losing him.

This is the third day in a row I've been summoned to Ms. Davis's classroom. So far, I've told her that Jonah doesn't bring lunch to school, he works full-time, and that his sisters turn to him for money. Three simple details that reveal almost everything.

Jonah won't forgive me if he finds out. That should be a good thing. When our friends find out about our "breakup," the nagging will stop.

So why does my heart keep stinging when I think about it?

Maybe I should ignore Ms. Davis's request and pretend like I don't know her. Maybe I should let her run with the information I've given her and wipe my hands clean.

But it's a chance. *She's* his chance.

So I return to her classroom after second period and stand before her, ready for the next questions.

"I'm going to ask you to do something for me," she says, sitting on the edge of the desk nearest to me, a soft frown curving her ruby red lips. "It might feel wrong, like you're betraying his trust. But . . . I'm hoping I can ask you a favor."

A favor is more than asking a couple questions. I fumble with my hands, anxious, waiting. How is she going to make me dig a deeper hole?

"I found Jonah's address in our system yesterday. I want to have a look around his place." There's desperation in her gray eyes. "I know I'm asking a lot of you, but . . . can you make sure he's home after school?"

I swallow hard. Jonah and I were planning on going to my place for a rendezvous about upcoming fake date ideas.

"I understand I've placed you in an uncomfortable position." Her voice wavers. I wonder how heavily thoughts of Jonah and his sisters have been weighing on her. "But I need to see for my own eyes that they're okay."

I draw a deep breath. Since she's depending on me for this, maybe now is my chance to flip the tables—to interrogate *her*. "What will you do if you don't like his living situation?" I ask sternly.

This gives her pause. "I . . ."

"Jonah is protective of Mik and Lily," I explain, my voice tight. "If you decide you don't like what you see, does that mean you'll involve Child Protective Services?"

Ms. Davis's eyes expand with astonishment. "How is it that CPS is the first thing that comes to mind for *both* of you?"

Jonah must've asked her the same question. "His sisters are his whole world," I explain. "If CPS got involved, and suddenly there was the threat of Mik and Lily being taken away . . ."

Ms. Davis kneads a knuckle into her temple. "CPS is the last thing I would ever force on them, Dylan. But, if I decided they were in some kind of trouble, I'd . . . have to figure that out, honestly."

I grimace.

"I'm going day by day," she says weakly. "Jonah doesn't trust me. But I promise you I want nothing more than what's best for them. And I would never do anything to tear them apart."

I stand there for a few minutes, deliberating. Her strained face, her desperate emotions . . . she's genuine about this. She wants to help Jonah.

"Okay," I say. "I'll . . . make sure he's home."

Her smile is frail but kind. I decide, suddenly, that I trust her.

"Thank you, Dylan."

JONAH

"We can't stay at your place for long," I say, dropping my backpack between my feet in Dylan's car. "Mik and Lily will be getting off the bus in—hey, you listening?"

Dylan is sitting rigid in the driver's seat, staring out at the clutter of cars in the parking lot. His eyes are glazed. "Hmm?" he asks.

"You good?"

"Oh. Yeah." He pulls his car into reverse, then swings toward the main road.

"You seem distracted," I say, eyeing him. His jacket buttons are mismatched, and his hair is disheveled, like he's been running his hands through it. I wonder if he's still weirded out about Saturday night. I'm still flustered, too, but I don't want it to keep getting in the way. If this tension stretches on much longer, interfering with our "dating," people will start noticing.

"Can we do this at your place?" he asks suddenly. "I . . . don't want to be home."

I analyze him again. His features are strained with anxiety. "Tomás's letter?" I ask softly.

His knuckles go white around the wheel. "Yeah."

"Okay." I nod. "Let's go to my place."

The ride to my house is painfully silent, aside from drizzle tapping the windshield. I can't help but want to dissect him. What is he thinking about? He's been acting distant, anxious, since Monday. Is it because he thinks I'm pissed at him for Saturday? Or has he just been consumed with thoughts about Tomás?

When we park on the curb and head inside, I'm glad to see my dad isn't home. I don't know if he actually goes into the office during the workweek, but he must get money from somewhere, because we haven't been evicted. I decided a while ago not to worry about his source. Trying to get words out of him is like pulling teeth, and I have way too many other things to worry about.

Dylan and I sit on the living room couch.

"I work night shifts all week," I tell him, crossing my legs under me. There's a single cushion between us. "Maybe we could plan an early group thing on Saturday?"

Dylan nibbles on his knuckle. "Yeah."

I squint at him. "What's going on in your head?"

He's quiet, his gaze far away. Then, to my surprise, he asks, "What are we, Jonah?"

It feels like forty-five minutes before I'm able to comprehend what he's asked me. What are . . . *we*? Like, me and him? Jonah and Dylan? Us? Together? My bewilderment is overtaken by my heart, which quickens, pumping blood into my face. I can't manage any words other than "Huh?"

"What do you think of me?" His eyes find mine, and they sharpen. He's nervous. For my response? Or something else? "Do you hate me?"

I laugh, but it sounds more like a forced cackle. "That's the whole point behind the fake dating. Because we . . ."

I trail off when I realize how serious his expression is. My face is burning hotter. Why is he looking at me like that?

"What do you want me to say?" I croak. "Don't tell me you've finally come to your senses about how amazing I am—"

Dylan catches my wrist, stopping me midsentence. I watch, stunned, as he presses his fingers to the base, feeling for my pulse. But he doesn't look panicky, so I don't understand what he's looking for. "Do you hate me?" he asks again.

Smoke is about to start pouring out of my head. "I . . . Dylan, I don't . . ."

"Your heart is racing."

I tremble with embarrassment. I try to wrench back, but he pulls against my resistance, dragging me forward until our faces are inches away above the middle couch cushion. He uses his other palm to frame my chin between his thumb and index finger, refusing to let me look away.

I'm not sure I want to.

"Do you hate me?" he asks for the third time.

His brown eyes are so big. And warm. I might melt in them, if I keep staring.

"Do you . . . hate me?" I ask softly.

Silence hangs between us for a moment. I can feel his breath fanning gently over my lips. Dylan opens his mouth, and I think maybe, just maybe, he's about to say something that could change everything.

Then I hear the hum of an engine rattling the far wall. The sound of a door slamming shut.

"Oh. Um." I wriggle away from him, then scramble to my feet, breaking whatever spell he just coaxed me under. "We should move to my bedroom. That's probably Dad."

Dylan stares blankly at the couch cushions.

I head to the window and peek through the blinds. My father's unpredictability is one of my least favorite parts about him.

My eyes settle on the car parked near the garage.

Wait.

My heart nose-dives into my stomach.

Why is Ms. Davis in my driveway?

DYLAN

Jonah Collins needs help.

I've brushed that thought away because I know he won't accept it. Now, though, as I watch him scurry through his house, tidying up, covering bottles of alcohol, reorganizing his cabinets, nearing the precipice of panic . . . I'm seeing the severity of it.

I don't know what Jonah thinks of me. If it's anything other than annoyance, he's too stubborn to admit it. I should be in the same boat. He's *Jonah*. The loudest, most pigheaded person alive. His insults are juvenile. Everything about him is over-the-top and cartoonish.

I should be. And yet . . .

He's not afraid to speak his mind. His smile could power the stars. His eyes are gray tornados, always reeling, always sucking you in. His walls are brick, but his skin is soft. His face is painfully honest. His love for his sisters is unconditional. He's . . .

A lot.

I don't know what we are to each other. It doesn't matter. What matters above all else is this.

Jonah Collins needs help. Maybe there's a way I can make him take it.

Even if it means smothering the warm, fluttering heartbeat of a flame that never should've kindled in the first place.

JONAH

My last-ditch attempt to make my house presentable is a waste of time.

Ms. Davis falls through the damn porch.

I watch it happen through the window. She gets out of her car, dressed in a peacoat and slacks, and I run through improvised responses to cycle through.

The fridge is empty because tomorrow is grocery day. The house isn't long term, we're moving once Dad has the money. We keep the heat low when we're away.

The first porch step collapses under her foot.

Normally, the sight of someone yelling and windmilling their arms would have me hunched in laughter. Today, all I can say is *"Shit."*

Dylan, the heroic prince he is, rushes outside to help. "Ms. Davis," he greets, offering his hand.

The rotted wood has folded completely around her ankle. "Thanks," she says, taking his palm and allowing him to hoist her onto the porch. Her eyes flit to me in the doorway.

"Dad and I were going to fix the porch this summer," I lie, hiding my trembling hands behind my back. "What . . . are you doing here?"

"I knew you moved after Kim died, but I never saw your new place." Her gaze wanders behind me. "I figured the only way I could see it is if I surprised you. Otherwise, you'd board your windows and pretend you weren't home."

My heart is pounding in my head. This is bad. But I have to remain calm. I function well under pressure, so I can definitely wheedle my way through this if I choose my words carefully.

"Let's head inside! It's starting to rain again," she says, shielding her hair from incoming droplets.

Hesitantly, I back up and try to smear on my charming customer service face. "Uh . . . welcome to our humble residence, then."

It's not impressive. The floor audibly protests her every step. Everything is old, worn, and barely functional, from the TV to the cabinets to the walls. Ms. Davis's eyes rip apart each fragment of the place in painful detail.

"It's dry in here." She presses a palm to her throat, then meets my eyes. "Do you have any juice or pop?"

The weight of her gaze tells me she's looking for more than hydration. But, what, am I supposed to say *no* and heighten her suspicion? "Tomorrow's grocery day, so we don't have much," I say, fully aware that she's following me to the fridge. I swing it open, fumble around the half-empty racks for the last remaining can of Diet Coke, then thrust it into her palm. "There."

I can tell from her slight frown that she saw everything over my shoulder.

"Thank you, Jonah." She pops the top and takes a sip, then ambles down the bedroom hallway and peeks into Dad's room. "Pretty sparse in here," she notes. "Whose room is this?"

"It's . . . Dad's." No point in lying about that.

"How often is he around?"

"Often enough," I mutter.

Dylan huffs from the mouth of the hallway. I shoot him a glare, then refocus on Ms. Davis, who's moved to Mik and Lily's room and is observing the pinned pictures with a smile. She swerves into the bathroom and flicks on the fan, which rumbles overhead. Then, she's at my room.

I slide in front of it.

"Move, please," she says.

"It's *my* room."

She grinds a palm against her forehead. "I'll give you twenty seconds to hide your dildo."

"Oh my God."

"Nineteen. Eighteen."

"Ugh, just go in!" I groan, stepping aside.

The first thing she pinpoints is the blanket I threw over my window, which she tugs down. It slithers over my telescope, exposing the taped crack.

"Mik's been using our glass as a soccer net," I say, which isn't a total lie.

After putzing around a while longer, she heads for the living room and takes a seat on the couch. "Jonah, can we have a minute alone?" she asks.

"No." Instinctively, I find Dylan's shirt, tugging him toward me.

"Fine. But his presence won't stop me from asking questions." She tucks one knee into her chest, sets the pop she's barely sipped from on the coaster beside her, and peers up at me.

And, yeah, it really doesn't. Suddenly, she's bombarding me left and right, asking if I feel safe, if we're here alone often, how frequently I need to hire a babysitter when I work, if I constantly find myself low on food, or with a lack of funds to buy new clothes. I swear she wrote a checklist and memorized it before coming here.

I try to fend her off as best as I can, attempting to make my answers detailed enough to satisfy her, but vague enough that she won't be further concerned. As I talk, though, Dylan seems to grow more and more tense, until he looks like a wound-up toy soldier. I wonder what he's thinking about, but try to not let it distract me.

"I know this place isn't a mansion," I tell Ms. Davis. "It's a fixer-upper, sure, but we're managing just fine—"

"Jonah," Dylan says, tentative.

I whirl toward him. His expression is strangely calm, almost grim. "What?"

"You're a terrible liar," he mumbles.

I stare at him, unblinking. He didn't just say that out loud, did he? Right in front of her? What . . . ? Why would he . . . ?

No. I won't let him.

"Get out," I whisper.

"Ms. Davis, Jonah is—"

"Get the hell out, Dylan."

"Jonah's hanging on by a thread," Dylan says, speaking over me. "He spends his week working to provide for his sisters. His dad is an alcoholic and isn't around to help him manage anything, so he's basically raising his sisters by himself."

I'm going numb. My palms shiver violently. He's not doing this to me. I'm hallucinating this, right? It's the only explanation I can think of.

"He won't ask for help, but if there's anything you can do . . ." Dylan takes a steadying breath. "He needs it. You said you won't contact CPS, but I don't think he believes that. So, maybe if you tell him some other options . . ."

You said you won't contact CPS.

I'm beginning to understand.

Could we do this at your place? I just . . . don't want to be home.

I feel like I'm choking. I shoot to my feet, coming within two inches of Dylan, trembling. I can't gather words in my mouth. None of them are powerful enough. He's got this soft, pained expression, and I recognize it.

Pity.

I beeline for the door, shoving through it. The gray skies are vomiting, and rain smashes the concrete in angry, shattering bullets. I leave their voices behind, heading into the street. The rain glues my hair to my forehead and my T-shirt to my chest. Dampness seeps through the bottoms of my shoes. I shiver without feeling cold. Or anything.

But then Dylan gets one hand around my wrist. Feeling bleeds outward from my chest, reaching in writhing ribbons across my body. I whirl on one heel, crunching my fingers into fists.

"Fuck you." I can barely squeeze the sound out of my throat. "Oh God. *I hate you.*"

"Jonah—"

"Don't you dare!" I wrench his shirt so I'm seething in his face, tears and rain blurring into one sloppy mess on my cheeks. *"Who said you can decide my life for me? How could you talk to her behind my back? How could you do that to me?"*

"I can't watch you struggle if I can help!" Dylan snatches my shirt as well, pulling me until I'm nearly on his toes. "What could she possibly do other than make things better for you? Why . . . why are you *so damn stubborn?*"

My jaw locks. Every vein tightens in my body.

"Why won't you accept *help?*" he cries out. "You're so . . . ugh! I can't stand it! It's so frustrating, the way you think you're some single parent! You can't keep doing this on your own—"

"Yes, I *can!*" I shriek, ripping out of his grip.

Dylan looks between my eyes, his teeth gritted.

"I can do it!" I half yell, half sob. My shirt sags and my body itches from rainwater, but I don't care. The things I'm feeling within me are far worse, far more painful. "I have the resolve! It's all I've ever had! I have *me*! *I* take care of them! *I* protect them! *It's my job to stay in control, and nobody can take that away from me!*"

Dylan's eyes are webbed with red veins, and his entire body is shaking. "Your resolve," he snarls, "isn't enough. And you know it."

It's like he's punched a hole through my chest. The breath rushes out of my lungs.

"You take care of them," he says darkly. "You protect them. But who takes care of you? Who protects *you*?"

I can only stare at him, my vision smeared with tears.

"You're not fine," he snaps. "You're tired, and sad, and cold. You're a *kid*. Quit pretending like you're handling things, because you're not. You're *failing*, Jonah."

Every word is like a shiv to my exposed heart. I know the hole isn't there, but I press my palm over it anyway, trying to hide it. The words leave my mouth in a raspy whisper, drowned by the rain roaring against the pavement.

"I'm . . . failing?"

Silence crushes us. Dylan fidgets. I stare at my soggy shoes, dazed.

"I didn't mean that," he mumbles. "I . . ."

He reaches for me, but I smack his palm away. "I'm done," I whisper. "It's done."

Dylan's expression is blank. Like he doesn't understand. As if he still thinks anything could ever come of us after these last few minutes.

"So everything that's happened lately," he says dryly. "None of it made a difference?"

That startles a laugh out of me. It's painful, though. Desperate. Angry. "You know what? Maybe it was starting to. Maybe I was *actually* beginning to think you weren't a pile of shit. Maybe I was *actually* convincing myself that being around you somehow made me happy. So, thank you for reminding me of the kind of prick you are, and for waking me up from this ugly-ass nightmare!"

I stride back to my house, chilled to the bone, drenched, aching, sourness burning my throat.

"Fine." His voice is icier than me. "Then fall apart, Collins. Alone. Just like you want."

I stagger to a brief stop on the sidewalk. A choked sob escapes my lips.

It *hurts*.

Once I'm in my house, I take his jacket, car keys, electric blanket, and backpack, then throw them onto the porch. Ms. Davis stands near the front door, watching me with a pensive expression.

"Bye." I wave in her face. "Goodbye."

There's sternness in her eyes, and something cracks inside of me, causing a fresh wave of tears to scour my cheeks.

"Just go," I plead, stuffing my face in my hands. "Just go . . . please . . . ?"

She lowers my shoulders and presses her lips to my forehead. "I'll make things right with you," she murmurs. "You, Mik, and Lily."

She leaves, taking the warmth with her.

I sit in the open doorway of my house, staring at my faded jeans,

ignoring Dylan when he grabs his things and takes off without a word.
Rain continues slicing through the atmosphere and beating the concrete. I'm freezing and soaked, and I can't even take a hot shower. I can't
even do that.

I hear footsteps on the porch. Mik stands there with an umbrella,
Lily clinging to her arm, and they're both staring at me with wide eyes.
I didn't even hear the bus rumble by. Seeing them drives another stake
into my chest, and I shouldn't—not in front of them—but I start crying.

They both shed their backpacks and toss them aside. Mik falls to my
left and swings her arms around my sopping shoulders. Lily sits in my
lap and curls up tight against me.

"I'm sorry," I sob, pressing Lily's head into my collar. "I'm sorry I
can't be better. I'm sorry I'm a failure. I'm sorry . . ."

I don't know how long I stay there, bawling, Adult Mode a distant,
inaccessible memory. Mik and Lily cloak me in all the towels they can
find, then push me to the living room couch. My head falls into Lily's
lap, my feet fall into Mik's. Lily fiddles with my hair, humming. Mik's
knees bounce under me. I think, for once, I'm warm.

At least until I remember him lying next to me. The feeling of his
hand in mine. The heat of his skin close by.

No. I'm not warm.

And maybe I never will be again.

DYLAN

I don't remember driving home. Silence pounds in my ears and sits thick in my throat. I cup my hands over my mouth. Hot, gasping breaths punch against my palms.

"Dad," I say when I walk through my front door. "Mom. Tomás."

The quiet is cold.

"Chocolate cheesecake." I wander into my kitchen, white splotches skittering around my eyes. "Sugar. Chocolate chips. Cream cheese. Vanilla extract. Cookie crumbs. Preheat to . . ."

I thumb through my recipe book, seeing but not absorbing.

"Preheat to," I repeat. "Preheat to. Preheat to three hundred and fifty."

I click the oven on.

"I'm going to melt the chocolate chips," I say, but then I burn them. "I'm going to combine the crumbs, sugar, and butter," I say, though I accidentally use flour instead of sugar. "I'm going to beat the cream cheese and flour," I say, but I don't have enough flour now.

Ah. I messed up. This is my fault.

Everything is always my fault.

But, no, this is what we wanted. Right? The opportunity to never have to talk to each other again? After today, we won't have to worry about our friends nagging us, because they'll feel too guilty. We accomplished our goal, so I should be feeling great.

Except I'm nauseous, and tingly with panic, and fuming, and tired, and *sad*.

I press my hands over my mouth again. Control it. Breathe. Focus on anything. My eyes find the new molcajete Mom brought home from her trip. Her ceramic bowl from Isla de Vieques, embedded with chunks of sea glass. My recipe book. The drawer with the letter.

My thumbs wander along my phone screen. It rings. Rings.

"You have reached the voice mailbox of—"

I disconnect, then exit Dad's number and pull up Mom's.

It rings.

"Dylan? I'm in the middle of a meeting. Can I call you back?"

I end the call. My fingers type out the next name.

Big Tom.

I swipe to call before I can stop myself. Before I can realize it's been over a year since I've even said *hello*, or seen his face. For a moment, everything in my body screeches to a stop. My breathing. My blinking. My heartbeat.

"We're sorry. You have reached a number that has been disconnected or is no longer in service—"

"Ah, fuck," I say, but it comes more like an angry sob. "Are you fucking kidding me?"

The robotic voice is still talking, so I scream over it.

"Shut up! Shut the hell up!"

I hurl my phone at the floor. It doesn't break, but it wouldn't matter if it did. My parents would buy me a new one without questions. Since they don't have time to ask any.

"Tomás," I cry, hunching over the counter, quivering. My eyes find the drawer again. "Tomás . . . wh-what do I do? What do I . . . ?"

I wrap my palm around the handle. The ache of missing him tears through my chest as I scoop the envelope up with clammy hands. My fingers hover at the fold, waiting for my brain's next command, but I don't know what to do. I run the words through my head—*I'm going to read this*—but they feel empty. I can't put any force, any strength, behind them. No matter how hard I pretend, I'm still incredibly, pathetically weak.

I pinch my shivering lips between my teeth. I'm seeing it all again. Reliving it. His slow, methodical disappearance from my life. From our family. Because of me.

He doesn't deserve this. I should be the one removing myself from the family. I'm the reason behind this turmoil. The reason he served time. The reason he's stuck in Detroit.

I know what the letter says. I've always known. I think that's the reason I've never been able to open it. The reason I never will.

It's not your fault.

"It is," I choke out. "It's my fault."

I tear it in half.

"It's my fault."

I tear it into fourths.

"It's my fault."

The fragments of the letter drift down the sink drain. My index finger flicks the garbage disposal, which grinds it into ribbons.

I shove my feet into my shoes and my arms through my jacket, then stagger out to my car, still shaking viciously. He has to understand. Everything that happened . . . it happened because of *me. I'm* the one who should've spoken up. *I'm* the one who sat there and took it like some pathetic rag doll without a voice.

The country roads pass me in a nonsensical haze of gold, and the radio fades in and out between static and miscellaneous stations. City lights are blurred splotches of red and green around me. The hum of the engine rings in my ears, and it's the only noise I can hear, aside from my own repetitive thoughts.

My fault. *It's my fault.*

I blink, and I'm pounding on an apartment door until it swings open.

"It's my fault," I say, stumbling forward against him, burying my face into his shoulder. "I'm sorry. I'm so sorry."

My brother's lanky arms swing around my back.

"Oh my *God*, Dylan."

"You don't remember a single moment of your drive?"

I can barely comprehend Tomás's words. The air around me is suffocatingly thick. My eyes flit around his apartment, trying to register that I'm *here*. And so is *he*. For once, I'm grateful that I still remember his address—something I'd tried valiantly to stomp out of my memories.

I watch from the futon while he stands at the kitchen counter, stirring two cups. He's shuffling foot to foot, the muscles shifting in his back, all lanky limbs and long fingers and . . .

He's the same.

My lips waver into a smile. Tomás still overflows with energy, unable to slow down and stop moving. When he turns to me with the cups, he's wearing that cheeky, familiar grin I haven't seen in over a year. His black hair is as full and thick as always, like Dad's before he buzzed it. He's wearing a white tank top, sweatpants, and a golden cross—his casual style.

"I . . . think I had a two-hour panic attack," I admit, taking one of the mugs from his hand. I peer into the brown liquid.

"Hot chocolate," he says brightly. "Cinnamon, a hint of cayenne. Specially frothed with the molinillo."

I swallow hard. "You remembered."

"Like I'd forget my brother's favorite hot chocolate recipe?" He flops onto the cushion next to me. The shadow of a mustache and beard combs across his lower face, but otherwise . . .

He's still Tomás.

I bring the hot chocolate to my lips. The sweet warmth and spicy kick nearly make me melt.

"So." He shifts, facing me. I can't muster the courage to hold his gaze longer than a couple seconds, so I keep glancing around the apartment. It's a nice space with a view of the Detroit skyline. Picture frames of our family are scattered around, most from years ago when everybody was happy. Or, "happier." We were never a perfect family, with Mom being the way she is, but we were at least . . . together. "Feeling better?"

I clutch the mug with tight hands. "I think I might be . . . dissociating. Or derealizing? Can't remember what Jenna called it . . ."

"Well. Take your time," he says, still smiling. He hasn't stopped since I got here. "I'm not going anywhere. Except to the kitchen soon, because I'm dying of starvation. Bought a week's worth of chicken shawarma from Olive Shack."

Immediately, I start salivating. "Olive Shack's still open?"

"Of course. It's one of the busiest restaurants downtown."

"Ansel still work there?"

"Nah. His sister's running the place, though. Gets me that thirty percent discount when I flash a smile." He grins once more for emphasis.

I hug my knees. I know I'm having a conversation with him, but it doesn't feel . . . real. Probably because I don't remember arriving in the first place. "I ripped your letter up," I whisper, bracing for his reaction. The atmosphere is going to change. When I next look at him, he's going to be scowling, or sighing with anger, or averting his eyes.

Tomás scratches his chin. "I sent you a letter?"

I stare at him in horror. He smirks and sticks his elbow out, nudging my arm.

"Kidding, Lil Dyl."

"Don't scare me like that!" I snap.

"Sorry, sorry," he says lightly. "Still. Can't believe I sent a handwritten *letter*." He shudders.

"Well, it was probably because . . ." The sound dissolves in my throat, but I push through. "Because I wouldn't answer your calls or texts."

"Yeah. You little shit." He winks, and the sight settles my worried thoughts down. Just a little. "Look, Dylan. Yes, I wrote you that letter because we were losing contact." He rests his head back on the couch, his voice softening. "I wrote it to tell you it's okay if you need time away from me. I know seeing me makes you relive those traumatizing moments with Tío Ramón. Especially . . . when I lost control." He swallows audibly. "I wrote it to tell you nothing was your fault. Because you were a child, and I was your big brother. I should've . . ."

He sighs, then clenches his jaw.

I peer out the window over the couch. The sun's mostly set, so there's little more than a splash of orange peeking over the horizon. "It's hard," I whisper, blinking through the acidic wetness in my eyes. "I . . . I *want* you to be part of my life. But whenever I think of you, and remember happy moments of us, they get cut off by this horrible feeling, and this memory . . ."

I visualize it. The blood-soaked bat. I hear it. The shattering bones.

I sip the rest of my hot chocolate. "I shouldn't have cut you out," I mumble. "Because of me, you isolated yourself from the family. We celebrated Día de Muertos for the first time in five years with Mom's cousins, and I thought you'd come, even if it was just to eat all of my jamoncillo de leche. But you didn't show. Not for Christmas, either."

Tomás takes my cup, bringing it to the kitchen. "My personal choices are *my* choices, Dylan," he says earnestly. "You're a victim. You keep forgetting that."

A victim. It sounds so . . . bizarre. Wrong. So what if I was just a kid? The family wouldn't have fallen apart if I'd just had the balls to tell my parents what was going on. If I had said something the first time it happened, they could've shut it down instantly. Tomás wouldn't have been the one to discover everything when he came to Tío Ramón's house for a surprise visit.

I should've said something. Instead, I was useless.

I watch as Tomás pulls the chicken shawarma out of his fridge. After reheating it and throwing it all together, he hands me a warm wrap. "Thanks," I mumble.

He brandishes his wrap at me like a sword, and I bump mine against his, before diving in. Despite not being fresh from the restaurant kitchen, it's as delicious as I remember it. The seasoned chicken, warm garlic sauce, and crunchy pickles fill my mouth with a rich, nostalgic taste of the past. Of struggling to keep up with his long strides as we walked to the restaurant. The feeling of his hand on the cuff of my shirt as we crossed streets, since I was too preoccupied with eating to pay attention. Sitting in his car while the stereo hummed, struggling to lick the sauce dribbling over our fingers so it wouldn't stain his seats.

Everything feels normal, like it used to. I feel . . . safe. Comfortable. My tight posture loosens, and I sink back into the couch, making myself cozy. When I glance over at Tomás, I realize he's watching me with a slight smirk.

"What?" I ask defensively.

"Nothing." He lifts his wrap to his mouth. "Just nice to see you looking like you're at home."

I can't help a smile. *At home* has always been wherever Tomás is.

I can't believe I ever forgot that.

Tomás and I speak well into Wednesday night. We've already convinced Dad to call me in sick on Thursday, because there's no way I'm leaving tonight for *school*. Tomás sends an email to his boss to request an emergency personal day. Above us, someone's bass thrums through the ceiling, but I'm too invested to pay it attention.

Tomás still can't hold down a girlfriend. He's an employee at the nearby university, which means he gets discounted tuition for the computer science degree he's working toward. He's also been participating in a ragtag street basketball team every Friday afternoon.

I catch him up on my life, too. Though, there's not much to report. Most of my news focuses around Hanna, Dad, or Jonah. I tell him about our fake dating scheme, our double date, the Halloween party, our breakup.

"Hang on." Tomás throws a palm up. "You telling me your stubborn ass fell for this boy?"

I choke on my next breath. "No! I mean, things have changed over the last few weeks, sure. But it's just because his face is cuter than I realized. But I'm not . . . I didn't *fall* for him. Hatred like that doesn't just go away."

"Yeah. You think I can't see the way you've been talking about him?" Tomás asks skeptically. He gestures at me from across the futon. "Let's see a picture."

I scowl, but reluctantly thumb through my gallery and open a selfie we sent to the group chat. He examines it in thorough detail, then pops his eyebrows at me.

"Cute indeed. And definitely your type."

"Shut up."

He tosses his head back in laughter, and I dig my face into my palms, groaning. "So, are you going to apologize for outing his shitty life to his aunt?" he asks.

"I . . . yeah." The thought makes me swallow painfully. "I don't know when, though."

Tomás makes a "tsk" noise. "Get on it, niñito!"

"I know! It's just . . . he won't want to hear it," I say wearily. I'm not sure he'll ever let me speak to him again, to be honest.

"Give him time." Tomás reaches out to pat my head, then shifts to his stern older brother voice. "He'll come around when he realizes why you did what you did."

Will he? Jonah's the obstinate type, so I'm not sure. And yet, I hope what Tomás is saying is true. Regardless of whether our relationship (or whatever you'd call it) is officially over after this, I still want to apologize. For what I did behind his back, and for the cruel things I said in the rain.

By the time I look at the clock, it's after midnight. We lay down the futon, which he covers with sheets and a blanket.

It's not easy to sleep, since I get anxious in unfamiliar places, but I'm close to Tomás for the first time in months. The thought eases my shoulders.

I think I fall asleep smiling.

JONAH

I'm numb through Thursday. Every blink and breath takes effort. My pen barely makes indents in my notebook paper. Words are muffled in my ears. During English, I know she's going to hold me back, so I don't bother leaving at the end of the period with Casey.

Ms. Davis is clicking away on her computer. "You can leave, Jonah," she says.

Oh.

I stand and head for the door.

"Take this." She sets a paper bag on her desk.

I take it.

That's that, I guess.

I head to lunch, stomach already groaning. There's a plastic container inside filled with pasta, accompanied by a dinner roll and a note.

> This is Myron's famous pesto pasta salad. It's got basil pesto, pine nuts, mozzarella, parsley, and tomato. Did Kim like to cook for you? Neither of us were talented in that department.
>
> Please bring the container to Myron when you see him for sixth hour. Also, favorite soups?

I poke the plastic fork into one of the curly pasta noodles. It's tasty enough to make me salivate. I scarf it down, because holy *hell*, that's good, and then I rip into the roll. Dylan isn't here, so there's nobody to distract me from the deliciousness. I haven't seen him once today, actually.

That's fine. That's good.

I check off the soups she's listed, because I don't have the energy to fight her on this. Andre tries comforting me (I texted him about the breakup last night—or, my fingers did without my brain's knowledge), but I don't want to talk to anyone, and thankfully, he catches on.

When early childhood education comes around for sixth period, I approach Mr. Kelly's desk, fumbling with my backpack straps. He's wearing these thick, dorky glasses on the bridge of his nose.

"Here." My voice is cracked and weak, but it's there. I place the container on his desk. "Th . . . thank you. For making it."

He tilts his head. "You filled out the checklist?" he asks sternly.

I fish it out of my backpack and hand it to him. "You don't have to . . . you and Ms. Davis shouldn't worry about making me food—"

"You can take your seat, Jonah."

My cheeks glow like coals. I want to argue. But my usual writhing flames are little more than smoldering embers. I turn to walk away, but he calls out to me again.

"One more thing."

When I twist back, he's holding out a slim, colorful book.

"For Lily," he explains.

I take it from him. I don't know why, but my eyes are wet.

I sit down without another word.

"She rarely cooked homemade things."

Ms. Davis looks up from her work on Friday, two braids sitting neatly on her shoulders. I'm propped on the desk in front of hers, swinging my legs.

"She didn't like cooking," I mumble. I've been having difficulty raising my voice above "barely audible." "It was mostly frozen store-bought stuff. But she was busy, so I can't blame her for not wasting time on making things from scratch."

Ms. Davis doesn't say anything. I wish she would, because I'm feeling awkward.

"Anyway . . . yeah." I climb off the desk to leave.

"Jonah." She reaches under her seat, then places another lunch bag in front of me. The sight of it perks me up and drains me. It's lunch. But . . .

"What did I do?" I whisper. "To . . . earn that."

She folds her arms over her desk and levels me with a strict look. "You're a seventeen-year-old boy," she says softly. "You don't have to *earn* food."

The breath hitches in my throat. "But—"

"Your only job is to be provided for. Basic necessities should never have to be requested, earned, or fought for."

". . . Okay." I don't know what else to say. She's wearing this grave adult expression I don't have the strength to combat—especially because it looks like Mom's. Every time I see her, I'm forced to witness the resemblance. The eyes. The nose. The widow's peak.

After all this, I can't help but wonder . . . why did things ever end between them? I'm nothing without Mik and Lily. How is it possible that Mom and Ms. Davis ruined their relationship so badly that they cut communication with each other?

I trail to the door, though my fingers pause above the handle. The question tingles on the tip of my tongue. "Ms. Davis? If you'd known Mom was going to . . . um." I glance back. "Would you have done anything differently?"

She sighs, but it's more thoughtful than annoyed. "Your mother was the most stubborn person in my life." She offers a frail smile. "I'm not sure there's anything I could've done that might've saved our relationship. Stubbornness is our family's fatal flaw."

I wince. Dylan's voice swirls into my head. *What could she possibly do other than make things better for you? Why are you so damn stubborn?*

"Mom never talked about her family," I admit. It's something I always questioned, but anytime I neared the subject, she tended to divert me elsewhere. Eventually, I got used to steering clear of it altogether. My mom's walls were thick and guarded—like a fortress—and it was difficult to get her to lower the drawbridge.

"There's a reason for that." Ms. Davis sounds solemn. Wistful. I wonder how much pain she's had to carry alone over the last few years.

I want to pry. But then my stomach growls, and she waves me along.

"Go on. I'll see you tomorrow."

I don't feel like reminding her tomorrow's Saturday. Instead, I head to the cafeteria, then pull out a thermos filled with chicken noodle soup. While I sip it, my eyes wander across the table. Dylan is gone again. He hasn't texted me since our fight, which is fine. Still . . . where is he? Why hasn't he been coming to school? If it was serious, Hanna would probably tell us, but she's been secretive.

Does he care at all about what he did?

I close my eyes. I envision him sitting across from me on my rickety old couch, gripping my wrist.

Your heart is racing.

Do you hate me?

I shake my head, scowling, despising the goose bumps crawling up my arms from the remembrance. Whatever. It doesn't matter what my answer was going to be, because he proved to me he's exactly the kind of person I thought he was. A princely prick who thinks his opinion is the only one that matters in a room.

He almost had me fooled. Almost.

I polish off the soup, then fumble for the note.

> I'm stopping by your place tomorrow at six to take you, Mikayla, and Lily to dinner.

My heart nose-dives into my stomach. I scrunch the paper in my fist. I knew it. She doesn't trust I can take care of my sisters. Because, despite having managed everything single-handedly since I was thirteen, I'm nothing more than a child to her.

"Hey." Andre's hand falls to my back. His brows are knitted. "Come over after school. I have homework, but no meetings or anything. We can pick your sisters up, and you can stay for dinner—"

"No." I squeeze my hands in my lap, despite desperately wanting to say *yes*. "I don't want to intrude. And I know you have a lot to do, so I'm not trying to get in the way."

"Jo-Jo, you're freaking me out. I know it was a bad breakup, but have you even slept? Besides, it's been forever since we got to hang out one-on-one."

"That's your fault, too," I say, sharper than intended. "With your student council meetings and AP homework . . . I'm not the only busy person in this world. My lifestyle is perfectly normal."

Andre stares at me, bewildered. I tear my eyes away, guilt stirring in my chest.

"Sorry," I mumble. I scrub my hands over my face, smearing away the exhaustion. "It's a rough week. I'll get through it."

I always do.

The end bell for lunch rings, and I scoop my backpack up, trudging away.

DYLAN

Tomás and I spend Thursday together, mostly talking, playing video games, and eating out at our old favorite local restaurants. On Friday, we're given a surprise when my father appears at the door with two suitcases—one packed for me, and one for him.

"Figured you could only last so long in the same clothes," he says, greeting us with his massive grin.

"Dad!" I throw myself at him, giving him the tightest hug I can muster.

"Okay," he chokes out, patting my back. "You're not Dylinho anymore, so ease up . . ."

Then Tomás lunges into us, and his weight nearly slams all of us into the floor.

Together, we spend the day being an actual family. Despite the crisp November chill, the skies are clear, so we wander Detroit. We take selfies along the riverfront, trying to get the Renaissance building or the bridge to Canada in the background. Tomás and I listen as Dad rambles about work, whether it be how George flubbed something again, or how he had to remove a pair of drunken guests, or other turmoil. Then, we're crouching next to the mighty Joe Louis fist, re-creating a picture from years ago.

We visit the Eastern Market, too, where we pass under the rust-red brick arches and wander between vendors, gathering vegetables, produce, cheeses, salsas. Tomás guides us to his favorite Mexican goods shop, where Dad and I parse through everything up for grabs—from black clay pottery, to beaded jewelry, to Otomi embroidery.

"Does this place feel familiar?" Tomás asks, nudging me.

I glance around the brick building, but nothing's coming back.

"I brought you here once when you were like . . . six." He picks up an intricately painted calavera, smirking. "I chased you around with one of these. Told you it was cursed and if you touched it, La Catrina would steal your soul at night."

It's ringing bells and making me frown deeply. "Getting the faintest memory of sheer terror," I say, and he grins.

"I made it up to you in the end."

"How so?" I ask, dubious.

"Bought you one of the alebrijes." He gestures to a nearby table of tiny, colorful, carved sculptures. "You liked this creepy porcupine one. But by the time we got to my car, it had already fallen out of your jacket pocket."

"You didn't go back to buy me a new one?" I ask accusingly.

He bursts into loud, boisterous laughter. Every noise out of his mouth sounds more and more like Dad. I smile, looking at my feet.

"Here." He drags me to the shelf of alebrijes. "Pick one."

I give him a skeptical look, then glance between the painted wooden sculptures. There's a cute sea turtle with multiple shades of blue and geometric shapes painted on its shell, so I pick it up. He brings it to the counter without comment, and they wrap it for him, then place it in a goodie bag. A moment later, he's stuffing it into my hand.

"Don't lose this one, menso." He winks at me.

I hold it tighter. There are sudden, inexplicable tears in my eyes. "Thanks," I whisper.

His brows arch with surprise. Then, he slings an arm around my shoulder.

"You know, Lil Dyl, you haven't really changed at all."

JONAH

I'm a wreck on Saturday, and it shows in my tips.

Tonight.

My teeth are chattering. I try eating at the restaurant, but every bite nauseates me. How much longer will I have with my sisters? I'm almost eighteen. Can I convince Ms. Davis to leave us in peace until then? Once I'm legally an adult, I'll work multiple jobs and find an apartment for the three of us. I can send Mik to that summer soccer camp she keeps mentioning. I can start a fund to help with a potential medical transition for Lily, once we have that conversation. From the research I've done, puberty blockers are expensive as hell, but if I find a job with insurance, I can work on trying to get Mik and Lily covered as dependents. Maybe it would help with the cost? If that doesn't work . . .

I don't care. I'll find a way. I just need *time*.

Eventually, I collect my money from Sherry. She's been cold and distant since what happened with Ms. Davis and Mr. Kelly, and she scolds me harsher, but it's fine. In fact, I prefer it.

On my way home, I try preparing a speech. What can I say to make her believe I can handle this? I walk through the door, my chewed fingertips bleeding, and find Dad in the kitchen.

He looks lost, like always. Like he's not sure why he keeps coming back. He's stirring mac and cheese on the stovetop. Mik and Lily must be in their room—they usually go there whenever he comes around, and I can't blame them. The sight of him . . .

It's exhausting.

Shit. Why does he have to be here right now?

I'm so *tired*.

I pass around him, my shoulders slackening. I snatch the bottle of whiskey atop the fridge, and when my fingers curl around the neck, I swear I see him flinch in the corner of my eye. By the time I look back at him, though, his gaze has returned to the pot. I probably imagined it, since I doubt he even knows I'm here.

I amble out to the porch and sit on the steps beside the hole Ms. Davis created, then unscrew the top, tipping the bottle into my mouth. It burns. Once the fire trickles further down, and I've stopped coughing and hacking, I bring it back to my lips. The liquid bubbles and froths in my empty stomach.

"He's a piece of shit," I say to the bitterly cold air, goose bumps flecking my arms. "What were you thinking, Mom?"

I chug another couple gulps.

"Thanks for pissing off into the void. Bet you didn't regret running back into that burning building with your damaged equipment. Bet you felt like such a hero, huh? Well, none of that matters. Mik and Lily are going to be taken from me, and I'll be left alone." I lift my bottle to the sky. "Cheers!"

I throw it back again. This time, I don't taste the burn.

When Ms. Davis's headlights assault my eyes, my body is numb with ice on the outside but fiery hot on the inside, and I'm trashed. I rock back and forth, tilting the whiskey bottle with me, the world a blur of mashed colors.

Her heels appear in front of me. I look up. She's staring at the alcohol.

"Makes you stop feeling things," I explain, unscrewing the top again. "That's what it does to him. Figured it'd do the same for me."

I try lifting it, but Ms. Davis plucks it from my hands, tossing it into the yard. She crouches, rests her hands on my knees, and looks up at me. Her gray eyes are glistening.

"I'm here," she says quietly.

I stare at her, hardly able to absorb her features.

"I'm here." Her hands tug my face forward, so my forehead rests against hers. "I'm right here, Jonah."

My shaky hands fall atop her warm ones. Ms. Davis . . . no, Aunt Noelle . . . is here. With me. I'm not . . . alone? My nose and cheeks are scorching. I try to gather the words I've been swallowing all these years. "Aunt Noelle, I . . ."

In one flimsy, pathetic breath, I choke it out.

"I need help."

The sentence feels like boiling oil on my tongue.

"I can't do this anymore," I cry, every syllable cracking pathetically in my throat. "Aunt Noelle, I can't . . . please help me . . . please . . ."

Aunt Noelle wraps her arms around me. I lean my weight against her jacket, shivering into her shoulder. "Pack your bags, Jonah." She draws back and sweeps her thumbs under my eyes. "You and your sisters are coming with us."

I wasn't sure what Aunt Noelle meant when she said "us" until her husband steps out of the passenger seat while I'm midbreakdown.

"Oh," he says when he sees how hard I'm crying against Aunt Noelle. She motions violently at him, her expression venomous. "Hmm. Well. I'll just."

Mr. Kelly—or Myron, I guess—climbs back into the car. Honestly, it's funny enough to break me free of my relentless sobs. I think I even laugh.

Then I blink, and time has shifted. Dad sits on the couch while we dart around, shoving things into bags. Well, I'm wasted, so I'm mostly staggering. Aunt Noelle moves between me, Mik, and Lily, reminding us of things we might need. "Toothbrush and toothpaste," she says down the hall. "Comb. Deodorant. For the love of God, don't forget deodorant."

At one point, I try to go into Mik and Lily's room to help them, but a giant hand catches my shoulder. "Focus on yourself now," Myron says with a scolding look, and he gently turns me by the shoulders, guiding me back to my room. I didn't even realize he came inside to help us.

I pack my necessities and bury my cracked telescope in my clothes.

Then, we're at Aunt Noelle and Myron's condo complex. They're in Delridge's "downtown" area, and they're on the second floor, so their balcony stands over the main street. They have one master bedroom and two guest rooms, though why they need so much space, I wouldn't know.

I take everything in while Aunt Noelle frantically tidies up Diet Coke cans and takeout boxes. "I know it's smaller than your house," she says. "But our heat's functional. Jonah, you'll have the back bedroom. Mik and Lily, you're in the one across from ours."

Lily crushes her stuffed giraffe into her chest.

"Shall we take a look?" Myron asks with a warm smile, offering his hand.

Lily fumbles with her fingers, then nods, returning his smile and placing her palm in his. Together, they head down the hallway, followed protectively by Mik.

I wander the living room. Soft white string lights are pinned to the

walls, and two colorful lamps shed pinkish light over the soft gray furniture. I step onto the balcony, peering over the iron railing. My vision is
fuzzy, but I can see couples and rowdy groups strolling under the streetlights, wandering into restaurants and bars, or heading to their cars.
Down the road, I see the glowing sign for Mr. Ramírez's churrascaria.
It's a cute area.

"They have parades down this street." Aunt Noelle ambles up beside
me, pressing a glass of water into my palm. "It's busy, but it makes us
feel . . . connected. Lots of good food, too."

I glance around, sipping. A round table with folding chairs sits to
my left.

"Myron and I grade out here when it's not too cold," she explains.

"Oh . . ." I fidget. "Speaking of school, will they care if we're staying
with you for a bit?"

"We already spoke to the administration."

I reel back, startled. *"What?"*

"Myron and I mentioned it yesterday after school. We've been planning on inviting you to live with us." She taps the bottom of my water
glass, and I lift it to my mouth obediently. "That's why we wanted to take
you all to dinner. To discuss it."

"Oh . . ." I rub the back of my neck. It feels kind of . . . invasive. How
long have they been married? Less than a year, right? And we're already
in the way, taking up their space and time?

"Speaking of, dinner!" She whirls back into the condo, her voice
bright and merry. "With you being shit-faced, going out isn't our best
move. But we can have something delivered. What are you in the mood
for?"

I trail inside, rubbing my frigid upper arms. Myron, Mik, and Lily haven't returned from the bedrooms. "Fast-food places usually have good deals—"

"Don't worry about what's cheap. Just say what you're hungry for."

"Well . . ." My brain scrambles to comprehend this. "Mik and Lily like—"

"*You.*" She takes my shoulders. "What do *you* want?"

I search her expression, swallowing. I'm not used to having to think about what I like. What my preferences are. Do I even have any? I ponder for a moment, then hesitantly say, "I like fettuccine alfredo. Is that . . . okay?"

"It's perfect." She heads down the bedroom hallway and calls out, "Girls! Husband! We're ordering from Ida Mancino's Italian Eatery. Look at the menu on my phone. And *you.*" She twirls back to me. "Keep drinking water."

While she and Myron help Mik and Lily get situated, I take my water glass and suitcase to my room. It has a white-and-gray color scheme, with a full bed, closet, dresser, and nightstand. The window on the far wall allows moonlight to cascade onto the carpet. I trail to the panes, peering up at the sky. I can see Orion's Belt—a few speckles of light in the pocket of space.

I set my broken telescope beside it.

"Not so bad, right?" a voice says, and I whirl around. Myron is leaning against the doorframe, examining me closely. I feel like he's always doing that—scrutinizing my facial expressions and body language to decipher what I'm thinking.

"It's . . . It's great." I clap one hand on the bed, not sure what to say or do. "Um. Thanks for letting us stay here. For now."

Myron's mouth twitches, and he steps further in, eyeing my suitcase. "Is there anything I can help you wi—?"

"No," I blurt. There's no way I'm forcing him to help me unpack when we're already upending his life. Besides . . . I'm not sure how much I *want* to unpack. This is just a temporary living solution, right? I don't want to get too cozy. "I'm fine. I've got it. Thanks."

I figure he'll insist (he seems like that polite kind of person), but instead, he nods in understanding. "Let me know if you change your mind."

With that, he heads out, leaving the door cracked behind him.

I know I should head over to Mik and Lily's to make sure they're doing okay, but I desperately need a few minutes of alone time. I grab fresh pajamas and toiletries, then head into the bathroom. Perfume, makeup, and aftershave clutter the sink, and the mirror is framed with pictures. There's a selfie of Aunt Noelle and Myron licking ice-cream cones at some carnival. A picture of them standing around a group of children holding books. A picture of her and Mom.

My breath catches. With Aunt Noelle's natural hair, it's incredible how similar they look, despite their ten-year age difference. It's weird to think Mom would be forty-three now. I reach out, grazing my finger against Mom's face. "Sorry," I whisper.

I place my shampoo and body wash on the shower ledge, stepping in. It's warm. It's so *warm*. I stand there for several minutes, letting the water carve streaks down my back. It stays hot, which is extra impressive. I should really check on Mik and Lily. But . . .

I huddle further under the water. Maybe it's okay to stay here a bit longer.

When I reenter the living room, bundled in my pajamas, our food is here. My pasta is creamy, thick, and perfect. It eases my nausea and clears my head. A bit later, after I've been sitting on my bed, thinking nonstop about everything and nothing, Aunt Noelle and Myron come in.

"You should sleep," Aunt Noelle says, sitting on the edge of my mattress while Myron sets a trash can beside my bed and more water on my nightstand.

"Goodnight, Jonah." He nods at me with a smile and leaves before I can muster the strength to say, "thank you."

Aunt Noelle smooths her fingers through my hair, pecks my forehead, and follows him, closing the door behind her. I realize something for the first time.

I'm not shivering anymore.

I still feel sickened from everything that happened. The way Dylan exposed me, despite knowing my fears, and ripped my heart into two. Still . . .

I lift my comforter over my chin, half-wishing he was here so we could hash it out. Half hoping he's already moved overseas so I never have to think about him again. I'm not sure which side is more dominant. The only conclusion I come to, as I drift unconscious, is that I'm warm.

I'm actually warm.

DYLAN

The only thing that gets me out of Tomás's apartment on Sunday is the threat of receiving zeroes on all my homework. Dad left earlier to make it home before his closing shift, so it's just been the two of us.

In the doorway, Tomás throws his arms around me, drawing me to his chest. "I'll see you for Thanksgiving," he says. "Whip up that tres leches de fresas, got it?"

I nod, resting my forehead in his shoulder. I've missed my brother's hugs more than I remembered. "Okay."

"You have my new number, so reach out whenever." I can hear solemnness in his otherwise light tone, and I realize what he's saying. He's planning on leaving our communication up to me. To ensure I'm always mentally prepared for it.

I'm not going to disappoint him. "I will." I tug away from him, and he says, "One more thing."

I peek back at him. "Yeah?"

"This might be random, but . . . go easier on Mom." Tomás examines me, a smile playing at his lips. "She says you've been ignoring her."

I furrow my brows.

"Do you remember when I first started serving time?" he asks, leaning against the doorframe. "Mom didn't come to the first couple visitations."

"How could I forget? She wouldn't talk to either of us."

"I know you have resentment for her." His voice is tentative. "I know you're upset she's rarely around. But . . . you inherited the whole 'I blame myself so I have to distance myself' thing from someone. And it wasn't Dad."

My heart sags into my stomach. Jonah said something similar before the Halloween party, subtly suggesting I must've gotten my knack for pushing people away from someone else. Despite now hearing it from Tomás's mouth, I'm not any closer to forgiving her than I was before.

"When Mom pushed me away, I chased her," he explains. "I know it's different with you, since you were so young, but . . . we've made things right. She wants to make things right with you, too. So when she calls . . ." He ruffles my hair. ". . . pick up the phone?"

I look him over and nod. "I'll try," I whisper.

"That's my Dyl."

With that, I head back to the parking garage across the street. I'm not sure I told Tomás everything I wanted to say—about how I still can't help but blame myself for what happened to him, no matter how many times he insists I shouldn't—but we'll have plenty more opportunities for conversation now.

I'm moving forward. Even if it's inch by inch.

One step at a time.

JONAH

When I wake on Sunday, there's a feast for breakfast.

I stare in disbelief. It's like Myron cooked the whole farm. There's a pile of scrambled eggs, a bouquet of sausage, a pound of bacon, a mountain of hash browns, a tower of buttered toast, a gaggle of pancakes.

"Holy *hell*," Mik says.

Lily lurches into the nearest chair, curls messy as ever, and begins to slather two pancakes with peanut butter.

"I made the toast," Aunt Noelle says with a proud smile.

"You did great, sweetie." Myron stoops over to kiss her cheek, then winks at me. I can't help but return the smile. There's food on the table, and I didn't have to make it or buy it.

"You like to cook, Myron?" I ask, plucking a piece of bacon free.

"I started learning a couple years ago since your aunt's cooking is atrocious." Myron looks at me grimly. "Now I do it for enjoyment. And to stop her from burning the condo down."

"You have no faith in me," Aunt Noelle grumbles.

"I'm a sensible man."

She checks to make sure Mik and Lily aren't paying attention, then thrusts her middle finger into his face. He kisses it. My respect for him shoots through the roof.

We sit around the kitchen table, munching through the surreal morning before Aunt Noelle tells us to get dressed. "We're going to the grocery store!" she says with enough enthusiasm you'd think she was taking us to Disney World.

So I go to my—their—guest room and fumble through my suitcase.

I'm still in a daze. This day feels like a hallucination. I climb into a sweatshirt and jeans, and once we're ready, we pile into Myron's truck. It's early November, but most of the tree branches have been stripped of leaves, creating colorful playgrounds in grassy lawns.

When we get to the store, Aunt Noelle pushes the cart, Lily holds Myron's hand, and Mik darts between shelves, requesting dozens of sweets. The food is piling up—boxed goods, meats and cheeses, pastas and sauces, breads and butter, veggie trays. This is a lot. It's . . .

I massage my forehead, scowling.

It's too damn much.

My phone dings, drawing me out of my stupor. I pluck it from my pocket, and when I see the name, my heart plunges into ice water.

PRISSY PRINCE
I did it.

There's a selfie of Dylan, who's wearing a peacoat, his loose curls stirred from wind. Next to him is a young man with dark brown skin, sharp facial features, and long limbs. His smile outmatches Dylan's.

Tomás.

My head fills with the sound of my pounding chest. My thumbs hover over the keyboard. *How? When? Why?*

But the more I will myself to type, the more anger begins to thicken in my stomach.

I shove my phone into my pocket without responding.

In the checkout line, I watch as the cashier swipes food across her censor, hiking the price. The higher it goes, the larger the lump swells in my throat. Are we even going to be able to eat all of this shit?

Aunt Noelle shifts in front of me, nonchalantly blocking my view.

It doesn't end. Now we're at a department store. Aunt Noelle guides Mik to the training bras section, and I wander away, ambling aimlessly between racks and shelves.

"Find anything you like?"

I crane my neck back. Myron is standing there, flowery skirts dangling off his arm. Lily holds his belt loop, her head tilted curiously.

When I don't answer, he starts yanking out shirts and pants. He ushers me to the men's dressing room and tells me to come out wearing each item. I do, because I'm still only half-aware of what's going on. He's giving me thumbs-up and thumbs-down, but for what, I'm not sure.

We get to the checkout line. Again, I'm watching that price climb higher, nibbling my nonexistent nails, my face paling. I can't pry my eyes away from the number.

Myron swipes a credit card. Why is he paying? What the hell?

We return to his truck, and I'm lagging behind, unable to keep up with their long strides and positive energy. This all feels so . . . *wrong*. Mik and Lily crawl into the back seats, and Aunt Noelle says, "Let's stop somewhere and pick up new toiletries—"

"Stop," I snap.

Aunt Noelle and Myron turn to me. My jaw is clenching, and my eyes are watering.

"I . . . you can't just . . ." I don't know where the sudden emotion is coming from, or why it's only now just bubbling to the surface. I've been coasting by under the radar of *feelings* the entire day, not allowing emotion to catch in my chest. Now, though, despite knowing it's a completely unreasonable reaction, my vision is blurring. With anger.

Why? Why am I *angry*?

"Jonah, are you—?"

"It's too expensive!" I say fiercely, interrupting Myron. "Why are you both flinging money left and right like it's nothing? What did we do to deserve . . . ?"

Basic necessities should never have to be requested, earned, or fought for.

Aunt Noelle's previous words swirl into my head, causing the rest of my sentence to dissolve. I cuss, aiming my face at the ground.

"Noelle," Myron says quietly, and she gives a subtle nod, then climbs into the car, leaving us.

"What?" I snarl at him.

"Nothing." He reaches out and bumps my chin with his index knuckle. "Deep breaths, kid."

I don't realize how hard I'm breathing until that moment. I close my eyes, steadying myself, drawing air through my nose and exhaling through my mouth. Like Dylan taught me. Ever so slowly, my sudden bout of rage begins to fizzle.

"Can you explain why you're upset?" he asks, unbearably calm.

"I already told you. Why are you spending so much money?" I demand. "You're not even family!"

I know that last bit is unnecessary dickishness, and I regret it as soon as I say it. It's my fault we haven't gotten closer to him over the last couple years, since he and Aunt Noelle started dating.

"According to the laws of marriage," he says, nudging his glasses up his nose like a giant dork, "I am legally your uncle. Sorry to break it to you."

I purse my lips. He's right. "Still, you barely know us," I mutter. "What makes you feel obligated to pay for all of our shit?"

"This *shit*," he says, so adult-y it nearly breaks me out of my stubborn irritation, "is stuff you need. I understand we may have overwhelmed you with this, and I apologize for that. But living with us doesn't just mean sitting around isolated in our spare bedrooms. It means we're going to provide for you. We're going to make sure you're well fed, clean, and properly clothed." He cocks his head at me. "Understand, nephew?"

It's a jab at me, but for some reason, my respect for him rises again. "Did Aunt Noelle make you do this?" I ask quietly, shuffling around. "Like, was letting three noisy kids completely flip your life around her idea?"

"It was a mutual decision. In fact, I'm the one who brought it up first."

I take that information in slowly.

"And really, noise is the last of my concerns," Myron says, with a skeptical smirk. "I grew up with five siblings on the Atlantic Coast in Florida. I've got fourteen nieces and nephews. Noise is home."

Florida? I look him over with curiosity. I wonder if it's too early to ask him why he left.

"Besides," he says, opening the back passenger door, "don't you think there's a reason Noelle and I decided to rent a condo with three bedrooms?"

He gestures to the back seat, where Mik and Lily are sitting, peering out at me.

I don't know what that means exactly. They must've rented that condo months ago, so it's not like they could've anticipated that their nieces and nephew would suddenly move in with them. But it's clear he's not going to go into further detail right now. Reluctantly, I climb in next to Lily, and he closes the door, then gets into the driver's seat.

I close my eyes, leaning against the headrest. I'm still not sure why I got so pissed, when I should be grateful. Maybe . . . I don't know.

Maybe I'm envious.

In a single day, after years of treading water, all of our troubles have been solved. I shouldn't resent Aunt Noelle's and Myron's wealth, since they're whole-ass adults with whole-ass careers and whole-ass salaries. And I'm just some huffing seventeen-year-old counting my tips off the clock.

I didn't have to fight for anything today. I didn't have to consider my precarious budget, or think about how a single purchase might impact me two weeks down the road. It's relieving, and yet . . . no matter how hard I fought, how many hours I put in, how much I penny-pinched . . .

I never came close to being able to do what Aunt Noelle and Myron did today.

Lily must notice my fists curl in my lap, because she folds her palm over mine. When I look down at her and see her chipper smile, the tightness in my face relaxes.

Right. None of it even matters. Because my sisters are being provided for.

That's all I've ever wanted.

DYLAN

"This is adorable," Hanna says, looking over my new alebrije with a fond smile. She peers up at me from the couch cushion beside me. "I'm proud of you."

"For not breaking it?" I tease, and she bumps my shoulder with her head.

"For seeing your brother, dipshit." She kicks her legs up into my lap, reclaiming her grip on a slice of the frosted chocolate cake we made. She forced me to put on her favorite messy island-based reality TV show ("It's good for killing your brain cells when you want to get away from the world"), but at least it's on mute, so I don't have to hear people sobbing and making out. "Did Jonah respond to your selfie?"

My amusement wavers. "No." Not that I'd been expecting him to.

It's been a few hours since I returned from Tomás's, and I've already unloaded on Hanna. She's been familiar with Jonah's situation awhile, apparently. To be fair, being burdened with information like that is tiring, and if you have to get it off your chest, Hanna's the best person to vent to. She's the world's greatest secret-keeper.

Jonah's reluctance to accept help is something that's been grinding quietly at Andre for years. I haven't spoken to him since our brief conversation in the cafeteria, but according to Hanna, he's grateful that I cared enough about Jonah to take that extra step. To force help onto him, even if it meant . . .

Losing him.

"He probably just needs time," Hanna says.

"That's what Tomás said," I mumble.

"Put yourself in his situation." She fiddles with the end of her ponytail, looking at me carefully from beneath her varsity softball cap. "You've been on your own for years, without help, without adults. You have no reason to trust anybody but yourself. Then, your boyfriend of a few weeks flies in and reveals all your well-kept secrets to someone with the power to upend your life."

I swallow hard. I still haven't told her that everything between us was technically fake. Or, well. It was supposed to be. "He'll never forgive me."

"I don't know," she admits. "Jonah hangs onto things. But it's just a matter of hoping, one day, he sees that you did this for his benefit."

I draw my legs into my chest. "I . . . want to talk to him. About Tomás." I hate that it's the truth, and I hate not knowing why. Jonah despises me again. To be honest, I'm not sure he ever *stopped* despising me. Why am I so desperate to share something so deeply personal with him?

"Even if he wants to respond, he probably won't." Hanna smirks. "He's stubborn."

I press my forehead into my knees.

"Has your therapist gotten back to you?"

I don't respond.

"Did you even send her the message?" Hanna demands, pointing her fork accusatorily at me.

"Uh . . . anyway, how are you and Andre? Things good?"

"Don't try to change the subject." She gestures at my phone on the arm of the couch. "Hand it over, da Costa Ramírez."

"Wait!" I plead, lifting my plate high as she lunges over my lap for it. "If I drop my cake—"

"It's a perfectly fine message," she says, unlocking my screen. To my horror, she begins to read it out loud. *"Hi, Jenna, this is Dylan Ramírez. I'm not sure if you remember me, but I was your client last year. If you're available, maybe we can schedule an appointment soon? Thanks!* See? Perfectly fine."

"It sounds terrible now that you've read it out loud," I whine, grasping for it.

"Too late. It's sent."

"Hanna!"

"You made it this far," she says, sharper. "There's no need to stop here."

I scowl, twisting away from her and unmuting the TV.

Which I immediately mute again when my phone buzzes.

Hanna waits, motionless, while I pick it up. *"Of course I remember you, Dylan,"* I read, my voice cracking. *"So nice to hear from you. I'll take a look at my schedule when I'm in the office and let you know of any openings.* Smiley face."

I exhale shakily.

"How does it feel?" Hanna asks, jostling my shoulder. "To finally be getting your shit together?"

I laugh.

I don't say, *I feel like I want to tell Jonah.*

JONAH

The days begin to pass, and suddenly, winter is rearing its jingling, luminescent head.

Mik, Lily, and I have been living with Aunt Noelle and Myron for over a month. Even though we've spent so much time with them, I'm too scared to ask how long we'll last here. Because I'm starting to feel . . . happy.

I wasn't sure they would be able to handle us. Mik—her belligerence and her inability to tolerate authority figures. Me—a rowdy pain in the ass who's way too loud and annoyingly overprotective of his sisters. Lily—well, she's the only perfect one.

But they can handle it. All of it. Aunt Noelle tucks my sisters in at night, and Myron breaks out his homemade mac and cheese frequently for Lily. She's started calling him "Uncle Myron," which makes his eyes shimmer every time he hears it. The girls love our new headquarters, though it takes time to readjust. Twice, I've found Lily crouched in her room with glazed eyes, unresponsive to my voice. Mik tells Aunt Noelle to *suck it* enough times to get her confined to her room. But they're smiling more.

Thanksgiving comes and goes. We cook a gargantuan feast, during which Myron tells Aunt Noelle to please, God, *stop* pulling ketchup out of the pantry. Charlie Brown plays in the background, and we take our loaded plates of sweet potato casserole and turkey onto the balcony, watching the early afternoon parade march by.

I've seen Dylan around school, but any time I glance his way, resentment surges in my chest. I want to yell, push him, cuss him out. I want to make him feel the way he made me feel.

That doesn't stop my heart from leaping when he sends me a selfie on Thanksgiving.

PRISSY PRINCE
Dad and Tomás are screaming at the Lions in
the other room. This place is louder than it
was during homecoming lol. Hope Thanksgiving
is going well at your aunt's.

I guess him finding out about my living situation was inevitable. He's smirking at the camera, looking annoyingly mature and handsome in a collared shirt and tie. Behind him, Mr. Ramírez and Tomás are midpose, focused angrily on something out of view.

Dylan looks . . . lighter.

I want to rip my hair out. I'm so *pissed*, but I still desperately want to know what's going on with him and Tomás. But I won't let myself acknowledge why I care. So I don't text him back.

I've been spending more time with friends over the last few weeks, since Aunt Noelle made me quit my job. ("I'm glad your co-workers got the wrinkly manager bitch fired, but I still want you to focus on sleep and schoolwork and socializing.") I see a terrible reboot with Casey, and go out for ice cream with Maya and Rohan after school. Since my workload is so much lighter, I've been able to sneak into the gaps in Andre's busy schedule. He and I have been hanging out more, doing homework, playing video games, marathoning shows that he's been begging me to watch with him for years, and taking walks around the wooded area near his house. He seems more energetic than usual, if that's possible. Or happier? Maybe both?

"What's with you, lately?" I ask him at one point, looking up at him from my position on the tree we've been attempting to climb. "Acting all giddy and shit. You're not planning on, like, proposing to Hanna out of high school, right?"

Andre snorts so loudly it could shake the branches. "I get to hang out with my boy. That's a good enough reason to act giddy, isn't it?"

I can't help but smile.

So then December is here, and Christmas music thrums through the condo. A soft blanket of snow has accumulated on the balcony outside. Myron sets up the tree, which fades between different multicolored lights. The entire condo glitters with tinsel. Soft yellow candles that smell like gingerbread and sugar cookies scatter the counters.

"I used to put up our tree," I tell Aunt Noelle, watching the shifting lights. "There was a short in it, though, so most of the lights were out. And I never found the tinsel after we moved. So . . ." I clear my throat. "This is nice."

Aunt Noelle wraps an arm around my shoulders, hugging me.

That evening, as I'm pulling on fuzzy pants and a T-shirt before bed, there's a knock at my door. "Jonah?" Aunt Noelle says. "Mind joining us at the table?"

Anxiety spears my chest. This is it. They're going to tell me about our future. That we've overstayed our welcome, and they can't continue to afford us, and they've decided to start their own family, so we would be in the way—

Except, that's not what they say.

"If we're lucky, your father will go along willingly, and we won't have to open any investigation," Myron says, palms folded on the table. "We'll need to petition the court, though."

My brain's scrambling to understand. Several binders are open on the counter, stuffed with nonsensical legal jargon, highlighted in places my father would need to sign.

"We may have to undergo post-placement supervision, but it'll be okay." Aunt Noelle's eyes are soft and searching. "There will be a finalization hearing. Jonah, since you're over the age of fourteen, your father legally has no power over whether you consent to the adoption. Unfortunately, your sisters are too young to have a say, so the decision lies with him. But we wanted to talk to you before approaching them—"

"You . . ." I blink. "You want to adopt us."

They're quiet. "When you moved in," Aunt Noelle says, slow and careful, "you wondered why there were two guest bedrooms."

I don't acknowledge this. I can't.

"It's because we knew, one day, we were going to start participating in home studies," she says gently. "Because, eventually, we were hoping to try foster care . . . and, if the stars aligned, adoption."

I can't swallow or blink. I'll start crying if I do. I stagger to my feet, my heart pounding so loudly in my ears I can barely hear my own thoughts. I can't go over the details right now with them, I can't ask questions, I can't focus. I just need time.

So I croak, "Can I borrow your car?"

Aunt Noelle and Myron exchange a subtle glance, but it's gone before I can properly read what passes between their eyes. "Here," Myron says, grabbing his keys off the counter and handing them to me. "Just . . . be careful. The roads are wet. Pay attention to your surroundings."

"Thanks," I manage to sputter out. I slide into my new winter boots and jacket, push through the door, descend the steps to the parking lot, and climb into Myron's truck.

I'm driving. My brain steers me down familiar side streets, past closed businesses, ignoring the voice in the back of my head that's telling me I'm headed to the last place on earth I should be right now.

They want to adopt us.

I try to draw level, steady breaths. I'm trying to digest it, from one syllable to the next, but it's impossible. My head is urging me to feel joy and celebrate. That I should be jumping in excitement and flinging myself into Aunt Noelle's and Myron's arms—not taking an impulsive drive across town.

Suddenly, I'm in his driveway, and then I'm on his porch, knocking on his front door.

It swings inward. Dylan Ramírez's eyes are wide.

"Jonah?"

DYLAN

Jonah Collins is standing at my front door at ten o'clock on a Saturday night.

He looks like he's not sure how he got here. He's dressed in long, fuzzy pajama pants and a bulky winter jacket. His gray eyes are watery, and the tip of his nose is pink.

His gaze rakes me head to toe, from my tank top to my boxer shorts. His face pinches into a familiar grimace.

"Piss," he says. "Shit. Balls. *Fuck.*"

With that heartfelt message, he swivels and stomps back down to the snow-slicked driveway.

"Collins, what the *hell*?" I demand, staggering into my boots and trudging out after him. "Why are you here?"

"I don't know!" he snarls, climbing into the driver's seat of the truck.

"Seriously?" My confusion is dissolving into irritation. "You're leaving?"

He grabs the door handle and slams it as loud as he can, then audibly cusses, staring at my garage door, hands tight around the wheel.

I rap my knuckle against the driver window. Jonah lowers it, still staring ahead.

"What happened?" I ask.

A tear escapes the crook of his eye, which he swipes away. "Aunt Noelle and Myron want to adopt us," he says flatly, his voice strained.

I take this in. Slowly, I lean forward, folding my arms over the open window. Jonah turns further away from me.

"That's great," I say quietly.

He fidgets, like he's fighting something off.

"You're happy, but something's bothering you," I say.

Jonah slumps into the seat, sniffling. "Quit pretending you can read me so easily," he whispers.

As if his face isn't constantly exploding with every thought and emotion he's ever had. "Does your dad know about this?"

"I . . . no." Jonah gnaws on his lip. "He'll have to sign all these adoption papers, though. Give his consent. Otherwise Aunt Noelle and Myron will petition the court. Or something. I don't know if he'll sign them, but . . ."

I avoid raising my eyebrow at that, because I don't want skepticism to come across on my face. I don't know much about the man, but from what I've gathered, Jonah gave up hope that his father would step up to be in their lives long ago. "You're sure you don't know?" I ask, keeping my voice level.

Jonah slaps the back of his head against the headrest. The tears in his eyes glint under the gold of the porch light. "He probably won't care. Like, unless the threat of us being taken away suddenly wakes him up—"

"Wait," I say, looking at him sternly. "Is that something you'd want? After all this time, would you be ready to give him a chance?"

There's a hint of distress in Jonah's eyes, like he wants to say *no, of course not*. But I can still see conflict in the tightness of his jaw.

"What's bothering you?" I ask quietly.

"I . . ." He scowls. "It's nothing."

"You came all this damn way, so you might as well tell me."

Jonah squirms, like I'm poking him with pins and needles. "I don't want to . . . like, I don't know if I'm ready to . . ."

"If you're ready to *what*?" I prompt.

The veins are tensing in his neck, and I wonder, then, if he even knows what he's trying to say. If he currently understands his own feelings. I lean my face in my palm, continuing to analyze him. "Your dad having a change of heart is the only way for you and your sisters to get out of the adoption process," I say. "I don't know that much about your relationship with him, but from everything you've told me . . . why would you be looking for a way out? Don't you want things to change?"

"Of course," he snaps. "But, like . . . I've been doing things my way for years at this point, and I know what my sisters need, and I—"

"Oh," I whisper, my eyes widening with understanding. "You're worried about losing control?"

Jonah's eyes shift, and I think we both realize, in that moment, that I've hit the nail on the head. "Why would I?" he grumbles.

"This adoption is going to strip you of any power you have in taking responsibility for your sisters," I point out, leaning further into the window. "You're a stubborn brat, so you're trying to find any loophole that'll let you hold onto it—"

"Shut up," he snarls, pushing my arms off his car.

I take a deep breath. Patience, Dylan. "It won't be easy," I say tentatively. "Like, he's your dad. It's going to take time. But . . . I don't know. Maybe you need closure with him so you can move forward?" I falter, then tack on, "I could come with you. If you want."

"Why would I want that?" he growls. "Why do you think I'd want *anything* to do with you?"

"I don't know," I admit. "Why am I the person you came to see tonight?"

Jonah's cheeks turn rosy. "You suck, Prissy Prince," he says, rolling up the window and forcing me to retreat. I watch as he flings the car in reverse and backs into the street. His tires screech and slip against the snow as he guns it, zooming away.

"Stubborn ass," I mutter, heading inside and kicking my boots off. I shouldn't be annoyed with the way he's acting, since I haven't apologized for betraying his trust. But I had a feeling that wasn't what he wanted to talk about.

Still . . . why *did* he come to me?

I don't know. I'm too relieved to care. Finally, he won't have to battle on his own. He'll relearn what it's like to be safe, warm, and happy. To not worry about anything other than *being*.

I don't know if he'll want me to be part of that journey.

All I know is, maybe, after all this, I wouldn't mind being part of it.

JONAH

"Can't sleep?"

Mik is in my doorway, dressed in her pajamas. The condo complex is dark, quiet. Which makes sense, since it's two o'clock on a Monday morning.

"You neither?" I guess as she ambles into the room. Aunt Noelle and Myron told them about the adoption last night, and while Lily immediately began to cry with happiness, Mik's reaction was more reserved. I haven't been able to gauge it.

Mik climbs onto my bed. Together, we sit on the edge of my mattress, watch sparkling snow flutter from the sky, adding to the pile gathering on the roads, parked cars, and trees. She flops onto her back, sighing.

"Why can't you sleep?" I ask.

"Can't help it." She shrugs. "I'm excited."

I'm not expecting that. Maybe Mik senses uncomfortable energy around me, because she shifts sideways so she can nudge my shoulder with her foot.

"You're not gonna have to worry about us as much anymore," she says.

"Yeah." I smile weakly. "Lily's already stopped asking me to tuck her in."

Mik graces me with a giant, dramatic sigh. "I'll tell you a secret."

"Hmm?"

"The only reason Lily cared about being tucked in at Dad's house is because it made her feel safe. So . . ." She waves her hand. The implication is clear, and it makes me feel all the more guilty.

"I didn't know that," I whisper.

"Course not. It was a secret." She pushes against my arm with her foot again, smiling. "You'll always be our big brother, okay? That's not going to change because Aunt Noelle and Myron become our legal guardian people."

I fumble with my fingers, unable to muster a response.

"I still want you to come to my games," she continues, peeking up at me. "Lily is still gonna draw you pictures. But things will be easier. So, like, when I hit another ugly-ass boy at school, you don't have to come get me. I know you're gonna worry, because you're Jonah, but we just gotta get used to it."

It's a long, winding way of saying, *we'll be okay.*

"I appreciate you, kid," I whisper, lying down beside her.

"You better. I'm pretty great."

I laugh. Then, the door hinge squeaks. Lily peeks into the room, bleary-eyed, dressed in her nightgown. "Hey, Lilypad," I say, gesturing to her. "Come in."

She yawns, crawling into the bed on my other side. She rests her head on my extended arm and curls up against me. Mik is already snoring.

My eyes flutter shut, and I drift off beside them, smiling.

I told myself I would be rational and calm. That I would go in there, slap the papers before him, and demand that he sign them in my fiercest, most unforgiving voice.

And yet, as I eye the binders stacked in the passenger seat of Aunt Noelle's sedan—both of which I stole while she and Myron weren't looking—my well of confidence is quickly draining. The ten-minute

drive to his house feels quadruple that time, and I swear I hit every goddamn red light in Delridge on the way over.

In through my nose. Hold. Exhale through my mouth.

It's going to be fine.

Deep within me, I know these words are true, even if they feel empty
right now. It's the only thing that coaxes me into the driveway of the
house we haven't seen since we came to collect the rest of our belong-
ings. I try to convince myself I'm closing a chapter in my life—not
opening a new one. There's no way my dad looks at this legal jargon and
suddenly realizes all his past mistakes. Right?

Seeing his car in the open garage makes it even more real. I stare at
the front door, numbness battling dread, determination battling confusion. I don't know what's going to happen. What am I expecting out of
this?

I know the answer to that. I'm expecting that he's going to sign the
papers without asking any questions, without a single care.

But what if that's not what happens? What if I walk in there, and the
house is tidy and warm, and he's clean-shaven, and the alcohol is gone,
and he greets me with a surprised smile? What if he says something
like, "There you are. Been missing you around here. You kids ready to
come home?"

What if . . . ?

I'm not sure how I'd respond to a situation like that. If I'd even want
it. To be honest, I'm not sure *what* I want out of this interaction. Do I
want him to sign the papers and get this over with? To hesitate and ask
questions, to show that there's some tiny fragment of him that actually
cares about us? Or would that just rekindle my ridiculous little flames
of hope that maybe he'll remember once, long ago, before Mom died,

before Lily was born, before Mik could form memories of him, he was
the kind of father who took time out of his schedule to sit in the stands
at my Little League baseball practices?

I'm not going to find the answers I'm looking for just by sitting here.
So, I gather the binders and force myself to my feet. My knees wobble
before the front door, and every breath rattles my chest.

Maybe I shouldn't be here. The only person who knows I'm doing this
is Dylan, since I texted him that I'm going through with his idea of getting "closure," or whatever. He offered to come again, but . . .

I need to do this alone.

I swing the door open and head inside.

It's not tidy. It's not warm. My father is where he always is, slumped
on the couch, watching some sports rerun, his hand curled around a
whiskey glass, his eyes bruised and far away.

It's what I expect, and yet, the sight of it all carves out the rest of the
emotions weighing on my chest, leaving me cold and hollow.

"Um," I mumble. "Dad?"

His gaze flicks to the door, to me, to the papers in my hand, before
returning to the TV. I haven't seen him in weeks, and this is his greeting.

It's what I expect, and yet, the sight of it burns my eyes.

Hesitantly, I continue into the house, closing the door and tucking
myself into the couch beside him. We sit in silence for a few minutes.
I'm not sure if he's waiting for me to speak first, or if he's already forgotten that I'm here.

There's no point in beating around it. "Aunt Noelle and her husband
are going to adopt us."

He doesn't seem to register this at first. Then, slowly, he pries his
stare away from the screen, shifts toward me, and looks me in the eye.

If he's feeling any emotion, he's not showing it. Sticking to his detached guns, I guess.

I want to be cool and confident as I explain the situation to him. But as I sit there, fumbling through papers, pointing to forms and high-lighted sections, my voice cracks. I'm beginning to feel the weight of the situation. My father has all the power in the world—he can turn our plans upside down with a simple shake of his head. I'm not sure he even realizes that, but the thought weaves a knot in my throat.

When I conclude my rambling, my father examines every inch of my face. I don't know if he's realizing what a screwup he is as a dad, or if he's thinking hard about what I've told him, or if he's merely using me as an anchor to keep from losing focus.

When he picks up the pen, a jolt rushes through my body. He begins to sign the documents, and I watch him, tense and rigid, waiting for . . . I don't know. Something. Anything.

He finishes within a few minutes, and nudges the binders back to me.

I look at his empty expression. This is one of the most important mo-ments of my life, and he can't offer a single word. No apology. No well wishes. No goodbye. I should feel angry, but I can't.

I'm sad.

My father is gone. He's lost. And though I gave up years ago on trying to form a connection with him, it still hurts to see that everything hap-pening right now is because he lost control with a single substance he was using to take the edge off.

And maybe . . . maybe he realizes that, somewhere deep down. Maybe that's why he signed the papers with such ease. Because he knows he can't take care of us. That we're better off in somebody else's arms. For the first time in years . . . maybe this was his chance to prove he could make the right choice and be responsible, one last time.

I'm not sure if that's true. But believing in the thought is far less painful than the alternative.

I rise to my feet, collect the documents, and beeline for the door. I don't take one final look around the house, or spare a glance back at him to see if he's watching me leave. I'm not sure I could handle it, either way.

When I step onto the porch, something old and weathered shatters inside of me.

Closure.

My lower lip trembles.

Isn't closure supposed to feel good?

DYLAN

He's already inside.

I'm sitting in Jonah's driveway, my engine humming. I received his text during therapy, where I was already anxious, sweating bullets at the mere thought that I was there. For the rest of the session, I couldn't think about anything aside from his text. Thankfully, Jenna never made me feel bad for anything, whether it was my distraction or the fact that I haven't seen her in a year.

The only thing that matters, she said, *is that you recognize you need help. I'll be here as a support system for as long as you'd like.*

I comb my hand over my face, sighing. I've been here ten minutes, dying to know what's going on in there. His father wouldn't get angry, right? Or lash out?

Now I'm *more* worried, so I get out of my car. The air isn't as bitingly cold as yesterday. We're supposed to get more snow tonight, so the clouds are thick, heavy, and gray overhead.

The front door opens.

I freeze. Jonah ambles out, a collection of paperwork in his arms, expressionless. He wanders down to his car, which is parked adjacent to mine, and stuffs the binders into his passenger seat. He looks like he's moving without thought.

"Jonah?" I say quietly.

He looks up at me. His apathetic face doesn't change.

"I . . . know you said you wanted to do this alone, but . . ." I walk toward him, until I'm a couple feet away. "I wanted to be here in case . . ."

Jonah's lower lip wavers, and suddenly, he smiles. But it's not Jonah Collins's smile. It's not wide and eye-crinkling and sparkling with fiery warmth. It's frail. Exhausted.

"He . . ." His voice comes equally as weak. "He didn't even read the paperwork."

Jonah's head sags. He takes a careful step toward me, then leans his head against my collar. Hesitantly, I wrap my arms around his trembling shoulders.

"Fuck this," he whispers, his voice muffled in my jacket. "Why am I crying? He n-never cared about us. He makes me miserable and cold and angry . . ."

"But he's still your dad," I murmur.

Jonah crumbles against my chest, soaking my jacket with gasping sobs. I tighten my arms around him.

"I want to leave," he croaks, hugging my waist. "I don't ever want to see this place again."

"Okay." I lean my chin against the top of his head. Being this close to him is giving me all kinds of conflicting feelings, but none of them matter right now. The only thing that matters is that I'm strong enough to support both of us. "Do you want to go home?"

"No . . ."

"We could drop your car off and take a walk?" I suggest.

Slowly, he parts from me, sniffling frantically. Without another word, he collapses into the driver's seat of his car. I get into my own, then follow him through the town until we're at a modest, two-story condo complex.

I wait for him to climb the stairs of his aunt and uncle's condo with the paperwork. Within a minute, he's returning to my side. He continues past me toward the main street, and I follow.

It's peacefully quiet, aside from the snow crunching under our feet. We follow the twinkling bulbs strung throughout town, passing closed restaurants, businesses, parking lots, and galleries, with no destination. The world is now cloaked in a blanket of night, the remaining light having been wrung from the sky.

Suddenly, Jonah wanders to the side of the street and lies by the curb, nestling into the snow. I plop down beside him, squinting through the flakes beginning to fall.

"I want summer," Jonah whispers. "I want the stars back."

I tilt my head to see him. He's back to being deadpan.

"There's this place . . . I haven't been there since Mom died. It's this dirt road in the middle of hay fields. We used to lie in the road for hours. She would point . . ." He raises his finger, drawing patterns in the clouds. ". . . and teach me about constellations."

His hand drops. Snow collects in his hair, and his breath swirls away in lazy white puffs.

"You saw your brother," he says.

My heart flip-flops. "Yeah."

"Tell me what happened."

I clear my throat. Briefly, I go over everything that took place after our fight—from my panic attack, to shredding the letter, to driving to Detroit in a daze, to spending time with Tomás and my father. Jonah stops me only to ask for more information, and I don't know why, but the fact that he cares enough to want details warms my chest.

When I tell him I started seeing my therapist again, his brows arch.

"Wow," he says, peeking over at me. "We break up once and suddenly you're thriving."

I snort. "More like fake dating you gave me courage to stop running away from my issues."

At first, he's quiet. Then, "Whatever steps you took to get to your brother, you took them on your own. I had nothing to do with it."

I don't argue with that, even though he's wrong. I don't tell him that I've been feeling more comfortable since we started this scheme, or that he made me feel safe enough to talk about Tomás.

He doesn't need to know.

"What's going on in your head?" I ask quietly. "Normally, everything comes through on your face. But . . . I can't figure you out."

He grimaces. "I'm pissed. Upset. Tired. Maybe grateful. But still mostly pissed."

"At your father?"

"Both of you."

I wince. His stare is wary but pensive. "I shouldn't have meddled," I whisper, eyes flitting between his. "I didn't have the right to make that decision for you. I regret hurting you. But if it gives you a better life, I don't regret my decision." I swallow. "I hope you understand. But if you never want to talk to me again, I also get that."

I can see Jonah deliberating, mapping out his options. He rises to his feet and swipes the back of his jeans. "Do you . . . *want* to talk to me?" he asks, clearly skeptical. "The fake dating was so we could have a blowup, and our friends would stop nagging us to get together. We're at that point, so shouldn't you be taking this opportunity to run?"

"Well . . . just because we got what we wanted doesn't mean I shouldn't apologize for the pain I caused you," I say, shrugging.

"Okay. You've apologized. So . . ." He stuffs his hands in his pockets. "We go our separate ways now?"

I fling myself upright and blurt, "No."

Jonah waits for an add-on, but I can't think of anything. Why did I say that?

"I'm going back." Like that, he begins walking toward the condo complex. He throws one final glance over his shoulder. "My birthday is on Tuesday. Andre's coming over, and we're celebrating at the condo. If you want to come . . . bring me a present as part two of the apology . . . I won't stop you."

He's giving me a chance. Another opportunity. The thought makes me smile. "I'll be there."

He continues on. I let him go, because I think he needs space. Once he's far enough ahead, I get to my feet, readjusting my clothes. My phone buzzes.

COLLINS
Thanks.

I pocket my phone, my smile widening. Faintly, I can see his retreating back. Then I'm wondering why I'm smiling, and my face is warming, and suddenly, Tomás's words are clanging around in my head.

You think I can't see the way you've been talking about him?

My back straightens. My eyes bulge.

Wait.

No.

My heart freezes midbeat.

Right?

No.

Sure, he's been cute on a rare occasion. Maybe I lingered once on thoughts of cuddling him or talking away the night. It's possible I've fallen asleep to the thought of his smile, but that doesn't mean I . . .

My hands curl.

Oh.

Oh, *no.*

Except now my heart is pounding, and I'm flooded with thoughts of Jonah smiling and laughing and whispering and kissing and sleeping and oh *shit.*

I slap my hands over my face.

Fuck.

JONAH

"Happy birthday to you! Happy birthday to you! Happy birthday dear—"

Several names rise from my lunch table. Andre says Jo-Jo, Dylan says Little Brat like an asshole. The rest of the cafeteria screams incoherent sounds. I'm standing atop the lunch table, bowing to everyone until a supervisor shouts, "Get down, Collins!"

Reluctantly, I do, and the cafeteria roar simmers to a hum.

"Now, *cake!*" Andre whoops while Hanna breaks out plastic forks and a kitchen knife.

My eyes glisten. "You didn't have to buy—"

"Buy?" Maya scoffs. "When we have a professional baker in the group?"

". . . Oh." I glance at Dylan, who's pulling a gigantic cake lathered in fluffy white frosting and sprinkles onto the table. Everyone waits eagerly for my reaction, obviously hoping I'll fling myself into his arms and beg him to bone me. (Okay, it's probably more like they just want us to reconcile, but whatever.) "Uh," I say. "Thanks."

As the cake slides closer, I swallow. It's clear he spent a painstaking amount of time on it. The evenness of the frosting—the meticulously placed sprinkles. When Hanna cuts into it, I realize it's three layers deep.

It's ridiculously delicious.

"You like it?" Dylan's voice is meek.

"It's perfect," I tell him, stuffing another forkful in my mouth. "It always is."

Dylan presses a hand over his smile, staring at his lap. I don't know why he's acting like a shy, modest schoolgirl in front of her crush. Maybe this is part two of his apology.

I'm feeling a bizarre mixture of regret and eagerness after I invited him over the other night. All I know is that I owe him after he showed up for me at my dad's house.

When Aunt Noelle, Myron, and I arrive home following their after-school prep, Dylan and Andre are already there, chatting outside their cars. We tackle homework first, to get it out of the way. Andre sits between Dylan and me on the couch, and because he has a talent for easing tension, the atmosphere isn't as bad as I expected. Dylan is unnaturally quiet—even for him. It helps that Andre is playing some upbeat sports anime soundtrack to help propel us through our suffering.

When Mik and Lily get off the bus, they react to Dylan as if they haven't seen him in years. They lunge into him, hugging his waist, squealing in excitement. He takes it all with a friendly smile.

Everyone loves Darling Prince McGhee.

Eventually, Myron and Aunt Noelle offer to take us to dinner, anywhere I want.

"Let's try Brazilian," I suggest.

Dylan lights up like a Christmas tree. Dork.

We walk down the street to his father's churrascaria. It's a cozy but fancy restaurant with warm orange walls, wooden pillars, and dim, colorful lighting. Mr. Ramírez comes out of the kitchen to meet us, and I know immediately where Dylan gets his sturdy build.

"Dad!" Dylan dashes up to his father like an excited kid. The man is wearing an apron smeared with flour, and his hair is buzzed close to his scalp. But he's got Dylan's bottomless warm irises.

He also radiates chaotic, cheerful energy. Guests lift their glasses in greeting when he passes. He snags a wine bottle from the bar, then fills Myron's and Aunt Noelle's glasses, one arm dangling over Dylan's shoulders. He does this manly handshake with Andre, like they're chummy even though they've just met, and when he gets to me, he examines me thoroughly.

"Jonah!" he says. "I've heard so much. I didn't realize you were so handsome!"

I hack on my Sprite. Dylan smiles apologetically at me.

I get over the comment quickly, though. Mostly because the food distracts me. Dylan explains everything in enthusiastic detail while the rest of us listen with rapt attention.

"This is bolinho de bacalhau," he says. "Dad salts and boils pieces of cod, then deep fries them. And that's pão de queijo. The dough's made from cassava flour and queijo Minas, so it's like cheese bread! It'll fill you up quick, so try not to eat too much. Ah, and these are bacon-wrapped scallops. They don't actually eat scallops in Brazil, but it's something Americans love."

I didn't know he was so passionate about this. I don't realize I'm smiling until he catches my eye, to which I instantly flatten my face.

Then, the meat shows up. Dylan tells me it's picanha—some kind of barbecued, smoky cut of beef they cook over open flame—and it's worth puking over.

It totally is.

"We *have* to come back," I say, leaning against Andre as we stagger to the condo. Myron carries Lily on his back, since she's "so full her legs won't work."

"I'm going to shit for days," Andre groans. "I didn't even get to the chicken heart . . . or the beef ribs . . . or the crème de papaya . . ."

I glance at Dylan. "Your dad is cool. Cooler than you, anyway."

He rolls his eyes, but he looks about as happy as I've ever seen him.

When we get back to Aunt Noelle's condo, I have *presents*. That's a first.

I plop down on the floor, resting my back against Andre's legs, and begin to open them. Lily got me a galaxy coloring book, and she's already filled the pages with vibrant marker. Mik got me a mug that, when filled with hot liquid, causes constellations to appear. Aunt Noelle and Myron bought me decorative lights for my room, flannel pajamas, dress shoes, and wireless earbuds, which seem excessively fancy. Andre gives me a game I can play on Myron's console.

When I think I'm out, Dylan says, "I . . . also got you something."

I blink in surprise. "It's not the cake?"

"You thought my present was *cake*?" He scoffs, then jogs to the door with his car keys. Moments later, he returns holding a long, bulky box. Eyeing him warily, I pry the wrapping paper away.

It's a telescope.

"I know your old one is special," he says, as if I need an explanation. "It's got four-hundred-millimeter focal length and eighty-millimeter aperture, whatever that means. I don't know if that's good or not, but I made sure it wasn't, like, a dollar-store telescope . . ."

I can't hear what he's saying. I can only stare at it, mesmerized. I haven't been able to look up at the moon and stars in years. Since when did Dylan get to be so . . . so . . . like this?

Well, no. He's always been like this. I've just been pointedly looking away to avoid seeing it.

"It's nice," I say, blinking frantically. "I really . . . like it."

I've hugged everybody for their gifts. Maybe Dylan thinks I'm going for it, because he leans forward, and sudden panic spirals through my head. I say, "Thank you for the thoughtful gift!" and stick my hand out.

Dylan stares at my extended palm. Then, he chews his lips, like he's biting back laughter. "You're welcome," he says, shaking my palm.

It's the most awkward and pathetic moment of my life.

Andre roars with laughter. "Oh, come *on*! Can't you losers make out already? Watching you act all hot and bothered around each other is *painful*."

Mik, Lily, Aunt Noelle, and Myron snicker. I know my face is burning red, so I scoop up the telescope, garble something unintelligible, and dash to my bedroom. As soon as I'm inside, I collapse next to my broken telescope and curl around the legs.

No. I'm definitely bothered, but hot? For *him*?

Mik eventually comes to retrieve me when Aunt Noelle breaks out the remainder of Dylan's homemade cake. I refuse to talk to him for the rest of the night.

Mostly because I don't know what to say.

Christmas arrives shortly into winter break. Aunt Noelle tells us they were planning on flying to Florida to visit Myron's family but canceled the trip to spend time with us. Apparently the Kelly family is incredibly eager to meet us, to the point where his eighty-two-year-old grandmother threatened to drive herself all the way across the country from Florida to get to Delridge. Myron merely laughed through the phone and said, "Things are hectic right now. But we'll get out there this spring."

The thought makes me tingle with excitement. If all goes according to plan . . . we're going to have a whole new family to meet.

We throw on Christmas movies and bake dozens of cookies. Then, we suit up in boots and snow pants, and head to the backyard—a massive lawn shared by everyone in the complex. Most people are away with family, so we have the whole place to make snowmen and forts.

I'm still recovering from my pitiful, final interaction with my father. I try spending more time with my friends and sisters, and less with my thoughts about the adoption. I don't know where Aunt Noelle and Myron are in that process, but I'm steadily learning to trust they can take care of it.

Steadily. I'm not sure I'm to the point of "acceptance" yet. But I'm making progress, and I think that's worth celebrating.

On New Year's Eve, Andre's parents host a party. Aunt Noelle and Myron encourage me to go and be with my friends, since I'll have plenty of other holidays to spend with them. The thought makes my heart flutter.

"But no drinking," Aunt Noelle snaps, handing me her car keys. "And if you do drink, text me and I'll pick you up in Myron's truck. And then I'll kill you."

She gives my forehead a fleeting kiss. It makes me feel like a kid when she does that. I guess I don't mind.

The house is overflowing with energy when I get there. The bass of the TV announcers pounds through the house alongside music. Mrs. Lewis sweeps through the place, offering appetizers to guests and scolding anyone who says no. Mr. Lewis and other adults are discussing politics in the kitchen. Maya isn't here—she has some party going on at her mansion—but Rohan, Casey, Hanna, Andre, and Dylan are in the living room, munching on appetizers and chatting while the television flashes to the glowing Times Square Ball.

"Finally!" Andre snaps when I sit down. "I thought you were going to miss the ball drop."

"What? It's only . . ." I squint at their hanging clock. "Eleven thirty. There's a whole half hour left! Are you all really that lost without me?"

This triggers an assault of berating and snarky comments from everyone aside from Dylan. When I look at him, he merely smirks and turns his eyes away. He's wearing jeans and a pale gray Henley shirt, the buttons undone and the sleeves rolled up, because of *course* he needs to look sexy at all times every day.

As the remaining few minutes until the New Year tick down, people rush into the living room, surrounding the giant TV, yelling over the noise, laughing boisterously, clinking glasses. I soak in the atmosphere—the mesh of vibrant noises and upbeat vibes—and smile.

For once, I'm looking forward to a new year.

"Practice kiss," Andre says beside me, grinning down at Hanna. "In preparation."

"So dramatic." She tsks, but leans in, allowing him to smooch her.

I glance sideways to where I last saw Dylan. He's gone. I frown, my eyes searching the sea of bodies crowding the TV. Did he leave? Right at the good part? Or . . . no. Maybe it's too loud and crowded around here for his comfort? "I'll be back," I say, beginning to worm through the throng.

"What? The ball's gonna drop in five minutes!" Andre cries out, but I continue on.

Dylan isn't in the kitchen, and the basement lights are off. Hesitantly, I crack open Andre's bedroom door. Normally, the silhouettes of four massive men staring me down through the dark would make me scream, but I've been in here enough to know that it's just cutouts of the three variations of Peter Parker and one of Miles Morales. My boy's hyper-fixation shows no signs of slowing, and I love that for him.

As I expect, Dylan's sitting on the edge of Andre's bed in the dark, alone, staring at the smaller, quieter television in front of him. It's on the same channel, projecting every possible angle of the Times Square Ball, and the thousands of people spilling away from it.

Dylan sees me and scrunches his hands around the comforter. "Just . . . needed a minute," he whispers.

I step inside, nudging the door closed. He turns his attention back to the TV as I prop myself beside him, keeping my knees together so my leg won't accidentally touch his. His body language is lax, and his eyes aren't struggling to focus, so I don't think he's panicking. But I extend my arm to him anyway. Just in case.

He looks down at it, then sideways at me, his eyes pouring into mine. He's close. Too close. But I can't shrink back and ruin these last few moments before the New Year. And I'm . . .

I'm not sure I want to.

Dylan's palm grips my wrist. Slow and careful, he smooths his thumb up the veins leading into my palm, seeking my pulse. When he finds it, it quickens against my will.

"You don't have to sit here with me," he says softly. "You should be where you want to be. Out in the crowd."

"Who says that's where I want to be?" I ask, returning my attention to the TV. I can't afford to meet his eyes again. Not while he's listening to my heart rate.

"Me." Dylan reaches up with his other hand. Tenderly, he brushes some of the hair away from my brow. "Because I know you."

The volume of the crowd in New York grows, as does the group in the living room. Dylan and I sit in darkness, unspeaking, watching as the Times Square Ball begins to descend.

"*Fifty-nine! Fifty-eight! Fifty-seven!*"

The numbers ricochet through our ears. The glow of the TV casts his face in pale colors.

"*Twenty! Nineteen! Eighteen!*"

Beyond Andre's window, I can faintly hear people spilling into the yard, screaming the countdown, banging pans. My heartbeat is quickening as I feared—my cheeks are flushing. He can definitely feel it. Does he know why? Do *I* know why? Hopefully he'll chalk it up to the countdown.

"*Ten! Nine! Eight!*"

"You should be out there." Though Dylan says that, his thumb presses deeper into my wrist—like a quiet, subconscious plea to stay.

"*Four! Three! Two!*"

"I'm fine here," I mumble. Instinctively, I loosen my tensed knees, allowing them to spread, just enough that the fabric of our pants is nearly grazing.

"*HAPPY NEW YEAR!*"

People stomp and jump around, shrieking, yelling. A champagne bottle pops. More people join the pots-and-pans crowd outside, and party blowers are going off. I'm sure several people are making out right now.

Dylan stays quiet. Motionless.

We stay that way another minute. The celebrations are still going. I can hear the faint cracks of fireworks in the distance.

"Happy New Year," I say, wishing it didn't sound so pathetic. I stand, gently remove my hand from his grip, and trail to the door, hating that I'm somehow . . . disappointed.

"Wait." Suddenly, Dylan has me by the crook of my elbow. He spins me, then nudges me back against the door and lifts my chin.

He kisses me.

It's quick. It's sweet. My thoughts, my complicated feelings, dissolve into meaningless nothing. His lips burn against mine, and the sensation seeps into my chest, heating my heart. When he draws back, my instinct is to move forward—to remove that space.

"Happy New Year," he says softly, the words brushing my upper lip. I stare at his mouth, then hesitantly move my gaze to his eyes. He holds me with his warm stare for only a second, before breaking away.

He steps around me, slipping into the hallway.

Disoriented, I press my fingers to my lips. Where his voice touched me. I feel pressure around my wrist, like my body is clinging desperately to the sensation of his grip around me.

I press my back to the door again, sliding down the wood until I'm sitting. I hug my knees into my chest. My stomach flutters, then sinks with a final, burning realization that drives my face down into my palms.

"Kiss me again," I whisper.

DYLAN

I *had* to step away.

He *had* to follow me.

I groan, reeling my head against the driver's headrest. All of this happened because I was social'd out and needed some silence. Seeing my mom's extended family from Texas is fun during Thanksgiving, even if their presence reminds me that my grandparents haven't visited since the incident between Tomás and Tío Ramón. Her cousins' kids are older than me—most are around Tomás's age—but they always help me feel included. Whether it be in conversations or impromptu soccer matches in the backyard.

Seeing them for Christmas, though, a mere month later, is exhausting. Mostly because we've already talked about everything, so what's there left to do? Other than cram everyone in the kitchen to make Bacalao a la Vizcaína and a surplus of green chili chicken tamales?

I'm still recovering from the barrage of questions. I should've expected I'd get overwhelmed at Andre's, since I never had the chance to recuperate. If I'd declined his invitation, Jonah wouldn't have found me in Andre's room, and I wouldn't have kissed him while he's still upset with me. And yet . . .

I could've sworn, as he was leaving, he was disappointed I hadn't kissed him at midnight.

I sigh, shutting my car off and clambering out. Snow is trickling from the sky once more, and the fresh blanket sheds the night in a bright gray. My neighborhood is so silent it's nearly eerie. With the sky and ground being as white as it is, it feels more like midafternoon than midnight.

I crunch my way to the front door, fumbling for my keys. Mom and Dad left this morning to attend a co-worker's party, which is far enough away that they decided to get a hotel. So, for once, I'm actually grateful I'll be alone. It'll be time to recharge. To bake my stress away, and try valiantly not to think about how it feels to kiss Jonah.

I start pulling out random ingredients. I have no idea what I'm going to make—only that it needs to be complicated and force me to focus.

There's a tapping noise at my front door.

I blink, waiting. Did I . . . imagine that?

No. There it is again, louder.

I frown, jogging to the door. Maybe it's some drunken neighbor trying to unlock the wrong house after celebrating across the street. I unbolt the door and swing it open.

Jonah Collins is standing on my porch. His face is gnarled with anger and distress. I'm feeling déjà vu with him standing there, looking ready to tell me off for something completely unreasonable.

"You," he growls. *"You piss me off, Dylan Ramírez."*

Ah. Definitely déjà vu. Right down to my muscles clenching with irritation and my jaw locking tight. Just because I have feelings for him now doesn't mean he can't still annoy the shit out of me. "Really?" I demand. "You're here to insult me?"

Maybe I'm imagining it, but I swear his face is deepening in color. "You've always been this goddamn *thorn* in my side," he continues, his words tight with anger. "You've scolded me like I'm a child . . . you think you're better than me at everything . . ."

My blood is starting to boil. "I can't believe you drove here just to—"

"But as much as you've made me angry," Jonah snaps, overpowering my volume, looking up at me with desperate, watery eyes. "I can't stop thinking about you."

The words hit hard enough to stun. I stand there, speechless.

"You broke my trust, and I told myself I was going to hate you forever for that," he cries out, and suddenly, he's pacing on my porch, scratching his hands through his hair, looking at everything but me. "I'm trying to stay mad at you, but you keep being this stand-up person. You keep showing me how kind and supportive you are, and how much you go out of your way for other people. And it's so hard, because I know you now, so how am I supposed to hate you? How can I hate *anyone* like you?"

He takes a giant, gasping breath. I stare at him, my mouth agape. "Um," I say numbly, but then he starts up again.

"I'm so annoyed, because anytime I think of you, it's all these moments we spent together, the quiet and the loud ones." It looks like he's caught between seething with anger and crying out of frustration. I can't tell which emotion he's feeling harder. "And then I think about the way you look at things you like, and the way you smile, and the way you're so warm, and how I want to sleep on you all night. And then I think about how you kiss me all soft and sweet, like you actually care about me or something, and it pisses me off all over again."

My heart beats against the walls of my skull, trying to wake me from this stupor.

Jonah whirls toward me, jamming his index finger in my face. "I hate how safe you make me feel," he says sharply. "I hate that I can't stop wanting to be around you. So, what I'm trying to tell you is . . ."

He freezes. His eyes are giant discs, his face and neck and ears all flushed.

"What I'm trying to say is. Fuck you," he croaks. "Goodnight."

Jonah spins on his heels and dashes toward the driveway.

I hardly have enough sense to recognize he's about to get into his car. The realization that he's actually about to leave coaxes me into motion.

"Wait!" I wrench my boots on, but I don't have time to tie them. I sprint out after him into the night, my teeth latching with furious disbelief. *"Jonah Collins, you can't tell me that and then run away!"*

"It was a mistake!" he shouts, scrambling for the keys in his jacket pocket. "I wasn't expecting to say all of that . . . oh, *shit*."

Just as he's pulling the door open, I skid to a stop beside him and slam it shut. He tries to sprint around to the other side, but I hook my arm around his chest, yanking him back. "You're not leaving!" I yell, my voice shattering the still silence of the night. "I won't let you!"

I seize his wrists, turn, and pin him flat to the side of the car, leaning my weight against him. His struggles against me taper off. He glares up at me.

"You're so loud," I snap at him, my furious stare flicking between his eyes. "You won't stop acting like a clown until you have everyone's attention. You'll cause a scene wherever you go just to get a laugh out of people. And you're stubborn. God, you're so damn *stubborn*. You fight against everything, even if you know it'll help you, which is so *aggravating*."

"Let go!" Jonah seethes, twisting his hands against mine. "I'm leaving! Get off me—!"

"But . . ." My voice is quavering, but I'm not sure if it's from anger or nervousness. "You're resilient, and passionate, and intense. You share this bright, chaotic energy with every person you're around. The reason you're so cold all the time is because you're *always* giving everybody your warmth. You're like this fireplace that makes everyone comfortable and cozy."

Jonah's struggles falter. Water glazes his eyes, glistening under the dim gold of the garage light and the pale blue of the falling snow.

"Your protectiveness of your sisters is beautiful," I say insistently, leaning further into him. He doesn't lean away. The thought makes my chest thrum with anticipation. "And how you insist on taking care of everybody but yourself, and the way you're so shamelessly *you*. You never stop being Jonah Collins. You're . . . you're just . . . *fuck*, I want you."

Jonah is silent aside from his quick breathing. I wonder if he's like me, feeling every emotion under the moon right now. The world is quiet, calm, as if it's listening in, waiting for whatever happens next.

But I don't want to wait anymore. I'm done waiting.

I tug Jonah along the edge of the car and hoist him up onto the hood. I lean in, so our noses are grazing. His breath is short and warm against me.

"Kiss me," he whispers.

Oh Lord, do I kiss him.

I drive forward, crushing my lips against his, nearly flattening him against the slanted hood of his car. He knots his fingers in my hair and squeezes my waist tight between his thighs, drawing me against him. I feel like I've been waiting for this moment for ten years, and yet my brain can only conjure two words.

Holy shit.

Every second of fiery, livid passion contrasts with sweet, soft lips. My fingers claw up underneath the back of his jacket. His skin is silky and cool and inviting, but his hands leave hot, scalding imprints against the nape of my neck and the edges of my face.

We part every so often, sneaking quick, zealous glances at each other as we catch our breath, trying to make sure this is all real, before one of us breaks the gap and advances again. At one point, he takes too long to catch up, and I lurch into him anyway, catching his neck under my lips. He arches his head, his eyes fluttering.

"Inside?" I mumble against his jaw.

His blush deepens. "Inside," he agrees.

We stumble into the house, kicking off our boots, tossing our jackets on the couch. As soon as the exterior clothing is off, leaving him in a V-neck sweater and jeans, I hoist him up, yanking his legs around me again, and heave him against the front door. I've never been into the whole "pinning my partner against a wall" thing, at least until now. Maybe it's because I like combating his writhing, always-moving personality. Or maybe it's because of the way he falls so comfortably into my grip, like he doesn't trust anyone more than me.

He doesn't seem to mind. He meets my lips with a frantic hunger, and I drive my hips forward, holding him aloft, sighing into his mouth as adrenaline courses through me in disorienting shock waves. Kissing him . . . it's unexplainable. It's like his entire persona fractures, and he forgets about his fierce stubbornness, his rigid nature. It's like holding M&Ms. The fiery reds and oranges bleed into your hand, leaving soft pools of warm chocolate.

I comb my fingers beneath the waistband of his jeans. His skin is a smooth canvas of warmth beneath the denim. He shivers again, but it's because of me, rather than the cold, and the thought pumps heat into my veins.

I carry him to the staircase and begin to ascend to my bedroom. Jonah throws his arms around my neck, clinging to me.

"This is the sexiest thing that's ever happened to me," he hisses in my ear.

I laugh so hard I nearly drop him.

Eventually, though, I make it upstairs. I sprawl him on my bed, and he makes a shrill noise when I tug my shirt over my shoulders, tossing it aside. "Yours, too?" I whisper, hooking my finger around the dip of his V-neck sweater.

It looks like steam is about to start rolling out of his ears. "Uh-huh," he says faintly.

He arches his back slightly so I can wriggle it off him, and I'd be lying if I said the sight doesn't nearly drive me into a frenzy.

I lie down sideways with him and yank his knee over my hip, while he smooths his fingers up my chest and over my shoulders. I kiss him slowly, deeply, massaging the length of his leg, keeping it hooked around me.

I sense the first trace of his exhaustion when his legs slacken. When his grip falls limp in my curls. I kiss both of his palms, then each of his fingers. He watches in a daze as I work my lips up his forearm, his shoulder, his jawline, until I'm back at his parted lips.

"I want . . ." Jonah falls quiet.

"Hmm?" I fold my fingers through his, lifting his knuckles to my lips again.

"I want to sleep here tonight," he says, "but I don't—"

He can't seem to force the words out. I laugh and say, "I promise I'm not scheming to have sex with you."

He sighs with relief. "I've never . . . and this whole thing is new . . ."

"Hey." I press one slow, tantalizing, lingering kiss to his lips, and he relaxes. "You don't have to explain yourself. Ever. Okay?"

He hesitates, then nods. "Okay."

I collapse beside him, then open my arms, allowing him to crawl between them. He rests his head against my upper arm. "I want to try again," I say. "But this time . . . without the *fake* part."

Jonah smiles that smile with a hint of mischief. I can read what he's about to say before he actually says it. "Maybe." His voice is light. "I'll have to sleep on it."

I smirk, flicking his nose. "You little brat."

He wriggles deeper into my arms, making himself cozy. "*Your* little brat," he whispers.

I nestle my chin into his hair. At least he's mine.

The night begins to flutter by in silence. I'm so happy, my pounding chest won't allow me rest. I'm not sure how Jonah falls asleep so quickly with my heart hitting him repeatedly in the head. But he does, and his slow, steady breathing is a comfort.

"Sleep well, cariño," I say softly.

For the first time, the word feels right.

JONAH

That was . . .

Last night was . . .

Wowie.

When Dylan opens his eyes, he finds me staring at him, buried under his comforter, flabbergasted. "Did you know you can fit a million earths inside the sun?" I blurt.

He blinks slowly.

"One million," I emphasize. "Isn't that interesting?"

He offers a sleepy half-smile, which, paired with his fluffed-up messy curls, nearly sends my heart into overdrive. I shift closer to him, allowing him to reclaim his grip on me and feed me his unending warmth.

I'm not sure what I was planning on doing last night when I followed him to his house. I definitely hadn't been intending to . . . well . . . *confess*. But the moment I saw him in his doorway, puzzled but a little eager, I had to stop being stubborn. To stop fighting my feelings.

Before I knew it, I was rambling, insulting him, complimenting him, blushing, acting like a fool. He followed me to my car and restrained me so I couldn't leave, which was way sexier than I care to admit. Then, we were making out on the hood, and he was literally *carrying* me upstairs, which was even more exhilarating, and . . .

It was a good night.

"Did you sleep okay, real boyfriend?" he asks with a cheeky smile.

Boyfriend. I'm not used to that word being used legitimately, especially not in reference to me. "Yeah," I admit. "You're like a goddamn space heater."

He laughs. I unwind against him, snuggling my head deeper into his neck.

We lounge around for the next hour, and by that I mean neither of us move, except to reposition on the bed when his arm falls asleep under my head. It's lazy and warm and perfect. I could stay here all weekend.

But I already woke to a heated thread of texts from Aunt Noelle, who claims she would've called the police if I hadn't had my location on and I hadn't previously told her where Dylan lives. I realize I forgot to text her I'd be spending the night.

I know you're not used to telling people where you're going or what you're doing, she typed. But when you're with me, you need to ask before doing whatever you want.

Which . . . ugh. Going from independent to partially dependent is kind of annoying.

But at least she cares.

She asked me to return home by noon, so eventually, I depart from Dylan's arms and stuff my clothes on from last night, then trail downstairs with him.

"I . . . uh." I peek up at him, hating how weirdly shy I've been feeling. "Do you think . . . we could have our first real boyfriend dinner tonight?"

He smiles, and my heart does a pirouette. "I know a good place, so I'll pick you up around six. Sound good?"

I nod awkwardly and trail to the door.

"Wait. Take this." Dylan wriggles a bulky Delridge Wildcats Track and Field sweatshirt over my head, the sleeves of which hang past my fingertips. I know RAMÍREZ is stitched across the back. "Since you can't survive without my warmth."

"But . . . I shouldn't just take your sweatshirt," I say uneasily, wrapping my jacket over it.

He knocks my chin up with his knuckle. "We're boyfriends, so you need a boyfriend hoodie." He presses a fleeting, mischievous kiss to my lips. "So everyone knows you're my property."

I dry heave with revulsion. He winks, then shuts the door in my face.

He's still a Prissy Prince after all.

When I get back to Aunt Noelle's condo, I have to sit through a hearty scolding from her while Myron gives me a subtle thumbs-up behind her shoulder.

Then I mention I have a date tonight, and her entire persona shifts.

"What?" Her eyes glitter. "With Dylan?"

Hearing it makes me fidget. I've had crushes on people, but I've never had time to pursue relationships. Now, though, the realization is catching up to me. I have a *boyfriend*. I shouldn't be nervous, because Dylan is obviously super extremely lucky to have me, but . . .

Oh, God. I'm going on my first *date*.

I shower triple the time I need, scrub myself ten times, accidentally shave my armpits (don't ask), and wash my face viciously enough to make my skin glow red. Once Aunt Noelle and Myron help me pick out an outfit, I spend the rest of my afternoon pacing, nibbling my nonexistent nails.

Though it's a torturously long wait, Dylan eventually texts that he's waiting for me outside. Mik straightens out my sweater, and Lily climbs up on the couch to smooth my hair down, since I've been ruffling it all day.

"You got this, Jo-Jo!" she says.

I jog down the staircase outside of the condo, slip not once, but thrice, and stagger to his car. He's standing in front of it, a turquoise dress shirt poking out from beneath a black fleece. His curled hair looks stiffer, but neater, like he put product in it. The thought that he took that extra step makes me weirdly giddy.

"Have I ever said turtlenecks are one of the sexiest things a guy can wear?" he asks.

My soft black turtleneck suddenly feels like it's choking me.

He steps forward and plants a soft kiss on my lips. Like I'm not flustered enough already. "Ready, cariño?"

I shake my hands out and nod. "Let's do this."

We start to the restaurant. I'm glad he offered to drive, because I'm way too nervous to pay attention to the road. Instead, I stare at his palm on the compartment between us. It's open, facing up. An invitation? But what if I'm gross and clammy? The last thing I want to do is make him gag over my moist hands before we even enter the restaurant. Instead, I focus on the ice-slicked trees and the passing snow-dusted buildings.

Dylan shifts both palms to the wheel, his smile flinching.

Great. Now I'm sweaty *and* a jerk.

Dylan calls it a "hibachi" restaurant. It's a wide, open space painted in soft yellow hues. The tables are set up in half rectangles, each wrapped around silver grills that hurl smoke into the vents above. People shuffle around under chef's hats, pushing giant carts filled with plates of meat, vegetables, and sauce. I watch in awe as a nearby chef juggles his cooking utensils.

"Whoa," I say.

Dylan smiles, swinging his arm around mine. "Just wait."

We're seated at the corner of a table next to a family of five—parents, two young teenage daughters, and a boy who looks around Lily's age. "So," I whisper to Dylan. "Is this normal? Sitting with other people?"

"Yeah."

I tap my feet agitatedly. The atmosphere is great—vibrant, fun, noisy. That could be why he chose this place. I'm naturally loud, so maybe he was hoping he wouldn't have to tell me to keep my voice down? Otherwise, wouldn't he have preferred somewhere more private?

I'm overthinking things. Still . . .

Dylan starts knitting his fingers, massaging his palms. Is he . . . nervous? He seemed unfazed earlier, when he was waiting for me outside his car. Has something changed? Is it my fault?

When the grill chef arrives in a black chef's uniform and a tall hat, it's the perfect distraction from my bumbling thoughts. He does that juggling act I glimpsed earlier, only now, I'm front and center, watching in awe as he tosses around his utensils. He flips an unbroken egg up into his hat like a cartoon character. Then, he sets a tower of onions on fire, which makes me scream. When I look over, I see Dylan shaking with laughter into his palms.

As he's cooking the vegetables, the chef gestures for me to open my mouth, then proceeds to hit me in the face with three chunks of zucchini. He moves on to my boyfriend, who catches it dead center in his mouth, because Dylan Ramírez is good at everything.

Eventually, I receive the largest pile of rice, vegetables, chicken, and shrimp I've ever had in my life. I drizzle it with some of that pinkish sauce, and when I take a bite, I moan so passionately that the mom of the boy next to me covers his ears.

"You like it?" Dylan asks, eyes gleaming.

"I'm in love."

". . . With the food."

"Uh, duh? What else?"

He jabs my side, and I squeak.

We receive our bill, and I allow Dylan to cover us this time—the only stipulation being that I can pay for us next time.

After we pack ourselves full, we head to the parking lot with our leftovers. He's holding his in his left hand—a strategic move, since mine is in my right. My fingers itch to reach over, but . . .

Ugh. I'm thinking about sweaty palms again.

"Do you want ice cream?" Dylan asks when we're both seated in his car. "We can go to that place you like over on—"

"No," I say quickly. I've already overeaten, and there's no way I'm going to explode on my first real date.

He sits there, his expression unidentifiable, then says, "I'll take you home."

The ride back to Aunt Noelle's condo is brutally silent. I don't know what to say. Besides, why is it up to me? Why isn't *he* talking? He's wearing this bothered look. Did he have a wake-up call and realize he wasted an hour and a half of his life?

As soon as he shifts into park in front of Aunt Noelle's condo, I go to shove the door open, but he catches my wrist. He strokes my knuckles with his thumb, which makes my heart scream.

"What's wrong?" he asks sternly.

"I . . . nothing. It's just . . ." I squirm, but he squeezes my hand tighter, keeping my focus on him. "I was wondering if you brought me to a steakhouse because it's loud? And I'd be less likely to draw attention to us? But I probably did anyway."

Dylan rubs his available hand over his face and sighs.

"Sorry," I say hastily. "Was it because I screamed over the onion volcano? To be fair, that was the coolest shit I've ever seen—"

"Hey." His lips tilt into a little smile. "I know you enjoy being around groups of people. I know you like loud environments over quiet ones. So, I thought bringing you to a hibachi restaurant would make you comfortable. I'm sorry if that ruined the night."

Oh my God. Oh *fuck*. I'm such a prick. I'm such a fucking piece of—

"It was perfect," I say, nodding earnestly. "Thanks for being so considerate. Sorry if I gave off weird vibes."

"Nah, it's cute. I kind of like that you're nervous." He gives me a knowing grin. "Did you think about me all day, Collins?"

". . . I've changed my mind. This is the worst first date of my life."

The haughty asshole laughs and catches my lips before they can form other violent words. Which honestly fixes everything.

"Can I walk you to the door?" he mumbles against my mouth.

I peek out his windshield, and though darkness has already laid siege to the town, the skies are clear. "Are you . . . up for a drive?" I ask.

He cocks his head. "Where to?"

I lean back, smiling, and gesture to the main road.

"I'll show you."

DYLAN

I don't know where I'm expecting Jonah to take me. It's getting late, so everywhere nearby is closing up shop.

Fifteen minutes later, though, we're passing beyond the city limits into country road territory. The streetlights and lampposts sputter out, until I'm relying only on my headlights and the reflection of the snow as we crawl through the dark. I haven't seen a car in ten minutes—the only signs of life are the occasional barn and farmhouse.

Jonah says, "Okay . . . here."

I look over at him, skeptical, because we're in the middle of a deserted dirt road slick with ice, surrounded by rustling frost-dusted fields. But . . . no. His face is solemn. It hits me all at once where we are.

I haven't been there since Mom died.

My eyes glisten. "This is . . . ?"

He offers a frail smile. "This is where she taught me about the constellations."

For several seconds, I can't move or speak. I merely watch as Jonah leans forward, gazing at the luminescent stars through the windshield.

"We would lie out here." He gestures to the road. "I was always afraid someone might run us over, but she told me it was our secret spot, where nobody could find us."

He shifts his eyes to his lap, his smile widening.

"She would bring this tray of brownies with her. Frosted, with sprinkles. She always knew when to take them out of the oven, so they were still a little gooey." He kicks his shoes off, then tucks his legs onto the seat. "We'd stay out here for hours, taking the galaxy in."

I absorb this in silence. Until Jonah says, "Can you open your moon-roof?"

"I . . . yeah. Sorry." My fingers stumble over the controls, until I find the one that pulls back the cover, revealing the glass in the ceiling. Jonah lays his chair back, getting comfortable. I do the same, gazing upward. The sky . . . it's overflowing with light. Every star is vibrant, puncturing the blanket of blackness.

For several minutes, we lie quiet, the silence broken only by the hum of the engine. Jonah's moved his left hand onto the compartment between us. I take it as an offer, and reach over, intertwining our fingers.

"I'm grateful," I say softly. "It means a lot that you'd let me share this place with you."

He smiles, his thumb stroking mine, from my knuckles to my wrist.

"If you decide to let me come here again, I'll bake brownies," I tell him. "I'll frost them and even add sprinkles."

"That sounds really nice," he whispers.

Silence again. I try to imagine little Jonah out here, lying on the road with a woman who looks exactly like him, his eyes glittering with every new fact he can add to his arsenal, chocolate frosting smeared on his upper lip. I want to know more about his mom—what she was like, and if he's a mini version of her. I don't remember ever meeting her, even though she was still alive when I first moved here.

"I . . . don't have anything special like this to share with my mom." I wince as soon as I say it. This moment shouldn't be about my prob-lems—it's about exploring what this place means to him.

But Jonah doesn't seem annoyed. He shifts to look at me, his gray eyes piercing through the darkness of the car. "It's not too late, right?" he coaxes.

I shrug. Kind of feels like it.

"If you want to make progress, you have to stop pushing her away."

"She pushed me away first," I say defensively.

"But don't you think she's trying to fix that?" His gaze turns stern. "I've seen how you react to her texts and calls. I know she's busy, and that's part of the reason you're irritated with her, but she's also making time to reach out to you. Even if those times are inconvenient."

I squirm in my seat. He's not wrong, but . . .

"Did I ever tell you . . . my mom died after a fight?" Jonah strengthens his grip around my hand, his voice soft. "It wasn't a big blowup, like the movies. But Mom and I were stubborn, so the littlest of things could keep us mad. I forgot to take the trash bin out when it was overflowing. I think she'd had a stressful day already, and that pushed things over the edge."

I stay quiet, still, listening.

"She took my phone away," he continues. "Which was completely overdramatic, so I yelled at her. She kissed me before I went to bed, though, like every night, so it wasn't *that* bad. Still . . . things were tense. My phone was in her jacket pocket when she died."

Jonah looks at me with tired, exasperated eyes.

"It's cool," he whispers. "Having a mom. So if you have the chance to fix things . . . take it."

I don't know what to say. Part of me wants to argue that Jonah's mom was always involved in his life, so it's not the same. But this is supposed to be a good night, so I merely lift his hand to my lips and kiss his palm.

"Okay, cariño."

Jonah and I spend the rest of the night in my car, watching the stars atop our warmed seats, talking, holding hands, smiling, bantering, kissing. I tell him more about my time with Tomás, and he tells me about his time with Ms. Davis and Mr. Kelly. The nervous energy plaguing us earlier has completely dissolved, and it's so . . . comfortable.

Maybe too comfortable, because Jonah starts falling asleep. When he wakes, we're back at the condo complex, and I'm standing next to his seat, poking his nose.

"Come on," I say. "Let's get you inside before your aunt puts together a search party."

Together, we walk up the stairs to the second story.

"I *am* treating you next time," he says, rising to the tips of his toes and sliding his arms around my neck. "Thanks for making this . . . um. You know. Special."

He plants a final, prolonged kiss on my lips. I sneak two fingers up the back of his turtleneck and dig them into the knobs of his spine, arching him into me. I can almost feel the sudden warmth radiating from his face.

"See you," he says, stepping back to the door.

I wink. "Buenas noches, querido. Que descanses bien."

He has no idea what it means. I hope he'll look it up later.

He heads inside, waves at me in this cute, unusually bashful way, then closes the door.

I head back to my car, feeling lighter and fluffier than the clouds above.

I plow carefully through the snowy roads until I'm back home. The house is flooded in darkness, aside from a single light pouring out of the kitchen. Faintly, I hear clinking, so I trudge forward and poke my head around the corner.

Mom is at the sink, handwashing dishes, dressed in an inky black blazer over a gray blouse. Considering the amount of pots and pans overflowing in the drying rack, they had people over for dinner. She has her phone wedged between her shoulder and ear, and she's speaking in stiff Spanish to someone on the receiving end. Judging by her tone, it's probably my grandma (though I'm not sure what either of them are doing up past midnight). They call each other once or twice a year, mostly out of formality, despite their estranged relationship.

Just as I'm considering sneaking away, her voice rises, and she yells, "¡Dios mío, eres tan ridícula, Ma!"

She slaps the phone down on the counter.

"Um," I say, shuffling around. "That was . . . abuela?"

She cocks her head over her shoulder. Her expression is already level again. "Yes."

She doesn't offer anything more, so I ask, "What are all these dishes from?"

"We hosted your father's staff for dinner." Her voice is still rigid. "He cooked, so I offered to clean the kitchen."

"Oh." Wow. It's pretty rare that they're both available to host things. I'll feel like a jerk if I leave now, so I amble over and snag a hand towel off the oven, then begin drying the plates and putting them away.

For a few minutes, neither of us says anything. I want to sprint far away from this situation, but I can't stop both Tomás's and Jonah's words from nipping at the back of my head. Tomás telling me that maybe I can't see it, but she *is* trying, in her own strange way. Even if it means random calls in the middle of the night to check in about school, because she doesn't know what other subjects she can bring up. Jonah telling me I shouldn't take her presence for granted, because one day, it might be too late to change things.

I don't like sitting in this discomfort. But if both of them think this might be a way to move forward . . . maybe I can give it a shot.

Instinctively, I sigh. How would I even begin to "fix" things? Talking to her would be a start, but about what? I don't care to know about work, because that's half the reason our relationship is messed up. Maybe mentioning Tomás is a good idea? I bet she's happy he's started coming around again. Or maybe not. Her face doesn't reveal much.

"So," I begin, but suddenly, she's speaking over me.

"You need to tell us when you go out."

I blink at her. "Huh?"

"This evening," she says flatly. "I texted you to be part of this dinner. You never answered. Your father and I had no idea where you were, or what you were doing, or who you were with." She slaps a wet serving plate into my palms.

Her words stun me. Why is she acting like she's around often enough to even know when I'm gone? "I was on a date," I say, equally as stiffly. "With Jonah."

"And you couldn't take two seconds to text me? It's disrespectful."

"I didn't see it," I admit. "I might've swiped the message away without looking—"

"As you do with most of my texts, right?" Her voice sharpens. "Either way, you should work on sparing time for your family. We could've used the extra hands tonight. Besides, it's not often we get to eat dinner together."

Incredible. There's no way she actually just said that to me, right?

Surely she has to be a *little* self-aware. "Um," I say, the familiar sting of bitterness on my tongue, "do you really want to talk about putting other priorities before family, Mom?"

"Dylan Mauricio da Costa Ramírez," she says, deadpan as ever. "You won't disrespect me any further tonight."

My blood begins to simmer. "So when you call me out for skipping a random dinner, that's fine, but when I call you out for skipping out on half my life, that's too far?"

"Dylan—"

"I'm done." I slap the next plate back into the drying rack and whirl toward the living room. I won't let her ruin this day for me. "Goodnight, Mom."

I try to stride away, but she snags the back of my shirt, pulling me to a halt. She slides in front of me, and for the first time, she looks up, eyes searching my face.

"I . . . apologize for snapping," she says hesitantly. "If you're upset, we should discuss it. Right, mi amor?"

Seriously? *Now* she wants to have some open conversation with me? I go to storm past her, but once more, she steps in front of me. Her insistence sends a bullet of rage tearing through my chest, and I shout, "¡Ya, quítate, ma! *¡Estoy harto de esto!*"

I try pushing her aside, but she catches my wrist. Her face contorts with brief desperation, and she says, of all things, "Don't run away from me."

I rip out of her grasp. "Running away," I breathe. Familiar white buzzing encroaches on the back of my head.

"Let's . . . talk about this," she pleads.

"About *what*, Mom?" I don't know why, but it's all coming to the surface—the anger, the resentment, the pain. "About school? The weather? Your next trip? Or are you finally ready to talk about Tío Ramón?"

"Dylan . . ." Her hands hover, like she doesn't know where to put them. Around my face? On my shoulders? It doesn't matter, because she doesn't have the gall to touch me. "I . . . wanted to be there for you, but . . ."

"But you weren't." The words come in a frantic, unexpected rush. "I *needed* you. Just as much as I needed Dad. Because . . . B-because I was . . ."

My brain fights the words burning in my mouth. *My fault. My fault.* But Tomás's comforting voice is with me, overpowering my self-doubt. I rip through the mental blockage and snap, "I was a victim, Mom. I . . . I needed your support. But you weren't there, so I learned how to stop needing you. Now you're just in my *way*!"

I go to shove past her, but she steps aside on her own. There are red veins in her eyes. Her mouth is open, like she's scrambling for something else to say, but I don't want to hear it.

I storm toward the staircase.

"I thought . . . you hated me," she says, letting out a breath.

I stagger to a stop.

"I thought you blamed me," she whispers. She's barely audible, and I have to strain my ears to catch her words. "Because I'm your mother, and I should know how to protect you. And I . . . failed you."

Tomás's words scorch through my head. *You inherited the whole "I blame myself so I have to distance myself" thing from someone. And it wasn't Dad.*

I try to soak this in. This . . . *reasoning*. The distancing, and acting aloof, and avoiding my eyes . . . how am I supposed to accept that? Nausea stirs in my stomach, and finally, I whirl on her. "I was just a kid," I croak.

She doesn't respond. She's focused intently on the floor, unable to lift her eyes to mine.

"Tomás saw you pulling away, and he chased you. But I couldn't. I didn't have the legs, Mom." My words are choked and haggard, and I'm blinking rapidly to keep the tears from escaping my eyes. "You put your guilt before my trauma. And I . . . I don't know if I can forgive you. Yet."

Unlike her voice, her expression hasn't wavered. Even now, after everything I've said, she appears perfectly level, far from cracking or unraveling or breaking down. I wonder if she's ever done any of those things. But then, finally, she pries her gaze off the floor, and she looks up at me. My breath catches in my throat.

There are tears in my mother's eyes.

They aren't sad, or angry. No, there's something almost . . . hopeful in there. For the first time in my life, I can actually read the thoughts hiding behind her mask.

Not yet. But maybe one day.

I blink, and suddenly, my own tears are grating against my cheeks.

I yank my feet off the ground and move up the staircase to my room.

It's done. It's all done.

I eye the facedown picture on my nightstand. The alebrije sea turtle next to it.

At least . . . for now.

JONAH

In March, Noelle Davis and Myron Kelly become our official legal guardians.

I've never sat down and assessed my own happiness. I've always focused on Mik and Lily. Their future, their contentment, was the only thing that mattered.

Now I can look out for myself.

April is here, which means the days are getting longer, the skies are turning from white-gray to pastel blue, and spring creeps into town in tantalizing bursts. I'm fighting for straight Bs (screw that grade on my essay, Aunt Noelle), and I get to see my friends whenever I feel like socializing. All of them have been busier, lately, what with deciding between colleges. Dylan's looking at a few in state, Andre wants to study abroad (to the reluctance but steadily increasing acceptance of his parents), and Hanna's favoring the West Coast.

I'm not sure what I want to do with my life, now that I have one. I think Aunt Noelle and Myron are secretly hoping I'll either take a gap year or go to community college, so they can continue building their relationship with me. Honestly, I'm okay with that.

Dylan and I . . . yeah. It still feels weird to say we're dating, when a few measly months ago we were archenemies of all time. Whether we're in the cafeteria, studying in the library, baking in his kitchen, or playing games with Mik and Lily at the condo, we see each other nearly every day. Aunt Noelle lets him spend the night sometimes, but only if we keep the door open. Which is fine. If I want to get frisky, we can go to his place.

I still haven't . . . well. He still hasn't . . . um. I'm still a virgin. Whatever. I'm nervous.

He's fine with that. He tugs me playfully, inch by inch, into this new, unfamiliar world. There's no pressure. His consideration makes me want to throw my reluctance to the wind, but he mentioned one night that he prefers to be. You know. The quarterback. Which means I have the honor of being. You know. The wide receiver.

I mean, he said above all else he just wants me to feel comfortable, and he's totally open to changing things, so it's not as if I'm stuck doing something I don't like. But I don't have a desire to be any particular position on the field. As long as I'm *on* the field and not, like, watching from the sidelines, it's fine. So. What I'm trying to say is that I don't mind catching his . . . football? Sports? Uh.

It's just that, at this point, I've seen all of him. And I'm not sure . . . how it's going to . . . work.

"You mean *fit*, right?" Andre asks, laughing hysterically when I voice my concerns.

"It's not funny!" I cry out.

He wipes tears from the crooks of his eyes. "You told him yet?"

"What?"

"That you're afraid of his enormous package?"

"Who the fresh hell do you think you're talking to?"

He doubles over again. I bury my face in my knees, thoroughly humiliated. "Well," he chokes out. "Baby steps, Jo-Jo. Work your way up the ladder."

I don't feel like telling him Dylan's already nudged me up a few rungs. I can't help myself around that jerk. His skin is so soft, and he smells so good, and his hands are so warm, and his house is so empty.

My favorite nights are the ones in his sunroom—a wide, glass-paneled space looking out over the backyard. Once, I come over and find a trail of glow-in-the-dark stars winding out of the living room. This immediately irritates me, because what *right* does he have to act so cute, and how *dare* he be so romantic? I storm through the house, following the trail, and see him sprawled out in the sunroom on a fluffy quilt.

"I know it's not the best town to stargaze in," he tells me, smiling. "But we'll be warm."

I collapse beside him. "This is so corny. I could eat this shit off the cob."

But I still snuggle up against him, and point out as many constellations as I can, despite the interference of the town's light. I tell him my mother's favorite was Orion. The simplest constellation, but one of the brightest and easiest to recognize. Dylan lets me spout off all my space knowledge, and plays along when I ask him how amazing it is.

"Yes, yes," he says, stroking my hair as I rattle on about the mass of neutron stars. He's not even looking up anymore. "Space is cool."

Dylan knows exactly how to handle me. He knows when to move the conversation along, how to trick me out of my anger. He's patient. I never realized that. Nor did I realize I *need* a patient person, because I'm . . . a lot.

But he can handle me, all of me, from my best aspects to my worst.

I'm learning more about him, too. I grow familiar with the signs of his panic attacks—the sudden, deadpan expressions and unfocused eyes. Tomás and I are both really good at nagging him to make therapy appointments. I tag along for emotional support when I can. Mostly, I sit out in the waiting area, but he tells me my presence nearby is soothing. It helps that he's back to doing track, which gives him something to add consistently to his schedule. If he ever needs assistance with his workouts, I'm readily available. To, like, sit on his feet when he does crunches, or watch from the bench while he lifts weights.

"You could join," he says every so often. "Or do something other than stare."

I raise my brows. He's shirtless and shimmering with heat. "I'll keep staring," I tell him, "but thanks for the offer."

He rolls his eyes, smirking. The only reason he doesn't complain further is because he can take it out on me later with his unending stamina.

Seriously. Over the last few months, as I've been gaining weight, I've been getting better at *keeping up* with him. With more food and sleep, I feel more energetic. Since his relapse into consistent workouts, though . . .

This guy wears me *out*.

We quickly determine in our budding relationship that we need to be way more careful about where we're doing these naughty things in his house. One Friday, Dylan's mom walks in the door with a suitcase and comes to the pleasant sight of two teenage boys making out on the living room floor, one with his shirt splayed open and the other with his pants unbuttoned.

Yeah. Great first impression.

Mrs. Ramírez is *way* different than her husband. She has this atmosphere reminiscent of Hanna's, only more intense and mature. I think she'd happily use me as a mop, and I would thank her for it. Her dark eyes make me feel like I'm being dissected.

It's awesome.

"Ah," she says when I hastily button my shirt. Her black hair is curled neatly against her shoulders, her skin is a soft bronze, and her winged eyeliner is sharp enough to slice through my soul. "Dylan, this is your boyfriend?"

Dylan smacks his forehead. "Why are you home?" he grumbles.

"Our retreat is over." She sheds her sleek peacoat and drapes it over the coatrack. I feel the tension mounting uncomfortably quick. "Jonah Collins, will you join us for dinner?"

I shiver. She makes my name sound *cool*. When I look over at her, I realize she's watching me from the staircase, eyebrows cocked. It's not a question.

"Yep," I squeak, for fear of vaporization if I say anything else.

"Six o'clock." She trails up to the second floor, taking the stiff atmosphere with her.

When dinner does happen, I feel like I'm suffocating. Dylan and I sit across from his mom in a nice Italian restaurant, fighting over the bread and olive oil and watching her swish her blood-red wine. She's wearing a pinstripe suit and heels (a power move), and grills me about my life.

"Can't you back off, Mom?" Dylan snaps, smacking my hand aside so he can seize the last bread slice. I have the primal urge to throttle him. "It's like you're interviewing him."

She cocks her head. "I am."

"*Why?*"

"To make sure he can take care of you."

"I can take care of myself." Dylan shoves the bread in his mouth and chews angrily. I fold my palm over his on the booth between us, and his tensed fingers relax. "Yeah," he sighs. "Jonah takes good care of me. Don't worry."

Mrs. Ramírez offers a fleeting smile.

Ultimately, she comes away from the night telling me to keep an eye on her son. I guess that means I've been accepted.

I've been shown off to Dylan's father and all of his restaurant staff, too. I love going there, partially because we get things for free, and mostly because Dylan lights up adorably whenever he sees his dad. The third visit, Dylan pulls me into the kitchen, where skewers of meat cook over open flames.

"Are we supposed to be here?" I ask nervously, before hearing an uproar of voices as the kitchen staff rushes over. They hover, clearly wanting to hug us but also not wanting to grease us up with their aprons. Dylan speaks to them in rapid Spanish, and I can tell he's introducing me. They all giggle and talk at once.

This is my world now. Meeting random people in Dylan's life and hoping they're not saying anything terrible about me while he hunches over in laughter.

Everyone shakes my hand and gives thumbs-up to Dylan, before scurrying back to work. He's still grinning as we walk out, and I realize I don't actually care what they were saying. If it keeps his face like that, they can talk trash all they want.

"George said your butt is flatter than the state of Kansas," he tells me.

Fuck George, though.

I've been officially dating Dylan Mauricio da Costa Ramírez, the Prissy Prince of Delridge High, for four months. It's reached this "honeymoon phase" where every time I see him, I feel nauseating happiness that makes me want to shank myself and get it together. I don't even care that Andre, Hanna, Rohan, Maya, and Casey are constantly up our asses about how they *knew* we would solve our differences, that we were *obviously* made to be the perfect lovers, that we fit together *effortlessly*, like two puzzle pieces, like the sun and the moon, like peanut butter and jelly, like *blah blah fucking blah*.

I'm not actually mad that they were right. Obviously. I'm just mad that they love smearing their arrogance directly across my face.

Dylan takes it all in stride, and cools me down in these instances by squeezing my palm or kissing my temple. Do I act flustered and overheated in front of our friends just to have these moments with him? Maybe, but nobody's ever going to know that sappy shit.

It's spring break now, and hopefully, I'll get to show him just how head-over-heels I am for him.

My friends, family, and I are staying up north at a ski lodge with an indoor water park.

And Dylan and I get our own hotel room. For an entire *weekend*.

Aunt Noelle and Myron offered to pay my way, with the only stipulation being that they could come with my sisters, too. "But don't worry," Aunt Noelle says. "We won't intrude on your romantic getaway, or try to hang out with your friends. Oh, and take these."

She tosses a sealed box of condoms at me.

Which pretty much makes it the worst day of my entire life.

On Friday night, Dylan and I drive up in his car and check into our room separately from Aunt Noelle, Myron, Mik, and Lily. At that point, we're both exhausted, so we wash up, dash the lights, and crawl into bed. I'm fully aware this is the first time we've ever truly had a place to ourselves, without the threat of someone walking in. The thought makes me jittery.

We sleep soundly and meet up with Andre, Hanna, Casey, Rohan, and Maya at the indoor waterpark the next day. Near the lockers, I find Aunt Noelle and Myron helping Mik and Lily with their cover-ups and swim shoes. Myron catches my eye, then winks and waves.

And, man, this place is *fun*.

We heave inflatable tubes up an exhausting amount of stairs, only to spend ten seconds riding them back down. When we're tired of that, we head for the open pool, where Mik is experimenting with the diving board and Lily is rolling around in the shallow end with a pool noodle. Normally, they'd lunge for Dylan at the mere sight of him. But Andre is here, too, so . . .

"Watch out, little losers!" Andre sprints up the diving board and somersaults through the air, landing with a giant splash. Instantly, Mik and Lily are scrambling toward him, laughing maniacally and shielding themselves against his waves. While they gravitate to his energy like moths to a flame, Hanna watches with amusement from a beach chair nearby, sporting a glittering black bikini (the pinnacle of badassery). I can tell she's taking full advantage of this break, considering she's been tormented with varsity softball practices every day after school for the last several weeks on top of leading the efforts for prom. Next to her, Aunt Noelle and Myron read their own books, glancing up at my sisters every minute in unison.

I wade through the water toward Dylan, who's sitting on the edge, kicking his legs.

"Hiya." I grip his palms and pull, drawing him into the water. "You don't want Mik and Lily climbing you like a treehouse?"

He allows me to tug him closer to the deeper end, where I have to stand on my tiptoes to keep my chin above the surface. "I think I'll let Andre have their attention," he says, smirking.

"What should we do for the twenty seconds they're distracted?"

"Feels like you already have an idea." He raises his brow as I slink my arms around his neck. I'm always more daring when he's shirtless. On top of that, droplets of pool water shimmer against his skin like little jewels. So I don't stand a chance.

"At least it's easier to hold me up in the water," I point out, when he props me on his hips.

"It's always easy to hold you up."

"Um, *no*. It's gotten very difficult for you over the last few months." How could it not? Now that I'm not overthinking how much a basket of mozzarella sticks costs, I've been stuffing my face to my heart's content.

He nods thoughtfully. "Your extra five pounds do numbers on my arms."

"It's been more than that!" I squeak, and he laughs, then meets my lips with an instant hunger I've learned not to battle, because he always wins. Always. It's been like that since the start, when he slapped me with that +4 in Uno.

Our pool passion doesn't last ten seconds before a lifeguard screeches her whistle, then yells at us to stop making out in the pool. Which is very biphobic of her, but I'm in a good mood, so I'll let it pass.

This weekend is amazing. I can be with the people I love, have fun, devour as much gross processed food as I want, get closer to my boyfriend, and just be *me*. The freeing sensation is enough to make me giddy.

I float on my back in the pool, smiling at the ceiling. When I peek over, I see Dylan holding Lily on his shoulders, pretending like he's falling over, back and forth, and causing her to shriek with laughter. He catches me watching him and tips his head.

Tell you later, I mouth to him.

Okay, he mouths back, before "slipping" backward and dumping himself and Lily into the water.

I'm definitely going to tell him.

DYLAN

Jonah swore he was going to interact with his family as little as possible, since it's supposed to be his spring break trip. And yet, there he is, wrestling with Mik in the pool, holding Lily's hand while she climbs to the top of a kid's waterslide. He's laughing, putting on his usual performances, making a complete ruckus with Andre. Amazingly, I've never seen him with so much energy.

"You ever think they'll leave us for each other?" Hanna asks, watching as Andre slings his arm around Jonah's neck.

"I think that's a possibility we'll be living with for the rest of our lives," I admit.

Hanna laughs, but there's something wistful there, like she's thinking deeply.

"What?" I ask, raising my brow.

"Hmm? Nothing. I guess . . ." She leans her head playfully against my shoulder. ". . . it's just nice to see how it all worked out. As I foretold."

I smirk, rolling my eyes. "Right. *Foretold*."

"Have I not been begging you to hit it for the last couple years?"

I haven't hit anything yet, I think, but I merely say, "Sure, sure. How many times do I have to say *you were right* before you stop reminding me of it?"

"Mmm . . . gonna go with two million." She winks. "Though, to be fair, I'm guessing it's more like you accidentally fell for him after you started *dating*. Right?"

Immediately, my heart begins to thrum quicker. I don't like the way she emphasized the word *dating*. "Accidentally?" I ask, laughing weakly.

"Well, it was a mistake, wasn't it?" She cocks her head to the side, her ponytail dripping down her arm. "You didn't start dating Jonah because you liked him. You started dating him because of how much you hated him. Am I wrong?"

My God. After all this time? After *everything*?

"I . . . you . . ." I can't formulate any words. I'm scrambling for the next step. Do I tell her? Deny her? Should I ask Jonah first?

"I know you, Dylan. And I know how you love." Hanna smirks, flips her ponytail triumphantly over her shoulder, and says, "I'm going to the hot tub. Care to join?"

"I . . . um. Yeah." I practically have to shake myself out of the previous conversation. Seriously. I can't believe she guessed our intentions from the get-go. Were we that visibly uncomfortable around each other? "Just . . . one minute." I wave her along, then trail back to our locker, digging through my bag for my phone. My heart skips when I see I have a text from Tomás. I'm glad it's skipping, now, instead of sinking, like it used to. It's his response to the selfie I sent him of Jonah and me. We're dripping with pool water, and he's kissing my cheek while I grin at the camera.

> Cute little shits!! You two having fun? You
> treating him well??

I laugh down at my screen and text back, Trying my best.

I glance up. Jonah is kneeling beside Lily, readjusting her goggles. My smile widens.

```
Seems I'm in love with him, after
all.
```

I haven't said it yet. I told Jonah that the first "I love you" and the first "let's have sex" are in his court. He's jittery about both of those things, so I think this is the best way to handle it. I'm okay with waiting. Being with him—holding him, bantering, going on dates, kissing, visiting his stargazing spot, baking sweets—is so far beyond any of that.

I'm in love with Jonah Collins.

Maybe admitting that sounds immature. We've technically only been real-dating for a few months, and we're both teenagers enjoying a lengthy honeymoon phase. But I don't think that matters. Whether we're young, naïve, wearing rose-colored glasses, or whatever . . . I think people should love at whatever pace suits them.

And I've never felt as comfortable around anybody as I have with him.

There are still steps I need to take on my own, of course. With Tomás, my mom, therapy. But, lately, my confidence in myself has been growing, and I've been more willing to try. Maybe it's just the fact that spring is showing its face, but I'm finally looking forward to things again.

It's been half a year since Jonah staggered into my room after homecoming, demanding a fight and then passing out on my mattress. Maybe it's wishful thinking, but I can't help but feel that one day, Jonah and I could build an amazing life together.

It's a day I can't wait to see.

JONAH

We all go back to the waterpark on Sunday. I'm extra loud and annoying today. My banter with Maya is unending. Casey swears I shatter their eardrums, supported by the fact that Lily covers her ears when I shout hello to my family. Hanna has to put her hand on my head to stop me from shuffling around and slipping while we're in line for waterslides.

Dylan understands why I'm being obnoxious even before I do.

"Why are you anxious?" he asks, his arm draped around my shoulders while we're cuddled up in the hot tub. "You're acting like a stand-up comedian with a gun to his head."

I scoff at him, but he's right. I'm nervous. Because it's our last night before we have to drive home, and I have a lot of feelings. Maybe Dylan knows what I'm thinking (he usually does), but regardless, he lets it go.

By the time we're dried off and dressed for dinner, I'm a wreck. I have to read the menu six times before I can comprehend it. My fingers bleed from the gnawing. I'm hyperaware of every sound, every scrap of conversation.

Relax. Relax.

Dylan folds his hand over my upper leg, which nearly sends me flying out of my seat. "What's wrong?" he murmurs. "Seriously, are you okay?"

"Peachy," I squeak.

I don't even realize we're done with dinner until people start standing to go get ice cream. "Headache," I sputter. I need to get to the room—take some time to cool down. Maybe do more research. Even if I *have* read every article in Incognito mode and watched every informative video I could scavenge from the dark side of Google.

"I'll go with you," Dylan says.

I shake my head rapidly. "You should get ice cream."

"I'm full. Besides, I'm trying to maintain some kind of figure for track."

As if his figure isn't perfectly flawless. Nonetheless, he won't budge, so I give everyone a hasty goodbye and wobble to the elevator. I feel his concerned eyes glued to my back as he follows.

The ride up is painfully quiet. We get to the room, and I stand uselessly in the doorway.

"Um," he says. "Can I . . . come in?"

"*I'm still dressed*," I wheeze.

"I mean. Like. The room."

Oh. I inch forward. He steps inside, closing the door behind us.

"I'll hop in the shower." Dylan grabs a pair of boxers from his suitcase, then heads for the bathroom. "Need anything?"

"Nah, I'll just throw up in the vents," I croak.

He scrunches his brows, but closes the door without comment.

"God," I choke out, collapsing onto our bedspread. "Yeah. Throwing up in the vents. Really romantic and sexy. Great dialogue."

I stare at the ceiling, counting breaths. The tingling in my hands ebbs away.

Okay. I've got this.

I fumble through my suitcase and put the necessary products on the bedside table. I have a Ziploc of fake rose petals, which I scatter across the mattress. I spritz myself with cologne, then do jumping jacks to loosen up, which probably negates the cologne. I smooth gel in my hair, but regret it immediately, because now I look like a teen heartthrob from a '90s boy band.

My mouth.

Crap. None of this will work if I'm not minty fresh. I creep to the bathroom door, nudge it open, and maneuver to the sink. Dylan is still in the shower, the glass door so fogged I can barely see his outline. Good, because it means he can't see mine, either.

I slap toothpaste on my toothbrush and jam it into my mouth, scrubbing violently. When I'm sure I've ravaged every crook and crevice, I bend over to spit.

When I pull up, the glass door is cracked open, and Dylan's staring at me around the edge. "Hello," he says.

I squawk, tossing my toothbrush aside. "Don't mind me! Uh. Have a . . . nice wash!"

Oh God. I need to get out of here. I need to pack my bags and flee to Canada.

"Come here, Collins," Dylan says, calm as ever. There's a trace of shampoo in his hair. I'm trying desperately to keep my eyes on his face.

I stagger toward him, heart skidding around my body. "Yo."

He opens the glass door further, takes my hands, and pulls me, fully clothed, into the shower. Before I can even protest, he scoops my face up and tilts it, kissing me. Water rushes over his head and back, dousing me, matting my shirt and pants to my body. I stand there, unmoving, trembling in his grip. "Look at me," he says gently.

I don't realize I've squeezed my eyes shut. Reluctantly, I pry them open, meeting his gaze. His soft, understanding smile burns my cheeks.

"I told you, don't ever feel pressured about sex," he whispers, smoothing his damp thumb over my brow. "Take your time. And, if you're ever ready—"

"I am," I say.

He blinks. Water droplets collect in his lashes. "Huh?"

"I . . . that's why I . . . um. Fuck me?"

I gag on my words. Dylan's lips quiver, and I know he's about to howl with laughter.

"I didn't mean it like a question!" I gargle. "I meant it like, *fuck me, why is this so hard.*"

"Well. It's not hard yet," he says.

I feel like I'm about to explode in the least sexy way possible. *"Dylan?"*

"Sorry!" He briefly pinches his wet lips between his teeth, very clearly holding back a grin. "The joke was right there."

I give a shaky, angry huff. "Ass."

He gets this mischievous twinkle in his eyes. "Are you insulting me, or making an observation?"

Oh my God, *he's naked.* I try to lunge through the door, but he slings an arm around me, drawing me back to him. I stagger into his bare chest, groaning.

"Relax, cariño." He lifts my hands to his mouth, pressing his lips to my knuckles. "And stop chewing your nails."

"Hmph." I can't come up with a better response. My eyes move on their own, communicating with my poor, agonized heart. He shifts his lips to the base of my hand, each kiss slick with water and warmth. His tongue traces a slow line along the indents of my palm. He kisses the veins of my wrist.

I'm numbingly warm, but still shivering. Watching, helpless, as he works his mouth to my shoulder, to the exposed skin at my collar, to the droplets slipping down my neck, to my jaw. He kisses the edges of my lips teasingly, invitingly. Waiting.

Of course, I meet him. I push forward, and he wraps his arms around my back, yanking me up against him. I scratch my fingertips gently against the muscles in his back—the jutting roll of his shoulder blades. He doesn't allow an inch of space between us, his tongue slipping along mine every time I start to forget about it, his waist grating mercilessly against my hips.

I'm going weak—my thoughts turn to mush. I barely have enough sense to slide a palm between our mouths and whisper, "The bed."

His eyes flit between mine. "You're sure?"

"Yeah." I smile, nudging his nose with mine. "I love you, Ramz."

I'm not expecting that to slip out of my mouth. I was going for *want*. But . . . well. It's okay. It's the truth.

It seems like he's having trouble comprehending what I just said. But then his eyes glitter, and a gigantic grin breaks out on his face. He backs me through the bathroom, through the bedroom, then tosses the comforter aside and presses me into the sheets. He lowers himself over me, painting me with whatever leftover water still clings to him. "I love you," he breathes, before kissing my forehead. "I love you." He kisses my nose. "I fucking *love* you." He kisses my lips, even as I laugh.

"You've been hanging onto that?" I guess.

He rests his arms on the sheets on either side of my head. "A little while," he admits.

"Sorry for keeping you waiting."

"Oh, God, no." He draws me into a long, deep kiss that makes my stomach tingle. "It's perfect."

My fingers find his, and I thread our hands together. He squeezes gently.

"You sure you're okay with this part?" he whispers. "If you want to switch positions, we can. I know I told you what my preference is, but I don't mind trying something else, honestly. I just want you to be—you're laughing again."

"Sorry!" I can't force back my smile. "It's not *at* you, I promise. It's just . . . you're cute."

"Cute?" he demands.

"As I've told you sixty thousand times over the last few months, I'm comfortable doing anything. I have no preferences. I promise that hasn't changed in the last two minutes." I loosen my grip from his so I can knead my palm through his curls. "Can we keep going?"

He blinks at me in apparent surprise. Then, he leans down once more to meet my kiss.

It's not quick and easy, but it's about what I expect. There's a lot of very unsexy waiting, and waiting, and more waiting. Dylan grips the headboard over me with one hand and uses it as an anchor, listening carefully to my body language and responding accordingly. The sheets become a tangled, sweaty bundle beneath us. He whispers in my ear. *Keep breathing. Relax. Tell me what you need.*

I love you.

I exhale, because those words steal the air from my lungs. He's looking at me with that tiny grin that used to make me squirm with anger. Now, it makes me squirm for an entirely different reason. "Say it again," I breathe.

"I love you." He lowers his lips until they're grazing mine. "Te amo, mi amor. Eres el dueño de mi corazón."

I don't know what it means. But I can almost feel it in the way he holds me.

Though I push against the lethargy, Dylan draws away on his own, his knuckles grazing my cheek. "It's your first time," he whispers. "Don't push yourself."

I sigh into the bedspread. He lies beside me, flipping me so I'm facing him and cradling me against his chest. Neither of us are ready to fall asleep, though, so we pull our pajamas on, then draw a cozy armchair toward the window overlooking the parking lot and slope of the mountain. He sits back, and I nestle in beside him, tucking my legs up, using him as my personal radiator.

Together, we gaze out at the lights of the ski lift and the clumps of people ambling up and down the street.

"Think we'll ever tell them?" I murmur.

"Hmm?"

"Our friends." I peek up at him. "Should we tell them that it was supposed to be fake? Like, I know Hanna probably knew from the start, but . . . are we ever going to fess up?"

". . . Nah." Dylan nuzzles his nose against the top of my head. "Let's keep it our little secret."

I nestle my head under his chin, still smiling. "Our little secret," I agree quietly.

Below us, I see a familiar group wandering toward the hotel. Hanna and Andre must've caught up with Mik, Lily, Aunt Noelle, and Myron, because they're walking back together, chatting. Everyone is bundled in winter attire, which makes me feel even warmer. The sight of them all . . . it excites me, despite my fatigue.

My gaze wanders up. Beyond the street, beyond the ski lift and waterpark building, beyond the points of the nearby trees, beyond the tip of the mountain. I stare at the sky, meticulously painted with flickering specks. Usually, it's awe-inspiring. Now, though, it's merely an ever-shifting canvas, meant to stay where it is. Maybe because I've spent the last several years always looking up for comfort. Always reaching for something far away—always daydreaming about something unattainable.

I don't have to reach anymore. I don't have to look up.

Now, I can start looking forward.

ACKNOWLEDGMENTS

To acknowledge my success in becoming a traditionally published author after ten years, I should first acknowledge the shitstorm that was 2020. Without it, this book wouldn't exist, nor would I be sitting here, overwhelmed with the number of people I want to thank for staying by my side while I waded through the query trenches and grappled with my identity. While the world was on fire, while a literal plague devastated the globe, while the political climate was at its most toxic, I wanted to write a story that would make people smile. That would take them away from the pain of the world and give them a reprieve, if only for a little while.

So, thanks, 2020. For sucking so much ass. I guess.

I dedicated this book to my parents, which means they probably deserve a paragraph. Not that it could ever be long enough to encompass everything they've done for me. Mom and Dad, thank you for being my support system, my joy, my everything. I've already rewritten this section multiple times because I can't seem to find words that can remotely grasp how much I love you and how lucky I am to have you in my life. I feel that I've come so far, and that's all because of your love and faith in me. I will forever be grateful for the close relationships I have with you both, for the support you've shown me through my entire life, for the sacrifices you've made for my happiness, and for the unlimited booze.

Jenna. Sweet baby sista. I would never be where I am today without you. You're my biggest supporter and my best friend. Thank you for always talking me down when I get in my head and for listening to my rants and ideas. Your encouragement has gotten me through my toughest moments, and I'll never forget what you've done to get me to this point. Thank you for being one of my favorite people in the world. (By the way, your ideas are never bad.)

Nicholas, thank you for being my first reader. Or my first listener. Back in elementary school and middle school, it meant the world to me that you could sit still long enough to listen to me read off my stories about the Big 7. Whether we were traveling to another planet, gaining superpowers from a pool (the Triple A Double K JENP Team!), or saving Jenna and Paige from pirates, you were always the first person to receive my creative ideas. Thanks for giving me the courage to share my stories out loud.

Laura, what would I do without you? You have been the most constant, supportive light in my life over the last few years. You're not only the best critique partner I could've stumbled across, but you're now one of my best friends. It feels strange to go longer than two or three days without talking to you. I'm so honored that we get to work together, rant together, and support each other through the hard times. I can't wait to see where this industry takes us both.

V, you followed me all the way from the *W* website and read all of my cringiest writing yet stuck around anyway. Thank you for being one of my longest-running readers, for being one of my favorite supportive people, for helping me to shape Dylan and his background. Thank you for reminding me of why I do this and who I do it for.

To my superpowered lit agency duo, Suzie Townsend and Sophia Ramos. Oh boy, where do I begin? Suzie, I don't know how you managed to sell my book so quickly in the heat of the pandemic. You have helped me bring all of my dreams to life, and I can't thank you enough for taking a chance on me and my writing. You're one of the best advocates I could've ever asked for, and my appreciation is bottomless. Sophia, words can't express how much I adore you and everything you do, be it answering my silly newbie questions or offering amazing advice and moral support. You both are incredible, and I'm so lucky to have you! I can't wait to work on further projects with you and see what comes next down the road.

I want to thank the entire team at Viking Children's Books for taking this book through every step of its journey, from marketing to design to publicity. But I especially want to recognize the best editor in existence, Dana Leydig. You saw potential in my little rom-com and dedicated so much time to helping me scrub it down and wring it out until the book reached its fullest, shiniest potential. You have guided me through this process with such kindness and understanding and have made my debut experience phenomenal. I am so incredibly honored that you fought for this book. I truly couldn't have asked for a more supportive editor, and working with you has been an enlightening experience that I'll never forget. Thank you for making my dream come true. Thank you, thank you, thank you.

Ash, Tay, Bree, and Katrina, thanks for having more faith in me than I did. You've constantly shown me so much support by reading my words . . . even when they haven't been your usual cup of tea, ha ha. Thank you for being my sounding boards and for encouraging my aspirations every step of the way. I'm so lucky to have you as my friends. (Ash, you could make your connection to Tay and me permanent if you got the air tattoo. Just saying.)

Leni Kauffman and Theresa Evangelista, you brought my boys to life in a far more beautiful manner than I ever could have anticipated. Thank you for giving me the bi cover of my dreams.

To my lovely Twitter friends, you have shown me so much love on this journey. I could not have done this without all of you—especially Diana (my queen), Elba, Anthony, Juli, Lore, Kris, Rod, Bee, Rogier, Dezirae, Anahita, Kamie, Gabi, Miriam, Emery, Gabriele, and Deke. There are so many more of you, and I'd name you all if it wouldn't increase the length of my book by another two thousand words. Thank you for always being there for me and for showing me how much you care.

Thank you also to my amazing authenticity readers, Stephanie Cohen Perez and Julian Winters. Your feedback was so thoughtful and invaluable. I can't thank you enough for taking the time to review my work.

To Alyssa Stein—yes, you. So many years ago, you introduced me to the *W* website. It was there that I learned that I wanted to make this my life. Thank you, my friend. I miss the hell out of you and hope you're doing well.

To my extended family who has shown me wholehearted support on my journey to publication, your words mean so, so much to me. Looking specifically at you, Kaitlyn, Abbey, Aunt Renee, and Mary. Thanks for being so awesome and vocal.

Lastly, to Grandpa Joe, who isn't here to read this but who never doubted that I'd make it this far. I'll love you always.

Thank you to everyone who has ever had faith in me, who has ever stood by my side, who has ever defended me or voiced support for this book, who has ever held my hand along this lengthy, winding journey. I will remember this kindness forever.

ALSO BY AMANDA WOODY

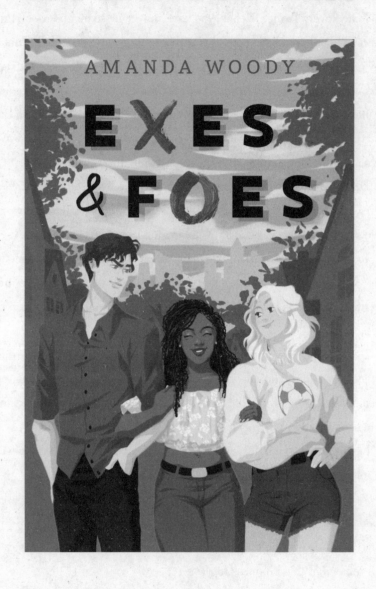